Anne Borrowdale has spent many years working for the church in theological education. She is well-known as a speaker, writer, and occasional broadcaster, and works closely with the St Albans and Oxford Ministry Course. She lives in Oxford with her family.

Other books by Anne Borrowdale

A Woman's Work
Distorted Images (short listed for the Winifred Mary Holtby prize) and
Reconstructing Family Values

all published by SPCK.

Praise for Anne Borrowdale's writing:

'lively and entertaining'

Life and Work

'intelligent, perceptive and thorough'

Church of England Newspaper

'balanced, refreshing, eye-opening and extremely well-researched'

Church Review, Dublin

'very readable and strongly recommended'

Derby Diocesan News

Messiahs Don't Fly

Anne Borrowdale

Ashton Pickering Publications

First published in Great Britain in 1999 by
Ashton Pickering Publications
44 Hollow Way Cowley OX4 2NH UK

British Library Cataloguing-in-Publication Data
A catalogue record for this book is available from the British Library

ISBN 0-9534755-0-6

© Anne Borrowdale 1998

Cover illustration 'Incarnation' © Craig Russell 1998

The moral right of the author has been asserted

Printed by *Manuscript ReSearch Printing*
PO Box 33 Bicester Oxon OX6 7PP UK
Tel: 01869 323447/322552   Fax: 01869 324096

For
Mike and **Richard**

Author's Note

My thanks are due to the various people who provided background information for this story, in particular, David Julier, Mark Kirkbride, Mary Nichols, Philip Sutton, Nancy Wallace, and Pat Willis. Needless to say, they bear no responsibility for the way I have used (or misused) this information. My thanks also go to my editor, Sonia Ribeiro, for her helpful suggestions and hard work.

All characters in this publication are fictitious, and any resemblance to existing institutions, or to real persons, living or dead, is purely coincidental. In my experience, those involved in ministry training are far too dedicated, and too busy, to do anything scandalous; which is why this story has to be set in an entirely imaginary diocese.

Anne Borrowdale
Oxford, 1998

PART ONE

November 1992

COME WIND, COME WEATHER

Who would true valour see,
Let him come hither;
One here will constant be,
Come wind, come weather;
There's no discouragement
Shall make him once relent
His first avowed intent
To be a pilgrim.

John Bunyan 1628 - 1688

One

It is a truth universally acknowledged that a young man who attends church with the slightest degree of regularity must be in want of a vocation. Michael Turner, waiting with easy confidence for acceptance into his chosen profession, had had a lifetime of people suggesting his suitability for ordination. The son of a clergyman, without any obvious talent for anything else, and with an uncomplicated faith that had never wavered, what other path had there ever been to consider? So, after a few years of dedication in low-paid jobs and voluntary work, he offered himself to the system which would test his calling. He glided through interviews in his diocese, winged his way to a provisional place at theological college, and soared through a selection conference, only to crash-land with the letter that awaited him on his return home on an otherwise ordinary October evening.

Michael saw the letter as soon as he came in through the door. One of his parents had propped it up for him beside the telephone, aware of what the official diocesan stamp might signify. He was smiling to himself as he pulled off his coat, tossed it onto the rack, and prepared to have his future confirmed.

A tug at the flap, the rip of a disintegrating envelope. A single bare paragraph glimpsed through the back of the paper; but such paltriness was to be expected. The Director of Ordinands was the one who told you the detail.

Michael unfolded the letter, and read:

'I regret to inform you that you have not been recommended for training.'

He read it again. It made no sense. '*...not been recommended*'.

The hall receded; the air evacuated from his lungs. For a full minute he stood staring at the sheet of paper, unable to think.

Reason. There must be a reason. He had to ring and find out what the selectors had actually said.

The Diocesan Director of Ordinands was not available. Michael left a hesitant message on the answerphone, and placed the telephone back on its stand. A sound at the kitchen door at the other end of the hall made him look up. His mother was looking through the glass with an expression of enquiry. He met her eyes, and what she saw brought her through the door.

'I've been turned down,' he said.

Meg's hand went to her mouth. 'Not for ordination?'

He nodded. 'Oh, Mike.' She came down the passage and put her arms round him.

He'd always been slightly built; he could rest against her and draw what comfort he could from her embrace.

'Does it say why?' she asked.

'No. I've been trying to find out, but the DDO's not in.'

'I expect it's something very simple,' she said, ruffling his hair. 'It must be, you're the ideal candidate, everyone's said so. Have you told Kate?'

'Not yet.'

'You should ring her.'

'Later.'

'Come on, Mikey, you need her here. It's a setback, but she'll help you through it.'

Dutifully, Michael picked up the phone, and dialled his fiancee's number.

He was sprawled on the sofa in the front room when Kate came in a few minutes later.

'Oh, you poor baby,' she said, coming over to kneel on the floor beside him. 'It's absolutely stupid. I don't know what they're playing at. We'll have to get the bishop to overrule.'

Michael blinked back tears. 'I don't know ...'

'Don't be defeatist. We've got it all planned. You're going to college, and I'm going to get a teaching job nearby. We're not going to let some stupid set of incompetents spoil everything. What do they know!'

He observed her as she spoke. She was beautiful, he'd thought so from the start. The daughter of the latest curate to descend on the parish. Michael had been twenty-four, and temporarily back living at home. Meg had invited the curate and his family to supper, and there was Kate. Tall, slim and seventeen, with long, light-brown hair shining on her shoulders, and deep-blue eyes that met his own with a return of interest.

'I couldn't believe it,' she'd confided weeks later. 'I had a real thing about blokes with dark hair and brown eyes, and I looked up and there you were, ogling me. I never stood a chance!'

'I didn't ogle,' he'd insisted. Yet he'd asked her out the following day, before any of the other lads in church could get in, and they'd been together ever since. Four years of loving her, of being constructed by her. But her schemes, the ones he'd thought his own, had fallen to dust, and he had nothing to say.

She held out her arms to him. 'Oh, baby, come here.'

He embraced her, touching her lips with his own, lowering his face to seek solace in the curve of her neck, smelling the familiar traces of her perfume. His body moulded itself intimately to her, as it had done this past year of being lovers, yet he felt curiously detached from her. It came to him with sickening intensity that she was not enough. The Michael who had been engaged to her had died out there in the hall. Whoever he was now had no need of her.

He tasted her skin, and knew he no longer loved her.

Michael struggled through the days that followed, hoping that he might somehow recapture the feelings for Kate that had been a part of his life for so long. Yet with each conversation they shared, each embrace she offered, he knew himself to be drifting further and further away.

'I don't know what to do...' he'd say.

'Of course you do. We look at the things they failed you on, and work on them so you can try again in a couple of years. Once we're married, that'll answer them thinking you never commit yourself to anything, and you'll seem more mature. Then you could go back to college to retake your A Levels, show you're capable academically. And you could start doing more things up front in church, so it shows you'll make a good leader.'

'I think I've lost my faith ...'

'Don't be silly, of course you haven't.'

He could not carry on with her. She had no imagination. He was a problem to be solved. She could not enter into the way this catastrophic rejection had ripped all meaning from his past, wrecked his faith as well as his future.

In the end he had to tell her, aborting a half-hearted attempt to make love on the back seat of his father's Astra. 'I can't do this, Kate. I don't love you any more.'

'What do you mean? We're going to be married. We've got the date set and everything. You're depressed about this ordination thing, that's all.'

'No, it's not all. We're not right for each other. I don't love you. I'm sorry.'

She wept, pleaded, reasoned, held on to him, struck him, until he too was in tears, but he held firm. At last he drove her home, in a silence broken only by his own sniffs, and Kate's uneven, trembling breathing. There was nothing left to say. As she got out of the car and walked up the driveway, his last claim to have a future vanished with her. God knew what his parents would say.

Meg and Edward were side by side on the sofa when Michael returned from work the following afternoon. Over in the corner, the television relayed to them the Church of England's latest, and definitive, debate on women priests. Meg had been an assiduous campaigner for years, and had been looking forward to this climactic day, but her thoughts were clearly elsewhere.

She turned on Michael as soon as he came in. 'How could you! Kate's such a nice girl. She's practically one of the family already. I cannot understand what you're thinking of. She rang me at school - she's in an awful state!'

He sat down. 'I don't love her any more.'

'You can't say that. Not when you've been taking advantage of her in the way you've done. She's so much younger than you, and to sleep with her and then throw her aside like this ...'

Michael felt his jaw tighten. 'She had no right to tell you.'

'Supposing she'd got pregnant? What then?'

'She was on the pill,' he said, wearily. 'It was a decision we made together. We loved each other. We thought it was for life. It hasn't worked out. Look, Kate's not the only victim in this. It's painful for me too ...'

'Rubbish! You're upset about not getting selected, so you take it out on Kate. It's not fair.'

'Perhaps you should consider,' his father put in icily, 'whether you might have been turned down because of your sexual misconduct?'

'I don't accept it's misconduct, not if you think you're going to marry someone. Anyway, the selectors didn't know.'

Edward's long face became portentous. 'God knew, Mike. And given the way you've behaved since, I'm beginning to think their decision was thoroughly wise.'

Michael leaned forwards, his head in his hands.

Back at Church House, Westminster, the Archbishop of Canterbury was asking for the result of the synod's vote to be received in silence.

Meg slipped her hand into her husband's. Michael heard her gasp as she began to grasp the implications of the figures being recited. As the Archbishop declared the motion passed, Michael turned to his mother to share her delight.

Her eyes were wet, but she was glaring at him. 'This should have been the happiest day of my life, and you've ruined it!'

His smile fell away. 'Perhaps I should leave,' he said.

'Perhaps you should!'

The coach journey from Croydon to Greathampton was a straightforward one, pulsing around the M25, along the M1, and across busy through roads to the town. Michael spent the journey staring out of the window, feeling more battered than he could ever remember.

It was late November. He had taken time to leave home. Another two weeks of trying to avoid Kate, whom his mother continued to encourage to call at the vicarage practically every day, in the expectation that Michael would change his mind. Another two weeks of not knowing what the hell he was supposed to do with the rest of his life. He would gain some respite this week with this visit to his godparents, but after that, he had no idea.

'Have faith,' everybody said, but he could find none. The God who had once been more real to him than his heartbeat had been transmuted into a Great Absence who teased the edges of his mind: if you really had been suitable for ordination, you wouldn't have lost your faith so easily. You're a failure. You're nothing. You've been deluding yourself. You're not wanted.

A series of minor traffic jams signalled the outskirts of Greathampton. Eventually the bus pulled into a bay near the end of the high street to allow passengers to leave. Michael waited while two elderly women, a young couple, and a mother with three sullen children made their way out onto littered grey pavements, then he trailed out of the coach after them. His rucksack dragging at his shoulders, he pushed his way through the Christmas shoppers invading the high street, until their ranks thinned as the shops gave way to garages and housing. He turned down the side road leading to St Martin's, whose modern spire poked up behind a small, neglected row of shop units.

The housing estate around the building had a rough reputation. Although the church served as a community centre, there was a perennial problem with youths hanging around the premises: breaking windows, spraying graffiti, occasionally breaking in to look for non-existent money, damaging cars, and generally intimidating members of the congregation.

As he passed, Michael noticed some boys - sharp, white-faced, and jacketless despite the winter chill - kicking a ball desultorily among themselves on the grass that surrounded the building. Thirteen or fourteen year-olds, he reckoned, observed by a bored-looking girl of full figure but indeterminate age, sitting on the low wall that enclosed their playing area, her thick bare legs blue with cold under a short skirt. Long, light-brown hair straggled over her heavy, pale face, and fell limply onto her baggy, patterned jumper. She was chewing an insanitary strand as she flicked her eyes across Michael, who had stopped at the entrance to watch them.

Aware of his presence, the boys shouted more loudly as they carried on playing:

'Give us the fuckin' ball, Kev!'

'Fuck yerself, dickhead!'

Kev, a skinny youth with tightly cropped dark hair and a single earring, turned suddenly and fired the football in Michael's direction with surprising velocity: a gauntlet thrown down to the prying stranger. Michael was good at football. He imagined himself trapping the ball, flicking it up off his trainers, bouncing it on his knee, and executing a perfect lob back in Kev's direction. In reality, his lack of preparedness and the imbalance of the rucksack on his back meant that the ball went through his legs, and was deflected out into the road.

'Who d'you think you are? Fuckin' Gary Lineker?' yelled a fair boy in a Spurs shirt.

'Fucking Bruce Grobelaar, more like!' Michael shouted back. 'OK, I'll get it.' The ball had bounced off a car parked on the other side, and was rolling back into the gutter. He dropped his rucksack and went to retrieve it, spinning it in his hands as he walked back to the group.

'D'you support Liverpool, then, mister?' asked a freckled boy with dull, gingery hair.

'Not with a goalkeeper like they've got, no. Crystal Palace.' Michael grinned as the lads made derogatory remarks. It was a fate Palace supporters were used to.

The fair boy fiddled around in his pocket and produced a small pack of cigarettes. 'Got a light?'

'No,' said Michael. He stopped spinning the ball and held it out to Kev.

''Ere, Robbie, I got matches. Give us a fag, would yer?' the girl said, heaving herself off the wall, and coming to join them. She lit up with an experienced hand, using her bulk to shield the fragile flame from the breeze that threatened it.

'Want one?' she asked Michael. The eyes that regarded him through the smoke drifting upwards between them were an interesting shade of greeny-brown, and her expression open and friendly. Her lack of sophistication caused him to revise his estimate of her age downwards. She was probably not much older than the boys around her, for all her physical maturity.

'No thanks,' he said. 'Do you hang round here a lot?'

'Wha's it got to do with you?' Robbie said, as he lit his cigarette from the girl's, and inhaled ostentatiously.

Michael sat down on the wall. 'Don't you have anywhere else to go? What do you do if it rains?'

'Get wet, mister,' said the ginger-haired boy.

'Aren't there any youth clubs or anything round here?'

'Naah,' Kev said. 'Wouldn't go to them any'ow. All bloody rules an' ping-pong, innit?'

'Doesn't have to be,' Michael said. 'What would you want?'

'Booze, drugs an' sex,' said Robbie, taking another drag. 'Hey, Lise, drop yer knickers an' get on yer back. D'ya want a piece, mister? She's not much cop, but she'll spread her legs for anyone for a fiver ...'

'Piss off, Robbie,' Lisa interrupted sharply. She turned to Michael, looking uncomfortable. 'You don't wanna listen to them. They're really stupid. Are you from the council, like?' she asked. 'Are they settin' something up?'

'Not that I know of. I'm just interested. It doesn't seem fair you not having anywhere to go.'

'Oh, nobody bothers about kids round here, 'cept for slaggin' us off cos we're hangin' around. There's this, what d'you call him, vicar here, comes poncing round saying "you can't play here, you might break the windows", but he don't do nothing about gettin' us somewhere we can go.'

'I thought there was a park round the corner,' Michael said, trying to conceal his amusement at her uncannily accurate representation of his godfather's parsonical tones.

'Oh, yeah. A lump of grass with a broken swing, covered in dog shit an' full of druggies an' winos. No one goes there. It's alright up in the Rows, they've got this bloody great youth club, but tha's too far for us.'

The boys agreed with her, attending to the conversation in sporadic bursts as they carried on kicking the ball among themselves.

Michael stayed for several minutes talking to them. As their interest waned, he took his leave, pausing only to intercept the football and dribble past two of the boys, to restore his self-respect. Then he swung his rucksack back on his shoulders, and headed for the road.

'Hey!' said a female voice behind him. He looked round to find the girl staring at him, biting her hair.

'I in't a slag, you know, tha's just Robbie windin' me up.'

'I'm sure you're not.'

'You won't tell no one what 'e said, cos me mum'll kill me if she thinks it's true. She thinks I'm after her boyfriend, stupid cow. As if! Wha's your name, anyway?'

'Michael. Michael Turner.'

'I'm Lisa.'

Michael held out his hand, and smiled at her. 'I guessed that. Pleased to have met you, Lisa.'

She looked down at his extended hand and then back at his face with an undisguised suspicion that fell away as she caught the amusement in his eyes. She returned his handshake with excessive politeness. 'I'd offer you a drink, but I in't got the facilities,' she said, nodding her head at the bolted doors.

Michael laughed. 'I know people round here. I'll have to see what I can do for you. Cheers, Lisa.'

He made his way across the road to the purpose-built vicarage behind its high fence, unexpectedly encouraged by his encounter with her.

Two

The television screen in Jenny Furlong's house was showing a heated studio discussion about women priests; a small, fair woman in a dog-collar was trying to sound reasonable in the face of severe provocation.

Jenny's Aunt Deidre was nodding in agreement. 'Nan is such a dear woman,' she said. 'We have our disagreements, but I do admire her tremendously. To be so dedicated to the campaign, despite losing her husband so tragically! So brave!'

'Really.' Jenny was getting fed up with Deidre's potted biographies of practically everyone in the invited studio audience. Strange how they all seemed to be Deidre's personal friends, or at least all personally indebted to her as head of the Leathwell Diocesan Training and Education Department. Except for the viper Ridgefield, of course, the most public opponent of women's ordination. Not merely sadly misguided like his allies, but, according to Deidre, positively evil. Jenny had been struck by his expression on the night of the vote a fortnight before as the cameras had caught him: the pale skin hanging haggard on his face, eyes bleak, gutted at the verdict.

'I feel sorry for him,' Jenny hazarded, as he launched into a bitter rebuttal of Nan's argument.

Deidre looked at her pityingly, but she had spent most of her visit doing that; most of Jenny's life, come to that, as if it was one of life's little ironies that her niece should be such a plain, awkward, unremarkable person.

'Oh, he'll be alright,' said Deidre. 'He can devote himself to his precious ordinands at St Barnabas. Make sure the place stays untainted by women. And if he fails, he can always fall back on his compensation package.'

The presenter drew the discussion to a close. Jenny turned off the television with relief. She had not been able to refuse her aunt's request to see so relevant a programme, but she could not quite see what all the fuss was about. She could see no reason why, having lumbered itself with the Reverend Deidre Rutt, the Church of England should not make her a priest, an archdeacon, and who cared what, if it so desired. There were surely more important issues in the world.

'It's certainly nice to see the little place you've got here, Jennifer dear,' Deidre said, smirking as she finished off her cup of tea. 'Of course, it will be much better when you've had a chance to get it straight. Well, I must be off.' She gathered her handbag and stood up. 'You really must come and see me soon. Tyrone will be back from the States shortly, you know. He's got a job with Radio Leathwell. He'd love to see you.'

'Thank you,' Jenny said non-commitally, as she showed Deidre out. She had never had much in common with her younger cousin, other than the misfortune of having one of the Rutt sisters for a mother. Tyrone had got the worst of that, having had Deidre undiluted for fifteen years since his father had divorced her. At least Jenny's dad had added something to her childhood.

She closed the front door and watched Deidre's figure, distorted by the thick, patterned glass, departing down the short driveway. As the sound of the car engine died away, she took a deep breath and let it go. Passing through to the kitchen, she trailed her hand along the bannisters, and the reassuring solidity of the walls, as if comforting the house for the recent invasion it had suffered from Aunt Deidre: the tapping of the woodwork, the feeling for damp, the criticism of the choice of decor, and the complaints about the lack of Lapsang Souchong.

'I'm working my way round,' Jenny had explained. 'I've had the kitchen fitted out, and got the central heating in, but this is the only room I've decorated so far.'

It was Jenny's first house, this two-and-a-box-roomed nineteen thirties semi on one of Greathampton's middle-ranking estates, and she loved it. Years of being a medical student had meant poky hospital accommodation, or the furnished flats of variable quality which she had occupied as a GP registrar or locum. Now she had secured a partnership with the practice that served this part of town, and oh, the bliss of being able to buy her own house, of being accountable only to herself. Since she'd moved in at the beginning of the year, she had slowly been making it her own. She revelled in the planning and the physical work in the odd times she had leisure, for it was not as though she had friends to fill her time.

She bent to free the catch on the cat flap, then opened the door to see how her cat had taken the exile enforced on her through Deidre's allergy to anything feline. Celestine, a long-haired tabby of extravagant proportions, stalked in, disdainfully omitting her usual twine around her owner's legs. Jenny picked her up and buried her face in the haughty fur, but the cat struggled free. As she walked back into the living room, she licked the scratch Celestine had left behind on her hand, and grimaced as she tasted blood.

Caroline greeted Michael on the doorstep with a hug, relieved him of his rucksack, and ushered him into her living room. Credits were rolling for the end of a television programme. Caroline turned it off.

'You've just missed a good bloodbath. Nan was putting Ridgefield in his place. It's been such an exciting couple of weeks...'

Michael let her talk, while he accepted the tea and carrot cake she proffered. Motherly, curly-haired and solid of figure, Caroline had provided a refuge for him more than once in his life when pressures at home had become too much. Her husband Peter emerged from his study for a brief greeting, the bright-blue clerical shirt straining over his expanding figure indicated he was, as always, on duty.

Caroline waited until they were alone again, and said, 'Meg says you broke your engagement. She says you've been cruel and callous, and completely gone off the rails. But as I said to Peter, that doesn't sound like you.'

'They liked Kate, you see. Such a nice, suitable Christian girl - well, you've met her, haven't you? We had it all worked out, and then I go and blow it all by getting turned down. Everyone says I'm being silly, and I should marry Kate and get a job and try again in a couple of years, but somehow none of that's what I want any more. I've changed, and I can't see myself ever going back.'

'There's really no chance you might get back with Kate? I've known other couples who've had a long engagement and felt the need to split up for a while, but then they've come back together stronger than before.'

Michael sipped some more tea, and helped himself to another piece of cake. He could sense Caroline's puzzlement, but at least he could talk about it without being shouted at.

'I can't see it,' he said. 'I have this recurring dream that I wake up and find I've married her after all, and it's become a nightmare. Packaged up, organised, everything mapped out for ever, and .... and nothing to dream about any more. Supposing it happens? You know what I'm like, I've always been inclined to do what anyone tells me, if it makes for an easy life. And there's Kate still thinking I'm the Lord's intended, and Mum going on at me all the time - what chance have I got? Especially as I miss her. It's been a big chunk of my life, and ... I suppose you know we were lovers. You can't just forget that overnight.'

'No. That's why some of us believe sex belongs in marriage. But you don't want a lecture,' she added, seeing his grimace. 'Anyway, I think you're stronger than you know. You're not completely malleable. I've had enough worried phone calls from Meg about you over the years to know that - you've never quite done what she's expected. I'm sure you're right to give yourself a breathing space, but if Kate's still that sure you're right for each other, you ought not to shut the door on her altogether.'

'Yeah.' Michael put his cup down, unconvinced.

'Will you stay on in Croydon?' Peter asked over supper.

Michael chased an elusive twist of pasta round his plate. 'I don't know. I can't really, it's not fair on Kate. But what do I do next? I suppose I'll have to get a proper job, but I'm not qualified for anything. I've not got a very impressive CV to offer.' He gave up on his food and put down his fork. 'I feel completely lost. Everything I've done has always felt like a preparation for ordination. Being turned down has wrecked all the plans I've ever had for myself.'

'You can try again, though. Give it a couple of years.'

Michael shook his head. 'I don't know if I want to any more ...'

The doorbell resounded through the house. Peter sighed. 'Here we go again.'

'Oh, that'll be Nan,' Caroline said. 'She said she'd drop an article off for me. Go and put the kettle on, love. I'll go.' She went out into the hall, patting Michael's shoulder as she passed.

Michael went through to the living room. Almost immediately, Caroline reappeared, followed by Nan Patten, inelegant in a tracksuit, with her shoulder-length light hair tucked untidily behind her ears.

'We've got Michael staying for a few days,' Caroline was saying. 'Do you remember Nan, Michael? She's at St Jude's up the road, and working for the Leathwell Programme for Ministerial Training.'

'I think you've been around when I've been here before, but not for a few years now,' said Michael, smiling a greeting. 'I've seen you on the telly often enough.' Nan was shorter than he'd remembered, but exuded vitality. He could never imagine her being ignored.

Nan held out both hands to him, brown eyes dancing in a strong face. 'Hello, Michael, nice to see you again. Actually, I'm not starting with the Programme until April. Fancy letting me loose training ordinands! I suppose they don't think I can do too much damage since it's a part-time course, and the students are theoretically as mature as I am.' She kissed

Michael's cheek as if they were old friends. 'Excuse me butting in, but I was just sitting down to relax on my one evening in this week, when I remembered Caroline wanted to see this.' She waved a magazine at them, and dropped it on the table beside the door. 'Did you see me on the telly this afternoon?'

'Of course I did,' said Caroline. 'I loved the way you patronised Ridgefield at the end, offering him a welcome in your church like that.'

'He lacked his usual fire, I thought. The fact that he's a loser has finally caught up with him.'

'Can you stay for coffee?' Caroline asked. 'Peter's just putting the kettle on.'

Nan hesitated. 'Unless you're wanting to talk to Michael?'

'There's nothing more to say about me,' he said, sitting down. 'I've just been turned down for ordination. I'm still in shock.'

'How very difficult for you,' Nan said, sitting on the armchair next to him, and leaning forward to look him in the face. 'You gear yourself up, and it all seems so right, and if you get turned down, it's a slap in the face. Knocks you right out. God's a bugger sometimes, don't you think?'

Michael laughed. 'Well, yes, I do, but I didn't think I was supposed to say so. I'm supposed to talk about how He's got everything planned in His infinite wisdom so that it will all turn out for the best.'

'But you don't believe it will, do you? You're bloody angry with God blundering about in your life, messing it up. Perfectly natural. You don't want to be pussy-footing about trying to talk yourself into feeling holy about it. Shout and swear at Him. I would.'

Caroline seated herself on the sofa, looking uneasy at her friend's language. 'Nan! Of course God's not messing Michael's life up. There must be a purpose in all this somewhere. When the Lord closes a door, He always opens a window. Don't take any notice of her, Michael.'

'That's all very well,' said Nan, 'but don't you think that when the Lord closes the door, He frequently manages to shut our fingers in it?' She winked at Michael, then turned to greet Peter, who came through from the kitchen with a tray of coffee.

Peter took a mug into his study to work, and the conversation moved to other, more domestic, arenas.

Michael sat back with his coffee. He felt at ease here, in this homely room, with its assortment of furniture inherited from relations with conflicting tastes. Photographs along the mantlepiece traced the progress of the Harts' three children from babyhood to the present: two at university, and one a frequently absent lodger as he did his A Levels. A large embroidered text hung above the fireplace. 'My God will supply all your needs'. All very well, but what if God didn't give a bloody hang for your needs? He looked again at the woman who had given him permission to be angry, laughing uproariously at something her friend had said, and decided he liked her.

The doorbell rang again, but before Caroline could rise, a female voice was heard in the hall calling out, 'Hallo?'

'It's Becky,' Nan said. 'She's staying over on her way to Wales.'

Becky appeared in the doorway, a well built young woman in her early twenties, with careful make-up, and dark hair parted to curve round her face.

'I decided "gone to Caroline's, back in a minute" was a contradiction in terms, so I came along.' Becky went over and kissed Nan's cheek, and sat down on the arm of her chair. 'Hello,' she said, looking across at Michael appraisingly.

Caroline introduced them, and Michael leaned across to shake her hand.

Becky raised her eyebrows at such old-fashioned courtesy, but she grasped his hand and held it longer than was strictly necessary. 'Hi, Michael,' she smiled. 'I remember you. I was passionately in love with you when I was thirteen and you came to run the church holiday club. You haven't changed a bit.'

'Why don't I remember you?' Michael asked. She was wearing jeans, and a tight top under a denim jacket which drew his eyes inescapably downwards.

'Probably because I was pre-pubescent. Men do somehow tend to remember me more now I've sprouted a bosom.'

'Becky...'

'It's alright, Caroline, Michael's not shocked. Are you?'

He shook his head. As she talked enthusiastically with Nan and Caroline, Becky's large brown eyes kept returning to him, inviting him to share her amusement. Her vitality was seductive; he found himself flirting with her, enjoying the dangerous freedom of being single, available, and unhampered by faith.

'I think I might pop down to the Bell,' Becky said, looking at her watch. 'See if any of the old crowd are around.' She looked across at Michael. 'Would you like to come?'

'Oh do,' Nan said. 'You don't want to be stuck with a couple of old women all evening.'

Five minutes later, he was with Becky, heading towards the town centre. Their conversation was easy, and by the time they were squashed together on a hard wooden seat in the corner of the crowded Bell, they were laughing like old friends.

'Have you got a girlfriend?' Becky asked, as he returned with their third round.

'No. I was engaged up until a few weeks ago, but I broke it off.'

'And I've just been dumped yet again, so we're both free to have fun. Do you have fun?' Her hand strayed to his thigh.

He looked into her face. 'It's been known,' he said, sliding a casual arm around her shoulders. The loud laughter and exuberant conversation around them had receded; his head felt light. He was aware of the solidity of her flesh, so different from Kate's bony slimness. Damn Kate. He leaned over and kissed Becky appreciatively.

'Why don't you walk me home?' she said. 'Nan won't be back for ages, not if she's at Caroline's.'

The invitation in her voice caused Michael's pulse to race, and why the hell not take advantage of the distraction Becky was offering him? 'OK,' he said, getting to his feet.

After that, there was only one way the evening could end.

Sitting in St Martin's the following morning, Michael tried not to think too hard about the evening before. The brief encounter with Becky in the small spare bedroom off Nan's hall lay heavily upon him. In his only two previous sexual relationships, desire had always gone alongside love. He was unfamiliar with the crude, straightforward lust that had compelled him to couple with someone he scarcely knew. Afterwards, he had wanted to run away as quickly as possible. Only he liked Becky, and did not feel he could discard her that easily.

'Can I see you again?' she'd wanted to know.

'Dunno. I don't know where I'm going to be.'

'Why don't you come to London to look for a job? You could doss down with me - there's plenty of room in the house I'm in.'

He'd been non-commital, but taken her phone number anyway. After all, why not London as usefully as anywhere else? Given that God had moved away leaving an indecipherable forwarding address, he wasn't likely to receive any guidance from that quarter.

And yet he had come to church this morning, so much was it the habit of his life. He looked about him at the faithful, loudly and cheerfully gossiping their week's news to one another. St Martin's was far too modern to be conducive to reverential quietness. The main part of the building was a large hall, with weekday services taking place in a small chapel partitioned behind wooden doors. On Sundays, the doors were folded back to allow the congregation to spread out into the airy lightness of the hall.

Michael watched Peter step onto the small raised platform in the chapel, and begin putting markers in the large service book on the unadorned altar. Above it, a giant tapestry showed a dove rising above tongues of fire.

Michael had taken a seat towards the back, near the end of a row of wooden seats. His head ached. He leant forward, elbows on knees, and sunk his head in his hands. But I'm not praying! he shouted mentally. And I'm certainly not going to pray for forgiveness. If you do still care about me, you can bloody well show it, instead of hiding out there laughing at me while I screw my life up. I hate you. Do you know that?

I shouldn't say that, he thought. Then he heard Nan's voice: 'God's a bugger sometimes. Get angry, I would.' It was alright for people like her, but he wasn't used to strong feelings; he could barely remember the last time he'd lost his temper. He'd never needed to.

With his face twisted beneath the shelter of his hands, he screamed soundlessly into the void:

It's not fair. You lead me all my life. I give you everything. My whole bloody life. Up to my eyes in tears and shit and other people, without asking for anything in return except the chance to serve you. And how do you reward me? You lead me on with visions and dreams, until I'm soaring in the bloody stratosphere, and then you abandon me. Let me down. Throw me to the ground, and you won't even speak to me. Not that I bloody well care. I'm going to forget about doing anything remotely worthwhile, and take the first job I can. Making cigarettes, or arms manufacture. Something you won't like, anyway. And I'm going to go to London and screw Becky just for kicks. And if you don't like it, it's your own bleeding fault! I've had enough. Do you hear? I've *had* it with you.

The intensity of his outpourings shocked him. He hadn't realised he was that angry. When he sat back up in his seat, he found his eyes were wet. He shivered despite the efficient heating in the building. With shaking fingers, he picked up the small red service book from the rack in front of him, and flicked through its pages, seeing nothing.

The woman who was to be his wife took her seat next to him without him giving her a second's thought.

26

Three

Jenny arrived at St Martin's shortly before the service started, slipping in to sit at the end of the row so that she could get out easily, since she was on call. She bowed her head briefly, but she never found it easy to concentrate surrounded by other people. If she had been thinking clearly, she would not have sat down next to this dark-haired young stranger, who was looking at the service books in confusion. A visitor, obviously, which meant she would be acutely aware of him throughout the service, wondering whether he needed help, and what he would make of the form of service. The young man made no move to find the first hymn, so she handed him her book. He glanced at her, and she noticed his eyes were wet. Please God he doesn't start howling in the service, she thought. I never know whether to pat people on the shoulder or leave them to it. He still seemed unsure of his place, so Jenny leaned across with her own service book, helpfully indicating the correct section. This time he whispered his thanks, and seemed able to follow the service on his own.

When the time came for the congregation to exchange handshakes, her neighbour looked much more relaxed.

'Are you a visitor?' she asked. He was a pleasant looking lad, now she could look at him directly. Slightly built, not much taller than she was - five-foot eight or nine, maybe - with thick, dark hair flopping around a fine-boned face, long-lashed brown eyes, and a wide, attractive smile.

'Yes. I'm staying with Caroline and Peter. Michael Turner. One of their many godchildren.'

'Oh. Oh, I am sorry. Showing you the right page and everything. I thought you didn't know. You must have thought I was so patronising.'

'Don't worry. It's nice to be made to feel welcome. I wasn't feeling like joining in, but you persuaded me.'

Jenny bit her lip; she hated embarrassing herself by getting her interactions with strangers wrong.

Michael smiled again. 'Really, it's alright. Thank you.'

Jenny was relieved when the bleeper went off in her bag, and she was able to leave before the end of the service.

Michael had been touched by the awkward care Jenny showed him, and amused that anyone could get so worried about being too helpful. As he'd shaken her hand, he'd realised she was younger than he'd first thought. Not the matron he'd assumed from his sidelong glance at her sensible, broad face with its slightly convex nose, and the short, limp, unstyled, brown hair that curled round her ears, but perhaps only a few years his senior. She'd been wrapped up in an off-white anorak, a plain-featured woman, with grey eyes, and a sprinkling of faint freckles on pale skin; the kind of face that would gain character as she grew older. When Michael first encountered her, she was nondescript. Once the service was over, he forgot all about her.

As the congregation departed, he wandered to the front of the church to ask Caroline for a key to the vicarage. Seeing that she was in the middle of an earnest conversation, he drifted over to the electronic organ, sat down on the stool in front of it, and fingered a few chords. He'd been quite good once; his single, scraped A Level had been in Music, achieved solely because there was a large practical element. Perhaps he should spend more time on it. Playing hymns and choruses with the music group at his father's church hardly stretched him. Very softly, he traced the first few phrases of Bach's Jesu, Joy of Man's Desiring, wincing as a discordant note reminded him of the time that had elapsed since he had last tried it.

'Play a bit, do you?' asked a voice behind him.

Michael looked up to find himself being addressed by the man who had played the guitar for songs during communion, middle-aged, with a black beard, and a stomach that stretched the boundaries of a faded red woollen jumper.

'Not so much now as I used to. Shows, doesn't it?'

'You're not thinking of joining St Martin's, are you? We're losing our organist after Christmas.'

Michael made a sympathetic noise. 'You work in Greathampton, do you?' he asked, deciding that Caroline was never going to be through, and swinging his legs round on the stool to talk more comfortably.

'I'm a youth and community worker over in the East End Rows. It's a local authority project. Does some good stuff. Petty vandalism has dropped no end since we started up. We're hoping to open a satellite project in the hall here in the new year. I've just heard we've got funding for two part-time posts, amazing!'

'I was speaking to a few kids round here yesterday,' Michael said. 'That must be what they were talking about. They said there was something

28

good further out of town, and they complained there's nothing for them round here. It would be brilliant if you got something going. What do the congregation think about it?'

'They're keen at the moment. They see the church youth group doing well, and they think I'll convert all the youngsters off the estate overnight. I'll let the truth dawn on them gradually.'

'I know what you mean. I often wonder what a congregation would do if they really did get a couple of dozen teenagers turning up en masse on a Sunday morning. Scare the hell out of them.'

Michael stayed talking for a few minutes until Caroline was free, then went back to the vicarage. Two days later he took the coach to London.

December raced past. Michael didn't look for a job; he did odd jobs around the house for Becky and her friends. When she wasn't busy with her work at one of the capital's smaller radio stations, he accompanied her to wine bars, clubs and parties, and extended his sexual repertoire with exhausting sessions on her bed. Sharing Becky's world brought temporary relief from his wretchedness, but he remained profoundly unhappy with the path he was treading, disaffected and out of tune with himself.

When a phone call dragged him from bed one morning shortly before Christmas, he was so hung over from a binge the night before that it took him some time to catch up with what was being said.

'I'm Baz Knight. We spoke at St Martin's last month. About youth work.'

'Oh, yeah. Hang on.' Michael grabbed his coat off the rack in the hall. There was no heating here, and he was shivering in the tee shirt and boxer shorts which were all he'd had time to put on.

'You sound rough,' Baz said.

'I am.'

'I won't keep you. I wanted to put a proposition to you. Do you remember I'd got everything set up for a new youth club at St Martin's? Well, the council's had an emergency meeting because they were going over budget, and they've withdrawn their funding. It's sickening - we've been raising a lot of expectations, and I'd hate to drop the whole project. I wondered whether you might come and help out for a while, so we can get something off the ground?'

Michael thought. 'You mean as a volunteer?'

'Yes. I know it's a cheek to ask, but Peter says you've been doing voluntary work for the last few years anyway, and he thought you were at a loose end. I'll be looking for alternative funding, so I might be able to offer a part-time job some time, only there's no guarantees.'

'Where would I live? How would I live?'

'Peter's sure someone at St Martin's would give you a room and feed you. They'd put you up themselves, but when Jane and Paul are back, they don't have the room. And we will have a vacancy for an organist, which would pay something. It all depends on what plans you've got.'

'Getting rid of my hangover, and after that, I've no idea. Can I have a think about it, and get back to you?'

Michael put the phone down and returned to Becky's room to crawl back under her covers.

'I've been offered some voluntary work in Greathampton,' he said. 'Running a new youth club at St Martin's.'

Becky moved over to hold him to her, warm curves pressed against him as if she owned him.

He put an arm round her perfunctorily. 'What do you think?'

'Don't let yourself be exploited,' she said. 'Typical church, trying to get things on the cheap. You ought to get a job. Get yourself sorted out. Train for something. You're not stupid.'

Michael turned onto his back, and shut his eyes. He needed to get away, to think, to consider Baz's offer. 'I think I'll go back home this afternoon,' he said.

'Why? I thought you were only going for Christmas Day.'

'I know, but my sisters won't be around this year, and I can't leave mum and dad on their own. Besides, they'll be short-staffed at the old people's home I used to help out at. I might as well do something useful.'

'Saint bloody Michael, eh?' Becky began to caress him, an unreadable expression in her eyes. 'I know your vices, though.'

He pulled away from her. 'I've got plenty of them.'

Kate cornered Michael in the kitchen on Boxing Day. Her family had come for lunch, and Meg had insisted Michael owed it to Kate not to run and hide the minute she appeared. He had, therefore, smiled and exchanged civilities with her before bolting to the kitchen on the pretext of checking the food.

'I got you a present,' Kate said, holding out a small parcel.

'You shouldn't have done. I haven't got you anything.'

'It's only little. Please, take it. The latest Terry Pratchett, that's all,' she added, as he hesitated.

He'd seen the hurt start to surface in her face, and took the present quickly, before she lost her carefully contrived control.

She leant against the worktop, biting her lip. 'What have you been doing with yourself?' she asked.

'Staying with friends.'

'Anyone I know?'

'Nan Patten's daughter,' Michael said, thinking it might help if she knew.

'Are you going out with her? Is she why you split up with me?'

'No. I only met her when I went to Greathampton.'

'You're sleeping with her, aren't you?' Kate added, still sensitive enough to his body language to read his guilt.

He met her eyes for the first time since she'd come into the room, and quickly looked away, wanting to deny it, but unable to lie. Kate looked so stricken that he wanted to explain: it's not serious, I'm only doing it to forget you. But such explanations would hardly help her.

'It's not your business any longer,' he said gently.

'I don't understand what's got into you. You don't seem to have any values any more. I don't know you any more.'

'I told you I'd changed.'

'Yes, but it's not even as if you're happy like this. If you were, I could maybe accept it, but you're miserable. I know just how your mother feels, seeing you go completely off the rails, and unhappy, and not being able to do anything about it.'

'Perhaps that's the problem,' he said, looking directly at her again. 'You want to treat me as if you're my mother, you've always wanted to organise me.'

'I could change, if that's what you want,' she said in a small voice.

'It's not about that. Oh, Kate.' He put his arms round her, wanting to comfort her, and for a minute they held each other.

Michael looked up to find Meg in the doorway. She smiled and withdrew tactfully.

He let Kate go abruptly. 'I'm sorry. I'll always be fond of you, but I can't love you. I'm going to be moving away, Kate,' he added, coming to a decision. 'I'm going to help with a youth club in Greathampton. I'll probably carry on seeing Becky sometimes as well. You'll have to accept it's over. We both have to start again.'

Four

Jenny sat in the congregation on the first Sunday of the new year, feeling the full force of Peter's persuasiveness. When your vicar explains that God is calling someone to offer up a room in their home for His sake, and you have, not one, but three, empty rooms sitting at the top of your stairs, there is not much point in arguing. Privacy was important to Jenny, but her sense of duty was well-developed. She'd lived in shared accommodation before; she could afford the extra expense. Peter was right, to refuse to share what she had would be selfish.

Back home, she looked again at her vacant rooms. She'd been living entirely on the ground floor until the upstairs had been refurbished: the bay-windowed front bedroom with its rotting window frames, overlooking the small front garden and the straight street of similar houses; the damp box room over the stairs, with empty cases and as yet unpacked boxes of her things; the back bedroom which got the sun, and gave a view of the narrow garden which she was slowly tending into shape. The windows there weren't too bad, although it would need to be decorated, carpeted and equipped. It was a reasonable size; Michael ought to be perfectly comfortable. She remembered him from their brief encounter. He'd not looked happy, but he'd controlled himself. As long as he didn't smoke, or play loud music, or want wild parties, it ought to be manageable.

'That's a very generous offer, Jenny,' Caroline said, when Jenny phoned her that afternoon. 'It will be good to have someone responsible like you to keep an eye on him. He got turned down for ordination a month or so back, and went through a broken engagement, and he's in need of a bit of encouragement.'

'I couldn't get involved,' Jenny said, 'I can't be responsible for him, I need some break from work. I can let him have a room, and I can provide food, but I wouldn't be eating with him. My hours are too irregular.'

'Of course. No, I was just thinking that you could encourage him to come to church, and perhaps have a word with us if he seems to be getting depressed. Not that it's likely, he's always been a cheerful soul before, but these things can knock you back temporarily, can't they? I'm sure he won't be a problem. In fact, if you want any odd jobs doing, he'll be only too happy to help out. And he's pretty sensitive about people, he's not likely to disturb you.'

Jenny put the phone down only marginally reassured. 'That,' she said to Celestine, 'is probably the most stupid thing I have done in my life. Please God it's only temporary.'

Jenny had intended to be at home, relaxed and welcoming, to settle Michael into his lodgings, but her home visits took longer than expected. She arrived ten minutes late, flustered, to find him waiting with Peter on her doorstep, discussing her front garden in the growing gloom of a January afternoon.

'I am sorry. I was running late,' she said, holding out her hand.

Michael removed a glove to return her handshake. 'I know who you are now,' he said, grinning at her. 'Dr Furlong sat next to me in church when I was here in December,' he explained to Peter. 'I hadn't realised that's who it was.'

'Do call me Jenny,' she said. 'Your hands are frozen. You'd better come in.'

Peter took his leave, and Michael followed her in with his meagre luggage. What was left of the pale, winter light filtered into the hall through the glass doors at either end, and receded as Jenny switched on the lights. Between them, they carted the near sum of Michael's wordly possessions up the stairs.

Jenny talked nervously as she led the way. 'I've given you the back bedroom upstairs. There isn't a sink, but I've got a downstairs shower and toilet, so you'll practically have the bathroom for yourself. Except that I've got my washing machine and tumble-dryer in there. You're welcome to use them.'

She opened the door of the back bedroom, which still smelt faintly of paint. Fitted cupboards lined the wall opposite the door. A single bed jutted from the nearest corner, with a shelf and wall light behind it. In another corner, there was a small kitchen unit, with a microwave, small electric grill, and tiny fridge. Under the window, a table and two upright chairs sat on the new, patterned carpet.

'You shouldn't have gone to all this trouble,' Michael said. 'You haven't done all this for me, have you?'

Jenny gazed at him anxiously. She felt as bad about doing too much as about doing too little. The key was to get the exchange between herself

33

and people exactly right, so that there were no outstanding obligations either way. 'I thought I might as well do it properly. I was going to do most of it except the kitchen things anyway. I'm happy to stock you up with food, but you'll have to prepare it yourself, because I tend not to have set meal times.'

'It's great. I really appreciate it, Jenny.'

She smiled more confidently. 'I did say to Peter that there would be some ground rules. You're not a smoker, are you?'

'No.'

'And you'll keep the volume down on that?' She indicated the ghetto-blaster he was removing carefully from his holdall.

'Absolutely.'

'I couldn't allow you to have overnight guests of the opposite sex. Or ... or the same sex if you're that way inclined. I'm afraid I don't agree with it.'

'Whatever you say. I'm not too bad, honestly. I'm a vicar's son, I took in purity with my mother's milk.' An impish grin tweaked at his mouth.

Jenny chose not to be drawn. 'Are you? I'm a vicar's daughter. I was going to say that doesn't guarantee respectability, but I've always been boring, so perhaps it does.' She looked at her watch. 'I shall have to go. This is a front door key for you. Settle yourself in. There's food and milk in the fridge, which should keep you going, and there's shops nearby, if you want to explore. Turn right out of the gate, then right and left at the end of the road. It's not far. If you've any problems, I'll be in later this evening. Only ...' She paused.

'Only you don't want to be interrupted by me banging on your door every few minutes. I'll keep out of your way, don't worry.' He held out his hand again, and she shook it. 'And thank you again.'

But a week later, there he was, pathetically angling for an invitation to inflict his company on her. Curled up in her armchair, with her feet tucked under her brown cord skirt for warmth, Jenny was finally relaxing after a late return from the health centre, when the rap on the glass door startled her. She had temporarily forgotten about the alien presence in her house. Coffee from the mug she was cradling spilled out onto the half-finished crossword in her medical newspaper, smudging the ink, and making her exclaim with irritation as she called, 'Come in!'

Michael shut the door behind him, and leaned against it, one hand in the pockets of his jeans, while the other scratched through the damp, newly-washed hair that flopped over his brow. 'Did you say I could use the washing machine any time, or should I ask you first?'

'Any time - I usually put my own stuff in on Saturday afternoon, but it doesn't matter.' She eyed him tensely, waiting for him to go.

His attention had been caught, however, by Celestine's indecorous sprawl in front of the gas fire. 'What a lovely cat,' he said, going over to squat beside her. The cat lay back, stretching to reveal a tawny stomach ripe for caress. Michael obliged, graceful hands obscured by the long fur. 'I love cats, only my dad would never have one in the house. What's its name?'

'Celestine.'

'Like in the Babar books?'

'Yes.' Jenny could have developed the theme had she wished, but she wanted him out. This was her room, a private place, the first room in her first house, decorated to her own design. Plain and neat, with cream coloured walls above the beige carpet; the discreetly patterned sofa and armchair; the shelves she had fixed herself in the alcoves to either side of the gas fire, with her books, hi-fi, television and video arranged over them. The painting of a bleak mountain which she had brought back from a Scottish holiday the previous year, immovable granite outlined against a slate-grey sky, while in the distance a shaft of sunlight promised transformation.

'Well, I suppose I ought to go back upstairs,' he offered, scratching Celestine's chin, and making no move. 'It seems odd to be living in your house, but not seeing anything of you. You alone down here, and me by myself upstairs. I mean, do say if you want to be left entirely alone, but if you want company any time, I wouldn't mind.' He was looking up at her, with that wide, teasing smile back on his face.

Too good-looking and self-confident by half, Jenny decided. She began to regret her generosity. 'I prefer to be on my own, actually.'

Michael's face fell. 'I'm sorry. I'll go.' He got up quickly and headed for the door. He opened it, then turned to address her again with a tremor in his voice. 'It's just that I'm going out of my head on my own up there.'

The door shut behind him, and Jenny tried to focus again on her marred crossword.

'Oh, bother him, Celly,' she said two minutes later, throwing the paper to the floor. Her concentration was gone. She was thoroughly disturbed by his intrusion, and would probably lie awake all night now worrying about how nasty, rude and unchristian she'd been. And the poor boy only wanted a kind word or two. 'Keep an eye on him' Caroline had said, and all she could do was send him to slit his wrists in despair all over the new carpet. She got up, and headed for the stairs.

'Hello?' His voice sounded tired as it answered her knock. Jenny went in. Michael was lying on his back on the bed, his hands behind his head, black socks protruding from his jeans.

'I was rude, throwing you out like that. I've come to apologise.'

'No problem. You wanted a quiet evening. I was wrong to disturb you.'

'Yes, but you don't know anyone yet, and you've had a difficult few weeks, and I shouldn't have been so unfriendly. Please, wouldn't you like to come down again, have a coffee or something? Otherwise I'll feel awful all night.'

He looked at her as if he was assessing her sincerity. 'OK.' He brightened suddenly, his face transformed. 'Only let me entertain you. I'm halfway through a can. Do you want one, or can I make you a coffee?'

He heaved himself off the bed, and picked a few clothes off the seat of the small easy chair beside the bed. 'Have a seat.'

Jenny sat down while he boiled the kettle, and prepared to be sociable. It might always be a second best to solitude after a hard day, but she was perfectly capable of holding her own. It was easy enough to smile and nod and make the right noises, as long as she didn't forget herself and prescribe continued bed-rest and a couple of aspirin.

'How do you find working with Baz?' she asked.

'Great. He's a good bloke. One of his part-timers in the East End Rows is leaving, so I'm applying to do a couple of paid sessions a week. If I get it, at least I can afford to go down the pub instead of harassing you for company.'

'You'll get to know people at church, too.'

'I suppose so, but it feels awkward. I'm not sure I believe in it all any more.'

'I thought you were going to be our new organist.'

'That doesn't signify anything. Organists are always cynics. It's all the weddings they play for. I mean, I think I still believe, but I don't *feel* anything. They said at my selection conference that I was spiritually naive, and it's undermined everything. It's as if my faith's been taken out and examined, and chucked away as useless, and I've nothing to put in its place. I wake up in the night wondering if I've been fooling myself all along, and whether the spiritual experiences we think we have really amount to nothing more than a chemical imbalance in the brain.' He handed her a mug of coffee, and threw himself back down on the bed. 'Only if I mention it, people say I'm being silly. That's all my fiancee ever said. Or they look at me as if I'm a heretic who should be burnt at the stake. Like you're doing now.'

'No I'm not.' She found herself stung into honesty. 'I just don't think you should rely too much on feelings. I don't go to church because it makes me feel better - quite the opposite, really. I come away realising how horrible I am most of the time. But I'm with people who do have the right feelings, and who have all the right answers, and that saves me from having to think for myself.'

'Is that a good thing?'

'Probably not, but I can't cope with being made to think at the end of a hard week. I'm brain-dead with exhaustion.'

'I thought things got easier once you qualified.'

'It's all relative. And I think I'll always find it draining being with people all day.'

'I'm sorry. No wonder you need me to keep out of your way. You can go now if you like. I shan't be offended.' He picked his can of lager off the floor and took a swallow. 'I might kill myself, but that won't be your fault. I shall leave a note blaming it all on the bastards at my selection conference.' He grinned and Jenny smiled back.

'You can live for a while yet - I've not finished my coffee.' She sipped at it again. 'Why exactly did they turn you down? Was it other things as well as saying you were naive? You don't have to say if you'd rather not talk about it ...'

'I don't mind talking about it, but I wouldn't want to bore you.'

'I'm interested,' Jenny said, and found she meant it.

'It wasn't anything much. Only that I'm thick, arrogant, self-centred, undisciplined, immature, naive, and a drifter. Easily remedied, don't you think?' He was watching her intently as he recited the list, and she sensed that her reaction mattered to him.

'But you don't recognise that picture of yourself,' she said slowly, straining to make sense of him. 'If you were someone like me, you'd be used to people misunderstanding what you were like, because you'd keep a lot of yourself hidden. But you're not like that, you're extrovert, you show yourself to people. So if they don't like what they see, if they reject that, you've nothing to fall back on.'

He nodded. 'That's it. I'm supposed to change, but I don't see how I can. They say I'm self-centred, yet I've spent years doing voluntary work, going wherever I could be of use. Sticking shitty sheets through the laundry, holding hands with old people who don't know who I am one minute to the next, digging gardens, running youth groups, and all I've ever had out of it is free meals and a bed for the night. Like you're giving me. They didn't see it as worthy, they thought it showed I was a drifter who couldn't commit myself to anything, or get down to any solid work. Actually, I have done a paid job. I helped a friend set up a burger van, and I've worked for him a few hours a week on and off for years. But that didn't count. That was evidence of how thick I am.'

'You don't talk as though you're thick. Have you not done exams?'

'I did alright with my GCSEs, only I failed at A Level. I fell in love and got distracted. Too much revision of physical education, and not enough of RE. I couldn't exactly explain that to the selectors, could I? They might have started asking whether I was sleeping with Kate, and I don't suppose they'd have approved.' He pulled himself upright, to lean against the wall. 'They thought I was immature, and didn't have leadership potential, but I've never had any trouble leading youth clubs. I realised my life might look odd on paper, but I was sure once they met me, and I explained I'd seen it as getting experience of different things before ordination, there wouldn't be a problem. All the others who interviewed me before my selection conference seemed to think I was an ideal candidate.'

'I'm not surprised you feel awful. It must have come as a real shock.'

'Too right. And now I feel absolutely stuck - I don't know what to do with myself, with my life.' He sighed loudly. 'Maybe you're right, I should stop expecting to feel good about anything, and simply get on with whatever comes my way. Baz'll keep me busy.' He stretched out a hand to her, and, because he seemed to expect it, she let him grasp her fingers. 'You know, you're the most helpful person I've talked to for ages,' he said. 'You haven't once told me what you think I ought to be doing.'

'I wouldn't dream of telling you what to do.'

'Exactly.'

Jenny withdrew her hand, a little embarrassed. 'I'd better go. It's nearly eleven.'

'Thanks for coming up, and for listening so patiently. And for letting me get to know you a little.'

She stood up. 'I hate to think what I've been saying. Do you always have that effect on people?'

Michael got up off the bed. 'Usually. It was one of the things I thought would make me a good vicar.' He stretched and followed her out onto the landing. For an instant, she was afraid he was going to touch her again, but he turned aside to the toilet, saying, ''Scuse me. I need a leak.'

He had not shut the door, and the sound followed Jenny downstairs. He had no problems making himself at home. Perhaps that easy assumption that he could be himself, and be welcomed wherever he was and whatever he did, was what had been taken as arrogance. In which case that experience of rejection was probably good for him. She saw herself putting the point to him, and wondered at how she could possibly have become that confident in his friendship in so short a time. She felt faintly disconcerted by the way he had thrown himself into the still waters of her contented, self-sufficient life, setting the first tiny ripples spreading from the impact.

The terrifying loneliness that lowered over Michael in his first week was dispelled as he began to form a network of friends in Greathampton: Baz, the other youth club workers, people at church, acquaintances at The Bell, and staff at McDonald's, where he did lunchtime shifts to supplement his paid sessions in the East End Rows. Surrounded by people, he was more himself, and his partnership with Baz flourished.

As February wore on, he and Baz finalised their plans for the youth club at St Martin's. Teenagers attached to the church had their own meeting on Sunday nights; this was to be something for those with no connections. Michael began to hang around the area in the early evenings to cultivate the potential clientele. The work suited him. He had always been able to mix with anyone, and it did not take him long to win the trust of Kev, Robbie, and their mates. By the time the club opened in the first week in March, there was a core membership of a dozen, and more who joined as the weeks wore on.

There was no sign of Lisa; the lads said she'd been ill, and when he did come across her on his way back from the town centre early one afternoon, she looked pale and tired. She was sitting alone on the low wall that surrounded the church, smoking. The heavy flesh of her thighs spread over the brickwork, unflattered by the cropped lilac leggings she wore under a bulky jumper.

'Hi, Lisa. Got a day off school, have you?'

'Yeah. Got a bad stomach.' She eyed him warily. 'Do I know you?'

'I met you here, before Christmas. We talked about youth clubs.'

'Oh yeah, I remember.'

Michael sat on the wall beside her. 'We've got a club here on Thursday nights. Would you be interested?'

'How do I know you're on the level?'

'Some of your friends are coming - haven't they told you? And there've been notices up in school.' Michael produced a bundle of brightly coloured leaflets about the club from the pocket of his black donkey jacket and passed one to her. Lisa studied it, losing her air of indifference as she questioned him. He was to discover that her capacity for throwing herself wholeheartedly into whatever emotion or activity was at the forefront of her consciousness was both her greatest charm and her most dangerous fault. She was planning the programme she would put on for younger kids when she became one of his youth workers, when their intimacy was interrupted by a shrill accusation:

'Hey! What are you doing here? You should bleedin' well be in school.'

'Gawd, it's me mum.'

Michael would not have guessed the parentage. The woman who had stopped to yell at her was nerve thin, her sharp face creased with deep frown lines. Her hair had been layered and dyed blonde perhaps two months before, and dark roots showed above the frowzy, dull strands brushing her shoulders. Kwiksave carrier bags bulged from each hand, and beneath her open coat, a checked pink nylon tabard with *Samsons* embroidered on it suggested she was on leave from the DIY store up the road.

Anger obliterated Lisa's career aspirations. 'I'm bad, you fucking old cow.'

'Hey! Watch your mouth! You get back home if you're bad, you don't hang around with bleedin' blokes. And get that fag out of your mouth. I told you before.'

Lisa inhaled deliberately, facing her down.

'Best go, Lisa,' Michael said, standing up.

'You can keep out of it!' the woman yelled, jabbing a finger at Michael as she took a step towards him, her voice a painful screech inches from his face. 'You keep your hands off her, you sodding pervert. She's fourteen, bloody little slag. You touch her and I'll have the law on you.'

Across the street, one or two people turned to stare, welcoming a colourful diversion on a dull day.

The woman turned on Lisa again. 'Get on home, now, you, or I'll take a bloody strap to you.'

Lisa hauled herself off the wall. 'Up yours!' She fitted a gesture to her words as she wandered off down the street with as much nonchalance as she could muster.

'I'm not trying anything on with Lisa,' Michael said politely. 'I was telling her about the new youth club we've got in the church here.'

'She's not havin' nothin' to do with no bloody religion.'

'It's not that sort of club, but it might keep her off the streets, stop her getting into trouble, if that's what you're worried about.'

Lisa's mother hesitated, and Michael tried his most charming smile. 'Take a leaflet, see what you think.' He tucked the paper into one of her bags.

'Huh.' The woman followed Lisa down the road. But at least she hadn't said no.

Five

'It's for you, Michael,' Jenny called up the stairs at teatime one Saturday towards the end of March. There was no movement from above, and she laid the phone on its side while she went to find him. She knocked, and put her head round the door.

Michael was lying on his bed, reading, with her cat sprawled across his chest, while pop music played from the radio next to him.

'Phone for you. Becky.'

'Right.' He looked at the cat. Jenny smiled and removed it from him. She followed him downstairs, while the cat purred floppily in her arms.

'Becky! ... Yes, that would be great,' she heard him say as she went back to her living room. She curled up in her armchair, and buried her face in Celestine's fur. Fresh from her adultery, the cat smelt of Michael's aftershave. Of course it was good that he had a girlfriend, and it wasn't Becky's fault that her mother was so strident. Nan had preached at St Martin's once or twice, and Jenny - who in any case disliked the tone of Nan's campaigning on women priests - had found her sermons far too personal and passionate for her liking.

'Becky's staying at Nan's,' Michael said, coming in after a perfunctory knock. 'I said she could come over and see where I'm living. Is that OK?' He sat on the arm of the sofa that straddled the wall between the doors to the hall and the kitchen, leaning back and looking thoroughly at home as he always did.

'Yes, of course, as long as it is only looking, and you remember what I said about not wanting anyone staying the night with you. I mean...' She coloured. 'It's none of my business what you do or don't do, but not in my house. I don't agree with it.'

'I know.' He regarded her quizzically, a half smile on his mouth. 'Would you like me to make you a coffee? You can't possibly disturb Celly again, can you?'

Jenny stroked the cat's fur firmly, feeling the static electricity crackle under her hand. 'Thank you. Make one for yourself.' He was so wonderfully transparent, that was probably why she had come to trust him.

'I suppose you've had a lot of girlfriends,' Jenny said as he sat down again, having handed her coffee and a biscuit from her own tin. It was a measure of how easy she had become with him that she could say it without any self-consciousness.

'Not that many. Only two, seriously. There was Victoria, who I went out with when I was seventeen. She was why I messed up A Levels. We were together over two years, then I called on her unannounced one evening and found her in bed with someone else, which broke my heart at the time. I carefully didn't get involved with anyone for years. I confined myself to flirting with the girls who came to events at the conference centre I ended up working at - four days of lingering looks, and passionate kisses on their last night.' He smiled. 'Then I went back home to help out with the youth work for my dad, and fell in love with Kate. Four years, that lasted. I took it slowly because she was young, and she had school and college to get through.' He paused, staring down into his mug. 'Becky's supposed to help me get over it, but I'm not sure it works like that.'

'Four years is a long time. However much you think it was right to break up, you'll miss not having her around.'

'Exactly. And my parents still haven't forgiven me, so they're not much support. They're certain we'll get back together. When I went back the other week, there was Kate looking tearfully at me, and my mother telling me I ruined her.' He helped himself to another biscuit.

'Poor girl.'

'I used to think that, but now I resent the way she's hanging onto me.'

'How old are you?' Jenny asked suddenly. 'All these lengthy love affairs you've had time for, and all these things you've done.'

'Twenty-nine in May. How old are you, if you don't mind me asking?'

'Twenty-nine in April. Funny, I put you down as much younger than that. You look about twenty-one.'

'So much for my cultivated air of maturity. Perhaps that's what misled my selectors. Mind you, you being a GP, and sensible and respectable, I thought you must be years older than me.' Jenny stuck her tongue out at him and he grinned. 'So, tell me about your exotic love life.'

'What about it? I've never had one.'

'Oh, come on, surely you've had a few boyfriends.'

Jenny thought back. 'Well, there was the disco I went to at school, when I was in the fifth year. I got myself a new dress for the occasion,

43

which my mother said made me look like a sack of potatoes. She was probably right. The only boys who wanted to dance with me were a weedy little third year half my height, and one of the sixth year boys who grabbed hold of me and smooched through one of the slow numbers. It was quite nice at the time, but I later discovered he'd only done it for a bet. And when I was in the sixth form there was a curate at my dad's church who was in love with me. He took me to a Church Missionary Society rally, and on the way back, he stopped his car and kissed me. He kept forcing his tongue in my mouth. I'd no idea men did that. Ugh. Then there was a drunken registrar who used to try to grope me on nights at the hospital. That's about it, really.'

'I find that hard to believe. You're good company, and you're not bad-looking. You could do something about how you dress, though. That's why I had you down as older. Those shapeless skirts and blouses don't flatter you. You don't mind me saying that?'

'Yes, I do. But you're wasting your time telling me. I've known since I was little that I wasn't the marrying kind. Why do you think I've nobly dedicated myself to medicine and doing good? One of my earliest memories is of my mother saying "It's a good thing she does seem to have a little intelligence, because she's really rather ugly, isn't she? If only she'd been a boy".'

'What a nasty thing to say in front of a child. I thought mothers were supposed to think their children were wonderful.'

'Neither of my parents thought I was any good at all. But then, they're like that with everybody, except my sainted sister. They spend their lives criticising everyone, especially me.'

'Surely they were pleased when you qualified as a doctor?'

'Not really. First of all, they thought being a nurse was a more suitable occupation for a woman. Then my mother kept telling me how hard I'd find the work, and since I did find it difficult, that wasn't what I needed to hear. Then finally, they didn't come to my graduation, because my sister was calling in after she'd been in Germany for a month, and "we really can't be away, Jennifer. I'm sure you understand. Besides, it would mean re-arranging the PCC".' The mockery in her voice was more intense than she had anticipated. She carried on, horrified to find her eyes filling with tears. 'Then her final contribution was to say "Of course, if it had been one of the London medical schools, like Stanley's boy, it would have been a different sort of occasion. But it *is* only Birmingham." Six years of my life, slaving away, and all she could do was dismiss it.'

44

'She sounds like a monster,' Michael said. 'Hey, don't cry.' He put his mug down and moved across to squat by her chair, rubbing her shoulder with one hand, while the other searched his pockets for a handkerchief.

Jenny produced one of her own. 'I'm sorry to be silly, it's a few years ago now, I've got over it really.' She blinked rapidly. 'Never cry with contact lenses in.'

'I didn't know you wore lenses. They don't show.' He stared into her eyes inquisitively, the limpid brown of his own eyes too close for comfort.

Jenny looked away.

'Do you have anyone else to talk to besides me?' he asked, sitting down on the floor, and leaning over her chair arm to caress Celestine, while he regarded Jenny sympathetically.

'Not really. Caroline tries to be friendly, and she's invited me for meals once or twice, but she will insist on asking a spare man to balance me, and that makes me angry, so I said "no" last time. Then people think I'm snobbish, because I don't say much, but it's only because I'm shy, and I don't find it easy to fit in. Or, of course, they're busy asking me about their bowels, which isn't my idea of social conversation.'

'I haven't found you difficult to get on with. I like you,' he said, moving his hand from the cat to pat her knee, and then back again.

'But I'm so dull.'

'You can't be that dull. What about that pornographic French film you took me to see on Wednesday?'

Jenny giggled suddenly. She felt her cheeks burning as her hand flew to her mouth. 'It was rather embarrassing, wasn't it? I'd no idea it was going to be like that.' She belonged to a film club in Leathwell, set up to show the more avant garde movies that didn't make the mainstream cinemas.

Michael had tagged along with her, expanding his education, he said. 'I enjoyed it,' he said innocently.

'You would.'

The doorbell interrupted their exchange.

'That'll be Becky,' he said. 'Are you OK?'

Jenny nodded. Michael squeezed her thigh companionably as he got up. She had been touched more in the last two months than in her entire life, and though she hadn't quite got used to Michael's tendency to embrace everything and everyone that came within his reach, he did it so naturally, so unthreateningly, that she had almost begun to enjoy it. She wondered what his girlfriends made of his indiscriminate friendliness, and tried not to listen to the voices and the eloquent silences as he greeted Becky in the hall outside.

45

Michael let Becky into the hall and kissed her. 'Nice to see you again,' he said, sliding his hands down her body. 'Let me get a jacket, then we can go.'

'Can't I come up and see your room?' Becky asked, inserting her hands in the back pockets of his jeans, and pulling him to her.

'I'm not allowed to entertain ladies. Landlady's regulations.'

'Can I meet her?'

'Who, Jenny?' Michael tilted his head back and searched her face. 'Not jealous, are you?'

'Course not. Just interested.'

Michael stepped away from her, shrugged, and went back down the hall to knock at Jenny's door again. 'I thought you might like to say hello to Becky,' he said, ushering her into the room. Jenny looked at him crossly. Colour crept over the normal pallor of her face, but whether of anger or embarrassment he wasn't sure.

He heard her making polite conversation as he went upstairs to fetch his coat, and hurried down again to rescue her.

'She's a bit grim, isn't she?' Becky said as they set off down the road.

'No, she's not. She's one of my best friends.'

Michael missed the quizzical look Becky directed at him, which suggested that for all the drabness of the bristling woman she had just met, she did not feel altogether safe. He was enjoying the quiet blossoming of his friendship with Jenny without analysing why he kept turning to her when she was such hard work a lot of the time. She hoisted 'no entry' signs about her as often as she allowed him to walk her private byways, but when she was prepared to attend to him, he felt whole without knowing why. She was intelligent, observant, talked about her work with dry humour, listened without trying to solve his problems or to organise his future. She worked long hours, and he was careful not to press his companionship, limiting the times he dropped by in the evenings, or walked to church with her, or accompanied her on trips to the supermarket, swimming pool or cinema. Such friendship did nothing to feed his need for bodily intimacy, however, which was why, every now and then, as winter turned to spring, he had returned to Becky for the energetic, uncomplicated physical gratification she offered.

'Why can't I come back to your room?' Becky asked, as they left the pub at closing time. 'It'd be easier than wondering when Nan was going to come barging in. Say I'm coming for a coffee. Go on. Even your old dragon can't object to that.'

'She's not a dragon. She doesn't want me having girlfriends staying the night, that's all. Let's go to your place.'

'No. I want to see your room. I'll be good. Promise. You can tell Jenny you'll leave the door ajar - that's what mum used to make me do when I took boyfriends home after a date.'

Reluctantly, Michael agreed, but he was relieved to find Jenny's little Peugot 205 absent when they arrived at the house. He led Becky up the stairs, put the kettle on to boil, and left her briefly while he went to the toilet. When he came back, her clothes were in a heap on the floor, and she was lying on his bed, laughing at him.

Alarmed, he shut the door tightly behind him. 'Becky, no! Put your clothes on. If Jenny finds out ...'

'Oh, come on, Michael, don't be such a coward.' She got up to kneel at the end of the bed, and grabbed hold of him. 'Just a little kiss. While she's out...'

She was already loosening his clothing, and his resistance crumbled. 'Maybe a quickie,' he said.

He awoke hours later to find himself still entangled damply with Becky's naked form. He should have known better than to expect her to be either quick, or quiet. He groped on the floor to find his bedside clock, dislodged there at some point in the night. Five thirty-five a.m. 'Oh, God! Becky.' He shook her. 'Wake up! You ought to go back. Nan'll wonder what's happened to you.'

She groaned, and reached out to kiss him again.

'Becky!'

She opened her eyes, protesting as he thrust her clothes at her and nagged her until she put them on. Pulling on his own jeans and sweatshirt over a complaining body, he steered her out of the house, and through deserted streets to her home. He hoped to God Jenny hadn't realised what was going on, or he'd be in big trouble.

'Look,' he said, as they neared Nan's house, 'I think it would be best if we didn't see each other again. I'm probably going to get chucked out if Jenny finds out, but it's not just that.' He took her hand. 'I like you a lot, Beck, but I don't feel happy about this ... arrangement we've got. I want something more ... more permanent, I suppose.'

Becky pulled her hand away. 'Like having it away with your frigid

47

little landlady? Worried she might have heard you sticking me one last night, are you? I should have guessed, you're always going on about her. Bloody Jenny this, bloody Jenny that. Well, you can tell her from me that she's in for a disappointment. You're a lousy fuck. I should know, I've had plenty of decent lovers to compare you with.'

'Of course you have. I've been a convenient bit of fun for you - but it's not enough for me. And it's nothing to do with Jenny.'

'Yeah, well.' They had reached her gate. Becky hugged him. 'I'm sorry, Mike. I didn't mean it. I don't like being woken up at this hour. It's been good while it lasted. Let's have a drink some time.'

'I'd like that. I'd like to stay friends. Good luck, Beck. God bless.'

He kissed her cheek, watched her slip into the house, and walked back to Jenny's. The break had been surprisingly easy to make. He let himself into the house as quietly as possible, pushed the door closed with a muted click, and prepared to tiptoe upstairs. As he put a hand on the bannisters, Jenny came out from her bedroom, her face drained and ashen. She confronted him at the bottom of the stairs, clutching at her fluffy white dressing-gown with agitated fingers.

'How *could* you? You *know* what I told you, you agreed. Half the night I had to listen to you. That woman calling out, and the bed going and ... it was dreadful. I've never been so embarrassed in my life. I thought you had standards. I thought you were my friend. How could you do it? You'll have to go. You'll have to find somewhere else.'

Michael received the onslaught uncomfortably. He didn't like being in the wrong. 'I am sorry, Jenny,' he said, taking a step towards her.

She moved back abruptly. 'Don't think you can coax your way out of this one.'

'Come off it, Jen, don't be so prudish. Even most Christians don't wait till they're married these days.'

'I do. I've got principles. I mean, not that I'm ever going to marry. It's obvious no one would ever want to go to bed with me. But even if they did, I wouldn't.'

'Well, maybe I'm different.' He glared at her, then abandoned the attempt at self-justification. 'Actually, I feel awful about it. I've only slept with girls I was really serious about. I should never have taken up with Becky.'

'I don't care what you do, or who you do it with, except when it's in my house. Screw who you like, but not in my house. Not under my nose.'

Jenny turned to go back into her bedroom. Michael, trying again to reach her, put his hand on her shoulder. She stiffened, then inclined her head back towards him. Their eyes met in the mirror on the hall wall. His face concerned, serious, hers miserable, with dark patches under her eyes. A thought flashed into Michael's mind, and disappeared before he could challenge it. You're going to marry her, it said. He laughed to himself, dismissing it as a joke of his subconscious, arising out of Becky's jibes. Sensible, unalluring Jenny. Dear Jenny. His friend. Who would he confide in if she threw him out?

'Please don't make me leave,' he said. 'It won't happen again. I've told her I don't want to see her again.'

'I can't have you staying, not with all that ...'

'Please?'

'Oh, I suppose you can stay.' She pulled away from his hand and went into her room, shutting the door firmly behind her.

The St Martin's youth club had grown in popularity since its opening, and there were regularly some twenty or thirty teenagers present on Thursday evenings. Though Baz was ostensibly in charge, he left it to Michael to run the club each week, with the help of a couple of other volunteers, one from the estate, and one from the church. Ten days after Becky's visit, Michael was leaning on the hatch to the kitchen, trying to have a conversation with a lad on the other side about his recent exclusion from school.

The volume of the music shaking the air from the loudspeaker nearby was making it difficult to hear; Charmaine had to shout to get his attention:

'Michael, I think there's something wrong with Lisa. She's been locked in the toilet for ages, and she won't come out. Me and Gemma have been talking to her, and Sharon's been in, but she keeps telling us to go away.'

Michael followed her across the hall and through into the passage where the toilets were situated. As the door swung to behind him, the music faded to an insistent thudding. Sharon, one of his helpers, was hovering in the doorway of the Ladies. 'Lisa won't come out. Do you think we ought to force the door? What if she's hurt herself?'

'Do you know what the matter is, Charmaine?' he asked.

'No. She was a bit down today in school, wasn't she, Gemma? But that's because she was on. Said she'd got a bad stomach.'

'Perhaps I'd better have a word with her,' Michael said. He left the girls gossiping in the passageway, and went into the Ladies.

The door of the end cubicle was shut, and he stood by it, calling gently. 'Lisa? What's the matter? Can I help?'

'I'm dying,' came a trembling voice through the door.

'Can you open the door? We can't help unless we can get to you.'

They had been solidly built, these cubicles, with no gaps above the doors and only a few centimetres of space at the bottom. Lisa had her bag beside the door, so he could see nothing of her. In any case, the bolts were inside, and if the occupant remained intransigent, there was no access short of forcing the door.

Michael sat down on the floor, the easier to direct his voice through the opening. 'Can you tell me what the problem is?'

He heard her moan.

'Lisa?'

'I'm bleeding,' she faltered at last. 'It won't stop. An' it hurts.'

'Is it your period, Lisa?' he asked, feeling out of his depth. Surely this was what Sharon was here for?

'It's worse than that.' She groaned. 'Owww. I'm going to die.'

'Shall I phone for an ambulance?'

'No!' The word was a shout. 'No! I don't want my mum to know. I won't come out if you do.'

'What about your doctor?'

'No! He'd tell my mum. She'll kill me.'

'Why should she kill you? You can't help being ill.'

Lisa said nothing, only groaned again. The sound frightened him. He wondered how long it would take to break the door down, and if they could do it without crashing against the girl inside. Inspiration visited him. 'I've got a friend who's a doctor, and she's only up the road. Would you let her see you, Lisa? I think you need help. If you let her see you and talk to you, your mum wouldn't have to know, would she? Can I ask Jenny to come?'

He had to strain to hear her reply, but it sounded affirmative. He went out to find a phone, praying that Jenny would be in, and that she'd come.

Six

Jenny resisted involvement at first, telling Michael to call an ambulance, or the girl's own doctor.

'She's locked in, Jenny,' he'd said, 'it'll take hours to get her out. I know you've not forgiven me yet, but you're the only one with a chance of getting Lisa to open up. I don't know what to do otherwise.'

She'd picked up the urgency in his voice, and in the end had driven to St Martin's with her bag.

Alone before the toilet door, Jenny put her bag down, and called the girl's name. 'Lisa? I'm Jenny Furlong. I'm a doctor. I'm a friend of Michael's.' She baulked at saying it, but the mantra worked. The bolt slid back, and Jenny pushed open the door.

Lisa had sat back on the toilet, but her brief step to the door had left blood in dark splashes on the floor. Her leggings and pants were round her ankles, with a sanitary towel attached, drenched with blood. Fresh red trails marked the inside of the girl's legs, and she was dabbing ineffectually at them with toilet paper, her hands shaking.

'I'm goin' to die. I can't stop bleeding. It just floods out. Ohhh, my stomach.' She bent double as spasms shook her.

'You're not going to die,' Jenny said, putting a hand on her shoulder. 'You'll be alright. How long have you been bleeding like this?'

'I come on this afternoon, and it's got worse. Owwww. I hadn't had it for a while, and it's like it's all coming at once. Ohhh, my stomach, I can't hardly stand.'

'Could you be pregnant?'

Lisa looked away.

'Is it possible, Lisa? Have you had sex with anyone?'

The girl looked at her through terrified eyes. 'January,' she whispered eventually.

'You're having a miscarriage,' Jenny said, 'but your body's having trouble getting rid of everything. You're going to need to go to hospital, so they can clear your womb out, and stop the bleeding. You've lost a lot of blood, so you may need a transfusion. Do you understand?'

Lisa shook her head, and began to sob. Jenny put an arm round her. 'You'll be alright. I'll take you in in my car, and then we'll get your mum to ...'

'No!' Lisa broke in. 'No! You mustn't tell my mum. She'll kill me.'

'She'll have to know, Lisa. I'm sure she'll be so worried about you, she won't remember to be angry. That's what mums are like. Come on, let's get you tidied up, and once I've got you to hospital, I'll go and see her and explain. Would you let me tell Michael? It'll be easier if I've got someone to help me.'

The girl consented, too weak to do much else.

The baby was lying on its back in a puddle on a filthy, grey, stone floor. Vast walls loomed in the darkened distance, meeting high above his head in a metal girdered roof. The baby was naked, except for a disposable nappy, yellow, swollen and sodden round its hips. It had been there for hours or days, crying intermittently, croaking brokenly, as if it knew no one would come. There were people around, somewhere in the building, but they were all turned away. He bent down and touched the baby's cheek. So icy, so chill, it was hard to believe that it belonged to anything living. He wanted to pick the child up, to remove the saturated nappy, and to warm the infant against his skin, to fill it with warm milk, to see the colour come back to its abandoned body. But he couldn't lift it, and there was no time left. He was too late.

Michael woke with a start, dragging the nightmare with him into consciousness. He sat up in bed, disturbed to the core of his being without knowing why; he usually slept too soundly to remember his dreams. It's thinking about Lisa's miscarriage, he told himself, but the power of his dream would not fade. In an effort to rid himself of the image, he got up to go to the toilet. Though it was past two, the landing was faintly illuminated from below. From the half-landing, he could see that a light was on in Jenny's sitting room, so he grabbed the elderly, baggy, green jumper he had purloined from his father to use in lieu of a dressing gown, put it on over his tee shirt and the pyjama bottoms that had been a Christmas present from his sister Ruth, and went downstairs.

He knocked lightly on the door, and went in.

Jenny was sitting in front of the gas fire in her dressing gown, holding a mug, and the face she turned towards him was bleak and drawn. 'What are you doing up?' she asked.

Michael went over to the fire, and sat beside her, extending his bare toes to the orange glow of the flames. 'I had a nightmare about an abandoned baby,' he said, examining the haunting image as he recalled it for her. 'Are you any good at interpretations?'

'You've eaten something, or you're under stress - or you're feeling abandoned. I don't know.'

'No, I don't. Whatever, it's fading now I'm down here. Couldn't you sleep either?'

'I can usually stay detached,' Jenny said, 'but I keep thinking about it - her mother. How could she be like that?'

Jenny had delivered Lisa to hospital, then collected Michael, and gone to fetch Lisa's mother. Impatient to return to the television blaring from the living room, the woman had listened angrily, said it was all the girl's fault for being such a slut, and sent them away. As they'd walked to the car, a young girl of about nine came out of the house, thin and shivering in a tee shirt, and pulled at Michael's arm.

'Is Lise gonna die?' she asked.

'She'll be OK,' Michael replied, 'but she could do with someone with her. Is there anyone else we could try?'

'You could call our gran over in Nottling. Lisa goes over there a lot. Do you want her number?'

So Michael had rung, explaining to a shocked woman called Stella Atkins as best he could, and offering to fetch her, since the last buses to Greathampton had long since gone. In fact, Jenny had had to drive, since Michael had neither car nor insurance, and she was so silent during the journey that he thought he had offended her yet again in assuming her co-operation. But at least they had delivered Stella to Lisa's bedside, and she had not been left entirely comfortless.

'I was remembering once when I was little,' Jenny said, gazing into the fire. 'Nine or ten, I must have been. My mother had a committee meeting, and I fell over and grazed my arm really badly. So I went into the meeting, and she bundled me out furiously, saying I *knew* never to interrupt her meetings, and how *dare* I drip blood on the carpet. So I sat on the back doorstep for ages, picking tiny bits of gravel out of my arm, and trying to clean it with a handkerchief. It was agony. Then I used a tea towel to wrap round my arm, because I didn't know what else to do, and when the meeting finished, my mother shouted at me for using it, and ripped it off, told me I was making a fuss about nothing, and sent me to bed without any supper. I don't ever remember being cuddled when I got hurt - or any other time, come to that. I have images of myself standing near my mother, wanting something, but not knowing what, and she'd tell me to stop getting in her way. It's not that it bothers me now, of course, but it's funny how memories like that come back every now and then.'

Michael moved closer to her, and put an arm round her shoulders. He felt her tense, but as he squeezed her shoulder, she let her head fall against him, and it consoled him to be comforting her as he had failed to comfort the child in his dream.

'I wonder what will happen to Lisa now?' he said. 'I do hope her mum lets her go and live with her gran, it sounded like a sensible idea. She's not a bad girl, really. Just ignorant.'

'But how can she be that ignorant? They get sex education at school, don't they? What were they playing at, experimenting with sex at that age, and thinking that if the boys used cling film it would all be quite safe?'

'Perhaps you could come and talk to the youth club about contraception, answer some of their questions. I'll bet you can spell parts of the body the rest of us have never heard of.'

'Perhaps you could try setting them a better example. How are kids supposed to know how to behave if people they look up to think nothing of bonking someone different every night, even people who are supposed to be Christians.'

Jenny pulled away from him as she spoke, and Michael dropped his arm. 'Why bring that up suddenly?' He looked at her profile. 'Why are you still so angry with me? I know I was wrong, but I've said sorry, and I've finished with Becky, and I'm not sure what else I can do.'

'I'm not angry with you.'

'Like hell you're not. I've been feeling your disapproval infiltrating its way through my ceiling for the last ten days, and you haven't smiled at me once.'

'Don't exaggerate.' She stared at the fire. 'Oh, alright, perhaps I have overreacted. It's not as if I haven't lived in shared houses and listened to people thrashing around in ecstasy before. I guess it's because I didn't think you were like that. You've always seemed sensitive and gentle, and I feel uncomfortable knowing you're a ... oh, what the heck, it's half past two in the morning, who cares what I say, you're a grown up man who has sex like a rutting stag.'

Michael burst out laughing. 'A sex fiend, no less, and in such innocuous guise.' He leant back, propped on his hands, looking down on the holed rib of his shapeless jumper. 'Actually, I'll tell you a secret, as it is half past two in the morning. All that vigorous rutting stuff isn't really my style. Far too tiring, and it inflicts all kinds of damage on my delicate anatomy. Though I have to say Becky has probably improved my technique. I shall be an amazing lover if I ever dare give up celibacy.'

'Michael! You shouldn't say that sort of thing to me.'

'Why not? You're a doctor.'

'Don't tease me.'

'Alright. I'll be serious. I've been hurt by you not speaking to me over the last couple of weeks. I really value your friendship. I wish we could go back to where we were before. I'd like to go out with you occasionally again, because I enjoy your company, and I can talk to you in a way I don't with other people.'

Jenny gazed thoughtfully at him.

'I do mean just as friends, I don't want a girlfriend. I mean, I like you, but not that way...' He found himself floundering.

Jenny smiled. 'I quite understand. I value your friendship too. You let me know when you're at a loose end, and I'll see if I'm free.'

In the tortuous years ahead, Michael was frequently to wonder how he came to marry Jenny. She always said it was simply because she was there, that it could have been anyone who offered him sympathy and security and steadiness in a world that stubbornly refused to have any religious meaning, but there was more to it than that. He was more himself when he was with her, needed the reflection of himself that she gave him. He missed her when he didn't see her. Each time he replayed that first year in his head, he could never see himself acting differently. Though there were many opportunities to discard their growing friendship, each time it was he who could not let it go.

He couldn't remember sexual attraction being a part of it, and honestly believed that the physical contact he had with her was no different from the way he touched and hugged others around him. That night, he put his arms around Jenny, and kissed her cheek, and returned to his bed to sleep untroubled, without considering himself disingenuous in the slightest. But Jenny sat for another half-hour looking into the fire, unsure whether she had the strength to cope with someone whose care and physical proximity so disarmed her. He would be an easy person to fall in love with.

Some six weeks later, Michael and Jenny were walking to the youth club, ready to introduce a discussion about sex.

'It's not really my area,' Jenny told him again. 'Everyone expected you were bound to specialise in Obstetrics and Gynaecology if you were female, so I decided not to Why are you laughing?'

'You're always telling me you're dull and boring, but you're a rebel at heart, aren't you?' He moved on swiftly as he saw her bridle. 'Anyway, you know a hell of a lot more than any of the youth club do, and they trust you. They were impressed with how you dealt with Lisa. All I need is for you to be a medical agony aunt for the evening. Can you get AIDS from sharing a toothbrush? Do babies come out of your navel? Is masturbation a route to hell, damaging to health, or a perfectly natural way to survive celibacy, that kind of stuff.'

'That last one sounds like your question,' Jenny said, turning pink, 'and if you've thrown it in to embarrass me, you've succeeded.'

'Not at all. It's the main form of sexual activity most of them know. The lads, anyway, I've never quite known what girls get up to. Maybe if you're embarrassed about it, you'd better not come.'

'I'm not embarrassed about the subject, it's when you talk about yourself. I don't want to know about your sex life.'

'Or lack of it,' Michael muttered as he held open the door of St Martin's for her.

'Or lack of it,' said her voice behind him as they made their way to the meeting room.

The discussion got under way. Michael sat in the circle of teenagers watching Jenny pretending she was entirely familiar with the peculiar language with which his charges talked about sex.

He intervened. 'Rather than completely confusing Jenny about what you're talking about, let's have a look at the words you use for different parts of the body, and different kinds of sexual activity.' He sent Robbie to find a flip chart, and before long, they had covered several pages with a collection of obscenities that chilled with their relentless brutality. He'd certainly have to make sure he removed them from the chart before going home.

'So is that what sex is really all about?' he asked them.

The discussion that followed was intense, though conducted with great ribaldry and humour. Michael could sense Jenny's discomfort at some of the views and anecdotes being offered, but she answered their questions with a practical authority that impressed him.

'Well, you can't let your feelings interfere when there's a job to be done, can you?' she told him when he commented on it during their walk home. 'You obviously don't go in for lectures on morality, so it wasn't for me to start.'

'I thought we talked a lot about morality, we just didn't give it that

56

label. They switch off immediately if anyone tries to lecture them, Jen. At least this way they think a little bit about things, and there's a chance they'll behave differently.'

'I can see that, but I still think Peter would have been horrified.'

'You mean you were horrified.'

She gave his statement some thought. 'Uncomfortable, maybe, not horrified. It's you, you're a bad influence on me. I knew where I was before you moved in.'

'Do you regret it?'

'Oh, daily,' she said, 'but I expect you're good for me.'

Michael slipped his arm through hers companionably, and they turned down the street towards home.

'Robbie, you never did!'

'Mike'll shit hisself.'

Robbie drained his coke can, threw it onto the pavement with a satisfying clatter, and belched loudly at Gemma and Kev, walking beside him, caught between horror and admiration.

'Yeah, but tha's a right laugh, innit? I can jus' see their faces. Wankers! Wan-kers!'

Robbie jumped in the air as he paraded down the street, chanting the word. Take the flip chart back, Mike had said, so he'd done it, but he'd had a bright idea on the way. The sheets they'd used had been carefully rolled up and folded into the bin, and it only took a moment to retrieve one of them, to smooth it down, and to stick it back in the middle of the pad with some of the Blu-tack he'd spotted on the window sill. And now the flip chart was back in its proper place, and he could not conceal his admiration of his own brilliance.

Seven

To call Nottling a village suggested a picturesqueness it had never had, even in the days when it had been a cluster of houses around a green. Two decades of housing development had turned it into a small town, though without the range of facilities. It took forty minutes by bus from Greathampton, on a route which wound through neighbouring villages, but Michael, staring out of the window, and dreaming about nothing in particular, wasn't noticing the time.

Lisa had gone to live with Stella during the Easter holidays, and he was anxious to see that she had recovered, and was settling in to her new school. She met him at the bus stop, waving to him over the heads of the Nottling residents disembarking the bus after a day's work in Greathampton. Her round face lit up as he took her hands, and then hugged her. Normally he held back from such embraces with the girls in the youth club, but her traumas and her move to Nottling had moved their relationship onto an altered footing.

Lisa looked little different, except that her delight in seeing him had brought a brightness to her eyes. She chattered all the way back along the road to her gran's house, and all through the egg and chips and sticky cake they had for tea. He had a private conversation with Stella while Lisa watched Home and Away, and was relieved to hear that she was coping after a difficult patch at school, and at last making friends in Nottling. After supper, Lisa walked back to the bus stop with him, taking a circuitous route to show him the village green, dull under a white sky. Two groups of boys were playing football: six or seven in one match, shrieking at each other as they strove to put the ball between the coats they had set down as goalposts; two smaller boys on their own, chasing after a ball with directionless eagerness. A dark-haired woman sat on a bench with a book in her hand, looking at them from time to time.

'That's Mrs Thompson, my history teacher. Those're her boys, she comes here sometimes with them,' Lisa said, crossing the grass with a wary eye on the footballers.

Michael followed her.

'Hello Miss. This is Michael from the youth club in Greathampton. I told you about 'im. He was good to me when I was in trouble.'

The woman dropped the furtive cigarette she'd been smoking, and ground it underfoot. A thin hand went up to brush the fringe out of her eyes as she sized him up. 'Hello. I've heard a lot about you. Lisa thinks the world of you.'

'I gotta go, Miss. I'm babysitting.'

'Thanks ever so much for supper, Lisa,' Michael said, with a hand on her shoulder. 'Take care. Give me a ring if you ever need me for anything.'

'Ta. I will.' She walked off across the grass with an ungainly stride.

Michael was about to take his leave of her teacher when he noticed the cover of the book she was reading. He sat down on the bench, intrigued. 'I've read that,' he said sitting down on the bench beside her. 'Is that school work, or are you interested for yourself? Because if you are, I know exactly what it's like.'

She stared at him in amazement. 'How very curious you should turn up saying that. I don't know, is the answer. Do you remember the Church of England voting on women priests? I was watching it, and when they announced the result, I suddenly had an incredibly strong feeling this was for me. I knew it was stupid. I mean, me! I've only been going to church for five years, and all I do there is organise the creche on Sunday mornings. It's not as if I've got anything to offer, and my husband's hardly going to approve. I've tried to put it out of my mind, but it keeps nagging away at me. Then I found this book about vocations in the library, and I feel confused again.' Her voice was low and husky, curiously attractive, even if it was only a symptom of the vocal demands of her profession.

He thought for a moment, studying the woman's face. She was slim and blue-eyed like Kate, though her hair was several shades darker, and lines worried around her eyes.

'You ought to go and talk to Nan Patten,' he said.

'Oh, I couldn't possibly. She wouldn't want to bother with someone like me.'

'Sure she would. I don't know her that well, but I do know she's had quite a few women coming to talk to her since the vote, to discuss whether it's something they should pursue. She's very approachable, and she works for the Leathwell Programme for Ministerial Training, so she knows a lot about it. Go and see her. Say I told you to, if you like. I can mention your name to her. Mrs Thompson, was it?'

59

'Alison. No, I couldn't. ... Though it's odd, isn't it? That I should be sitting here reading this, and you appear out of the blue to suggest what I can do about it? Almost as if it might be meant. I feel like that eunuch chap reading Isaiah, and having Stephen come up to his chariot and explain it all to him.'

Michael smiled. 'You definitely don't look like a female equivalent of a eunuch, and I'm not baptising you in the village pond, it doesn't look very sanitary. Look, give me your phone number, and I'll ring you tonight and give you Nan's number.'

Alison tore a tiny scrap of paper off a blank page at the back of her book, and scribbled her number on it with a pencil stub extracted from her pocket.

Michael tucked it into the pocket of his jeans. 'Good luck!' he said, holding out his hand.

She shook it with narrow fingers that were dry to his touch. 'Thanks for encouraging me. You'd better hurry or you'll miss your bus.'

Michael jogged across the grass and through the alley to the main road, just in time to board the bus. He might be utterly confused about his own direction in life, but there was the occasional sign that life had purpose. It was nice not to be completely forgotten.

May gave way to June. Jenny was busier than ever, and scarcely noticed the summer arriving through her surgery window. Though her caseload remained steady, her paperwork seemed to have multiplied, and she was doing a course on family planning, which left her with little free time. She was hanging on the telephone trying to sort out a hospital admission, while she munched a sandwich and dealt with her mail, when Margaret, one of the receptionists, put her head round the door:

'There's a young man asking to see you, says he's a friend, and can he have a word with you. Says he knows it's your lunch hour, but he'll be happy to share your sandwiches. He'd got such a nice smile, I said I'd see if you were available. Michael Turner, he says his name is.'

Jenny smiled. 'Oh, yes, send him in ... hello?' She turned her attention back to the phone, narrowly avoiding taking a bite from a letter headed Greathampton General Hospital, instead of her bread. 'What time did you say?'

Michael appeared in the doorway as she rang off. They had seen little of one another in recent weeks. When she arrived home, she was often too tired to talk to him, and in any case, he'd found some mates to play tennis with - and drink with afterwards - and what with the youth club nights and music practice, was rarely in.

'What a nice surprise,' she said. 'You'll have set tongues wagging through there. Here, have a sandwich.'

Michael took the sandwich box and sat down in the chair at the side of her desk, looking with interest around the clutter of her consulting room. 'Thank you. I hope you don't mind me popping in like this, something's cropped up, and I wanted to tell you before I saw Peter.'

'Go on,' she said. 'But excuse me if I yawn. I flag around lunchtime.'

'This'll liven you up.' He took a large bite of the sandwich and spoke through his mouthful. 'Imagine the scene. Monday afternoon. The Mothers Union are gathered in the Church Hall. Mrs Jennings is giving a talk on family values. She's written a beautiful list - respect, discipline, love, etcetera. Unfortunately, someone with a tidy mind has closed the flip chart, so she shuffles through it in front of her somnolent audience - this is two-thirty in the afternoon, remember - so as to find her list. She sees a page of black writing, and thinks, "Ah, good, this is what I want", and she steps away from the easel and says, "Here you'll find a list of what I mean when I talk about family values".'

Jenny's stomach dropped. 'No! It can't have been, you threw our sheets away...'

Michael held up his hand, and she stopped. 'There is a stunned silence from the members, horrified gasps rend the air. Wanking. Beating your meat. Jerking off. Spanking your plank. Surely Mrs Jennings is not recommending these for the Christian family?'

'Oh heck.'

'Heck indeed. I had a moment's hope that being mainly elderly ladies, they wouldn't understand what it all meant, but no such luck. At first they thought it was just kids having a bit of fun, but I'd put that bit about onanism, and a Bible reference to show it had been going on for thousands of years, and they didn't think kids would have done that. So eventually, I get a phone call from Peter, and I have to confess.'

'But how did it happen?'

'I must have missed one of the sheets somehow, though I was sure I'd checked. The trouble is, Peter's in one of his periodic fits of rigorism, and he's into stamping out sexual immorality. So the thought that I'd been allowing the youth club to discuss masturbation, rather than simply telling them it was a sin, got him more than a little irate. I explained it was part of an evening session on sex and relationships generally, but I think that made it worse. Then he said, did I know that Mr. Partridge found a used condom outside the West door last week...'

'Better than cling film.'

'Not to Mr Partridge. If all he finds is cling film, he merely thinks they've been indulging in an orgy of sandwich eating. Condoms is a tad more obvious. Anyway, Peter isn't sure the PCC is going to countenance the youth club continuing if this is the sort of thing we get up to, and I'm summoned to explain it all to him at five o'clock.'

'You shouldn't have to deal with it all yourself. I was part of that session, and Baz knew about it.'

'It was my idea, and I accept it's my responsibility, but I thought you ought to be warned in case anyone asks you about it. And I needed to talk to someone, because I'm worried. What happens if the PCC want to close us down?'

Jenny looked at her watch. 'I'll be in surgery again at five, or I'd come with you, but I could give Peter a call before then if you think it will help.'

'Would you? He still thinks you're sound, so if you say it was all above board, he might believe it. He knows I suffer from lax morals.'

'Well, then, he's wrong. Apart from that business with Becky, which you're not that proud of anyway, you're the most moral person I know. I wish I had half your dedication, especially when you've virtually lost your faith.'

'Thank you. That's one of the things that worries me, though. Am I working like this with the youth club because it's the best thing for them, or because I'm not a proper Christian, and I don't have the right motives any more?' Michael got up and went to the window.

'You have to judge it by its fruits, don't you?' Jenny joined him, looking out over the stream that ran behind the surgery, sluggish in its gully below a rusted and damaged wire fence. 'Lisa trusting you when she wouldn't tell anyone else. The way you talking about what it was like being in love with Kate got Robbie admitting there might be more to sex than a five-second screw. You're doing brilliantly. Don't let Peter bully you.'

Michael smiled at her, and put an arm round her shoulders. 'Thank you for that pep talk.' He was silent for a few moments, then let her go. 'Are you doing anything on the 26th?'

'Not necessarily.'

'It was going to be our wedding day. I'd like to get away, do something different - would you keep me company?'

She could hardly turn him down, though a whole day with him would be as painful as it was gratifying. She would dress her mediocre best, and walk with him, or sit across a table from him, laughing at his stories, stimulated into argument, and drowning in his eyes, and he would not be moved one iota by her beauty, intelligence and wit. In her dreams, he reached for her hand and declared his love. In reality, he dropped in and out of her life as it suited him. Took what she had to offer and left her hungry. Just like he'd done this lunchtime, she reflected ruefully, as she picked a single strand of cheese out of her lunch box. At least love was not quite such a finite resource.

Jenny's phone call and Michael's contrition went some way towards convincing Peter that the youth club had not yet been entirely corrupted, but he insisted that the PCC should consider the whole question of its programme. Baz and Michael were summoned to the next meeting to be told that what the youth club needed was a dose of sound moral teaching.

And the PCC, in the shape of Mrs Jennings, had the answer. 'You must get the Blatherwyckes along from St John's in Leathwell,' she said. 'They do some marvellous work with teenagers! They really speak the language of young folk. They explain the Christian teaching, and then ask the young people to take a pledge to stay virgins until they marry.'

Michael and Baz, hearts sinking, expressed caution, but they could make no headway against a PCC in the grip of an idea.

'I don't like it,' Michael said to Baz as they left the meeting. 'If they start preaching, they'll undo everything we've done over the last six months. Our lot'll never sit politely through something like that, but if they object, the club's future's on the line.'

'Don't be pessimistic, Mike. What about the power of prayer? Or if you're still feeling agnostic, bribe them. We usually have a summer outing from the Rows. Tell your lot we'll take them to Alton Towers if they come and behave themselves with the Blatherwyckes.'

It was a new approach to youth work, but Michael felt anxious enough to try it.

'You lot are bloody well going to be cooperative and polite,' he instructed them. 'Because if I can't tell the people who run the hall that you've got the message, they'll chuck us out of here, and the club'll be finished. On the other hand, if you behave yourselves, I'll give you all a free day trip to Alton Towers.' It would mean a lot of extra shifts at

McDonald's, but he could cope with that, if they could cope with the Blatherwyckes.

Around twenty regular youth club members turned up for the occasion. Gemma had brought Lisa, who lived up to the subject in heavy make-up and a tight denim dress that rendered her much older than fourteen.

Michael made his introductions, and found a chair. Bernie Blatherwycke sat on the edge of his seat, and began to talk. Tall and thin, with a long face broken by a drooping moustache and his dark hair worn long and swept back from a receding hairline, his appearance was not one calculated to instil confidence in anyone below thirty. His wife Midge sat next to him, smiling. Her long greying hair hung loose on her shoulders, and a long printed red skirt flowed over her knees. On her left, their seventeen year-old son Colin, brought to speak from experience, held himself rigidly in his chair. His eyes, half-hidden by the hair he wore long to conceal chronic acne, were directed unwaveringly at the floor.

'So why do you think it might be good to wait until we're married before we have sex?' Bernie asked. The teenagers slouched in their chairs, arms folded, looking at the floor. 'OK. You all think it's fine to have sex before marriage. Why is that?'

'Yer balls drop off if yer don't get yer rocks off,' Robbie contributed, to sniggers from his mates.

'Not that I've heard of,' Bernie said. 'Otherwise I think my wife would be complaining. I didn't have sex till I got married, when I was twenty-two, and I'm quite normal.'

A certain amount of sniggering greeted this statement. Michael put his head in his hands, but Bernie and Midge appeared to have taken it in good part, and some good-humoured banter followed.

'Colin, I think this is a good moment for you to tell your story,' Bernie said, wafting a hand at his son.

Colin, who had been methodically chewing the inside of his lip for the previous few minutes, looked up, alarmed. 'I had my first girlfriend when I was fifteen,' Colin began, with the nervous air of one who had rehearsed many times in front of a mirror and was thrown by having an audience of more than one.

'Blind was she?' Robbie shouted. For a skinny youth, he could generate a lot of volume. Michael glared at him, and Robbie whispered something to Kev that had them both sniggering.

'Wha's up with you lot?' Gemma asked them.

Colin ploughed on. 'We talked about how far we should go, and we decided...'

'He's got tits on his face,' Robbie stated loudly.

'... we decided...'

Lisa turned round in her seat. 'Leave it off, Robbie. You wanna watch it, you might get spots when you grow up. If you ever grow up. I wanna hear what Colin's got to say.'

She smiled encouragingly at Colin, who was blushing furiously. 'We decided not to.' He looked anxiously at his mother, and slumped defeated back into his chair.

'You see, sex is a gift,' Midge continued sweetly, 'and getting married is like Christmas. And who'd want to open all their presents before Christmas?'

'I would,' Robbie called. 'I'm always gettin' me hand down bloody stockings, me.'

'Shut up, Robbie. You promised Mike not to fucking swear,' Kev hissed.

'You c'n always feel the wrapping paper, see what's under it,' Gemma giggled, shooting a hand towards Kev's crotch. He fended her off.

Michael intervened with a sharp 'hey', and they subsided in their seats.

'So what can you do?' Lisa asked, directing her words towards Colin.

Midge answered for him. 'The rule a lot of people find helpful is "above the waist, and above the clothes". That way you can't get into trouble.'

'But...' Lisa began. Then she gave up and settled back in her chair, her face contorted in thought.

The other teenagers stared incredulously at Midge. Sensing his moment, Bernie moved in. 'I know it sounds difficult, but,' - his voice dropped into a more reverential key - 'I want to tell you that Jesus is here to help! And I'm going to ask any of you who want that help to come forward now.' He picked up a sheaf of papers from the floor. 'There's a form here that you can sign, pledging yourself to avoid sex until you're married. Then we'll say a prayer for you...'

Lisa was on her feet almost before he had finished speaking, a devout expression on her face as she knelt on the ground.

Bernie closed his eyes for a few seconds in prayerful gratitude or sheer relief. 'Don't be afraid of what anyone else will think,' he continued, gazing earnestly around the group. 'It doesn't matter what you've done in the past. Jesus will take it all away!'

Michael looked at his legs, stretched out in front of him. Oh my

God, he thought, talk about inappropriate. He was aware of a whispered conversation at his side, and then of a rustling. Kev got up and went forward to join Lisa, smiling sanctimoniously, followed by his mates. Before long, submitting to the pressure created by their example, every single teenager in the room was kneeling on the carpet in front of Bernie, until, apart from Sharon setting out the tuck shop in the kitchen, Michael was the only one left.

Midge fixed her eyes on him. 'This isn't just for teenagers. Come and join them. It'll mean so much to them to have your support.'

'Go on, we've all done it,' Kev said.

'Yeah, sign the fucking pledge!' Robbie urged him.

'I'm not signing anything,' Michael said, feeling uncomfortable. He got up. 'I'd better go and give Sharon a hand.' And he escaped into the kitchen.

'We were bloodly brill,' Kev said to Michael, once the Blatherwyckes had gone, elated, back to Leathwell. 'Alton Towers, here we come!'

'You didn't have to go that far. I'd have been happy as long as you didn't lynch them,' Michael said. 'You've really shown me up, haven't you? Even though I am probably the only person among you who really does intend to stay celibate for the next week.'

Afterwards, he drove Lisa home to Nottling; Jenny had added him to her car insurance, and it helped to have access to transport.

'He was rather sweet, wasn't he?' Lisa said.

'Who, Bernie?'

'Naah. Colin. I mean, he can't help his zits, but he'd got nice eyes.'

'He wasn't exactly chatting you up.'

'Tha's cos he's shy, innit? Naah, I don't fancy him or nothing, I jus' thought he was sweet. I'm one of them Christians now, in't I? I'm goin' to be good. Tha's goin' to be boring, innit? Still, I s'pose I have to give it a go.'

They stayed talking in the car for ten minutes after he'd drawn up outside her house, and by the time he left, she was contemplating becoming a nun. Michael smiled to himself as he drove back, amused by the intensity of her short-lived enthusiasms, though she could pick much worse ones. Characters like that were entertaining, but exhausting.

He was relieved to find the light on in Jenny's living room when he got back. He needed someone thoughtful to whom to unburden himself.

'How did it go?' she asked, as he flopped down on her sofa.

'It started off alright. The Blatherwyckes weren't as bad as I thought. Only then they decided to get evangelistic about it. God, I've never been so embarrassed in my life. That kind of thing's fine in its place, but it was completely inappropriate. Especially given my lot were only looking interested because I'd bribed them.' He described the evening, drawing some comfort from her amusement.

'...so there I was, being publicly challenged to offer my sexual organs to Christ.'

'You've signed the pledge! Well done!'

'How could I, Jenny? Even though it ended the way it did, I can't feel that Kate and I were wrong to sleep together. It was a good relationship for both of us for years. And if I fall in love again, if I'm engaged again, I'm bound to want to sleep with her. I can't pledge myself to something I'm not sure I believe in. Only what happens when it all gets back to Peter? The entire youth club converted, and pledged to avoid premature passion, while their leader remains stuck in moral turpitude. It's not going to look very good, is it? Yet another moral lapse from Michael. I shall probably get excommunicated, and they'll hand the dear young folk over to Mrs Jennings.'

'I don't see why. It's not as if you're actually doing something wrong. You didn't like feeling pressured into signing a silly pledge. I mean, I don't believe in sex before marriage, but I'm not sure I'd want to make a public declaration about it.'

'You always cheer me up. But anyway, Jenny, I'm not sure all this works. It's all very well making sex out to be special and holy, but what happens when you *are* married? How the hell do you get it up if going to bed is supposed to be a spiritual experience? You need a bit of lust somewhere, don't you?'

'I wouldn't know, would I?'

'No, well, I'm not sure I know either. Four months of celibacy, and I've forgotten what it's like. And it's all your fault.' Michael stretched and yawned. 'I think I'll have a bath and turn in. Good night.' He ruffled her curls as he left the room and headed upstairs to soap his redundant physique.

Eight

'Family planning? Surely that's a difficult matter for a Christian to undertake? What about those who aren't married?' Aunt Deidre, in a crumpled pink suit and clerical collar, sat on the edge of the sofa with her lips pursed. Beside her, Tyrone mirrored her position. Jenny's cousin had a figure as sturdy and ill-defined as her own, but in his case, it had run to plumpness. Periodically, he sneezed, allergic to the infinitesimal traces left in Celestine's absence. His fleshy face contorted in the effort, so that his already small, pale eyes disappeared. Lank, light hair brushed back from his brow revealed a tendency to spots, and dusted his shoulders with dandruff. He was not particularly attractive in appearance, a fault Jenny could have forgiven - for who was she to judge - had he been less prim and self-righteous about everything.

'Contraception is far too easily available, I think,' he said. 'It only gives people ideas.'

'Then why are there still so many unwanted pregnancies?' There was an argumentative tone in Jenny's voice. She should never have spoken of her interest in contraception, in one of her rare telephone conversations with her mother a few weeks before, but she had needed to fill the silence on the other end of the phone with something.

Now here was Deidre 'just passing, dear', on a Saturday afternoon, with Tyrone in tow 'to see your lovely little house', come to check up that she was not bringing the name of Furlong into disrepute. Well, Aunt D. was going to get another shock in a minute. From where she sat, Jenny had been watching Michael digging at the end of the garden, dressed only in shorts and heavy boots, with the small gold cross that never left its narrow chain round his neck, glinting in the sun. He was now sitting on the garden seat removing the boots - with some difficulty, since Celly was fascinated by the laces - which meant he was on his way in. Somehow, she had never got round to telling her mother than she had a young, attractive, male lodger, so Michael's entrance was going to be interesting to observe.

'God, I'm knackered,' Michael said, as he stepped in through the patio door. 'Give us a can of something, Jen.' He took a step towards the sofa to collapse, and, as his eyes adjusted from the brightness to the relative shade of the room, spotted Deidre and Tyrone. 'Sorry, I didn't realise you had visitors.'

'That's alright. Do stay, I'll get you a lager. Or would you rather have tea? I was just about to make some. This is my aunt, Deidre Rutt, and Tyrone, my cousin. This is Michael Turner, who lives with me.'

'I won't shake hands, I'm filthy,' Michael said, slumping to the floor against the wall opposite the end of the sofa.

Shock popped Deidre's eyes outwards, while her mouth opened and shut as she struggled to find something to say. Tyrone looked frozen in horror. Deidre agreed to tea, clearly torn between desire to wipe the dust of this immoral house from her feet, and to find out all she could about her niece's apparent lover.

'I know your name. You work for the diocese, don't you?' Michael was saying as Jenny went to the kitchen, unaware that his presence and her introduction had been capable of misconstruction.

Jenny chuckled as she put the kettle on and got the lager from the fridge. How perfect, to have Michael appear, slim, tanned, sweaty and bare-chested, behaving as if he owned the place. She could imagine Deidre contacting Joan with appalled urgency. 'Jennifer is living with *the* most frightful man.' What delight there was in being thought naughty. She went back in with her tray, and patted his bare shoulder with her hand as she gave him his can, hoping he wasn't being too polite. Michael shot her a surprised look.

'I'm hoping to become responsible for ministerial training in the Diocese too,' Deidre was saying, in her normal, queenly tones.

Bother Michael, he was thawing Deidre, taking an interest in her work. Typical.

'The Leathwell Programme for Ministerial Training is in utter chaos. Albright, the Principal, is a dear man, but no administrative skills. The students don't know what they're doing one week to the next.'

'Doesn't Nan Patten work for that?' Michael asked. 'I'd have thought she was a good administrator - isn't that what she used to do before she was ordained?'

'Dear Nan. Yes, indeed, such an able woman. Surmounted her personal tragedy so bravely. But she's not in charge. In any case, we're reorganising at Diocesan Church House, and the Programme is going to become part of my department. I have such visions of what can be done! I see every ordinand doing theology by correspondence course and learning on the job from their own vicar. There's really no need for the expensive central set-up they have at the moment. I've already started drafting a workbook for them. It's a tremendously exciting prospect for me...'

Jenny poured tea and sat back to listen to Michael at work. He even got Tyrone unbuttoning enough to explain his convictions about the way the Church ought to use the media. Smarmy little creep. 'I'm hoping to go for ordination soon. Then I can really use my influence.'

'Wonderful, isn't it?' Deidre said. 'Joan and Austin are so thrilled. Of course they always wanted a son to follow Austin into the priesthood, but with poor little Jeremy dying like that, and you girls with your careers, they've had no one to carry their hopes.'

'I didn't know you had a brother,' Michael said to Jenny.

'He died when he was eleven months old, just under a year before I was born. A cot death. It is *not* something we talk about.' She grimaced. 'In fact, I didn't even know about him until I was a teenager. You told me, don't you remember, Ty? You'd just found out, and you kept calling me Jeremy, and saying I wouldn't be there if he'd lived. I went crying to mum, thinking she'd tell you off for lying and teasing me, but she turned on me and said I shouldn't meddle with things that were nothing to do with me.'

'I got a rocket, though,' Ty said ruefully, almost human.

'Poor Joan found it very upsetting. But I saw no point in avoiding the truth. Well, dear, we'd better be off.' Deidre summoned her son to his feet with a single look, and headed for the hall.

'So nice to see you again, Jennifer, and to meet your, er ...' Deidre looked between the two of them.

'Friend,' supplied Jenny.

'Yes. We'll see ourselves out.'

'I do believe you were wanting your aunt to think you were living in sin,' Michael said when the door had shut behind them.

'Not at all.'

'You should have whispered a warning to me. Then I wouldn't have explained that I'm only the lodger. Mind you, I'm not sure she was convinced.'

'I shouldn't think any woman could imagine living with a body like that and not lusting after it,' Jenny laughed, pinching the skin over his ribs. 'It's a good thing I know you too well.'

Which is all very well, she thought, watching Michael as he went back into the garden. He thinks it funny that my relations should think I'm embroiled in a steamy relationship with my lodger, and so do I, really. It's

70

only that sometimes I think I am falling in love with him. I think about him far more than I should. Like a compass needle dragged to the north, I home in on his presence. I long for him to take my hand, or hug me, or kiss my cheek, even though I know that's how he is with everyone, and it doesn't mean anything. Oh well, it will pass. Who said love was like measles? You think you've been inoculated against it in childhood, but it can still strike you down. All you have to do is endure. It always gets better, given time.

She shook her head, and went upstairs to see if her washing had finished.

Michael's failure to commit himself publicly to sexual purity got back to Peter and Caroline, and led to him being summoned once again to the vicarage to explain himself.

'They weren't being serious,' he said to Peter, sitting in his god-father's study amid the piles of papers. 'They were trying to impress me so I'd take them to Alton Towers. If any of them are avoiding sex at the moment, it's more because of the talk Jenny and I had with them than anything the Blatherwyckes said.'

'That's hardly the point. All I and people in the church see is that you're failing to set a good example. I don't expect kids off the estate to have our values, but the whole point of having a youth club in the church hall is so that we can witness to them. We don't do that by you proclaiming it's perfectly alright to sleep around.'

'I didn't say that. I said it felt OK for me and Kate because we'd been together a long time, and were engaged. It's not as though I've even got a girlfriend at the moment.'

'Look, Mike, I realise you don't think it's helpful to preach directly to the young people, but you should be prepared to tell them about right and wrong, and right and wrong from biblical standards, not some watered down, liberal version of your own. I do wonder if I'm compromising too much by letting you have these responsible roles in the church, when you seem this uncommitted about the whole thing.'

'That isn't fair,' Michael said. 'I might not be finding faith easy, but I'm still committed. I'm giving my life to your church at the moment.'

Peter smiled. 'As Jenny pointed out to me very forcibly after that business with the flip chart. She clearly regards you as some latter day saint, because you have carried on with everything while it's been difficult. I'm not unsympathetic. I'm simply worried that we're failing the world

71

when we bend over backwards like this not to judge, and refuse to say where we stand.'

'I don't think judging others is a role that comes naturally to me.'

'Then you need to develop it. Wasn't that one of the things pointed out at your selection conference, that you didn't seem to have leadership abilities? You've got these kids' respect, now learn to use the opportunities that gives you. I'll leave things for now, but your behaviour is going to be under the microscope from certain people in the congregation, and I want to feel you're repaying the trust I'm placing in you.'

'Well, I'm alright for the next month, I shan't be here,' Michael said. He was due to spend ten days in North Yorkshire helping to run a Christian youth camp, something he had done regularly for the last six years. It was always exhausting, and apart from a possible light flirtation with one of the female students on the leadership or catering teams, he would do little but work and sleep, and pretend he was as devout as the rest of them always seemed to be. After that, he'd be back for a quick turn around before disappearing for a further three weeks' camping with his sister Sarah's family in France. Jenny would enjoy having her house to herself again for a while.

Jenny told herself that she was relieved that he had gone, hoping that her life would settle down around her again in some normality. She worked, and sat in the garden, trying to enjoy being on her own, completely uninterrupted, while she desperately denied how disturbing she found Michael's absence. As the days wore on, her longing for him was like an aching bruise. Once or twice, she found herself on the landing outside his room, wanting to go in. She resisted, until driven by an urgent need to spray the greenfly on the honeysuckle, which could, she realised, only properly be reached from his window. She felt guilty as she stepped inside, and stood in the centre of the room with her eyes shut, breathing deeply, trying to capture the scent of him. There wasn't really anything there, only the sun shining hotly through the window, reminding her of what she had come for. As she leant over the sill, spraying, Celestine appeared, climbing up through the foliage.

'He's not here, you stupid animal. Come here, you'll get soap spray all over you, and you won't like that.' The cat jumped on to the window sill, pausing to rub against Jenny's face before descending to the floor. Jenny finished the job, closed the windows and turned round. Celestine was sitting in the sunlight on Michael's bed, washing herself. Jenny lay down beside her, stroking the hot damp fur. Beside the bed was a photograph of Michael standing between his parents, with his arms round their shoulders. She picked it up and stared at him, loving his smile, and his ease with his body, and envying the closeness he had with his family. Her parents would have felt like that about Jeremy, had he lived.

'Why did he have to come here, Celly? What am I going to do about him? I've never had anyone have time for me like he does. How can I help loving him?' An acrid tear made its way to her eye as she turned her face into the pillow. She took a grip of herself.

'What will he think of me?' she asked the unresponsive cat, sitting up. Then she straightened the duvet and pillow, and left the room, closing the door behind them both.

Michael came home soiled and weary the following Saturday afternoon, and slept for nearly twenty-four hours. Jenny had been out when he arrived back, but the presence of a single stick of Whitby rock propped up against her living room door indicated he had returned. She saw nothing of him until the following Sunday lunchtime, as she sat in her garden after church, eating lunch at her parasolled patio table. Michael appeared without warning, crossing the grass on silent bare feet, and coming up behind her to blow in her ear. As she turned, startled, he kissed her cheek, and reached cosily over her shoulder to extract a piece of cheese from her plate. His physical proximity unnerved her, the warmth of his body, and the used smell that hung about him, as yet unwashed after his travel and sleep. He was dressed only in faded shorts, and looked fit and extremely tanned.

'Michael, please! You've hardly got any clothes on,' she snapped.

'Sorry. Doesn't it give you a thrill?'

'A tan's a sign of skin damage. You should cover up. Look, if you're hungry, go and help yourself to whatever you can find in the kitchen. Leave my plate alone.'

'Thanks, Jen. Then I'll tell you all about my holiday.'

He came back several minutes later with a plate of sandwiches, and the pot of chocolate trifle she'd been saving for her tea, and sat across the plastic table from her. In control of herself once more, Jenny listened attentively to his exuberant account of the camp. Celestine approached them slowly over the grass, as if she had much better things to do with her time.

Michael held out a hand. 'Here, Celly, have you missed me?'

The cat jumped on his lap, claws mercifully retracted, and rubbed herself against his bare chest and chin. Michael looked across at Jenny, as if struck by a thought. He leaned across the table and put a hand over hers. 'Have *you* missed me? I've missed not having you to talk to. Let me take you out tonight. We could go for a meal somewhere, out in the country. You're not on call, are you?'

'No. No, I'm not.'

'I'll give Evensong a miss, and we'll go to the White Swan. I'm not playing tonight. See you at seven?'

Cloud had appeared by the time they arrived at the pub that was set beside the river a few miles out of Greathampton. The air was muggy as they sat out in the garden watching the slow water drifting past. Trees bowed low over the opposite bank, fish rose, breaking the smooth surface of the river, while late birds picked off the insects clouding the air. A mosquito buzzed near Jenny's face. She swatted it away, and slipped her jacket back on over the silky red vest she was wearing, to protect her bare arms.

'Getting bitten, are you?' Michael asked, putting two glasses down on the worn wooden slats of the table, and dropping a packet of peanuts from his teeth. 'They don't usually bother about me.' He manoeuvered himself onto the bench next to her.

'Something nasty in your blood, I shouldn't wonder.' She sounded brittle, even to herself.

'You don't seem to be yourself today. Anything the matter?' Michael slipped an arm round her. 'It is nice to see you again, you know. It's all so manic and intense, that sort of camp, and you're nice and restful.' He squeezed her shoulders, and, as she turned towards him, planted a firm, affectionate kiss on her lips. 'So, what have you been up to?' he said, letting her go, and picking up his pint.

Jenny smiled philosophically as she answered him, with her dreams clattering around her on the ground once more. At each fresh demonstration that Michael's embraces meant nothing more than ordinary affection, she berated herself for her longings, but it didn't seem to help. It was just as well no one ever knew what she was really thinking. She ate and talked with Michael as the night turned their faces into shadow, and the next day, he was gone.

The elderly lady with blue-rinsed hair who was giving out service sheets as Jenny went into church the following Sunday, narrowed her eyes behind her glasses as Jenny said good morning.

'Michael's away, is he?'

'Yes,' she said, surprised by the aggressive tone of the question, for she knew Mrs Pitchers only by sight.

'I expect you're missing him.'

'Me? No, not specially, no.'

'I'm surprised you dare to receive communion,' Mrs Pitchers hissed.

Jenny opened her mouth to remonstrate, but the woman had turned to greet a new set of people, and so she took her seat. For the rest of the service, the words went through her head. The only explanation was that her name was being linked with Michael's, but why on earth should that be? Jenny heard little of the service, nothing of Caroline's sermon, and at the end, with her nerves stretched, she tackled Mrs Pitchers as most of the congregation waited at the hatch for coffee.

'Why were you asking about Michael like that before the service?'

'You know very well. I saw you out with him last Sunday. My son had taken me out for a meal, and there you were, slobbering all over each other. I always said it wasn't right to have a man and a woman sharing a house like that, and this just goes to show. No wonder he taught the youth club all those wicked words, and he couldn't take the pledge, he's living in sin with you. I can't believe that an organist at St Martin's could commit such shameful acts, and you certainly ought to know better, a doctor like you. I'm going to tell the vicar, you mark my words.'

'You're mistaken,' Jenny said, feeling increasingly sick as Mrs Pitchers' monologue went on. 'Michael lodges with me. There's nothing whatsoever between us like that.'

'Lying about it doesn't make things any better. I saw you, there was no mistaking it.'

'But that was nothing. It didn't mean anything.'

'That makes it even worse, then, doesn't it?'

'There is nothing in it,' Jenny said, angrily. 'And I'll thank you not to go spreading rumours.'

She arrived home shaking, trying to tell herself it was simply one nasty old woman, and nothing to worry about, but it hung over her all week, making her brusque with colleagues and patients alike.

The following Sunday, Jenny contemplated staying away, but decided she had to brazen it out.

When she walked into church, Mrs Jennings, with whom she had always got on, took her to one side. 'There's a lot of ill feeling about your relationship with Michael, my dear,' she said. 'People are beginning to say that that's why you were taking that rather questionable line with the youth club, because you're trying to justify yourselves. I don't like to say anything against Michael, with him being the vicar's godson, but I'm afraid he's not altogether as Christian as he likes to make out. I don't blame you, my dear. He's very charming, and I can quite see he's easy to fall for, but the fact remains, you are breaking one of the commandments, and people are talking.'

'There's nothing between us, Mrs Jennings, honestly. Mrs Pitchers must have seen me with Michael at the pub the other week, and he did kiss me, but you know what he's like. He's probably kissed you in his time.'

'There is a difference between that and what Eileen saw. I do understand. I have a daughter who's living with her boyfriend, so I'm the last one to want to throw stones, but I don't want to see you humiliated. It wouldn't help your professional life much, would it?'

'What do you mean? I really haven't done anything. Why don't you believe me?'

'I'm not saying I don't believe you. But I do think with all the talk there is, it might be better if you didn't go up for communion. Mrs Pitchers could well get up and say something publicly, and it could be unpleasant.'

'I don't believe this,' Jenny said. 'I shall go straight to Peter.'

'He's away for the next couple of weeks, dear. If I were you, I'd keep a low profile.'

'In that case, I'll stay away.' Jenny left the church, her eyes to the ground to avoid meeting the gaze of anyone coming in. I'm never going there again, she thought, struggling to get home before she broke down. It's so unfair. Everyone thinking I'm involved with Michael, and all the time I repulse him. I hate him. I love him. I wish he was here. But all she had of him was the postcard that arrived during the second week of his holiday. She propped it on her desk in the health centre, and reread it constantly, imagining each word to convey more than she honestly knew it did.

'Dear Jen, Enjoying Brittany,' he had written, 'especially the seafood & crepes. Weather variable. Lots of swimming & playing beach games with the girls - Sarah (35) Emma (12), Naomi (8), & Rachel (5). Hugh (38) spends all day trying to light the barbecue. Unfortunately they're all plebs - I wish you were here to investigate the local culture/history with me! Hope all's well with you & Celly. See you soon. Much love, M.'

Nine

Jenny's first thought when she woke on the Sunday before the bank holiday was that Michael would be back by the evening. A day without church stretched ahead of her, a waiting that would be intolerable, for all that she never wanted to see him again. She'd do something different, she thought, drive over to Leathwell, and go to the Cathedral. Have lunch somewhere, treat herself.

The sky was overcast as she drove over roads scattered thinly with traffic, for the weekenders had gone, and day trippers would not be lured out today. Fields gave way to housing, housing to garages and superstores, and then she was in the city, following signs optimistically designed to direct tourists to Leathwell's unremarkable cathedral. Grey stone blackened by pollution, a squat spire that was visible only to those who searched the city's horizon for it, and a dearth of stained glass windows - the result of bomb damage in the war.

There were few in the congregation as Jenny found a seat in the middle of the chancel, and sat, consciously relaxing her breathing, so that the cold stone, the vaulted ceiling and wooden carvings of the rood screen could calm her spirit.

The man who climbed into the pulpit to preach looked familiar, though it was a few minutes before she realised that this was Christopher Ridgefield. Of course, he was a canon, she shouldn't be surprised to find him there. Aunt Deidre would not be impressed to find her sitting at his feet, but then, her aunt had long since given up on her. From where she sat, Ridgefield was an indistinct pale face with dark hair above the white of his robes, but his voice, amplified through the building, was clear, and his faint northern accent easy to listen to. She detected little sign of the anger and arrogance that showed in his television appearances, and was surprised to find him thoughtful and inspiring - as if he was a man of faith after all, and not the fanatical heretic Deidre dubbed him.

She was one of the last of the congregation to leave and shake Canon Ridgefield's hand after the service. He was laughing with the verger as she approached him. A pleasant face with a hint of fleshiness, grey eyes and grey beginning to creep through the dark hair that was carefully brushed back from his forehead.

'I enjoyed your sermon,' she said. 'No, sorry, that's the wrong word. It spoke to me. Sorry, that sounds cliched. What you said about not expecting things to be easy - what was it? "Even messiahs don't fly". I needed to hear that. I appreciated your honesty about your own life.'

He had been about to turn back to the verger after giving her a polite smile, but he checked himself and looked at her more intently. 'Thank you. I used to think allowing the word "I" to creep into sermons was the ultimate sin, so it's nice to know at least somebody finds it helpful. Why don't you come and have a cup of coffee with me in the crypt?'

'I couldn't do that ... I'm sure you've got other things to do.'

'Not until after I've had my drink. Do come.' He smiled, surprisingly charming, so that Jenny was following him to the crypt before she realised she had accepted the invitation.

Ridgefield showed her down stone stairs to the cafe, where he sat her at a small table while he fetched coffee.

'You're going through a difficult patch yourself at the moment, are you?' he said, as he sat down and emptied a carton of cream into his cup. 'I'm happy to listen ... or I can talk about the architecture of the cathedral if you prefer. Or the weather.' He smiled again, and then, as she hesitated, said, 'I can be trusted. I am a priest. It won't go any further.'

Jenny looked into his eyes, weighing him up, believing him. She wasn't in the habit of unburdening herself to strangers, but she had a profound need to talk to someone. After all, anyone Aunt Deidre disliked so intensely ...

'There's this man who came to our church to help with the youth work,' she said. 'He was happy not to be paid, but he needed somewhere to live, so I gave him a room in my house. I thought I was being really noble, because I've done quite enough sharing of houses, but I felt it was something I could do to help. And Michael's been friendly to me - like he is with everyone. He's one of the kindest, most generous people I know. He'll help me with the shopping, or dig the garden, or take me out for a drink sometimes, if he can afford it. He's always got time for me if I need anything. And now I find everyone in church thinks we're having an affair. The one time I try and do something helpful, and everyone attacks me for it. I spend my life behaving perfectly respectably, I'm the dullest person you could meet, and yet people are ready to believe the worst of me on no evidence at all! I'll end up having to kick him out, and then I'll lose the only real friend I've got.'

'Gossip can be pernicious, can't it? What does Michael feel about it?'

'He doesn't know - he's been away the last few weeks. I don't know what I'll do when he hears. I'll never dare look him in the face again. He'll be horrified - he'd never think of me that way in a million years.'

'But you wish he would?'

Jenny grimaced. 'Does it show that much? I can't help it. But I keep it to myself. I'd never embarrass him by saying anything.'

'Why not? Perhaps he feels that way about you. He obviously enjoys spending time with you.'

'No, he's told me doesn't think of me like that. That's why he feels safe with me. I'd cope if it wasn't for this gossip.'

'So you're not sure what to do - carry on as you are, keeping quiet about how you feel, but finding it painful. Asking him to leave, which will stop the gossip but you think will lose you a friend. Or telling him you've come to care about him, and seeing whether you can find a way through it together.'

'I'd not dream of the third choice. I'd die of shame,' Jenny said, blushing. 'So don't go telling me that must mean it's the best one.'

'If it hurts it must be good for you? No, I don't go along with that. I'd simply ask you which of those options opens up more possibilities for growth for both of you? Perhaps it's not at all the right advice for you, but that's what I've been asking myself lately. I've become far too conservative and dull, so I've been trying to get myself to take a few risks. That's what I was trying to say in my sermon. I thought that was what you found helpful.'

'I wouldn't want to take it too far.' Jenny drained her cup. 'I'd better go. Thank you for your time.'

'It's been a pleasure meeting you,' he said, standing up and extending his hand. 'I'll remember you.'

It was the evening when Michael finally arrived back in Greathampton after a wearisome day's travel. He took his bags to his room, and smiled as he caught sight of himself in the mirror. He hadn't got round to shaving before they'd left their last campsite early that morning, and the stubble, combined with his brown face and dark eyes made him look distinctly Mediterranean. His tee shirt smelt of sweat, as Rachie had constantly and tactfully pointed out as they sat squashed together in the back of the Volvo, so he had a quick shower before going downstairs to find Jenny. He tracked her down in the garden, sitting on the step by the patio door, her face screwed up to read the *Sunday Times* in the velvety light of the late August evening.

'I'm back,' he said as she looked up.

'Hello.' Her grey eyes were dark and troubled, and she didn't smile.

'I've brought you a present, well, three actually. Some local honey, a beeswax candle, and a bottle of plonk. And a bottle opener and glasses, in case you want to start it now. Only they're not presents - I raided your kitchen.'

'Thanks,' she said dully, taking the items from him. 'You shouldn't have bothered.'

He sat down on the step beside her. 'You seem pleased to have me back.'

'Sorry. I've got out of the habit of social chat. Did you have a nice time? What was the journey like?'

He told her, stretching the story out while he opened the wine, and drank it with her as the first stars appeared in the sky.

'So how's things with you? Anything interesting happened at church while I've been away?'

'I wouldn't know. I haven't been.'

'Why not? What's wrong, Jenny?'

'I'm not wanted. I'm supposed to be living in sin with you, and if I show my face, I'm threatened with hordes of people denouncing me in public.'

'You're not serious! But Jen, that's awful. What do Peter and Caroline say?'

'They've been away. I don't know when they're back. I don't really care. I never want to show my face there again.' She explained what Mrs Pitchers had seen, and Michael laughed.

'It's just some silly jealous old biddy. Don't let it drive you away. We'll explain it's not true, and they can all come and inspect our living arrangements if they like. Not a johnny in sight - not a used one, anyway.'

She didn't respond, staring down at her glass, and swilling the wine around in it.

'Come on, Jen,' he said, putting a hand on her knee, 'you shouldn't take things like this so seriously. Laugh it off.'

'How can I?'

Her distress touched him. He took her glass, put it down, then circled her with his arms. She was rigid in his embrace at first, then tentatively put her arms round him, resting her head on his shoulder. He stroked her hair with his hand. It was soft and fine, like Rachie's, and he felt a surge of fondness for her.

A measureless minute went by before Jenny spoke again, emotion battened down as she struggled to explain. 'How can I laugh it off when I wish it was true? I've told everyone that there's no truth in it whatsoever, and you wouldn't dream of looking at me in that way. Why should you bother with someone plain and difficult like me when you could have anyone you choose? "Michael wouldn't touch me with a bargepole", I say. Only it hurts because I'd give anything ...' She faltered, and her longings hovered unarticulated in the gloom between them. 'I know you've said all along you've only been doing things with me as a friend, I know that. It's just that I'm not used to having someone, a man, being that sort of friend. You put your arm round me, and hug me, and kiss me, because that's how you are. But I'm not. I can't brush it off as if it doesn't matter...'

Oh, no, Jenny, he wanted to say, please don't be saying what I think you're saying, don't complicate everything. Instead, he continued to hold her, and spoke gently.

'What are you trying to say, Jenny?'

She pulled herself away, and looked at him directly for the first time, her face pale and indistinct. 'I've fallen in love with you, damn it. I didn't mean to. I'm sure it'll pass, but in the meantime perhaps you could stop wanting to do things with me all the time. Stop being so ... so demonstrative. I thought it would evaporate while you were away, but it hasn't. I'm sorry. I wasn't going to say anything, but I can't cope with it on my own. It's not that I don't want to see you at all. I'd hate it if you moved out, but I can't carry on like this.'

His hands fell to his sides. 'Oh Jenny, I am sorry. I had no idea. I've never led you on.'

'I know you haven't. It's not your fault. It's me, not being used to having friends.'

'But who can I go round with, if not with you? You're my best friend.'

'Perhaps now you know, I'll get over it quickly. I feel awful, making an issue of it.'

'Don't worry about that. It's my fault. I should have thought.' He stood up, feeling lost, and held out his hand to her. Jenny took it, and he pulled her up. 'The trouble is, I naturally want to hug you to show there's no hard feelings ... oh, what the hell.' He embraced her again. 'I am flattered, Jenny. I like you so much. I only wish I could return your feelings, but I can't force it if it's not there. I'm sorry.'

'Well, goodnight,' she said, turning from him and going into the house.

'Goodnight. I'll talk to Peter and Caroline about the rumours. It'll be alright. Don't worry.'

He slid the patio door shut against the night. Above the glow of the streetlights, the sky was peppered with stars.

As September wore on, the relationship between Michael and Jenny was strained.

Michael had visited Peter as soon as he and Caroline returned from their holidays to complain about Jenny's treatment, and found a ready ally.

'If I'd thought there was the slightest impropriety in your lodging with Jenny,' Peter said, 'I'd never have allowed it in the first place. 'It seemed important that you had someone sensible to keep an eye on you, and it takes a peculiar imagination to see you and Jenny getting romantically involved. She's simply not that sort of person, is she?'

'I know,' Michael said, and immediately felt disloyal. Poor Jenny, to have everyone, himself included, write her off as a woman incapable of feeling. 'She has been a good friend to me, though. That's why it's unfair to have these rumours going around.'

'I wonder if it would be sensible to find somewhere else for you live, all the same.'

'But that's making it worse, as if there really might have been something going on.'

'Hmmm. Perhaps you're right. I'll talk to Mrs Pitchers, and I think a stern sermon on the dangers of gossip wouldn't come amiss. Mind you, Mike,' he added as he got up to end the interview, 'I do wish you'd get yourself settled down. No one could gossip about you then. You know, for such a nice chap, you cause a heck of a lot of trouble.'

'Story of my life,' Michael said with a grin as he left.

Peter's intervention resulted in a written apology from Mrs Pitchers, and gradually Jenny was able to blend back into church life. Nothing, however, gave her back her old ease with Michael, and they were both awkward with each other.

Michael continued with his work, but lacked his normal enthusiasm. The depression that Jenny had helped to keep at bay since he had arrived in her house sagged back on top of him as he mourned the disintegration of their friendship. Everyone was suspicious of what he was doing with the

82

youth club, he wasn't fit to be the organist, his faith was still in a coma, and he had no idea what he was going to do for the rest of his life.

He needed someone to talk to, someone outside his immediate circle, and he thought of Nan. He'd been unsure, earlier in the year, how she would react to him after his liaison with Becky, but a conversation over the washing-up at Caroline's had cleared the ground, and he thought she'd understand his current predicament. He arranged to go and see her one Saturday afternoon towards the end of September.

'I'm seeing that teacher you sent me at lunch time, so come at two,' Nan had said.

After a dull beginning to the month, the weather had turned mellow, and the afternoon was warm. Michael waited for several minutes on the doorstep of Nan's house without a response to his ring. Then, hearing female voices laughing nearby, he let himself through the side gate and into the back garden. Sitting around a white plastic patio table alongside Nan was the dark-haired woman he'd met in Nottling, smiling and attractive in a summer dress.

Nearby, Caroline lay on a lounger with her feet up, and a guilty wine glass in her hand. 'I *am* working really,' she said unconvincingly. 'Look at the time, Nan, I ought to have gone half an hour ago.'

'Now, now, what have we been saying about women not going along with the same old work ethic? Take time to enjoy life, that's what I say. Come and join us, Michael, we're only nattering about our priesting. Only! Listen to me. You know Alison, don't you?' Nan rose and embraced him. 'This is one of the perks of the job, I always think. You can kiss gorgeous young men, and pretend it's entirely motherly.'

Michael laughed. 'Watch it, I might sue you for harassment.'

'I should reply that you're well known for cuddling anything that moves. At least you've got a healthy attitude towards the body and sex. Not like some clergymen I know. Did you see that piece the wretched Ridgefield wrote the other day? "As in sexual activity, the male takes the active role, and the female the passive, so in the priestly ministry, it is only men who are suitably well endowed". Well, I ask you!'

Alison giggled. 'My vicar says that too. Wishful thinking on his part, I guess. Not that I've had any opportunity to judge ...'

'Well, we don't need to worry about that lot any more. As from April, it's not going to matter in the least what they say. We'll be full-blown priests. There's wine in the fridge, Michael, if you want to help yourself.

83

We're nearly finished.'

Michael got his drink, and pulled a chair into the circle.

'Do you think Ridgefield will send a contingent of the Barney boys along to heckle us while we're being done?' Nan was saying. 'I think I'll take some rotten eggs stuffed up my cassock, and if they start trouble I'll let them have it.'

'Peter says St Barnabas is in a lot of trouble,' Caroline said. 'They've found asbestos all over the place, and they're facing a huge bill to get it removed. With their falling numbers, they're going to have difficulty raising the funds. They might even have to close down.'

'And wouldn't we all be sorry! Not that anyone would dare, when it's practically the only theological college that isn't sullied by women.'

'I hear you're getting some changes at the Programme too,' said Michael. 'Jenny introduced me to Deidre Rutt a few weeks ago, and she said her department is taking you over.'

'She what?' Nan exploded. 'When did she say that? Of course she's not. She's made some proposals, but we'd never accept being part of her empire! It would be a disaster. How dare she go round saying it's going to happen, the manipulative old cow!'

Michael cowered in mock horror. 'What have I said?'

'I can't stand the woman - all she's interested in is expanding her power base.'

'I went to a day she organised last year, and she seemed pleasant enough,' Alison said.

'Oh, she always appears pleasant, but it's not sincere for a minute,' said Nan. 'She got right up my nose when David died, saying she knew exactly what I was going through because she'd been divorced, and telling me how I was supposed to be feeling all the time. It still bugs me, even though it was nine years ago.' She knocked back a substantial swig of wine. 'Deidre is a good manager, I'll give her that. And she's right that the Programme is badly run - Roly Albright is a dear man, but he's more of a scholar than an organiser. Only she's not got the slightest idea about what's needed to train ordinands. She expects their parish priest to teach them everything, and thinks they can fill in any gaps by sending her essays through the post.'

'That would never work for me,' Alison said. 'My vicar doesn't approve of women priests, and I'd need some stimulation from other people on the same course.'

'Exactly! I mean, there are plenty of decent clergy, but what do you do if yours is a complete idiot? Still, whatever she's going round saying, I'm sure Bishop Derrick won't let it happen. He can't stand her either. Sorry, Alison, I shouldn't be talking like this in front of you.'

'I'm fascinated,' Alison said. 'I thought education was bad enough.'

'You should hear them when they really start being uncharitable,' Michael said, smiling across at her. 'How's term going?'

'Not so bad. My energy levels are usually quite high up to half term. Your Lisa's looking a lot more settled.'

Michael and Alison talked briefly while Caroline and Nan fussed with their diaries, and then Alison and Caroline left.

Nan came back and pulled her chair nearer to his. 'So how are things? I hear the new youth club is flourishing, but you've not had an easy ride with it.'

Michael sighed. 'It's like you say. Sex is the trouble. You can't mention anything to do with it without getting embroiled in a debate about the Church of England's moral teaching. It's been damned hard work, winning the kids' trust, and getting to the point where we can talk about things, and then I'm told I'm corrupting them. I've given most of my time to it, for free, because I thought it was important, and now I'm wondering what the point is.'

'I'm afraid that's the way the Church is going at the moment. A lot of people are drawing their lines in the sand, and if you don't use the right catchphrases about moral standards, you've had it. Peter's been feeling the pressure to show that St Martin's stands for something. Caroline's not so strict, but she goes along with him. I'd have thought they'd both understand that what you do with a bunch of kids off the estate can't be the same as what you do with churchgoers.'

'I think they do, but they're not sure about me, whether I'm quite sound enough. And they might be right - I've never really got my faith back. I mean, I go to church, and play the organ, and say all the right things, but I don't feel anything any more. I know lots of people don't, and Jenny says I shouldn't expect it, but I always had it before. I hate feeling this empty inside. It's like an amputation. I keep checking the place where my soul should be, and there's nothing there. Which only goes to prove the selectors were right, if I've gone to pieces so easily.'

'I'm not sure about that. A lot of people go through periods of doubt and dryness, and it often does them a lot of good, shakes them up and puts them back together again. And after all, you're still doing a lot of good, what with all your voluntary work.'

'I can't do this for ever. I thought it might all become clearer once I came here, but it hasn't. Baz says I ought to train as a youth and community worker, and get a full-time job in it, and maybe I should, but how do I know? The trouble is, in the past when I've changed direction, I've always had a strong sense of being called to do something. I feel completely defeated now it's stopped happening. I don't need to have great plans, I can live one day at a time, but I need to think there's some meaning to what I'm doing. I need some dreams.'

'Of course you do. You've got to believe you have a contribution to make to the world somewhere. You will get through this, Michael, I'm sure you will. It's like the pain of labour - you're giving birth to a new person, and it's bloody painful. Goes on for ever until you scream you can't stand it and you're off home, but you have to go through with it. There are times when all we can do is endure, but we're not abandoned completely.' Nan drained her glass, then sat back, looking sympathetic.

'That's how I *feel*, though. I feel as if I've taken a wrong turning somewhere and I'm hopelessly lost. Jenny's been the person who's kept me going, except that now I'm in a mess with her, and I'm scared I'm losing her.' Michael hesitated. 'That's what I wanted to talk to you about.'

'Not sex rearing it's awkward little head again?' Nan asked, smiling at him.

Michael laughed. 'Well, no. That's the trouble. It would be fine if it was. You see, after I broke up with Becky, I decided I wasn't going to get into another relationship until I'd got my life sorted out better. But obviously, I need friends, and I've ended up doing a lot with Jenny, because we share a lot of the same tastes, and as I said, she's encouraged me to keep going. Except that now she says she's fallen in love with me, and I don't know what to do. I'm very fond of her, I suppose I have kissed her occasionally, as a friend, but I can't think of her in that way.'

'You haven't exactly been wise, have you? You should realise that a good-looking man like you is taking a risk having a close friendship with a woman. What the hell is she supposed to think if you take her out, and probably touch her up all the time, knowing you?'

'I said from the start it was just as friends. She knew that. I've never misled her. And she's always said she didn't want boyfriends, she was too committed to her work.'

'Is she being difficult about it?'

'Oh, no, the opposite. She seems to think it's like having bad breath. She's very apologetic, and she's trying to treat it, so it goes away. She says she doesn't want me to move out, just not to see as much of me. Only now everything's awkward between us, even when we do go out. I feel I'm losing her, and I hate it. Actually, I find I'm angry with her for ruining everything. I want things to be back where they were before she complicated it all, because she's the best friend I've got.'

'What a selfish sod you're being. Where do Jenny's feelings come in all this? You mess around with her, and you're quite happy for her to say it's all her fault. You expect her to be available for you, even if it's tearing her apart, until, presumably, you get yourself a girlfriend, and suddenly it's "goodbye Jenny, don't call me". You're not being fair. If you really do care about her, surely you've either got to clear out, and give her a chance to recover, or go out with her properly, and see what happens.'

'I wish I could go out with her. I really like her, but I don't fancy her, and that wouldn't be fair on her either, would it? I don't know, do you think you can love someone without being *in* love with them?'

'I'll tell you what I find interesting. You love God, but you've lost the feelings. You love Jenny, but you don't have the feelings. Maybe it's the way you are at the moment. Or maybe you're expecting too much. I don't think we ever quite get the same romantic fireworks and passion once we get past twenty-five.'

'That's a depressing thought.'

'It is rather, isn't it? Perhaps I should carry on hoping I'll be swept off my feet by a red-blooded bishop.' Nan laughed, then became serious. 'Only I do think you've got to decide about Jenny. I know I don't know her, and I don't know you all that well, but if it was me, and I had someone who was as important to me as she is to you, I wouldn't let them go. There are worse things to build relationships on than solid friendship, and perhaps the fireworks would come later.'

'Yes, there are worse things,' Michael said thoughtfully. He remembered holding Jenny in his arms the night of his return from holiday, the softness of her hair, and the fondness that had filled him. It wasn't as if she repulsed him. 'Thanks, Nan. You've been a help.' He embraced her and kissed her cheek before wandering back to St Martin's to try to lose himself playing the organ.

Ten

It was warm inside the church. The sun poured through the large windows, and radiated through the glass of the central skylight. A faint smell of polish mingled with the scent of the flowers arranged in the vases standing on niches around the walls. Amid the quiet of the afternoon, the distant sound of traffic was the only interruption to the stillness. Michael's conversation with Nan echoed in his mind, and he had an impulse to try to pray again. He knelt and buried his face in his hands, pressing down on the wooden back of the chair in front of him.

It happened without warning. A flood of fire deluged him, bathing him from head to toe in happiness, the like of which he had never known. Laughter and light and languages and music bubbled round his head, his limbs danced within themselves. Despair evaporated. The knot of anger at the God who had left him directionless came free from its anchorage deep within, floated upwards like a bubble of gas, and was gone. He didn't know what was happening, only that it was good to be there. Motionless, he held his breath, absorbing the sensations. Then he straightened his head, and held out his hands, palms upward, smiling. Light and heat beat against his closed eyelids, a presence seemed to pulse around him. If he opened his eyes and turned round, he would see ... but he had no need to see. God had come back to him, like a lover once thought lost returning to caress skin and heart and mind. Like a mother receiving back the babe she thought dead, laughing with exquisite delight as she held it to her breast.

Questions crowded into his mind. Tell me, what must I do? What about Jenny? What about ordination? There was no answer, only a peace beyond understanding, and the knowledge that he was in the right place. That was all, but it was enough. He was still on the right road, despite the rough terrain and fog bewildering him. He had glimpsed a signpost.

Slowly, like the passage of an eclipse, the light was extinguished. The glare against his eyes faded. The warmth passed. He opened his eyes. Far above, the sun had gone behind a cloud.

There was a slight noise at the back of the church. He got up, and raised a hand to the churchwarden, returning mended hymnbooks to their shelves. Then he went over to the organ, and plunged into The Arrival of the Queen of Sheba, for the sheer joy of it.

That evening, he heard Jenny return after her evening surgery, gave her time to have supper, then went downstairs to knock on her door. She was curled up in an armchair with the local paper open in front of her at the 'Deaths' column: 'Looking to see who you've finished off?' he had teased when he'd first observed her undertaking the exercise.

From the strained look she gave him when he put his head round the door, he doubted she had been registering any of the information in front of her.

'Hello,' he said, shutting the door, and going to sit on the arm of the sofa. 'I've got my faith back.'

'Good.'

Her tone was hardly an inducement to share what had happened. I'm making her thoroughly miserable, he thought, Nan's right. Either I say I'm moving out, or I take a leap of faith. And what else are signs for, but to impel doubting believers into leaps of faith? She had bent her head to the paper again, so he waited until she looked up at him. 'Would you go out with me, properly?'

He had expected joy; instead she continued to stare unhappily at him. 'You're only saying that because you feel guilty.'

'No, I'm saying it because I'm very fond of you, and I think it might grow into something. There are much worse bases on which to build relationships than what we've got.'

'I don't think so. I should only end up getting hurt.'

'Aren't you being hurt anyway? You throw me out, or we carry on wishing each other a distant good morning when our paths cross in the hall. What use is that to either of us? I'd rather give it a go. If it doesn't work, at least we've tried. If it does work ...' The image of their faces in the mirror months before, and the knowledge that had come with it, sprang suddenly into his mind. It *was* going to work, somehow. He was going to marry her. His future wife remained unenthusiastic and silent.

Michael stood up and held out his hand to her. 'Come here.'

She rose and stood tensely in front of him, her arms folded across the thin fabric of a pale-print summer dress, her eyes anxious.

He placed his hands on her shoulders and bent to kiss her. She remained rigid, and her lips were dry and unresponsive under his.

He stopped. 'You have to try too, Jenny. You're confusing me. I thought you said you were in love with me, but you freeze when I touch you.'

'I'm sorry. I don't know what you want from me. You don't fancy me. I don't want to be played with.'

He studied her face. 'I'm not playing. I really care about you. That's the only thing this is about.' He unfolded her arms for her, and placed her hands on his shoulders, smiling. 'Come on, live dangerously. Take the risk. Give us a kiss.' His arms slid around her waist, and this time when he kissed her, she responded.

With his eyes shut, he concentrated on the sensations transmitted by lips and hands. I could get to like this, he thought. I'm not in love with her yet, but one day ... He opened his eyes and smiled at her.

'Was I ... was that alright?' Jenny asked.

Michael laughed and hugged her more closely. 'Well I enjoyed it.' He pulled her down to sit with him on the sofa, and tried again. 'You know,' he said, surfacing, 'for all you complained about the curate with the insistent tongue, you seem to have got the hang of it.'

She smiled. 'You remember that, do you? I was exaggerating for effect.'

'I guessed it. You've had hundreds of boyfriends. You will go out with me, won't you?'

'If you really want me.'

'I do,' Michael said, and meant it. He kissed her again, pushing her down against the cushions and caressing her breasts through the cotton of her dress, wondering how far he would get before she objected, if she objected. He'd undone three of the tiny buttons that stretched challengingly from her neckline to waist, when the blow fell: a substantial clout, with pinpricks of pain that pierced through his tee shirt and into the flesh of his back.

He jerked upright, sending the cat flying to the floor from her precarious perch. 'Ow! Who asked you to butt in, moggie?'

Celestine, washing herself hurriedly in a pretence of equanimity, glanced disdainfully at him.

He looked at Jenny, lying back in the corner of the sofa, giggling. 'She was protecting my virtue,' she said, doing her buttons up. 'Don't go too fast, Michael,' she added, more seriously. 'It's all new for me, and I'm shy about this kind of thing. Above the waist, and above the clothes, isn't that what the Blatherwyckes told you?'

'Ah, but I didn't sign up,' he said as he laid down next to her. 'But I'll do whatever you say. We've got plenty of time.'

Jenny touched his cheek tentatively. 'You said your faith had come back.'

Michael rested his head on her shoulder, and told her, at peace in the possession of her friendship once more.

Jenny could never quite let herself go over the first two months in which she was supposed to be going out with Michael, always expecting that he'd announce he'd had enough, or met someone else, and that would be the end of it. Certainly he was affectionate, both if he dropped in on her at the end of the evening, or on the few occasions they managed to find time to go out anywhere, but she saw no evidence that he cared deeply, for all the warmth of his embraces.

When she opened her front door on the gloom of a November evening to find Becky blinking in a pervasive drizzle, she assumed at once that it would mark the end.

'Hello, is Michael in?' Becky asked, pushing her damp hair back from her face, and wiping a drip from the end of her nose.

'Yes. Well, no. He's popped out to the shop, but he'll be back any minute.'

'I'm supposed to be staying over at mum's, but she rang to say she had an urgent meeting, and then she forgot to leave a key. I wondered if Michael might be free to go to the pub, or something.'

'You'd better come in.' Jenny stood back and let her into the hall. She felt inadequate beside Becky, despite having made efforts with her hair and clothes to make Michael less ashamed of her. 'Take your coat off, you can wait in my living room if you want. I'm going out in a few minutes, but he should be back. I expect he's got talking to someone. You know Michael.' Her heartiness sounded false.

Becky, hanging her dripping coat on the end of the bannisters, looked at her pityingly. 'It's very kind of you to make me welcome,' Becky said as she sat down on the sofa. 'I know I owe you an apology for earlier this year. It was my fault, Michael was trying to keep the house rules. It was a bad time for me. I did a few things I regret.'

Jenny stared at her, wishing it didn't matter to know that Michael had had sex with this woman, kissed her and touched her with a noisy passion he'd never dreamt of directing towards herself. She had to pull herself together, force her hands to unclench themselves, and strive to

91

find a friendly tone. 'That's alright.' She cleared her throat, and attempted a smile. 'It didn't happen again.'

'Is Michael seeing anyone these days?' Becky asked. 'I wouldn't want to intrude, but I thought he might give me another chance.'

'No he's not. Not seriously. He goes around with people, but he's not really involved with anyone.'

'Good.'

The sound of the front door opening and shutting broke into their enforced intimacy. Jenny got up swiftly and opened the door into the hall.

'You've got a visitor,' she said, before he could speak.

'I wondered whose the coat was.' He came through and Becky turned her most welcoming smile on him. 'Hello, Becky. This is a surprise.'

She stood up and went over to him, kissing his cheek as she explained herself.

Jenny left them to it. 'I'm off,' she said, reappearing at the living room door in her coat. 'You'll lock up if you go out, won't you?'

'Hold on,' Michael said to Becky, and followed Jenny to the hall. 'I don't have to go with her,' he said in a low voice.

'Go on, I don't mind. The poor woman looks as if she needs a drink.'

'Are you sure?'

'Of course.' Jenny kissed his cheek quickly, and opened the front door.

As she closed it, she heard Michael say, 'OK, let's go to the Bell. Only I haven't got much money, so if you want to eat, you're on your own.'

Michael found it difficult to give Becky his full attention as they walked to the pub through continuing spots of rain. He was too busy worrying about whether Jenny really did mind him going off with Becky, and how he would put things right with her if she did.

Becky slipped her hand through his arm. 'You're very quiet. Did I come at the wrong moment? The atmosphere between you and Jenny seemed rather strained, I thought. Did she think I might seduce you again?'

'Probably. I'll tell you when we get there. Where's Nan tonight?'

'She's at a meeting. Had you heard that the Diocese are wanting Deidre Rutt to take over the Programme? They've all been up in arms about it, trying to think of ways to avoid it, and now there's been a counter-suggestion that they become an independent body, and base themselves at St Barnabas. Apparently St Barnabas is in financial trouble, so having the Programme there would solve some of their problems too. This meeting tonight's for them to choose between Deidre Rutt and Christopher Ridgefield - what a prospect! Mum says she'll have to resign whichever way it goes, because either option is a disaster.'

Michael laughed. 'Not much of a choice, is it? Surely there's something else they could try?'

They tossed a few alternatives around as they completed the walk to the pub.

Only when they were seated in the corner of the Lounge bar of the Bell did Michael take a sip of lager and revert to the subject of Jenny. 'Jenny was finding it awkward having you call, because she's going out with me now, and naturally she was a touch uneasy about you coming to ask me out.'

'You're going out with *Jenny*?' She raised her eyebrows. 'But she said you weren't seeing anyone at the moment. "Not seriously", she said.'

'I hope that's only her being self-deprecating as usual. It's pretty serious for me.'

'That's a shame, I was wondering if you'd give me another chance. I wasn't behaving very well earlier this year.'

'Neither was I.'

'No, but I was into making conquests, proving to myself that I could attract anyone I wanted to, and I wasn't fair on you. I was thinking we might try again.'

Becky's basket of scampi and chips was delivered onto the table. Michael pinched a chip. 'It would never have worked. I could still fancy you, and I like your company, but I couldn't live with you for five minutes. I'd drive you mad. You'd want me to be ambitious. It was beginning to happen last December.'

'I wasn't going to propose living with you.'

'No, but that's what I want. I'm nearly thirty. I want to settle down, get married, have children. I want something long-term - I think that's what I'll have with Jenny.'

Becky shook her head. 'Well, well. I always said you fancied her, didn't I? So what do Caroline and Peter think about you shacking up with your landlady?'

'It's not like that. She doesn't agree with that kind of thing, as you ought to know.'

'Poor old Michael.' Becky patted his arm.

'I'll manage. It's early days yet. Actually, Becky, there's not many people know about us yet - except Nan, because I talked things over with her. It's not that it's a secret, but once Peter and Caroline know, they'll probably say I have to move out because it looks bad, so don't say anything, will you?'

'You can trust me,' Becky said. 'Just because I've landed a prestigious job with the BBC doesn't mean I'll broadcast everything.'

'Tell me about it...'

Michael left Becky with a group of her old friends, and walked back home. It was past ten, and Jenny was curled in her armchair with Celly on her lap, watching the news.

'Have a nice time?' she asked, without looking at him.

'I'd rather have been with you,' he said, sitting on the sofa, and removing his trainers. 'Why did you tell Becky I wasn't going out with anyone, and wasn't serious about anyone?'

'Well it's not exactly working, is it?'

He sat back, looking across at her profile. 'It's working for me.'

She said nothing.

'Don't you like me any more?' he asked.

'No. I don't. I don't want to go out with you.'

He couldn't believe she meant it, but her words knocked the breath from him just the same. 'What's the matter? You were fine before Becky came. You're not jealous are you?'

Jenny stared at the screen, taking an inordinate interest in the nation's economic affairs.

'Put the television off and come over here.' She glanced at him, thought for a while, and then obeyed. Michael put his arms round her and kissed her forehead. 'You don't really want to finish with me, do you? I couldn't bear it if you did. I love you.'

'You *say* that,' Jenny said, pulling away from him and throwing herself into the corner of the sofa, 'but you don't *mean* it. It's a pleasant game for you, but it's not the real thing. You don't want me, not really. Not like you used to want Becky, and still do, for all I know. What you really want is a proper relationship with a proper woman, not sexless cuddling with an old cow like me who you force yourself to touch, and get it over with as quickly as possible.'

'You can't have it both ways, Jen,' he said, taking her hand. 'You keep telling me not to go too fast, and slap my wrists when I do anything other than kiss you, and I've tried to respect it. You can't turn round and say it proves I don't want you. I'd love to be able to make love to you. I practically

94

have to tie myself to my bed at nights to stop me coming downstairs to your room.'

He wasn't sure exactly when he'd fallen in love, he could only remember getting back late one evening from the Rows to find Jenny in her kitchen making a drink, and knowing it had already happened. She'd let her hair grow, so that it brushed her brows and curled around her neck, softening her face. That night, she had on a scoop-necked top, and it had been the smooth, pale, erotic curve of her neck and shoulders that had moved him as he came up behind her, and touched his mouth to her skin.

She laughed and shook him off, saying he was tickling her, and because he was still trying to take things slowly, he had let her go. But the wanting had become stronger as the weeks had gone by, the desire to have her, to know her, to break through her self-sufficiency, to be needed by her.

He pulled her towards him and put his arms round her again. 'Not *want* you?' He cupped her breasts deliberately through her blouse, and kissed her with slow passion. 'Not *want* you?' he whispered in her ear. 'Come next door with me, and I'll show you whether I *want* you or not.' His lips found her neck. 'Please, Jenny, come to bed with me...'

Eleven

Jenny pulled away from Michael so that she could study his face. For a long time she gazed at him, through clear grey eyes, and he wondered how he could ever have thought her plain or ordinary.

'We don't have to go all the way,' he said, 'not unless you ask me to.'

'I might,' she whispered, 'in the heat of the moment. That's the trouble. And then I'd feel dreadful afterwards.'

Michael caressed her face with his finger. 'What do you mean?' he smiled. 'No woman feels dreadful after I've made love to her.'

'I'm not ready for it.'

He paused. 'I was waiting for you to say "yet".'

'Yet,' she said, holding his eyes, the tiny word committing her to something. 'You do promise not to, don't you, whatever I might say?'

'That's understood, Jen.'

He led her to her bedroom next door, and she put on her bedside light, angling it away, so that the bed was in shadow. Michael pushed the heavy cardigan off her shoulders, and drew her down onto the bed with him. They searched each other's mouths, another long, slow kiss of trust and hope and passion.

'Where's Celly?' he asked, drawing breath as he began to unbutton her blouse. 'I don't want to get attacked for doing this.'

'I was relieved when she stopped you. I didn't want you to see me. I'm odd.'

'Don't be silly.' He opened her blouse, reached behind to unfasten her bra, and pushed it up out of the way. She shivered a little in the air, nervous at the exposure.

'You've got pokey-in ones instead of pokey-out ones,' he said, tenderly examining the oddly inverted nipples of her well rounded breasts, with the intentness of a trainee midwife.

'I told you I wasn't much to look at.'

'It's a challenge. Do they pop out with encouragement?' He lowered his mouth to see what he could do.

Jenny stroked his hair timidly. 'I thought you'd be put off.'

'Why?' he said, looking up. 'It's all you.' He turned his attention to her other breast. 'I love you. I think you're beautiful.' He lay half on top of her, his mouth closed on hers as his hands ran over her body. His left hand found the button of her trousers, and began to undo it.

'No.'

Michael watched her face. It was hard to read her expression in the dimness. He extended his fingers under her trousers to tease at the springing mound of hair. 'No?'

'I don't think so. I'm not comfortable about that, not yet. I'm sorry.'

'OK.' He withdrew his hand and returned to his caressing of her breasts and neck and shoulders. It was difficult to stop, to have the half of her naked under him, and not to be able to lie between her thighs, driving into her, making her his own, but he forced himself to stay within the boundaries she had set. He lay over her, propped on his elbows, and kissed the tip of her nose. 'But never say you don't know what I want from you.'

Jenny smiled. 'I won't.' She pulled his head down again to lay on her breast. 'And I want you, too. You know that, don't you?'

Michael reached down and pulled the covers up over them, then settled his cheek contentedly against the soft mound of her breast. Some boundary had been crossed; they would never merely be friends again.

Though Becky discussed Michael and Jenny with Nan, neither of the women had any intention of mentioning it to the Harts.

'I'm not saying I approve if they're sleeping together,' Nan had said, 'but it's a private matter for the two of them to work out, and I don't see that it makes a great deal of difference whether they're living in the same house or not. If they want to, they will. If they don't, they won't, but Peter's a conservative old bugger these days. Best not to say anything.'

But three weeks later, when Becky was paying another flying visit to Greathampton, she managed to alert Peter to what was going on. She arrived to see Caroline during supper, and sat down at the table on the tail end of a conversation in which Peter was mentioning the problem of Jenny's relationship with Michael.

Not realising that Peter was referring to the events of the summer, Becky saw a chance to be generous to her former lover. 'I don't see why you should be negative about it,' she said. 'They're pretty well suited if you think about it, and Michael's obviously in love with her. Quite soppy if you ask me. I reckon he's been soft on her ever since he moved in, and that's why things never worked out with me. I wouldn't be surprised if there were wedding bells in the air.'

Becky stirred her coffee, registering only slowly that Caroline and Peter were staring at her in shocked silence.

'What are you talking about?' Peter asked.

'You were talking about Michael and Jenny ... Don't tell me. You still don't know, do you, and I've gone and put my foot in it?'

'You mean Michael's involved with Jenny?' Caroline said. 'The sneaky little toad. Why didn't he tell us?'

'Because he knows perfectly well what we'd say,' Peter snorted. 'I was bending over backwards to clear Jenny's name because he swore there was nothing between them, while all the time, he's going out with her behind our backs. Has been all year, you say? I've had enough, Caroline. He'll have to go. I'm not having him in any positions of trust any more.'

'I don't think he's doing anything wrong,' Becky said, trying to salvage the situation. 'They're not lovers or anything, and they've only been going out a few weeks. I don't think he realised he liked her till lately.'

'Excuse me, please,' Peter said. 'I have a phone call to make.'

With all his musical responsibilities in the run-up to Christmas, Michael proved elusive, and it was not until the week before Christmas that Peter was able to meet him to discuss his behaviour.

Michael, alerted by Becky, guessed what he was about to be grilled about, but he was too distracted by Jenny to worry overmuch about it. When he opened the door to Peter, he was looking his best, in a dusky-blue shirt, bright tie and smart trousers, newly showered and shaved, and ready to accompany Jenny to a Christmas drinks evening at the health centre.

'Come in,' he said brightly. 'You've not been inside before, have you?' Peter followed him down the hall with a tense smile fixed to his face. 'I was having a coffee, do you want one? I'm sure Jenny won't mind. She's getting ready - we're off out in half an hour.'

'No thank you.' Peter looked around the living room as Michael sank back on the sofa and picked up his mug. 'I thought you had your own room.'

'I do, but I can't invite Jenny into my bedroom, can I? I come here if I want to talk to her.'

'That's what I wanted to see you about. I understand that you're going out together.'

'That's right.'

'So why did you swear to me that there was nothing between you?'

'There wasn't, then. Jenny was in love with me, but I didn't feel the same way. I couldn't tell you that, it wouldn't have been fair on her. Now I've fallen in love with her.' He put his mug down. 'I'm really serious about her, Peter.'

'But you can't possibly carry on living here! You know all the fuss it caused when people only *thought* you were carrying on with her. If you really are, you'll have to move out.'

'Why?'

'Don't be naive. You know why.'

'Where am I supposed to go? I don't have any money.'

'He's not going anywhere.' Jenny said from the doorway. She was transformed by make-up, a softly fitted, dark-green dress and heeled shoes. Indignation made her face glow. 'Why should he?'

'I will not have my organist and youth leader living with his girl-friend,' Peter stated tersely. 'It compromises everything I'm trying to teach.'

'We're not living together,' Jenny said, 'and even if we were, I can't see that it's any of your business.'

'Of course it's my business as long as Michael does the work he does in the church. It's not a question of what you're actually getting up to, it's how it looks. It sends all the wrong messages. I can't make an exception merely because he's my godson. You have to find somewhere else, Michael. You can always stay with us once Christmas is over. It's either that, or give up the work.'

Michael met Jenny's eyes. 'There isn't anyone else to run the youth club, it might have to close down. I can't let that happen.'

'I know,' she said. 'You'll have to move out. But I think it stinks, Peter. You ought to be trusting us, not giving in to people who've got nothing better to do than gossip all day.'

Michael broke in before Peter could retaliate. 'I'm going home tomorrow, anyway,' he said. 'Maybe I can move into your spare room when I get back.' He rose, and showed Peter out.

'I've never seen you that fierce!' he laughed, as he hugged Jenny on his return to the living room.

'I didn't mean to be. I'm just fed up with being gossiped about, and with people who believe the gossip.' She adjusted his tie. 'Let's forget about it for tonight, I vote we enjoy ourselves.'

'I thought we were going to a deadly drinks party at the surgery.'

'We'll liven it up.'

Jenny was in a strange mood that evening. Michael knew her to be much more dynamic than her quiet, professional front suggested, but he was puzzled by her ebullience, wondering what lay behind it. She hung onto his arm, joking and teasing as she introduced him to her partners and the various members of the practice team, and repeatedly replenishing their glasses of wine. They swayed home two hours later.

Jenny dropped her coat on the hall floor, went through to her bedroom, and switched on the bedside light. Michael took off his shoes, jacket and tie, and came up behind her.

'You'll spoil your dress,' he said, drawing the zip downwards. The dress slithered to the floor, leaving Jenny standing in her long slip. She went to her handbag, and fumbled for a moment in it, then placed a small packet on the bedside table.

Michael glanced at it, then at her face. He swallowed. 'Are you sure?' he asked, through dry lips.

'Yes. I don't care any more,' she said, standing close to him and unbuttoning his shirt. 'If you're being victimised for sleeping with me, you might as well ... and, oh, Michael, I want to make it up to you.'

'You'll need to take more off than that.' He eased her tights and pants down her legs, then tried to remove the slip.

'I'll be cold,' she said nervously, clutching the silky material against her thighs.

'Hop into bed. I'll soon warm you up.' He wriggled free of his trousers and shirt and joined her under the covers. Within seconds he was lost, kissing her mouth and freeing her breasts, his hands roaming down her back, cradling the heavy flesh of her buttocks, sliding between her thighs. Sod foreplay, he thought, almost ripping his boxer shorts as he struggled free of them, I'm going to explode any second. He reached out for the packet she had left beside the bed, raising himself on one elbow as he tore it open.

Her face arrested him, capping his desire. Tense, anxious, her teeth biting into her bottom lip while she eyed the condom as if it were a knife held to her throat. Michael put it back on the table and collapsed on top of her, while his blood pounded wildly through his body.

'You don't really want this, do you?' he whispered to her ear, once he could get his breath back.

'I do. I want to give you something. I'm nervous, that's all. I will let you.'

He propped himself up on his elbows and gazed down at her, with his little cross brushing her chin. 'It's not a question of letting me, or giving me a consolation prize. You're not supposed to look like you're steeling yourself to jump out of a plane without a parachute.' He kissed her. 'I can wait. I love you too much to want the first time to be something you might regret. Besides, I promised, didn't I, not to give way, even if you begged me?'

'I shouldn't have led you on. Isn't that the worst thing a woman can do, leading a man on and then stopping him at the last minute? You'll hate me now.'

Michael rolled off her and lay on his side, tracing her breasts with his fingers. He glanced downwards and smiled as he replied. 'Does it look like I hate you? The worst thing you could do would be to leave me. You're necessary to me. Don't ask me why. I'm crazy about you. The question is, what are we going to do about it?' He had his own solution, but the telephone interrupted his intended proposal.

Jenny picked it up, and he smiled at the professional manner she managed to assume, despite her virtual nakedness.

'I've got to go out,' she said, putting the phone down. 'Patrick's been called out to one of my patients who's rather confused, and he won't let Patrick touch him. Insists he wants the girlie back. That's me.' She was dressing herself as she spoke.

Michael lay on her bed watching her pull out trousers and jumper from her drawer, words and senses whirling around him, not knowing whether to laugh at loving her, or mourn at losing her when he wanted only to lie with her till morning. He waited until the last throb of her car engine had faded, then dragged himself from her bed, tidied it, and climbed the stairs to his room.

The following morning, Michael was on the coach to Croydon, staring out of the window at grey skies and heavy traffic, dreaming of making love to Jenny. He'd barely had a chance to speak to her again before he left, since she'd not returned from getting her patient finally admitted to hospital until after midnight, and had disappeared to the surgery after a brief morning visit to kneel by his bed and say goodbye. She'd tasted of toothpaste when he'd kissed her, and she'd complained of the roughness of his chin as he wound his arms round her neck.

'I'll ring you every day,' he'd said. 'I'll miss you.'

'It's only a week, Michael,' Jenny smiled practically. 'You're a softie,

101

really, aren't you? I bet it's you who buys all those soppy Christmas singles, like It'll be Lonely This Christmas. What am I going to do with you?'

'Marry me,' he'd wanted to say. But she'd looked at her watch and said, 'Good heavens, I'll be late,' and with a final kiss, she'd been out of earshot.

The vicarage was bursting as Meg juggled relations, mince pies, mulled wine and parishioners and Edward rushed frantically around taking services. Sarah and Ruth were there with their families, squashed in, arguing happily, greeting him with affection: Ruth's children, ten year-old Sophie and nine year-old Jack vying for his attention with Emma, Naomi, and Rachel. He plunged into the festivities without his usual zest. Normally he'd enjoy it, they relied on him to keep things convivial, but he was too preoccupied to rise to the occasion.

'Are you worried about seeing Kate again?' Meg asked, fishing for the cause of his discomposure as he helped her prepare supper that evening.

'Kate? Of course not.'

'She is going out with Gary, but it's an off and on kind of thing. She still thinks about you. She'd have you back like a shot if you wanted.'

'I wouldn't marry Kate if she was the last person in the world. Besides I've ...'

'Come on, Mike, you said you'd help Emma and Sophie practice their song. They're waiting for you.' Ruth breezed into the kitchen, disposing of the moment in which Michael had been about to confide in his mother.

Somehow, no other opportunities arose. His parents knew nothing of Jenny, besides the fact that she was the respectable, spinsterish doctor in whose house he lodged. Not until she rang as the Turners were finishing a late Christmas lunch, and they saw the effect it had on him.

Meg was in the kitchen collecting cheese and biscuits for the final course when the telephone went. Michael went through quickly, but his mother had already answered, far too cheerful after her third glass of wine.

'Of course. Who shall I say is calling? ... Not ringing to say the house has fallen down, I hope! Hold on, I'll get him for you.'

'Is it for me?' Michael asked.

'I'm not sure it's anything to cheer you up. It's only your landlady.'

He snatched the phone, but did not put it to his ear straightaway.

Meg took the hint. 'Don't worry, I'm off,' she said, picking up the tray. He said 'hello' in a carefully neutral voice as the door swung to behind her.

'Was that your mother? I was nervous about calling you up, but I've been out so much, I thought you wouldn't have been able to get hold of me. You haven't told them about me, then?'

'Not yet. It's been so hectic, I haven't had the chance. Oh, Jenny, I do love you. I want ... I wondered ... ' He broke off as Meg came back in, purple paper hat stuck precariously on the back of her grey hair.

'Sorry, dear, forgotten the butter.'

'Hold on,' Michael said down the phone, eyeing his mother with annoyance, as if her reappearance was deliberate, as perhaps it was.

'I can't really talk here,' he said, as Meg departed. 'Can I ring you back in a little while, when I can lock myself in somewhere. Oh, Rachel, what do you want?'

'Diggies!' said his niece, pink-cheeked with excitement, getting biscuits from the cupboard, and going out, leaving the door open behind her.

'Happy Christmas, anyway, Jen. I'll ring back as soon as I can.'

Michael went back into the dining room to a phalanx of curious heads.

'What on earth does your landlady need to ring you about?' Meg asked. 'Did she want to give you notice?'

'Look at the state of him! I reckon he's in love. What's she like, this landlady? A buxom divorcee with brassy hair who says "I can do extras, for a price"?' Ruth thrust out her own insubstantial bosom as she attempted an execrable accent, and roared at her wit. Her husband looked at her pityingly.

'Hardly,' Michael said. 'She's a GP. She's been working all over Christmas.'

'How old is she?' Ruth asked.

'Oh, my sort of age.'

'Beautiful?' Ruth persisted.

Michael hesitated.

'Only to him,' Sarah laughed. Michael had mentioned Jenny a few times while they'd been in France, and she had her suspicions.

'Are you involved with her?' Meg asked.

'Yes. Kind of.' He looked at her anxiously, begging her to approve.

'I told you he was in love!' said Ruth. 'Come on, what's she like?'

'She sounded rather quiet,' Meg said, 'but pleasant, I'm sure.'

'She is a bit shy,' he said, 'but very nice. I think you'd like her. Her dad's a vicar, too, in Buckinghamshire.'

103

'You should have brought her with you, she could have gone in your room...'

'That's not fair,' Sarah said. 'You never let me and Hugh share rooms. Just because he's shacked up with her.'

'What does shacked up mean, Mummy?' Rachel asked.

'It means I live in my own room on one floor, and Jenny has the ground floor, and we meet in the hall,' Michael said firmly.

'I was going to say, and Michael could have slept on the sofa,' Meg said. '*Is* it serious, Mikey? Because we'd like to meet her if it is.' She smiled reassuringly at him. 'Surely she's not working all week. Why don't you ask her to join us for a day or two? And stay on a little longer yourself?'

'I suppose I could. But you'd have to be nice to her. I don't think she's used to big family gatherings like this.'

'No, Michael, we realise this is your last chance of settling down with someone worthy, we'll be good as gold, and we'll not let the kids ask you awkward questions,' Ruth said. 'Will we, Sarah?'

Michael left them to resurrect anecdotes for their husbands about the ways they had interfered in their younger brother's love life in the past, and went to use the phone in the study.

Twelve

Jenny drew up on the gravelled drive in front of the vicarage at around four on Boxing Day, as darkness began to obscure the sky. Michael was at the front door before she'd switched off the engine, the new, brushed cotton, red-checked shirt he'd been given for Christmas flapping over his jeans. He sensed his sisters watching him from behind the darkened landing window as he walked across to open Jenny's door. The security light, activated by his movement, flooded around him.

'They're all spying on us,' he said, as she got out. 'Would you be embarrassed if I kissed you?'

'Yes.'

'Tough,' he said, cupping her face in his hands, and kissing her as passionately as if they had been alone. 'Ready to meet them?'

'I'd put lipstick on for the occasion. I needn't have bothered.'

'I thought you tasted different. You look really nice.' She was wrapped in a thick, patterned cardigan over navy trousers. Hardly as glamorous as his family might have expected after Vicky and Kate, and her face would always be sensible rather than pretty, but he adored her.

The Turner clan welcomed her with enthusiastic curiosity. They shook hands, asked after her journey, made conversation about her work, pressed a cup of tea and mince pies on her, and appraised her as she sat on the sofa next to Michael.

Edward decided he must have met her father at some point, since they'd coincided in the Diocese of Peterborough twenty-five years before. He produced a tray of sherry and lemonade, and disappeared to help Meg with the supper.

The older children were playing Game of Life noisily in one corner of the room, while Rachel sat in the centre of the carpet with her new Barbie doll, her straight body in its worn, grey jog-suit the antithesis of the doll who was her current role model. She had been pausing from time to time to consider her Uncle Michael and the lady with him, and, having drained her lemonade, she wandered over to them.

'Are you going marry her?' she asked Michael, standing confidentially between his legs, sticky hands on his knees. 'Cos I want to be a bridesmaid, and I have to be before I'm six, or I won't have any teeth for the video.'

'Rachel, really,' Sarah said, ineffectually, since it was a question she would like to have posed herself. 'Her friend was a bridesmaid, but she didn't dare smile because she'd got her front teeth missing,' she explained.

Michael smiled at his niece, brushed her straggly light hair back over her shoulders and pushed her nose with his finger. 'I hope so, only I haven't asked her yet.' He fished a handkerchief out of his pocket, wetted it with his tongue, and cleaned around her mouth.

'You could ask her now. She's sitting next to you,' Rachel stated, with the clear-sightedness of the young, as she dodged his attempts to remove her hard-won stains.

'It isn't normally the kind of thing a man asks a woman in front of other people,' Michael said, feeling for Jenny's hand.

'I could ask her for you.'

'Rachel! Come here,' Sarah called.

It was no good, Rachel needed to know. She climbed onto Michael's knee and addressed Jenny. 'Are you going to marry him?'

'I hope so, only he hasn't asked me yet,' Jenny replied. He squeezed her hand, and she flashed a smile at him.

'I think he wants to, though,' Rachel said seriously.

'Do you think I should? Is he nice?'

'Well,' Rachel said, wrapping a strangling arm round Michael's neck, 'if you bounce up and down on his bed he shouts at you.'

The sound of muted giggling emanated from Sarah and Ruth on the other side of the room.

'I shall have to remember not to do that,' said Jenny. 'Anything else I should know about him?'

'Sometimes he steals your chocolates.'

'I don't,' Michael said.

'Yes you do. You took my last chocolate snowman.'

'I'll tell you something,' Jenny said, 'he steals my cat. He picks her up, and carries her off to his room, and I don't see her for days.'

Rachel wriggled across onto Jenny's lap. 'I've got a cat. He's called Fluff. What's your cat called?'

The conversation grew less personal. Meg appeared at the door to call everyone to supper.

'Michael and her are getting married,' Rachel called, running over excitedly to grab Meg's apron. 'I'm going to be a bridesmaid and have a dress with pink frills and a thing on my head like Barbie.'

106

Meg looked at her son inquiringly. 'That sounds exciting.'

'Rachel, you're a little terror,' Sarah said, swinging her child up and hugging her.

Michael had taken hold of Jenny's hand again. 'Be through in a minute,' he said.

Left alone in the room, they kissed slowly. 'Well?' he said. 'Are you going to marry me, Jenny? Make a little girl very happy? And make me happy too, of course.'

'If you're sure.'

'I'm sure. We're engaged, then?' he said, pulling her to her feet.

'We seem to be.' They laughed as they kissed, and went to the dining room hand in hand, to break their unstartling news.

'I'll make you a bed up on the sofa,' Meg said to Michael, as he boiled the kettle in the kitchen to make Jenny a chocolate drink before bed. 'I know you think I'm being silly, since you're living together anyway, but this is our house.'

Michael went over to Meg and leaned against the worktop next to her. 'I'm not sleeping with her. She doesn't agree with that sort of thing. Why do you think I want to marry her so quickly?'

He and Jenny had talked as they shared the clearing up after supper, and decided on a wedding in three months' time. Michael might have to move out to avoid the appearance of impropriety, but he wasn't going to stay with the Harts any longer than he had to. Jenny's house was his home.

'I'd wondered whether she was pregnant, actually,' Meg said, picking at a blob of grease on the worktop with her thumbnail. 'Oh, Mikey, it's not a very good reason for marrying, just for sex.'

'I was joking. She's been my best friend for nearly a year now, and I can't do without her. You do like her, don't you?'

'She seems pleasant. Not easy to get to know, though.'

Michael sighed. 'I know she's not who you'd have chosen for me.'

'I wouldn't dream of choosing for you. You are nearly thirty. I only hope she can persuade you to get a proper job, instead of all these bits and pieces. I know Jenny's got her career at the moment, but if you have a family you'll need to support her. And you'll never get selected for ordination if you can't get a grip on your life.'

Michael moved away to get a mug out of the cupboard.

'I'm sorry, dear, I wasn't going to say anything, but we worry about you.' She came over and hugged him. 'We *do* like her. We're delighted, really.'

107

He smiled a goodnight, and left to take Jenny her drink.

Jenny took her mug from Michael, and put it down beside the bed so that she could give him her full attention. She put her arms round his neck, and stared into his eyes, dark and absorbed by her, at the serious line of his wide mouth, the mole on the edge of his jaw that must make shaving awkward, the tousled hair that stopped just above the straight eyebrows. The thought that the next time she arrived at this house she would be his wife knotted her stomach. Impetuosity was alien to her nature, yet here they were sliding like a descending bobsleigh into marriage before they had properly understood what they were taking on in each other.

She kissed him. 'You'd better go. I'm tired. I was up half the night.'

As she undressed, she nosed around the room which had always been Michael's, and which still bore traces of his life there. Books and tapes that he hadn't thought necessary to have with him in Greathampton. A wardrobe with one or two jackets and trousers he obviously didn't consider fashionable enough. At the end of the bookshelf, there were some photographs in cardboard frames, face down, dusty. Michael as a toddler, his face round, but recognisable, hair a shade lighter, but eyes the same. An old school photograph, with a pre-pubescent Michael donating the same generous smile to the world. The last showed him in a studio portrait with Kate. Her left hand was displayed with a sapphire ring. It must have been done to mark their engagement. She studied the two faces. Kate was lovely, with that long brown hair swept back off her face, and wide blue eyes. Michael looked pretty much as he did now, a slight change of hairstyle, not much more. And he was in love, you could tell that from the soppy expression in his eyes, all too familiar, damn him.

So if he could fall out of love with someone as beautiful as this, what hope was there for a plain, dull woman like her? She shivered. Perhaps he'd once thought Kate necessary, too.

Michael and Jenny married at the end of March. There was some whispering in the church, but since Michael had stayed with the Harts since January, and everyone loved the excitement of a wedding in the congregation, there was general delight when their banns were read out. The church made a presentation on the Sunday beforehand, the youth club turned its Thursday session into a party, Lisa came over on the bus especially for the occasion, and Peter, his moral stance vindicated, he felt, conducted a low-key service at St Martin's at four o'clock one Saturday afternoon, for a small gathering of Furlongs, Turners, and friends.

Jenny hadn't known, until she had actually seen her parents sitting in the church, whether they were going to turn up. There had been a time when she had fantasised that in presenting Joan and Austin with Michael, she would at last be granted some approval, but from the moment she broke the news of her engagement to Joan, she knew that the same soul-destroying patterns were to be repeated.

Deidre had, of course, passed on her report of the shiftless, un-employed, rather too good-looking young man currently taking advantage of poor dear Jennifer, but Jenny had hoped that once they met Michael, they would like him.

Jenny had taken Michael to meet them one Saturday late in January, but unfortunately, the more charming he tried to be, the more suspicious they became of his motives for wanting to marry their ugly, graceless daughter.

'How do you do, Mrs Furlong?' Michael had said politely, extending his hand. He'd put on a shirt and tie for the occasion, and looked far too attractive.

'How very nice to meet you, Michael,' Joan said, smiling and returning his grip.

There was always something brittle about her mother, Jenny reflected, which wasn't disguised by her elegantly cut black skirt and matching cardigan, with her favourite gold necklace around her throat.

'We've heard so much about you!' said Joan. 'Do come in. I've made coffee, so if you'd like to take him into the lounge, Jennifer dear, I'll bring it through.'

'She seems nice enough,' Michael said, as Jenny shut the living room door behind them. He peered at the bookcases, wandered over to the piano in the corner and played a few bars of a Chopin prelude.

'She will be, to your face. It's what they say behind your back that counts. At a guess, now they've laid eyes on you, it'll be something like "Austin, that young man is up to no good. It's because she's a GP, he's after drugs, you mark my words".'

Joan ushered Austin into the room, and Michael turned from the piano and went to shake hands with him while she put a tray down on the coffee table. Joan made for the piano and shut the lid firmly. They spent an awkward hour making conversation. Austin, a reserved man with defeated shoulders, a hooked nose, and thin hair swept across a balding head, asked Michael about his work and his churchmanship.

Joan detonated ostensibly cheerful remarks under Jenny with unerring accuracy. 'Of course, we despaired of Jennifer ever having a boyfriend, she was such a dumpy thing when she was a teenager. Such a contrast with Diana. It's difficult to get clothes to look good on you with your figure, isn't it, dear? ... So how is your work going, Jennifer? She works very hard, of course, Michael, but I have to say I never thought she was really suited to a medical career. She's never been very good with people, which was such a disappointment, because Diana was absolutely charming as a child. You used to run a mile when I introduced you to our friends, don't you remember, dear? I hate to think what your bedside manner is!'

'I think Jen's beautiful ... She's very well respected in the town,' Michael would say, trying to stick up for her, but making little impression.

Jenny herself said little, merely sat with her face blank, counting the hours until they could leave.

Having had their offer to wash up refused, the two of them took a short walk after lunch, and on their return, went to find Austin and Joan still busy clearing up in the kitchen.

Jenny paused with her hand on the door, and waved Michael to her. Through the narrow opening, they could hear her parents' voices:

'...that ring he gave her. Cheap and flashy, I thought,' Joan was saying.

'Like him. Doesn't seem to have had any proper jobs, and sponging off Jennifer.'

'Bastards,' Michael mouthed.

Jenny shrugged. 'I'm used to it,' she whispered.

'You shouldn't be. I couldn't help hearing what you were saying,' Michael said, striding in. 'I'm not used to being suspected of being a fraud. I may be poor, and I may be cheap, but I'm not flashy. And if I am cheap, and poor, it's because I'm not asking for payment for all the work I do. Jenny was very generous in providing somewhere for me to live, so don't run us down.'

'Really, Michael, you must have misheard. We weren't suggesting anything of the sort,' Joan blustered.

'And while I'm on the subject, what I haven't misheard is the way that you talk about Jenny. You seem to find it impossible to believe that I could love her for herself, and do you know, I'm beginning to understand why she finds it difficult to believe as well. Have you always run down everything she does like that?'

'Watch what you're saying, young man,' Austin said.

'Please, Michael,' Jenny said, pulling his arm.

110

'I don't know what you're talking about,' Joan said.

'No, perhaps you don't. Shall I point it out to you next time you do it? Because I take exception to people making derogatory remarks about my fiancee.'

Joan was indignant. 'We never make derogatory remarks about anyone. What a very rude young man you seem to have fallen for, Jennifer. I know Diana had one or two unsuitable boyfriends, but they were never personally abusive.'

'I'm sorry, Mrs Furlong,' Michael said. 'I don't mean to be rude. I'd just like you to be clear that I am not a fraud, and that I love Jenny very much, and I'm proud to be marrying her. You don't have to like me, but I would like to be respected. My dad is in Crockford's, after all,' he added, with a grin.

'Is he?' Austin grunted. 'Turner, you say?' His hand went to his collar above his grey shirt, as if to reassure himself of his own credentials.

'Edward Turner, Ridley Hall and Croydon.'

'I must look him up.' Austin disappeared.

Joan turned back to the sink and plunged her hands back in the water.

Jenny went up to her hesitantly, and put a hand on her shoulder. 'It's alright, Mum. It really is.'

Joan froze at the touch. 'We couldn't afford to marry you from here, you know. Not without a lot of notice. When did you plan to do it?'

Jenny walked back to Michael, propped against the worktop. She leant back against him, and his hands joined in front of her. 'We wouldn't expect you to. We'll get married in Greathampton. It won't be a big do, but you can let us know who you'd like invited. You will come, won't you?'

'As long as we can get away. It depends what date you choose.'

'Now when you say that,' Michael had said slowly, holding her tighter, 'Jenny thinks you mean that you don't really want to come. She doesn't say anything, because she can quite understand that her wedding isn't important to you, but it hurts.'

Joan turned round and eyed him across the room, shocked by his honesty. Her well groomed face looked momentarily bleak. 'Don't be silly, Jennifer. Be your age. Of course we'll come.'

And they had, even if they kept themselves to themselves, and rebuffed the attempts of Michael's relations to get beyond formal politeness as they mingled over the buffet.

Jenny held onto Michael's hand as they circulated among their guests, the ordeal of the gathering mitigated when he was there to make conversation.

All she had to do was look radiant in a hired dress, and introduce people to her new husband, resplendent in the posh new suit she'd bought him when he'd hinted he might try the Oxfam shop.

'You remember my cousin Tyrone...' plump and pale, kissing her with moist lips.

'I've got through!' Tyrone proclaimed. 'I'll be starting my ordination training in September.' Difficult to believe, but clearly there were hidden qualities in her cousin that had impressed some particularly perspicacious selectors.

'Congratulations,' Michael said. 'Where are you going?'

'St John's, Nottingham, I hope.'

'Excellent.' Michael sounded genuinely pleased for him, though it must hurt to think a pretentious sod like Tyrone could succeed where he'd failed. When she looked at his face, though, he was smiling and relaxed. No, he'd never brood about anything.

'Aunt Deidre. Thank you for coming.'

'We wouldn't have dreamt of missing it. Who'd have thought you would end up getting married? But you look lovely, dear. Lovely. Though as Joan says, white's not really your colour.'

Michael squeezed Jenny's hand. 'I hear you're not taking the Programme over after all,' he observed to Deidre.

For an instant, her smile faltered, and her eyes simmered with disapprobation. 'It's appalling! Collaborating with St Barnabas! It can't possibly work.' She favoured them with her smile once more. 'Is that your father over there?' she asked Michael. 'I must have a chat with him. I know so many clergy in your diocese.' Deidre drifted away.

'...My sister Diana. And Miles, her husband.' An elegant couple. Diana had always been everything Jenny was not. Poised, fashionable, successful. 'She's a solicitor, and Miles is a corporate accountant. Are the children somewhere?'

Michael smiled and joked with them, but as they moved away he muttered: 'Your relations are a grim lot, aren't they?'

'Dire,' she agreed. It was almost light relief to move to sit with Kate and Gary, though they were not looking cheerful. Gary, with his cropped hair, earring and muscular frame, looked ill at ease in a suit, and it couldn't have been easy for him to watch his girlfriend's envious absorption in the proceedings. Kate had wanted to come, though, so Meg had said, in order finally to bury her relationship with Michael.

'So it's done,' Kate said to him, as if the others weren't there.

'Yes.' He placed his left hand over hers on the grey formica table;

the bright gold of his untarnished ring shone between them.

'I do hope you'll be happy. Really.'

'I hope *you* will be. Best of everything, Kate.' Michael embraced her gently across the glasses and plates, his lips lingering on hers as he kissed her and held her eyes with a half-smile that held no traces of regret.

Gary and Jenny watched them awkwardly, and caught each other's eye.

'And the best of luck to you, Mrs Turner,' Gary said. Then he leaned across the table and kissed her, hard lips and a rough chin against her skin. 'And thanks for removing the competition,' he added in an undertone. He settled back with an arm around Kate as Jenny and Michael moved on.

At nine-thirty, Michael and Jenny took their leave of their guests. The party would continue, but they had to be up early the following morning to fly off for their honeymoon in Italy. They kissed Meg and Edward, smiled at Joan, and shook hands with Austin.

'Jennifer,' Austin called, as they turned to go. She walked back to him. 'Here. Contribution for the wedding.' He pushed a small folded piece of paper into her hand.

'Oh, Dad, you don't need to.' Jenny unfolded the cheque. Five hundred pounds. 'We can't take it.'

'Please. That's what daughters are for, costing you.' Jenny hugged him. 'He's a nice man,' Austin mumbled. 'Reminds me of myself before I met your mother. I hope you'll be happy with him.'

Clumsily, he embraced her, and her vision was blurred as she and Michael took a taxi home.

They had altered the house during Michael's temporary exile, turning the newly decorated front bedroom into their joint one, and moving his things out of his room to spread them around the house. Their suitcases and travelling clothes lay ready for them. It remained only to get some sleep, or rather, to make love for the first time, and to sleep only if it came as a side effect. Michael helped her out of her clothes, and drew her beneath the covers to lie naked with him. He took his time caressing her, fondling and kissing every part of her skin with studied attention, his eyes dark and deep and vulnerable in the glow from the bedside lamp. She had not known that love could be so frightening.

His lips journeyed past her breasts, her navel, over the teazel of hair, exploring her, and moving back to find her lips again while he slid inside her. Jenny held him, a welter of unfamiliar, embarrassing, exciting, distracting sensations racing through her. So this is sex, she thought, this body crushing me against the mattress ... a wet mouth inside my head ... my taste on his lips ... human flesh taut under my hands ... I'm glad he knows what he's doing, because I don't.

'Worth waiting for?' he breathed, lying on her with his heart thumping against her breast as their bodies settled slowly back into normality.

'Once isn't enough to tell.'

'It'll get better. The first time's always peculiar.'

'I didn't mean I didn't enjoy it.'

'It's alright, Jen. You can be honest with me. I need you to be honest with me. I'd rather know the truth. And I hope I can always be honest with you.'

'I don't know if I want that,' she whispered. 'Sometimes I'd rather pretend I don't know, if the truth's going to be painful.'

'The truth is, I'm always going to love you. Why should that be painful?'

The avowal came easily from him, not yet confronted by the complex choices the reality of their married life would bring.

'Make love to me, Mikey, it can't be wrong.'

'I was never unfaithful to you, Jenny.'

Not really.

PART TWO

May 1994

WITH A GIANT FIGHT

Whoso beset him round
With dismal stories,
Do but themselves confound;
His strength the more is.
No lion can him fright;
He'll with a giant fight,
But he will have the right
To be a pilgrim.

John Bunyan 1628-1688

One

Even when you were thirty, there was still something exciting about getting a new bicycle for your birthday, Michael decided, riding out of the entrance to the health centre. He'd been thinking about picking one up second hand, but had never got round to it. Now Jenny had presented him with this wonderful machine, looking anxiously at him, and worrying if she'd spent too much.

He'd hoped his delight had been apparent, but in case it hadn't, he'd interrupted the lunchtime surgery meeting between his wife, her mail, and her sandwiches, and now he was off down the hill to the Hart's vicarage, with the wind racing through his hair.

'Hello! Happy Birthday,' Caroline said, hugging him on the doorstep. 'That's a splendid bike, isn't it? You'd better bring it into the hall, or some of your young friends might decide to borrow it. Come through. Nan's here, she's recovering from a trying morning at St Barnabas, but she won't mind watching you open your present.'

Michael dealt with his bike, and went to greet Nan, who was curled up on Caroline's sofa, looking smarter than usual in jacket and skirt.

'You're looking posh,' he said. 'Have you reformed now you're a proper priest?'

'*Semper reformanda*, that's me.' She waved a hand. 'One grows, one changes. Actually, I've been bearding the wretched Ridgefield in his den, and I thought I ought to look the part. I'm going to be working hand in glove with him from now on, have you heard?'

'I think Caroline said something.' He sat down.

'It was either St Barnabas or being taken over by the dreadful Deidre. Sorry, I know she's Jenny's auntie, but I've never been able to like her. We decided that at least Ridgefield would want to keep as separate from us as we would from him, so we opted for St Barnabas.'

'I'm surprised he agreed to it,' said Michael.

'You should see the conditions he's laid down. If I so much as mutter "Dearly Beloved Brethren" in their chapel, they'll lynch me. We're supposed to be sharing resources, but he says he hasn't decided whether to ask me to do any lectures for him or not. He'd prefer not to, but he has to try and cooperate. He'll go bust if he doesn't have the Programme bringing him extra income to pay for his asbestos problem.'

'It can't be too easy for him,' Michael said. 'All those things he's campaigned for, and he ends up having to welcome you into the place.'

'I'd feel more sympathetic if he hadn't been so obnoxious to me over the years. We've faced each other enough times at synods, or on the radio, or we've shared conference platforms, and you often form an alliance with someone under those circumstances. But he's always so damned supercilious and patronising. There's rare moments I've heard him speak on other subjects when he seems almost human, and I find myself thinking he might be quite pleasant if only he hadn't got his Y-fronts in such a twist about women priests. But when I have tried to be friendly, he's snubbed me like I'm some form of low-life. I tackled him about it this morning. I said "I know you don't want me here, and I'd prefer not to be here, but since we have got to work together, I'd appreciate it if you could try to be civil".'

'That was brave,' Caroline said. 'What did he say?'

'That he was in an impossible position, because all his allies thought he'd sold out in accepting the Programme at St Barnabas, to say nothing of me. He says he's trying to set up a trust fund to make the college financially secure, so he can kick us out next year. That means persuading donors that St B.'s has kept its integrity, so he can't afford to be too chummy. Nice of him to be frank about it, I suppose. Only don't spread that around - we don't want Deidre casting her predatory eye on us all over again. Anyway, in the meantime, he acknowledges that he and I are going to have to work together. He apologised very sweetly for being uncivil, and as a mark of our new-found respect, he is going to start calling me Nan, and I am to call him Christopher. I hope you're impressed.'

Caroline laughed. 'I can't quite picture Ridgefield being sweet.'

'Jenny thinks he is,' Michael said. 'She met him after a service in the Cathedral, and had a cup of tea with him. She was very impressed.'

'Oh, he can behave perfectly pleasantly when he wants to, he simply doesn't want to when he's with me. Ah, well, I expect I'll survive.' Nan smiled at him. 'How is married life, anyway?'

'Absolutely brilliant,' he said. 'I should have done it years ago. Only then it wouldn't have been with Jenny, would it, so what would have been the point? I'm sorry you were away for our wedding, because it was your advice got us together.'

'I didn't think I said anything much. You must both come round for supper sometime. I've not actually met her properly yet. It was so hectic last term, and what with all the palaver about moving to St Barnabas...'

'Give us a ring sometime. I'd like Jenny to get to know you, because she's been prejudiced against you ever since Becky led me astray. Thinks you brung her up wrong.'

He smiled, as he usually did when he thought about his wife. It was the third time in his life he'd been in love, but the intimacy was much more intense than any he had shared with his other lovers: living with her, sharing every part of his life with her, making love to her again and again, sleeping every night with her in his arms, and waking to find her face on his pillow. He had abandoned himself to her, like a bungee-jumper flinging himself into the air. He would be brought up short some day, but until then, he was in free fall, and revelling in it.

Jenny, by contrast, was climbing down a thin ladder with extreme caution - and a safety harness. She found it difficult to accept the depth of his desire for her, and it would take time for her really to let herself go. In the meantime, he enjoyed working on her, persuading her to unbend after a long day at work, massaging her neck, kissing the soft skin below her ear, loosening her clothes ... He loved her breadth, her solidity, soft flesh a man could grasp and bury himself in ...

'...Something tells me his mind's elsewhere,' Nan was saying. Michael forced himself to concentrate.

'I said, have you thought any more about what you're doing job-wise?' Caroline said. 'You don't want to be living off your wife permanently, do you?'

'Don't be old-fashioned, Caroline,' Nan said. 'You're still doing your voluntary stuff, aren't you, Michael?'

'I am. I've been opening the hall up for kids to drop in in their lunch break, and I've got the youth clubs on Sundays and Thursdays, as well as working with Baz up in the Rows, and doing the music. I'm busy enough.'

'Yes, but if you got a proper job, you might have more chance of being selected for ordination, mightn't he, Nan? It'll soon be two years since you last went, so it's time to think about it.'

'I'm not sure I'm ready for that yet. It's only in the last few months I've felt I've had my faith back, and I need to do some more work on it before I look at ordination again.'

'Why don't you study theology with the Programme?' Nan said.

Michael looked at her with interest, 'I didn't realise you could. I thought you only took ordinands.'

'No, we have a few who are sent direct by their churches. They do almost everything the ordinands do, bar some of the practical stuff. If you could get Peter and St Martin's to sponsor you, we could take you on. Then if you went back for selection, say in your second year, and got through, you'd have time to fit in anything you'd missed.'

'What a good idea,' Caroline said. 'It might be just the thing - answer the questions there were about your academic ability, and how committed you were to things.'

'What's more, we even have a couple of bursaries each year for lay people, so you'd not be sponging off your wife.' Nan winked at him, and he smiled thoughtfully back at her.

That evening, Michael laid the possibilities out before Jenny as they sat in the shade of their patio eating the supper he'd prepared for her return from the surgery.

'It sounds perfect,' Jenny said. 'It'll give you something to do, so you won't have to complain about me working late.'

'It'll mean being away - six weekends a year, and a week in the summer.'

'We'll appreciate each other all the more afterwards. Oh, do apply. Besides, it'll go down well with our relations - I've had Meg and Caroline and my mother saying how glad they are you've got me to take you in hand and make something of you.'

'And I've had my dad and your mum suggesting perhaps I should get a proper job to keep you in the manner to which you are accustomed. You don't think that, do you?'

'I earn quite enough to support us both, and I can't see you being happy in a nine-to-five job. You're brilliant at what you do now. Just because I get paid quite well for doing work I'm good at, while you don't, doesn't make what you do any less worthwhile.'

'Thanks.' He reached out to take her hand. 'That's one of the things I love about you. You're perfectly prepared to be unconventional.'

'Who, me? I'm very conventional.'

'You're not, you know. You like to be that bit different. That's why we married each other.'

Jenny frowned, and returned to the original subject. 'So do you see doing this as a step on the way to ordination?'

'Maybe. I still think it's something for the future, but not yet. What do you think?'

'I don't know. If it's what you want, I'll support you. As long as you don't end up like my dad. You haven't heard his sermons, have you? A triumph of hypocrisy over cynicism.'

'I don't think there's any danger of that. I'm a cheerful soul, it would take a lot to turn me cynical. All I need is for you to let me talk to you, and to cuddle me from time to time, and I'll be a bishop before you know where you are.'

She smiled. 'Well, you don't need to decide now. Get signed up for the Programme, it'll be worth you studying theology whatever happens. You always said you wanted to.'

Alison took a deep breath, and strove to keep her voice level. 'Are you saying you want me to withdraw?'

Steve turned a page of his computer journal. 'You do what you like.'

'You say that, but you're so gloomy about it, I dread what's going to happen.' She watched him, slouched in his chair, with his eyes firmly on the paper. Behind his greying beard, his lips were tense. If she pushed him, he'd become more and more withdrawn, but she had to try. They were supposed to be going on their summer holidays soon; they wouldn't survive if this was still hanging between them.

'You said when I first made enquiries about ordination that you'd support me if it was something I wanted to do. Why can't you be pleased for me now I've been accepted?'

'I don't see why I should be left to babysit for weeks on end.' He raised his head, though with the light from the window reflecting from his glasses, she couldn't see his expression. 'What happens when I'm supposed to work late, or cover weekends? "Sorry the computer's down, but I've got to mind the kids?" It's not on.'

'We talked about all that. It's only six weekends and one week in the summer, and you said you could arrange for one of the others to cover for you. And it's not as if the boys are any trouble these days.'

'You never told me you'd be away.'

'I did! I wouldn't have gone ahead if I hadn't talked it all over with you.'

Steve went back to his paper.

'Steve, please, I need to know. Are you saying that you aren't prepared to look after the kids sometimes while I'm away? Because if so, I'll withdraw from the Programme.'

'You might as well go through with it now you've got this far. I expect

121

I'll manage. As long as you don't expect me to be happy about it.'

She got up and left the room. Sounds from the garden suggested the boys' after supper football game in the garden would shortly be ending in tears. Alison went upstairs, and shut herself in the bathroom, where she sat on the toilet with her head in her hands, and allowed herself a brief cry.

The letter saying that she'd been accepted had arrived that morning, and she had been overjoyed. She had gone through the whole process expecting all the time that the door would be shut in her face, and each time people had held it wide open for her. She couldn't help thinking someone from the Almighty downwards had made a monumental mistake, and she still scarcely dared to believe.

She'd broken the news to the family over tea, and immediately Steve had started grumbling. Just for once, Lord, she cried, just for once, why can't he be nice to me about something, instead of always looking for the worst possible outcome? He might not be a church-goer himself, but he'd been so polite and reasonable when the Diocesan Director of Ordinands had made a home visit, that she dared to imagine him becoming a properly supportive vicar's husband. Now, she was reduced to wondering whether they'd still ordain her after her marriage had broken down. She couldn't go back ten years and unmarry him, she wouldn't be without the boys, but how she longed to feel cherished and understood instead of constantly undermined and frozen out.

She blew her nose on some toilet paper, flushed it away, and stood in front of the mirror repairing her make-up. Steve never noticed how she looked these days, but she tried to keep up appearances. What was it Lisa Gates had told her today? 'Lee Currie's got a crush on you, Miss.' Pathetic, when even the thought that a lumbering sixteen year-old was weaving adolescent fantasies about you, could cheer you up.

As she went out onto the landing, she heard Steve coming upstairs, and stood with her head bowed, waiting for him to pass by.

He stopped. 'Would you like me to fix you up with a desk and a computer upstairs, for your essays? Otherwise we'll all four be fighting over the one downstairs.'

'Oh.' She looked up at him. Behind the wire frames, his eyes were guarded. 'Yes, thank you. Can we afford a new one?'

'I could put one together from bits and pieces we're getting rid of at work.'

Alison followed him into their bedroom to listen with the appearance of attention while he described his alternative strategies for relocating the furniture. She'd rather have left him to get on with it, but this was Steve's way of saying sorry, and trying to show he cared, and she had to appear grateful.

Tonight, as predictably as broken nights followed childbirth, he'd be wanting sex. Kiss kiss rub rub thrust thrust and how was it for you, dear? He'd never ask. She'd never dare tell him the truth. She'd long since given up expecting even the tiniest of seismic quivers to attend their infrequent love-making. She hoped that the adventure of training for ordination might fill some of the hollows in her life, might drown out the dreadful fear that she was thirty-two, and this was as good as it was ever going to get.

Nan had made the mistake of booking her holiday during September. It meant that, while her colleagues disappeared out of the country as soon as the Programme's summer school was over, she found herself helping the Programme's half time secretary with their reluctant move into the new office at St Barnabas. They'd been allocated space on the top floor of the forbidding redbrick mansion that formed the centre of the college's complex of buildings. The series of shabby study bedrooms that occupied the narrow corridor alongside them were no longer used by college students, though they would be filled whenever the Programme was in residence.

Their own small suite of rooms had once been staff accommodation. Ridgefield had deputed a couple of the Barney boys to give the rooms a coat of magnolia paint, and Nan's first action was to fling wide the dormer windows under the eaves to rid the office of the smell.

'Everything satisfactory?' Ridgefield asked, putting his head round the door late one afternoon.

'So far,' Nan told him. 'Can I introduce Lin Wilkinson, our secretary?'

Lin, an elegant woman in her fifties with a taste for jewellery and smart clothes, left the box files she had been arranging, and came forward to shake Ridgefield's hand. After an exchange of pleasantries, he left them to get on.

'I didn't think he'd recognise me,' Lin remarked as she turned back to her files.

'Why, did you know him before?'

'I was in the parish where he did his first curacy. It must be all of twenty-five years ago. He and Bishop Derrick were there together.'

'I hadn't realised they went back that far. You should have told him you knew him.'

Lin made a face. 'I don't know that he'd have appreciated being reminded of it. He had to leave suddenly after he got into a mess with a married woman.'

'Ridgefield? Come off it - everyone knows he can't cope with women. I always assumed he was gay.'

'Not then, he wasn't.'

'So what happened?' Nan came and sat on the desk under the window, intrigued.

'I don't know if it's fair to say ... as long as you don't broadcast it...'

'I won't.'

Lin settled herself on a swivel chair. 'She was a nice girl, daughter of a bank manager. She got married at nineteen, to one of those smooth types who charm you at the time, but looking back, you wonder how you've been taken in. He worked at the bank, and ended up in prison for fraud. Meanwhile, she'd got to know Christopher, who was young, and good-looking, and shy, and had all the ladies of the church crazy about him.'

'Including you?'

Lin raised an eyebrow. 'Maybe a little. Not as bad as this lady. She used to confide in him, and he wasn't experienced enough to see what was happening. The whole thing blew up just after Christmas. The police were wanting to question her husband, and she went round to see Christopher. Normally Derrick would have been in the house as well, but he was away. I couldn't tell you exactly how it happened, but Derrick arrived back earlier than expected the following day to find the two of them in bed. Derrick and Father Teddy - the vicar - sorted it all out as quietly as they could. They asked me to look after her, but no one else got to know. She left the area soon after, and we lost touch. Christopher got shipped off to a church where there wasn't a woman under seventy-five, and presumably he's been a model of propriety ever since. If his books are anything to go by.'

'My God!' Nan said. 'No wonder the poor man's so screwed up about women. He's terrified he'll get seduced again. I can quite see why he can't stand the thought of the priesthood being invaded by voluptuous harpies like me!'

Lin laughed. 'I have wondered about that sometimes, whether that business was what made him so anti women priests.'

'I expect he'd have formed the same views whatever,' Nan said. 'But fancy Ridgefield messing around with married women. It's not at all the clean-cut image he projects. I shall look at him differently from now on.'

Two

Michael was singing to himself as he retraced the route of the bus back along the main road from Thorleigh to St Barnabas, where the Programme was holding its first residential weekend of the term. A passing cyclist peered round to identify the source of the offending noise; unfairly scornful, Michael thought, for he was generally agreed to have a good voice. He walked easily, his arms bare to the warmth of the September sun, and the small rucksack containing a change of clothing, a washbag, a couple of books, and his paper and pens, light on his back.

It had given him absurd pleasure to buy the notepad, hammering it home to him that he was at last getting the chance to study. Whether or not this was the first step on the road to being ordained no longer seemed to matter. He was at his happiest when he could let each day unfold in front of him as it came, and now, with a wife and home, new friends to be made ahead of him, and a sky of unclouded blue overhead, he felt no need to concern himself with a distant future.

On his left, large houses rested in the early evening light, and in the gaps between the traffic, birdsong broke from the trees and shrubs that lined the road. The leaves were beginning to turn colour, but were still thick, so that he almost missed the sign for St Barnabas poking out from its post on the inside edge of the pavement. He turned in through the high iron gates to follow the wide drive that wound through spreading trees to end before the lowering Victorian frontage of the college's main building. As Michael climbed the steps and passed through the heavy double door at the entrance, he was met by a slim, attractive woman with an apprehensive, familiar smile.

'Hello, Michael. You're not doing the Programme too, are you? Because if so, we have to go round the outside. I've just got into trouble for presuming to ask Father Ridgefield's personal secretary - apparently there's a sign.'

Across the hall behind her, he could see a dour, bespectacled woman with curly, brown hair, typing behind a sliding window marked Reception.

Michael made a face, and grinned. 'That's Gloria,' he whispered. 'Not to be trifled with. Nan says they don't have a cross on the building, they keep her in the front office. I know I know you, but I can't remember your name.'

'I'm Alison Thompson - we met at Nan's a year ago.'

He looked at her more closely as they went back down the steps. 'Of course. I remember, you're Lisa Gates' teacher. You're an ordinand? You got through?' She nodded. 'That's brilliant. I am pleased for you.' He held out his hand, and she took it.

'It's wonderful to find someone I know. I'm dead nervous.'

'So am I. Let's stick together.'

'I think it's round here ... ah, yes, there's the sign.' They followed the direction of the arrow on a small piece of yellow card attached to the brickwork. Round the building, past a side door with its terse message that this was the Principal's private accommodation, and any visitors should call first at the college's Reception. Past the sleek, black Audi drawn up beneath a wall plaque marked *Principal*, and on towards one of the modern blocks set amid the college's rolling grounds.

'So you're an ordinand too, are you?' Alison said

'No. No, I'm merely studying theology, for the good of my soul.'

'You'd make a good priest. I wouldn't be here today if it wasn't for you encouraging me.'

He smiled. 'Kind of you to say so. How's Lisa doing?'

'I'm not sure. She was fine up until the end of last term, but this year, she's been looking as if she's got the weight of the world on her shoulders. She's just turned sixteen, and I think she'd rather have left in the summer. Still, I'm hoping she'll pull herself together and do some work. She's got a chance of getting a few GCSEs if she tries. I see a fair bit of her, because she babysits for me.'

'Perhaps I should give her a ring - I haven't spoken to her since March.'

'You're a youth worker, aren't you? You don't ever take assemblies in schools, by any chance? There was a curate at our church who used to come in sometimes, but he's left, and I could do with finding someone to replace him. I imagine you'd be good at that sort of thing.'

'I'd love to,' Michael said. 'I used to go into my mum's school regularly. What would you want?'

By the time they stopped to register and to get their room keys from Nan, they had already formed an alliance.

Michael mixed easily with the rest of his fellow students as the weekend unfolded. Altogether, there were nearly forty of them across the three year groups. Since the Programme didn't take ordinands under thirty, most of them were older than he was; retired, or changing direction after a midlife crisis they took to be divinely inspired.

He watched Nan, endeavouring to look demure in a flowery dress since she was forbidden her collar on site, but unable to prevent a certain acerbity creeping into her manner as she brushed up against the members of the St Barnabas staff currently in residence.

'It's difficult for you, isn't it?' Michael said, taking his coffee cup over to join her after supper on Saturday as she stood with Jackie, a second-year student of statuesque proportions.

'Does it show that much? It's this place, and having to be polite to Ridgefield when he's being obstructive. He's supposed to be making us feel welcome, but he's been as bad as ever this weekend.'

'He was awful yesterday, wasn't he? There was Roly telling us St Barnabas was delighted to have the Programme meeting on its premises, and Christopher comes and talks to us as if we're contaminating the place.'

'He's a psychotic bully, that's what he is,' Jackie opined. 'Mind you, they do say if someone's being unpleasant, all you have to do is to imagine them naked.'

Michael was coming to realise that, though happily married to a man even more statuesque than she was, Jackie invariably talked about men as if she was desperate. 'I thought it was naked except for black socks,' he said.

'Whatever turns you on. I was going to give Ridgefield a mental striptease, but I couldn't decide whether he'd have black underwear to match his black suits, and then I started thinking tight black briefs could be kind of sexy, and I got distracted.'

'I sometimes wonder if all you ever think about is sex and naked men,' Nan told Jackie. 'How ever did you get through your selection conference?'

'By imagining all the selectors naked except for black socks,' Michael and Jackie declared together, laughing.

'Well, God help the Barney boys when they arrive tomorrow,' Nan said. 'Is your wife coming, Michael? It's time I met her properly.'

'Yes, she is. I can't wait to show her round, and introduce her to everybody.'

127

Guests for the buffet and service to mark the beginning of the association between St Barnabas and the Programme began arriving towards the end of Sunday morning. When there was no sign of Jenny, Michael went to hang around the college entrance to wait for her.

It was another beautiful day. Blue skies stretched over the trees, and gliders from a nearby club circled languidly above the birds. Every so often, wives, husbands or children of his fellow students wandered past him. Grim-looking young men with close-cropped heads, uniformly attired in jeans and tee shirts and the occasional earring, ungraciously unloaded boxes from the boots of battered cars. The Barney boys had been required to begin their term a day early in order to coincide with the Programme's weekend, and they were not pleased about it. They responded to Michael's greeting as they passed him, however, taking him for one of their own.

He had watched the woman making her way slowly through the ranks of parked cars for a full minute before he recognised her. The heavy-framed grey glasses, navy skirt and sensible blouse had proved an effective disguise, for he'd been looking for the creamy cotton print he'd helped her choose for the occasion.

'Jenny,' he said, going to greet her. 'What happened to the new dress? And what's with these?' He touched her glasses with his finger as he leaned across to kiss her, and she pulled away in irritation.

'I know, I know, don't go on about it. I broke a contact lens, alright? I've been up all night with one blooming patient after another, I've got a headache, Celly knocked my coffee all over my dress, and I don't want to be here. So unless you want me to turn straight round and go home, don't say another word!'

'I'm really pleased to see you,' he said, smiling at her ingratiatingly. 'I've missed you.'

She snorted dismissively, but she allowed him to take her hand as he led her round the corner of the building to where coffee was being served on the lawn.

'I couldn't even find my proper glasses. I hate these, they hurt my nose, and I so wanted to look nice when I met everyone.'

'I know. It's alright. You look fine.' He had seen her pass through such bristling moods before, and knew that his patient good humour, while it might irritate her at first, would eventually restore her equilibrium. It was just a shame that his new friends' first impression of his wife would be of someone who snapped at him, and behaved as if they were on the verge of divorce. He squeezed her hand.

Nan came up to them as they came away from the table with their coffee cups. 'You must be Jenny,' she said, holding out her hand. 'It's nice to meet you at last, when I've heard so much about you. I remember Michael sitting in my garden saying he couldn't live without you, but he didn't know what to do about it. I hope he's not always that thick, because we need him to stick with the Programme. We need all his talent for getting along with people if we're going to survive our cohabitation with St Barnabas.'

Jenny returned Nan's handshake with a polite smile. 'It can't be easy for them either, having to put up with female ordinands, let alone you.'

'Jenny was up all night saving lives,' Michael said, putting an arm round her shoulder, 'so you'll have to excuse her sounding cross. She's lovely really.'

Jenny pulled away from him, slopping coffee into her saucer. 'Oh, bother!' She looked at Michael with appeal. 'I'm not having a very good day, am I?'

'I'll leave you to it,' Nan said, 'but it would be lovely if you'd both come for a meal some time. I'd like to have the chance to talk to you, Jenny. I'm not really as awful as Michael makes out.' She left them with an amused smile.

'What did she mean about you in her garden? Did you discuss me with her?'

'I had to talk to someone. Nan pointed out how unfair I was being to you, and suggested that either I ought to leave you alone, or go out with you properly. I made the right choice.'

'I'm supposed to feel grateful to her for talking you into it, am I? Well, I don't. I hate the thought of you gossiping about me with her.'

'It wasn't like that. You *are* feeling prickly. Oh, here's someone you'll have to meet.' Michael had caught Alison's eye across the grass and waved her over. Like most of the students, she'd dressed up for the Sunday - Michael, in jeans and tee shirt, was one of the few exceptions - and the gaudy print of her strappy sundress drew attention.

'Jenny, this is Allie,' Michael said. 'She and I have been clinging together for support all weekend - or at least, sitting on the back row giggling. Teachers always make the worst pupils.'

'Don't be rude,' Alison said, laughing with him as she shook Jenny's hand. 'It was you causing the trouble, passing me notes like that. I thought we were going to get slung out in Ridgefield's pep talk yesterday.'

'I'll be on my best behaviour now Jenny's here. We'd better go in.'

They followed the other students and their families into the lecture room on the ground floor of the new block. Michael sat between Jenny and Alison as they listened to the briefing delivered by Roly, Nan and their other staff member, Robert, but it was to Alison he whispered more often than his wife.

Jenny sat back in her chair with her arms folded and allowed her mind to wander over the cracked and peeling paint in the lecture room, and along the metal-framed windows, open to the faint scent of the gardens outside where the huge trees juddered gently in the breeze. She was ashamed of herself for letting Michael down. She would have managed to be cordial if he'd been an unwashed vagrant with bad breath, however sore her head or tired her body. Since he'd done her the favour of marrying her, the least she could do was to look as if she was making an effort.

The version of their story she returned to most often portrayed her as the graceless, plain woman whom he had stooped to rescue out of his infinite kindness. Strong where she was weak, experienced where she was embarrassed, intuitively intelligent where she slogged, spiritual where she was earthbound, socially skilled where she was awkward, his loving her made no sense otherwise. It frightened her when Michael cast away all his defences, and came to her with need naked in his eyes. She wanted to push him away, despising him for his weakness, and hating herself for her lack of graciousness.

They'd had their first real row when he'd come home in the middle of his North Yorkshire summer camp because he was homesick. He'd signed up to lead the camp before their engagement, and when one of the other leaders had had to pull out after getting a new job, Michael had not felt able to withdraw. Four days into it, however, he'd become so miserable that the staff team insisted he go home for a night.

Jenny had been filled with intense, irrational irritation when she had unexpectedly found him waiting for her on her return from the health centre. She had not realised how difficult she would find it to live intimately with someone else. When her job drained her, she needed silence and space to recover; she didn't need Michael, all devotion and anxiety to please, requiring more of her than she could give.

'What on earth are you doing here?' she'd snapped.

'I missed you,' he'd said, getting up and trying to embrace her. 'I kept thinking about you, and I couldn't sleep without you to cuddle.'

'Good grief, Michael! You're behaving like a two year-old pining for his mummy. Grow up!' She pulled away from him, angry at the hurt on his face.

'Surely you missed me, too?'

Jenny sat down. 'Actually, I had a few good nights' sleep for a change without you breathing in my ear. Oh, don't look upset! I'm sorry, I find it difficult to think of you being so dependent on me, that's all.'

'Of course I'm dependent on you,' he said, going over to sit at her feet. 'I wouldn't have married you if I could manage without you. It's called being in love. If you can't accept that, then what the hell did you say "I do" for?'

She ran her fingers through his hair, needing to make amends. 'Because I couldn't manage without you, I suppose.'

'That's better.' He took her hand. 'You know, even the Bible allows a man to be excused from his other duties for a year after he's got married. I'm not that peculiar, wanting to be with you. Come to bed with me, and I promise I'll go back first thing in the morning.'

Well, he was surviving without her now pretty well, exchanging asides with Alison on his right. For the first time since her marriage, jealousy began to thread its tentacles through her. Alison might be married - Jenny had looked for the ring as soon as she saw her laughing with Michael like that - but she wished he hadn't gravitated towards the most attractive woman in the room quite this early on, and regretted having encouraged him to commit himself to the Programme and all it involved. As if she could have stopped him: he had been like a dog on a wild beach in his enthusiasm, and it would have taken more strength than she had to bring him to heel.

Once the briefing was over, the Programme students and their guests queued to fill their plates at the buffet set up on long tables on the grass. The twenty or so St Barnabas students collected around their own group of tables, resolutely isolating themselves from the Programme.

Jenny was casually noticing them when she saw a familiar face. 'Michael,' - she pulled at his arm - 'Michael, that's Tyrone. What's he doing here?'

Michael turned to look. 'I thought he was going to Nottingham.' He followed her as she wandered over. Several pairs of hostile eyes stared at them, and conversation ceased. Tyrone looked pointedly at his plate.

'Hi, Tyrone. I didn't know you were coming here,' Jenny said. 'Did you know Michael was on the Programme?'

Tyrone got up quickly and moved away with them. 'Hi, Jenny. Hi,

Mike. Change of plan. I wanted to be nearer home.'

'I wouldn't have thought Christopher Ridgefield and the Barney boys were your scene,' Michael said. 'What do they think of having a woman priest's son around the place?'

Tyrone's eyes darted round warily. 'They don't know. I've got my dad's surname, so no one suspects. Look, for God's sake, Michael, don't tell them. It's complicated enough talking to you - none of the lads wants anything to do with your lot, and I don't want to be ostracised.'

'Bollocks! Surely we can talk to each other, even if we don't agree on some things?'

'OK, it's bollocks, but that's the way things are. Be a mate, and don't let on we're related? Say you know me from somewhere, if you have to - say Jenny knows me, or something, but leave the cousin bit out.' He looked anxiously between them. 'Please.'

'If you say so. You must come round for supper sometime, mustn't he, Jen? I'll see you around, anyway.'

Tyrone scuttled back to the Barney boys, to explain away his apparent treachery.

'It's odd, him being here,' Jenny said as they walked on.

'Perhaps he's got a girlfriend nearby.'

'Who, Tyrone? He's even more priggish than I was.'

'He might be learning. You have.'

She didn't look at him, afraid of finding his eyes desiring her. She wasn't yet ready to relax her guard.

'Well, look who that is!' Michael said suddenly. 'It's one reunion after another.'

Jenny followed his gaze. Seated at one of the old wooden tables at the edge of the grass, was Becky Patten, squashed up with Nan, Caroline and Peter. Peter had been invited to this inaugural weekend as a member of the Programme's governing body, and Becky, presumably, had been in the area and come for the free lunch.

Nan left as they arrived, stopping only to say a few words before she rushed off, muttering that she had to prepare for the afternoon's service. Becky got up to talk to Michael, and asked, with an intimate smile, how he was enjoying married life.

The headache Jenny had been carrying all day throbbed in her skull; her glasses heavy on the bridge of her nose intensified the ache. She couldn't face plunging herself into sociability, even with Caroline and Peter.

'Would you excuse me a minute?' she said. 'I'm going to get my jacket from the car - it's turning cool.' She put her half-empty plate down on the table, and left before Michael could offer to go for her. Though it had begun to cloud over, it was still not that cold, but the walk to the car would give her a chance to pull herself together.

The front doors of the college were still wedged open as she passed, and through them, Jenny could see the dim, enticing interior of the hall. There was no one about, and she thought that if only she could sit for five minutes, and take some more pills for her head, she might be more of a credit to Michael for the rest of the afternoon. She stepped inside. Gloomy portraits of past Principals sneered down at her. Ahead of her, the front office at the foot of the wide staircase was deserted. On her left, the dining hall was already laid out for the evening meal, and clattering could be heard from the kitchens behind it. To her right, a panelled wooden door had the legend '**Fr C. F. Ridgefield, Principal**' inscribed in gold paint. She took a few purposeless steps towards it.

'Can I help?' came a clipped voice from behind her. She turned to see a dark-suited clergyman outlined against the open doors.

'I was wondering if there was somewhere quiet I could sit. I've got a terrible headache, and I didn't go to bed at all last night. I'm a GP,' she added, in case he thought her capable of dancing till dawn. As he stepped further into the hall, she recognised him as the Principal. 'I'm Michael Turner's wife. He's just started on the Programme.'

'You can sit in my study if you like. It'll be quiet.' His voice had lightened, as if reassured by the knowledge that she was not an ordinand herself. He veered to the right of the hall and unlocked the door.

'If you're sure I'm not intruding.'

'Not at all. I get headaches myself. I'm Father Christopher Ridgefield, by the way.'

'I know. I met you a year or so ago at the Cathedral. You won't remember me, but you talked to me over coffee.'

He led her into a large, gloomy room, its walls panelled with dark wood under a high, ornate ceiling. The sun glanced shortsightedly through the two tall, narrow bay windows behind a desk covered with books and papers, unable to penetrate the shadows that shrouded the rest of the room. Around the walls were glass-fronted bookcases. A worn brown leather sofa and two massive armchairs were arranged around the elderly, stained, gas fire that squatted in what must once have been an imposing fireplace.

Ridgefield turned to look at Jenny more closely. 'You didn't have glasses then. I do remember you. Jenny, isn't it? How nice to see you again. Did you solve your problem?'

'I married him,' she said, smiling genuinely for the first time since her arrival. 'I confessed I'd fallen in love with him, and eventually he decided he could tolerate the idea.'

'Good. Or at least I assume it's good. You say he's on the Programme?'

'He's studying theology. He's not an ordinand.'

He eyed her reflectively. 'It's not very relaxing in here, come into my sitting room,' he said, going to another door at the end of his study which led into the wing of the original mansion given over to the Principal's private residence.

She followed him through into a small hall. Ahead of them, a broad flight of stairs ascended towards a high window decorated with coloured glass that shone warm reds and greens onto the pale walls. To the right of the stairs was the front door, and another door, half-open, that led into the living room. The brightness and warm tranquility came as a stark contrast with the oppressiveness of his study. Large windows allowed much more natural light to infiltrate, and the furniture was modern. A light ash sideboard, with a matching dining table and chairs tucked away at the end of the room, a small three-piece suite in pale leather, and a television, video, and hi-fi. A single, abstract painting hung above the sideboard.

Ridgefield settled her on the sofa and disappeared to fetch her a glass of water for her pills. The tense aura that had surrounded him in the hall had dissipated as he set the glass down on the table beside her.

'You stay here, and I'll let your husband know where you are. I'll come and get you at quarter past two for the service. You've got nearly an hour.'

'You're very kind.'

'No trouble.'

Jenny swallowed some tablets, removed her sandals and glasses, lay back on the sofa, and closed her eyes. What would Aunt Deidre think, to see her sprawled so decadently in Christopher Ridgefield's private quarters? She wondered how many other people ever came into this room. Not many, she'd guess. He was like her, a shy person, who needed retreat from the world, and presumably the older you got, the more you reverted to type. What would she have been heading for in the absence of Michael's patient persistence? A long-serving lady doctor, dependable and unloved, having a sluice room in the bowels of Greathampton General named for her to

134

mark her retirement. She'd make it up to him once she'd had a rest.

She woke at the sound of her name.

'Mrs Turner? Jenny?' When her eyes opened, she found Ridgefield's face close to hers, gazing on her with an ache that was not for her, but for some loss and loneliness of his own.

He blinked, and drew back. 'I was staring, forgive me. I'm going peculiar in my old age.' He put the cup of tea he was holding down on the table. 'How are you feeling?'

'Better, thank you.' Jenny put her glasses back on, and picked up her cup. 'Did you find Michael?'

'I did. I hadn't realised your husband was one of the Hart-Patten camp. I'm surprised you dare to cross my threshold.'

'Michael doesn't belong to camps. I give him a couple of weeks before he's propping up the bar with your students, and they all think he's one of them.' She took another sip of tea. 'Anyway, I judge people for myself, and you've always been very kind to me.'

'Don't sound surprised. Rumours of my nastiness are greatly exaggerated.'

'So I've gathered,' she said.

Her rest had restored Jenny. She listened intelligently to Ridgefield outlining the history of St Barnabas as he showed her over to the chapel that extended out at the back of the main building.

Michael was waiting outside, and she went up to him and slipped her hand into his. 'I'm sorry I was being horrible earlier.'

'As long as you're feeling better now. I was quite jealous when I heard Christopher had taken you off to bed.'

'It was only a sofa.'

'Plenty can happen on sofas,' Michael said. 'I shall have to watch you.'

They went into the chapel, and found a space in one of the pews.

'Tacky, isn't it?' Michael whispered, seeing Jenny glancing round at the gold paint and numerous ikons decorating the high walls. 'Allie says it's like a child's painting. God says "thank you very much, it's lovely", but He can't wait for us to grow up and do better.'

'I wouldn't have thought it was Tyrone's scene,' she whispered back. She could see her cousin, squashed into a pew at the back with his fellow students, sedulously ignoring her

Michael lowered himself to his knees. Jenny closed her eyes briefly, but she rarely found it easy to pray in strange surroundings. Before long, she had opened her eyes and was watching Michael with his head on his arms, reminded of the first time she'd seen him. Even when he said he'd lost his faith, he was much more spiritual than she'd ever be. She sat back, studying the way his hair was cut into the nape of his neck, and the set of his shoulders under his tee shirt, and her stomach twisted with desire. In a couple of hours, they'd be in bed together, no doubt; perhaps this time she'd be able to let herself go, and be the kind of lover he deserved. She folded her arms, and tried to think of something else.

From the other side of the aisle, Alison was also observing Michael out of the corner of her eye, noting his abandonment to prayer, while Jenny sat morosely next to him. She had been taken aback to find his wife so plain and ill-tempered, and not at all what she'd expected for such an attractive, good-humoured and kindly man. Perhaps, as with her and Steve, things had been different when they'd married. Before time and change had drained their relationship of everything that made it meaningful. Poor Michael, no wonder he'd valued her friendship so much over the weekend. They'd have to stick together, give each other the support they lacked from their spouses. That was probably why they'd been sent on the Programme at the same time.

A rustling at the back of the chapel indicated that the Bishop's procession was assembled and ready to begin the service.

Alison was too busy looking round at them to see the gentle hand Jenny laid on Michael's shoulder, and the quick hug he gave her as he stood up. Even if she had, she would have found a way of misinterpreting it, for she was already clinging to him as to a lifeline, without knowing how costly her struggles for survival would be for them all.

Three

'Oh, Andy, I've been waiting for this so long.' Her mother had gone at last, taking Darren with her, and Kelly was out with friends. Lisa moved over to where Andy sat on the sofa watching the television, and put her arms round his neck. 'I've missed you ...' She tried to kiss him, but he turned his face away, and she caught only the stubble of his cheek.

'Bloody hell, Lise, cut it out,' he said, pushing her away from him roughly. Though small, he was wiry and strong, a seaman tanned by wind and sun, with close-cropped gold hair, tattoos and an earring. Lisa had loved him ever since he'd come into her mother's life three years before. Her toy boy, Tracey had called him, though he was twenty-four, and only four years her junior. The house came alive during his infrequent appearances, as he showered them all with presents, and treated them to trips out: the cinema, McDonald's, Alton Towers, the Aquapark; Tracey would lose the sharp frowns on her face and temporarily stop shouting at them.

Lisa's devotion had turned to infatuation soon after Darren was born, nine months after the weekend her mum first brought Andy home. Though she had barely seen him since she'd left home, Lisa had persuaded herself that he was her only reason for living.

'But you love me.' Lisa said. 'You said we could be together soon as I was sixteen, and I am. Two weeks ago.' She gazed at him, her eyes wide, knowing it gave her appeal. In the last year, her heaviness had evolved into curves, and with her long hair currently dyed a silvery blonde, she had become used to attracting attention.

Andy merely looked uncomfortable, alarm hovering in his pale-blue eyes.

'Look, Lise, you gotta cut all that crap out. What you an' me did was a mistake, and I'm not interested, right? I only said that stuff to put you off. I never thought you'd still be on at me two bloody years later. You're a great kid, Lise, but you are still a kid.'

'I'm not, I'm not. I'm a woman. I'd do whatever you like, I know how now, Andy, please...' Tears began to run down Lisa's face, smearing her make-up, and ruining the appearance of sophistication she had been trying to cultivate ever since she dressed up to come to visit Tracey, knowing Andy would be there.

'Don't cry,' he said impatiently, punching her shoulder gently. 'I got carried away with yer, tha's all. I should never've done it, an' it's not happenin' again. I'm thinkin' of leavin' the navy, and settlin' down with your mum and Darren and Kelly. I'll be yer bloody step-dad. I could end up in the bloody clink if I touch yer.'

Lisa blew her nose and wiped the skin under her eyes. 'You could end up there anyhow if I was to tell. You knocked me up.'

'What? What're you talking about?'

'When you an' me did it, I got pregnant, didn't I? Then I lost it, and that's why me mum chucked me out. Only she never knew it was you, she thought it was one of the lads.'

'Gawd! I never knew. Tracey said you was getting out of control, she never said ... Christ, I'm sorry, Lise.' He stared at her, stricken.

Lisa's resentment of Darren had started it. He was a sickly baby who cried all the time, so that she could do nothing with him, and Tracey had no time left for her daughters. Lisa started staying out late, for all the notice her mother took of it, messing around with her mates round the back of St Martin's, talking about sex and investigating each other's peculiarly different bodies. Andy stayed for a week that November, just as aggrieved as Lisa at one year-old Darren's whingeing and Tracey's constant attendance on him. Lisa saw her chance of hitting back. Finding him in the house alone one day after school watching an adult movie on the video, she lay down next to him on the sofa, and told him about her experiments in the church grounds, dramatising them to make her seem more experienced than she was. Then she undid his shirt, and said she wanted to know what it was like with a real man. Andy, angry and frustrated with Tracey, aroused by the film and Lisa's stories, and with an afternoon's drink inside him, hadn't taken much persuading.

Oh, but it had hurt. First his hand up her skirt, rubbing her, calloused, bony fingers working around inside her, electrifying, dangerous, uncomfortable. Then he'd put her hand on his cock, swollen and hard, fearsome and adult, and nothing like her pals with their adolescent willies prodding at her in the fumbling dark. He parted her legs and she cried out when he pushed himself inside her, a searing penetration that impaled her beneath him. When he withdrew, there was blood on him, and he'd wiped it off with horror.

'Bloody Christ, tha's your first time! You said you'd done it before. Fuckin' hell! Look, Lise, I'm sorry.'

'I have done it, but it wasn't like that,' she said, biting back her desire to cry. 'Oh, but I don't mind. I love you.'

'Don't you dare tell your mum. She'd whip me balls off. Christ! How old are yer? You're not even sixteen, are yer? You tell a soul, and I'm banged up for months.'

'Course I won't tell. You do love me, don't you?'

'Course I do. Only you're too young. Give it a couple of years.'

He'd gone back to sea a few days later, without coming near her again. The gory discovery of her pregnancy had come as a severe shock, for if she'd thought about it at all, she'd assumed that her already irregular periods had stopped because he'd damaged her in some way. But she'd kept her word and said nothing about Andy's role. After all, it could have been one of the lads, just about. Instead, she'd woven two years of fantasies around him, how she'd persuade him to leave Tracey and set up home with her, and they'd have a real, proper baby, rather than the underdeveloped glob that had streamed from her in pieces, and still haunted her dreams.

'Oh Christ,' Andy said again. 'Here, you i'nt said nothing to no one, have yer?'

'Course not. I wouldn't want to get you into trouble.'

'Well you'd bloody well better keep it that way.'

They heard Tracey's voice outside, and the kitchen door opened. Lisa got up, and Darren pushed past her as she went through to put the kettle on.

'Whatcha, old man,' she heard Andy say to him. 'You're a terror, you are.'

'You sit down, I'll make you a cuppa before I go, Mum,' she said, keeping her face turned away until she could get out her mirror to repair the damage to her face. She'd appear normal, show Andy she couldn't care less. What did she need him for anyway? He was a piece of shit, and she could have anyone she wanted.

Michael had last spoken to Lisa when she came to the party he'd thrown at the youth club the week before his wedding. As he watched her approaching the school gate one lunchtime some weeks after the start of the Programme's term, her physical appearance had not changed much, apart from a lighter shade of hair. Her expression had altered dramatically, however. In place of her friendly, open gaze, a sullen, sulky expression had been lowered over her features, and she looked at him guardedly.

Michael had cycled to Nottling that morning - a manageable twelve mile ride, despite the unaccountable undulations of a road that had always seemed flat by public transport. He was not, however, looking forward to the ride back.

Alison had quickly taken him up on his offer to help with assemblies, and it looked like becoming a regular thing. He'd eventually made contact with Lisa, and offered to buy her lunch, and here she was, looking as if the whole idea bored her rigid.

'Do you want to get a burger and walk up to the green?'

Lisa shrugged. 'If you want.' She got a cigarette out of her bag, and lit up.

'Workin' in yer lunch hour, are yer Lisa?' called a boy as they crossed the road outside the school.

'Piss off!'

I've been here before, Michael thought. He looked at her profile, her painful cultivation of nonchalance that shouldn't fool anyone.

'You can shag me if you want. Me gran's never in at lunchtimes.'

'How much are you charging?'

She looked at him, and blew smoke in his direction. 'You're all the same, in't you? Get a chance to get yer leg over, an' you couldn't care less about anyone else. What if I tell Jenny?'

'I've no desire to shag anyone except Jenny, though by the time I've cycled home, I shall probably be incapable of getting my leg over anything higher than a centimetre. No, I wondered what value you were putting on yourself.'

'Naah, I'm not on the game, I just in't that fussy any more.'

'Why's that?'

He stopped at the mobile van parked in a side street near the school, and bought them each a burger, a can of Coke, and a bag of chips to share. They carried on walking.

'You were enjoying life when I last saw you. What's gone wrong?'

Lisa chewed her burger thoughtfully, and he waited for her reply. 'Promise you won't tell?'

'Not unless you give me permission - unless you've murdered your gran or something.'

'Yeah, I've buried 'er six feet under,' Lisa said, with a flashed smile that was more like her old self. 'I'll tell yer when we get up to the green, OK?'

Michael phoned Alison that evening.

'You got back alright, did you?' she asked.

'I did, but it's given me a whole new insight into the phrase "groin strain".'

'You want to rub in some .....'

'Not where I'm hurting, I don't. I think I'll stick to consulting Jenny on that sort of thing, if you don't mind. Anyway, I rang to tell you about Lisa. She's given me permission to have a word with you, because I thought it might be helpful if someone at school knew the situation. It isn't to go any further.' Michael explained only that Lisa had been in love with her mother's boyfriend, and that she'd hoped to win him from her once she'd turned sixteen. 'He let her down somewhat abruptly,' he finished. 'Obviously she's feeling rejected, and she's upset, and angry, and jealous, and all the rest of it. I think I've persuaded her that she's not going to solve anything by sleeping with every male under thirty-five in Nottling - luckily she's only been at it a few weeks, so she's not gone too far. I think it's helped her being able to tell someone.'

'Thanks for telling me,' Alison said. 'I'll have a word with her, let her know I'm on her side. She's lucky to have you around. Not everyone would take that much trouble. And that assembly you did this morning was fantastic as well. You're a saint.'

'Hardly that. I'm a waster who has nothing better to do. Speaking of which, that sounds like Jenny's car, and I'm supposed to have her slippers warmed and her supper on the table, so I'd better go.'

He rang off, and hobbled through to the kitchen. He had not passed on Lisa's confession that it was Andy who had got her pregnant two years before.

'It was my fault. I threw myself at him,' she'd said.

'You were fourteen. He had no right to do it, regardless of what you did.' A thought had struck him. 'What about Kelly, if he's living with your mum now?'

'Oh, he'd never touch 'er. He's like her dad, same as 'e's Darren's dad. He never meant to have it off with me, an' he never touched me again. S'not like he's a pervert.'

'I was wondering if I ought to have a word with social services,' Michael had said. He'd done a day on child protection in Croydon a couple

141

of years before, and was trying to remember what he'd been told.

'You bloody well better not. Tracey'd kill me if she knew. Anyhow, I'd deny it, wouldn't I? Then they couldn't do nothing. Tha's what I said before, that I done it with some lads, an' I weren't saying which ones.' She tugged his arm. 'Look, Kelly'd tell me if he laid a finger on her, and he in't going to. He was drunk, an' I chucked meself at him.'

Michael thought about the dilemma Lisa had placed in his lap as he cycled home, and reached what he thought was the responsible conclusion, to respect Lisa's judgement, and to honour his promise to her. He said nothing, even to Jenny.

'You don't look too comfortable, Mike, my pet,' said Jackie, as they sat in the St Barnabas bar after their lectures on the following Wednesday. Michael had started the habit of Programme students staying behind at St Barnabas for a drink after lectures. He'd had half an hour to wait before his bus back on the first evening, and he'd wandered into the bar to kill time. There'd been a few dubious looks from the Barney boys at first, but as Jenny had predicted, it rarely took Michael long to be accepted. By the third week, Alison had offered to travel to Thorleigh via Greathampton, and give him a lift, so he persuaded her to stay for a drink with him too, and their numbers were growing.

'He's got a boil on his bum,' Alison said.

'And how do you know that?' Jackie queried. 'We all know he's the most beautiful creature to hit the Programme since ... well, since I arrived, but,' she continued loudly as the group at the table around her laughed, 'that's no excuse for rummaging in his boxer shorts...'

'I told her in confidence, to explain why cycling was painful,' Michael interrupted, 'and I wish I hadn't. A man should keep his boils to himself.'

'Is that why you two were giggling on the back row when we got onto the subject of plagues of boils erupting among the Egyptians?' asked Ijaz, another first year.

'Partly,' said Alison, giggling. 'The final straw was when the lecturer said that circumcision meant the Israelite men stuck out like a sore thumb.'

'You're a bad influence on her, Michael,' Jackie said.

'It's the other way round. Hello, Nan,' he added, seeing her at the entrance to the bar. 'Come and join us. Drinks are on Jackie.' He leaned back and pulled a chair into the circle.

Nan hesitated, glancing uneasily around her.

'Good God, Rick, was that you?' came a voice from a group of St

Barnabas students slumped in easy chairs a short distance from them. 'There's a distinctly disgusting smell in here all of a sudden.'

'Not me, mate,' Rick replied loudly. 'Coming from over there, I thought.'

Michael turned round to look at the trio boisterously wafting their malevolence towards Nan. Tyrone sat between Rick, a blond youth with the build of a prop forward, and Marcus, shaven-headed, staring over his pint with belligerent eyes. Tyrone met Michael's eyes, and smirked.

Michael opened his mouth to challenge them, but Nan touched his arm. 'It's not worth it,' she murmured, sitting down next to him. 'It's what they want.'

'I didn't realise it was as bad as that. I know they've been difficult in your lectures, but I didn't realise they were that offensive.'

Nan leant forward over the table, keeping her voice down. 'It's not all of them. That group's the worst. Do you know, Tyrone Nixon had the gall to swagger up to me after my session a couple of days ago to ask whether I'd ever thought of going on a course to improve my presentation skills, because he'd heard Deidre Rutt from the Diocesan Department of Training and Education was putting on a very good one next month. I nearly strangled him.'

Michael laughed. 'That sounds like he was deliberately winding you up.'

'I realised that - after I'd harangued him for several minutes. Then he had the effrontery to complain to Ridgefield that I was being disrespectful because I'd sworn at him. Fortunately Christopher took my side. You know Gerald, their senior student? Apparently he'd already been to report how uncooperative the Barney boys were being, so Christopher knew it wasn't all my fault. Not that you lot have been much better,' she added, looking round at them. 'Christopher said when he lectures for the Programme, you all sit there looking blank while he tries to get a flicker of recognition from you.'

'I don't like him, and I don't see why I should take what he says,' said Jackie.

'Except that he's a renowned specialist in church history, and you're lucky to be getting him.'

'I never thought I'd hear you praising Ridgefield,' Jackie said.

'I'm merely trying to be fair. He's been fair to me lately.'

'He does know his stuff,' Alison put in. Smoke from the guilty cigarette she had just lighted meandered upwards to the high ceiling, to add its infinitesimal particles to the yellow sheen that clung to what had once, years before, been white paint. Michael sat back in his chair, a little gingerly, listening to them dissect Ridgefield. He waited until Alison had stubbed her cigarette out, and stood up cautiously.

'Could we go, Allie? Jenny will be asleep before I get back, otherwise, and I don't think I've seen her to speak to since Sunday.'

'Not that she likes me to speak to her much on Wednesday evenings,' he added, as they made their way to the car park. 'She says there's nothing worse than being expected to get excited at second-hand, and the day she experiences a flicker of interest about whether or not Paul wrote Ephesians will be the day she finally knows her mind has cracked.'

'That sounds like enthusiasm compared to Steve,' Alison said. 'I told him all about Roly's lecture, and then quarter of an hour later, I mention Roly again, and he says "Who's he? One of your pupils?" I give up. That's why it's wonderful travelling with you, so I can have an intelligent discussion about everything.'

'I wish Jenny was more interested. I used to talk to her for hours when I first knew her, and I hate it when she looks bored and tells me to go away.'

'Had you known her long before you married?' Alison asked. They were out on the main road now, and the darkness encouraged confidences.

'I was her lodger for a year. I'd come to Greathampton after my engagement to a girl back home had broken up, so I needed someone to take an interest in me. I don't suppose I'd ever have gone out with Jen if I hadn't lived with her, because she's not easy to get to know.' He leaned forward to adjust the ventilation. 'You ought to meet her - I know she was being grim at the introductory weekend, but I think you'd get on. Hey, I know, why don't we have a get-together? I'd like to meet Steve, and I'm sure Pam and Jackie and Ijaz, maybe one or two of the others, would come, with partners. We're central, so you could come to us, everyone brings some food, so I don't have to do all the cooking.'

'Would Jenny mind?'

'I'll talk her into it.'

Jenny readily agreed to host the party, and they set a date two weeks ahead. Michael was shaking crisps into dishes spread across the kitchen worktop when she came in from work, regarding him with horror.

'But I thought they were coming on Friday.'

'That's right. Today is Friday. I was beginning to wonder if you were going to show up, given how uninterested you are in what I do on the Programme.'

'It's not that, you know it isn't. I want to meet them, it's just that I've been thinking it was Thursday all day. It's because I swapped my family planning clinic with someone. I am sorry, I meant to be here to give you a hand. What can I do? I need to change, and they'll be here any moment.'

Her anxiety dispelled his momentary irritation, and he ruffled her hair. 'Never mind. Go and have a bath, and I'll bring you a drink up. I've nearly finished everything.'

Jenny was lying almost submerged beneath a flotilla of fragrant bubbles by the time he arrived in the bathroom with her drink, with only her head and the tips of her breasts breaking the surface.

'Have you noticed,' she said, her eyes on the water, 'when the littlest plops of bubbles get a certain distance from the large ones, they suddenly rush headlong to join them? It must be gravity or something. You see them circling each other, and you want to warn them not to get too close, or they'll cease to exist.'

'What have you got in there?' he asked, as he put the glass of chilled white wine down on the wooden ledge at the end of the bath. 'A new line in existentialist toiletries from the Body Shop?'

'That's right. This one's called "Angst".' She looked up at him with a tired attempt at a smile. 'You're looking very smart, is that new?'

Michael smoothed the patterned waistcoat he'd put on over his white shirt and usual jeans, and squatted beside the bath, trailing his fingers through the bubbles and over her skin. 'Do you like it? Three pounds from the Oxfam shop. Not bad.'

'What should I wear?'

'You look pretty good like that,' he said, leaning over the bath and kissing her.

Jenny turned her head away. 'Haven't you got things to be doing downstairs?'

'Probably, but I haven't seen you all day.' He picked up her hand, and planted a series of kisses from her palm to the crook of her elbow.

She pulled it back. 'Oh, Michael ... you're getting wet. Stop it.'

'Am I not allowed to be in love with you?'

'No, not if it makes you stupid.'

'Why do you say things like that? Have I done something wrong?'

Any reply she might have made was pre-empted by the ringing of the doorbell. Michael sighed as he left her to her own company, and went downstairs.

By the time Jenny came down twenty minutes later, most of their guests had arrived. Steve and Jackie's husband Alan were on the sofa talking computers, Ijaz and his wife were eating with Jackie in the dining room, and Michael was exchanging holiday stories with Alison and Pam. He was facing the hall, and saw Jenny appear at the foot of the stairs, and pause, holding the newel post, before plunging herself into the party. She'd put on the cream dress which had failed to make it to St Barnabas three months before, and her cheeks were pink from her bath. He smiled reassuringly at her, knowing how hard she found it to socialise at the end of a day that had drained her of energy, humour and concentration. He beckoned her over, while he carried on embellishing the anecdote he was constructing out of their Italian holiday. Allie, animated by alcohol and company, was an ideal audience, and looking particularly gorgeous tonight, he thought. Not much up top, but she was showing it off well with that clingy top she was wearing with her skirt. He enjoyed flirting with her, secure in the knowledge that they were both safely married.

'Bit of a disaster all round, really,' he concluded, laughing. The organisational problems that had dogged their tour of Italy hadn't affected their enjoyment of the sites or each other, but they made a good story.

'I'd love to go to Italy, especially Rome, but it's too expensive,' Alison said.

'Well, it was our honeymoon, so we wanted to splash out,' Michael said, taking Jenny's arm to draw her into the group.

'I thought you said you went this year.'

'That's right. We got married in March.'

'Right.' Alison looked at him oddly. 'I'd somehow assumed you'd been married for ages.'

'That's my careworn expression,' Michael laughed. 'I've aged years.'

'I'm going to get a drink,' Jenny said, leaving abruptly and heading for the kitchen.

'That wasn't very tactful, was it?' Alison said. 'You say your honeymoon was a disaster, and then that marriage has worn you down. What is your poor bride supposed to think about that?'

He grimaced. 'You think I ought to apologise, do you?'

'Definitely.' She patted his arm, and Michael went through to the empty kitchen where Jenny was standing looking at the range of bottles on the worktop.

He came up behind her in the constricted space and put his arms

146

round her. 'The honeymoon part wasn't a disaster, as you know very well,' he murmured into her ear. 'And marrying you is the best thing I've ever done, as you also know. Except that you snap at me when I say so.'

'I'm a disaster myself, aren't I?' Jenny said, turning round and resting her head on his shoulder. 'It scares me when you seem to love me too much, and I hit out at you, then the next minute I'm terrified of losing you to all these dynamic beautiful women like Alison. I can't seem to handle it - you, marriage, everything.'

'Allie's tits are nothing like as sexy as yours,' he whispered in her ear, squeezing her breast surreptitiously. 'And anyway, she smokes. I could never lust after a woman who smoked.' He looked around, and finding no one near, proceeded to kiss her passionately.

'Now, now, Michael, kissing wives is definitely not allowed.' Michael turned with a grin to find Jackie in the doorway, large and flamboyant in a red blouse and white leggings that undulated over her curves. 'If what you're after is a decent snog,' she said, 'you only have to ask. I'm always available.'

'So I hear.'

Jackie laughed. 'Shame I don't get more takers, but I suppose my husband might have something to say. Did I hear you say Ty Nixon was coming tonight?'

'He told Michael he would. Michael asked a few of them from St Barnabas, but he's the only one who showed any interest,' Jenny said. 'I don't know where he's got to.'

'Slinking down the road with a blanket over his head, in case anyone sees him associating with us, I dare say.' Jackie reached across to fill her wine glass. 'Although I have to say he and I have been forming a deep and beautiful friendship ever since I saved his life the other week. He'd got that flu bug that's going around, and he'd passed out in the library, so I rescued him. Heaved him over my shoulder and took him to his bed. He must have thought he'd died and gone to heaven. Any time you want me to show you how it's done, Michael darling, I'd be happy to oblige.' Jackie blew him a kiss.

Michael could feel Jenny tensing under his arm. He shook his head very slightly at Jackie.

'No, only joking,' she said. 'I like a man I can get hold of, not a skinny little shrimp like Mike. I'll leave you two to get on with it.'

'And I don't fancy Jackie, either,' he whispered. 'She's a lovely person, but she should never wear Lycra. Tree-trunks dressed as saplings, I call it. Not at all erotic, not at all like you.' He kissed her again

147

'We ought to join the others,' she said.

Tyrone arrived half an hour later. He had at first intended to turn down the invitation, since he had spent much of the term delighting in fostering trouble between St Barnabas and the Programme, and did not wish to be seen to be friendly himself. His mother had been incensed by the way Ridgefield had filched the Programme from under her nose, simply, she alleged, in order to spite her. She had therefore persuaded her son to transfer to St Barnabas - easily done, given how desperate the college was for students - and to see what he could do. After all, if the Programme were to find it impossible to work with the college, there was a chance that it would have to return to the diocesan fold. Trouble at St Barnabas would certainly damage Ridgefield's reputation; it might even stop the path to episcopacy that everyone was predicting for him. The Barney boys had not needed much encouragement to be awkward, and Tyrone had been pleased to see the chasm opening up between the two sides. Then had come his brush with Jackie, when he had discovered her deep resentment at the Programme's being forced to come to St Barnabas, and at having to be taught by someone as conservative and misogynistic as Ridgefield.

'If we carry on the way we have been doing, I can't see the arrangement lasting,' he'd told her, waylaying her in the car park as she arrived for lectures, and steering the conversation towards his goal. 'I thought Nan was going to walk out after that argument in the library the other week. A few more incidents like that, and the whole thing will collapse. And,' he'd lowered his voice, though the cars around them were empty, 'we could make it happen. You could make it happen. Annoy Ridgefield, provoke a few confrontations ... it's easy.'

Jackie had laughed enthusiastically at the prospect, and he'd slipped back into college congratulating himself.

Now here he was approaching Michael and Jenny's house ready to cement his alliance with her. The sparsely set lampposts shed a cold white light as he made his way along the deserted street. On the main road, traffic continued to pass through the town, and a few pedestrians ventured out into a night already touched by frost. Here, the residents sheltered behind their double-glazing, numbing themselves with television. The figure who suddenly emerged from the shadows of the bare lilac tree by Jenny's front gate startled him.

'You goin' in there? To Michael's?'

Ty peered at the girl who had spoken, her face indistinct behind the fall of light hair across her cheeks.

'Yes. Why?'

'Is it a party, or something? Cos I was goin' to call, but I won't if there's people there.'

'There'll be quite a few, yes.' She sounded young. Probably some kid from the youth club, pestering Michael. 'He won't want to be disturbed. You'd best be off home.' He turned in at the drive, and didn't look back.

'You didn't see a girl out there, did you?' Michael asked, after he'd taken Tyrone's jacket and thrown it with the others in the spare bedroom.

'There was a girl spoke to me. I told her you were entertaining, and she ought to go off home. Do you have a lot of bother with kids hanging round here?'

'You sent her away? Damn.' Michael opened the front door, and looked around, but the girl had gone. 'I bet that was Lisa. She rang earlier. She was upset because her mum's getting married tomorrow, so I told her to drop in here. Thanks a bunch, Ty.'

'I was only trying to help.'

'Yeah, well, you weren't to know,' Michael said. 'And hopefully she'll be back. Come and have a drink. I'm glad you're here. I wish more of your lot had come.'

Ty gave him a withering look, but, being Michael, he didn't seem to notice.

149

Four

Frost had given way to blustery rain and chilling winds when the Programme students met at St Barnabas for their first weekend of the new year. Their journeys had been unpleasant, and by the time they had sat through their Friday night lecture, they were more than ready to relax in the bar. As soon as Michael put the tray of drinks down on the table in front of his friends, Jackie stretched across and grabbed her pint, gulping down several rapid swallows.

'I needed that. It was hard work getting my brain in gear again after all that excess at Christmas.'

'No fags, Allie?' he said, handing her a glass of wine.

'I've given up', she said. 'As from the twenty-second of December. And that took a real effort, I can tell you, what with all the relatives I had to endure over Christmas, and the boys being hyper for the entire time.'

'Well done!'

'Michael offered me an incentive, you see,' Alison said, turning to Jackie. 'He promised he'd kiss me if I gave up smoking, and it was an offer I couldn't refuse.'

'Did I?' Michael said.

'Don't tell me you don't remember! You bumped into me and the boys in Leathwell, doing our Christmas shopping, and took us off for a burger.'

'I remember that bit.'

'And I said I needed a fag, and you told me I ought to give up. You said you'd avoided me when we were all kissing each other at the end of term Eucharist, because you'd seen me nip out for a fag beforehand, and you thought I'd smell.'

'Tactful, isn't he?' Jackie said.

'So I asked if you'd kiss me if I gave up, and you said, of course, if that's what it took to inspire me.'

Michael laughed. 'I didn't realise my lips were such a valuable prize. Here we go, then.' He leaned across and kissed her briefly on the lips.

'Go and get us some fags, Jackie,' Alison said, 'it wasn't worth it.'

'Shame on you, Mike, you can do better than that! I've seen you in action.' Jackie nudged his arm, spilling drips of lager on his jeans. 'Give the poor girl a thrill!'

Michael let himself be swept along by their high spirits. 'If you insist.' He took Alison's face in his hands, and kissed her again, moving his mouth against hers with a theatrical flourish for ten or fifteen seconds, then he drew back, laughing with her.

'Much better. What else can I give up?' she said, but their eyes met briefly, in recognition that something more powerful had passed between them as her mouth had opened under his, and for a few electric seconds, their tongues had touched.

The episode disturbed him. Allie had been an entertaining friend to have through their first term, and he hadn't meant to complicate things. After all, he was happily married, and she had her vocation as a priest to consider; he had no desire at all to get involved.

'Can I join you?' Nan appeared at their table, carrying a glass, looking quite unlike herself in a black suit with a low-cut, russet body underneath that gave a hint of cleavage.

'Do.' Michael moved to allow Nan to come between himself and Alison. 'You're looking stunning.'

Nan beamed at him, her dark eyes shining. 'Do you like it?' she said, brushing her hand through hair now cropped short about her face, and rinsed with a deep gold tint. 'Becky gave me a makeover for Christmas, and I treated myself to some new clothes. I was worried I might have gone too far. I passed Ridgefield in the hall earlier, and he gave me a most peculiar look.'

'Poor man, fancy having you turn sexy on him,' Jackie said. 'He represses his urges all his life, and avoids women wherever possible, and suddenly there's you every which way he turns, a living advertisement for wonderbras, if I'm not mistaken.'

Nan laughed. 'He hasn't repressed his urges all his life, you know. There was an incident when he was in his first curacy...'

'Ooh, tell us more!' Alison said.

'No, I can't. I shouldn't even have said that much. Let's just say, he hasn't always hated women.'

Jackie punched her playfully. 'Shame on you, I want to know all the sordid details.'

Michael intervened. 'Come on, give the man a break. It's hardly fair bringing up stories from decades ago. You should judge people on what they're like now.'

'Prejudiced, misogynistic, reactionary ...' Jackie murmured.

'Oh, he has his moments,' Nan said. 'You know, it's very easy to assume that because someone is completely wrong about one thing, they must be wrong about everything. Whereas actually, Christopher is a decent man, underneath all that prejudice. He can even be fun to work with.' She paused, lost in thought, then she drained her glass. 'I'm off to bed. See you in the morning.'

Nan's room was over in one of the new residential blocks. As she made her way down the path towards it, she noticed a light had been left on in the lecture room she had been using earlier. Christopher got annoyed if they were too profligate with electricity, so she took a detour, to turn the light off. She had not thought of the possibility of the room being occupied, and was startled to find Ridgefield leaning over the papers spread across the table at the side of the room.

'I'm sorry,' she said. 'I didn't realise you were here.'

He turned, looking sheepish. 'I saw the light on,' he said. He glanced at the paper he was holding, and hastily replaced it on the table. 'I was being nosy.'

Nan came closer. 'Help yourself. It's only my guidelines to students for writing up their placement reports. You're welcome to crib anything for your lot if you want to. You don't have to tell them where it came from.'

He smiled. 'I should make a point of telling them. We mustn't confirm their prejudices, after all, must we?' He was keeping a straight face, but his eyes betrayed amusement.

Nan was unable to think of a response to teasing from such an unusual source.

Ridgefield turned back to scan the papers on the table.

'I could lend you the book that extract comes from,' she said, seeing him pick up a photocopied sheet.

Ridgefield was reading, and appeared not to hear. Nan found herself observing his profile: the straight nose, the hair with its creeping grey, the faint lines around his eyes, the way the pale skin was beginning to sag on his cheeks, the outline of his lips. I wonder what he'd be like to kiss, she caught herself thinking. Oh God, I want him.

He looked round. 'Pardon?'

Nan continued staring, unable to look away, or to remember what it was she'd said before that unbidden acknowledgement of desire had caught her out. She felt herself flush.

'Oh, nothing.'

For a few bewildering seconds, they gazed at each other.

'You look different,' he said at last. 'You've had your hair cut.'

'My daughter gave me a day at a beauty salon for Christmas. I got a makeover.' Nan smiled, and wished her voice didn't sound peculiar. 'I blame her if people don't like it.'

'There's no need to do that. It's very attractive. That style suits you.'

'Thank you.' Nan fiddled with one of the piles of papers, neatening its corners self-consciously. 'I ought to get to bed,' she said, looking up at him again. 'Can I leave you to lock up?'

Ridgefield hesitated, then nodded. 'Goodnight, Nan.'

She was shaking as she went to her room, berating herself for giving herself away so foolishly. Of all the canons in all the cathedrals in this godforsaken nation, I have to fall in love with him! She tried to recapture his expression when he had stared back at her. Had there been anything there? 'It's very attractive,' he'd said. 'It suits you.' Hardly a declaration. And Christopher Ridgefield would never contemplate having a relationship with a woman priest.

She spent most of the night persuading herself that the whole thing was a momentary aberration, not to be taken seriously. Only when she saw him looking across the room at her during breakfast the following morning, she was no longer quite so sure.

Michael behaved as normally as he could with Alison for the remainder of the weekend, but he noticed how frequently her eyes were on him. He'd kissed many women apart from his regular girlfriends over the years, with affection or faint stirrings of passion that didn't mean anything. That was what it should have been like with Allie; it shouldn't have sent him home from Thorleigh on Sunday afternoon feeling disturbed and guilty.

The warmth of Jenny's welcome only made it worse. They'd managed a few days off together over Christmas, and though she'd been working over this weekend, she was still looking relaxed. She brought him a mug of tea, and casually dropped an itemised receipt onto the coffee table in front of him.

'Oh, yes, I came across this in your shirt pocket when I was putting the washing in. What were you doing consuming two milkshakes, two coffees and four burgers in Leathwell just before Christmas? Wasn't that when we went shopping?' Her tone was inquisitive rather than accusatory, but he felt defensive.

'I ran into Allie and her sons, and treated them.'

'You never said.'

He gazed up at her. 'You don't have to look at me as if I'd committed a crime.'

'I wasn't. I don't mind, I'm sure it was innocent.'

'Well of course it was. Stop being so bloody jealous.'

Jenny sat down abruptly in her armchair, looking shocked at his uncharacteristic flash of temper. Michael sipped his tea, and stared out of the window, wondering what had got into him.

It was a couple of minutes before she replied, in a voice from which she had not quite eradicated the tremor. 'I wasn't being jealous. At least, I didn't think I was. Have I got something to be jealous about?'

'Don't be stupid.'

'Would you tell me, if you did find someone else?' She sounded sick at heart, but he felt he needed to recover himself before he attended to her.

'What's the point in talking to you if you never listen? I'm going to play the piano,' he said, and got up and left the room.

She'd bought the piano from her parents to give him for Christmas, and now it was ensconced in their dining room. He played it most days, often with Jenny sitting at the table listening while she worked, or read. Today, she stayed where she was.

Half an hour with his music restored Michael's equanimity. He came back into the living room where Jenny sat staring tensely at the newspaper, took it from her, and sat on the arm of the chair, hugging her.

'I'm sorry for getting cross,' he said. 'I didn't mention seeing Allie at the time, because I was meeting you for afternoon tea, and I didn't dare confess I'd already had something. I don't know why I overreacted just now.'

'It was my fault. I expect I sounded as if I didn't trust you.'

'You can surely trust me not to be unfaithful to you. You know I love you.'

'But you didn't, not in the first place. And I keep thinking you might find someone who you really fall for, like you never did with me.'

He drew back to look into her face. 'How long have you been thinking that?'

'Since you started going out with me.' She gave a little smile. 'And especially since you started the Programme, and suddenly you're with

154

interesting women again, whereas before you were out of circulation except for me. I keep remembering how quickly you ended up in bed with Becky.'

'That is so ridiculous I don't know how to answer it. Move over.' He slid into her chair, and pulled her back onto his knee, holding her tightly. 'I got involved with Becky because I was out of my head for a while, and you mustn't begrudge Allie my friendship. Steve isn't interested in what she's doing, her head teacher's a committed atheist who's always making snide remarks, and her vicar doesn't agree with women priests, so she needs all the support she can get. Maybe I flirt with her occasionally, and Jackie, and some of the others, but it doesn't mean anything. There's no way I'd ever be unfaithful to you. You're necessary to me.' He stroked her cheek, aching to drive the apprehension from her eyes. 'I don't function without you. Even when we're at odds, or you're shutting me out, underneath everything you're part of me. No other woman is ever going to be that.' He kissed her slowly, all thoughts of Alison fading as he kindled passion between them. 'I miss you when I'm away,' he breathed in her ear, as he slid his hand underneath her skirt. 'And we've got a couple of hours before church ...'

Alison had no such incentive to put Michael from her mind. She survived the loving greetings from James and Josh, and the subsequent arguments between them that always broke out within half an hour of her return; she sympathised with Steve over his ordeal in babysitting for an entire weekend, and finally sat down at the kitchen table with a cup of tea and the Sunday papers. Her fingers kept returning to brush her lips, for her predominant memory of the weekend was the moment that Michael had kissed her, and she was already dreaming of what it would be like when it happened again.

A flu bug ravaged the nation that February, taking its toll of many of the students and staff both at St Barnabas and on the Programme. With Roly away, Nan found herself alone in charge of the Wednesday evening session. The dining hall was sparsely populated, with such of the remaining Barney boys who were upright, out at a special service in Thorleigh.

As the Programme students talked to Nan over supper, it became clear that several of them were in the middle of personal crises, and they began asking whether Nan could make the service they'd be having at the end of the evening into a Eucharist.

'I could see if Ridgefield's about,' she said.

'Why can't you do it?' Jackie asked. 'You're a priest, aren't you?'

'You know I'm not allowed to, not here.'

'And why not? Why should Ridgefield be allowed to dictate to you? It's nothing to do with him. Please, Nan, this is important to us.'

'I can't. I'll go and see him.'

Nan made her way to Ridgefield's study, and tapped lightly on the door. While she was waiting, Tyrone came into the hall, his jacket dripping from the rain outside.

'I wouldn't do that,' he said. 'Father Christopher's got a migraine. He won't want to be disturbed.'

'Oh. I see. I'd hoped he might come and celebrate for us. The students want a Eucharist.'

'He'll be in bed. He gets really bad.'

'Hell! And all your other staff have got flu ... what am I going to do?'

'Can't you do it yourself? You're a priest.'

'I'm not allowed to.'

'Who'd know? Besides, it's mainly Ridgefield who's so anti. I agree with women priests myself, and so do half of the rest of us.'

'You certainly don't treat me as if you approve.'

Tyrone shrugged. 'That was last term. You've won us over.'

Nan was not sure, looking back, why she had accepted Tyrone's protestations so easily. Perhaps her sense that Ridgefield's attitude towards her had changed for the better made her less wary. Perhaps Tyrone was telling her what she wanted to hear, that she would be right to lay aside the unnecessary restrictions that had been laid on her. And so she nipped out to the nearest late-store for bread and wine, and at the end of the evening, gathered together like the first disciples behind doors closed through fear, the Programme got its Eucharist.

When Nan arrived at St Barnabas the following morning for a lecture, she found Ridgefield, pale, but up and about again, waiting in the hall.

'Are you feeling better?' she asked. He ignored the question, and she realised that his pallor stemmed as much from anger as anything else.

'Might I have a word with you in my study?'

He stalked across and held the door open for her, and she stepped inside, thinking: Oh, God, he's heard about it. He didn't even offer her a seat, but as soon as he'd closed the door behind him, he laid into her.

'You know that the Programme is only allowed to share our facilities on the strict understanding that you don't try and behave like a priest on our premises. Tyrone informs me that last night, he saw you attempting to celebrate Mass in the lecture room. How dare you!'

Tyrone! Oh, God, she'd walked straight into that. She tried to speak evenly. 'There were a lot of students with problems, and they pleaded with me, and there wasn't anyone else available with all this flu. I did knock on your door, but there wasn't any answer. Then I was told you were ill, too. I couldn't let them down, it was my pastoral duty. It was an exceptional case. I promise it won't happen again.'

'You're too right it won't happen again. I may not have been well last night, but I was downstairs - I'd have heard if anyone had knocked at my door. Don't make things worse by telling lies. How you can call yourself a Christian minister defeats me completely. Pastoral duty, indeed! You've been building up to this ever since you first came here. Being thoroughly obsequious to get me to relax my guard, and then you do this!'

'It wasn't like that. I didn't want to break the rules, but the students needed it. I'm sorry if I got it wrong.' She was striving hard to keep her temper, feeling that she still had a chance of drawing on the reserves of goodwill that had grown between them. 'Please, Christopher...' She looked up into his face. 'I thought we'd come to understand each other better than this.'

'You thought! I know what you've thought. Dressing yourself up, flaunting yourself, throwing yourself at me like some neurotic spinster. If you only knew how ridiculous it makes you look.'

Nan was rocked by this attack; wounded, she hit back with the only weapon that came to mind. 'Of course! Women have been throwing themselves at you all your life, haven't they? I suppose that's how you excuse how you behaved with that woman when you were a curate. And *you* dare to lecture *me* on pastoral care!'

His expression froze; red patches appeared on his cheeks as he struggled to cope with this unexpected ghost from his past. 'What are you talking about?' he asked at last, his voice rough. 'Who have you been talking to?'

'Got you worried, haven't I? You think you're so bloody holy. Mr Celibacy himself, when all you are is a hypocritical bigot!' Nan pulled the door open, and stepped into the hall.

Ridgefield's voice followed her. 'You won't get away with this! I shall be taking this to the highest levels, and if I have anything to do with it, you'll never work in this or any diocese ever again!'

She turned back. 'As if I bloody well care,' she yelled, finally losing the last vestiges of her self-control. 'I've had it up to here with your pettiness and arrogance, and as far as I'm concerned you can bloody well

157

fuck off! Right, Father Christopher bloody Ridgefield? Fuck off!'

And on that unoriginal but highly effective exit line, she strode across the hall and out of the building.

She was vaguely aware, as she left, that the sound of raised voices coming through Ridgefield's door had drawn attention, so that there were several students watching in shocked silence in the hall as the argument reached its finale.

Only when she was at home, and had calmed down enough to think straight, did she realise that the public nature of this row must inevitably lose her her job. She confessed her misdemeanour to Caroline over the telephone, but with Roly away, there seemed little she could do. On top of that, she remembered that Christopher was due to come to her house for an important meeting with Robert and the Diocesan Director of Ordinands on Monday night, and what the hell was she supposed to do if he turned up wanting to start round two?

After an awful weekend, with anxiety tightening her stomach so she could hardly eat, and what felt like the beginnings of flu tightening her head, Nan had resolved that she would talk to Ridgefield the moment he arrived, and crawl to him in abject apology, begging him to at least talk with Roly before making any final decisions. It all came to nothing, because he was late, and they had to start without him.

The meeting passed without her making much contribution. She told them she wasn't feeling well, and they seemed content to talk among themselves. Her occasional glance at Ridgefield told her that he was avoiding looking at her, and he certainly did not address her. They finished at ten. The DDO left, and since Robert and Ridgefield had some business to finish off, Nan cleared away their coffee cups, and crossed to the small spare bedroom that led off her hall. She kept an overflow of books from her study there, and occupied herself trying to track down a quotation. She sat back on the bed, with her legs tucked up under her skirt, flicking through the pages of a book, waiting for the men to go.

Robert poked his head round the open door. 'Goodnight. Thanks for your hospitality. See you on Wednesday'.

The door closed behind him. Ridgefield could be heard using the downstairs bathroom next door. Nan focused on her book, praying that he'd go without saying anything, because she was in too much of state by now to cope. No such respite was offered. Ridgefield came into the room, put his briefcase on the floor, and leant against the bookcase on the opposite wall.

Five

Nan looked up. Ridgefield's face showed a storm waiting to break over her.

'I thought you might like to know that your disgraceful language last week was witnessed by most of my students, and I have had a whole series of complaints. I've written to Bishop Derrick making a formal protest about your behaviour, and asking for your dismissal.'

'I ...'

'I will not be spoken to like that in front of my students. You want to call yourself a priest, yet you lie, and swear, and blatantly ignore any rules you don't happen to like. I've done my best to accommodate you, bent over backwards to treat you with respect, but I've had enough of your childish tantrums...'

'I was going to apologise for losing my temper,' Nan got in finally, 'but I'm bloody well not going to now. I'm the one who's bent over backwards, trying to accommodate to your prejudices, despite the way everyone's been harassing me, and hassling me. I've been forgiving when your mob have misbehaved - why do you have to come down on me like a ton of bricks when I do one thing you don't like? You've been waiting for this, haven't you? Sodding bastard!'

'Watch your language when you speak to your superiors.'

'Oh, "watch your language with me, my girl",' Nan mimicked. 'Call yourself superior! You're not even superior to bloody dog shit.' Her voice shook, and she could feel her eyes filling with tears.

'Oh yes, turn on the tears. You know you're completely in the wrong, so you go for sympathy. Well, you've picked the wrong person to try that on. I'm not moved in the slightest.'

'Of course you're not. You haven't got any human emotions in you. You're a fucking eunuch!'

'If you're going to continue to swear at me, you might at least try to pick your metaphors better.'

And suddenly it all caught up with her. She was too tired to keep on fighting, and tears rolled down her face as all the turbulent emotions of the last few days and weeks overtook her. 'Shut *up*! Can't you even let me lose my temper with you without telling me I'm doing it all wrong? I can't argue with you, I can't talk to you, everything always goes wrong. I hate it. I hate you hating me all the time. Why can't you just go away and leave me alone?'

She collapsed prostrate on the bed, her face buried in the pillow, her hands clutching the gold candlewick bedspread, and wept.

Ridgefield looked at her with a degree of annoyance, wondering why she had to make it all personal. He picked up his briefcase to go, then put it down again. But of course it was all personal. It came to him that it always had been. As the ignorant gardener recognises that the shoot is not a weed but a planted seed springing out through the earth, so he understood at last the depth of his feelings for her. He could no longer go away and leave her in this state. Her tears did have the power to move him, and he desperately wanted things to be right between them. He came over and knelt beside her, and put his hand on her back.

'I'm sorry, Nan.' He rubbed her shoulder. 'Don't cry.'

Still sniffing, she turned her head towards him. One eye, reddened by tears, peered up at him from under the bright hair that straggled damply across her cheek. He brushed a strand away with a gentle finger. 'I don't hate you, Nan.'

She rolled over onto her back, timid in the face of his kindness. Ridgefield smoothed the hair away from her other cheek, and stroked her face. 'I really don't hate you.' Then he leaned forward and kissed her.

That first contact released floods of desire to wash through him, driving away the bitterness. His hands roved over her, under her clothes, moving them aside. She was pushing off his jacket, throwing aside his collar and opening his shirt, to hold him against her, skin to skin. He thought of the arid years, of the decades through which he had forfeited this ecstasy of touch. And then there was no space left for thought, he did not want to think, only to follow the intolerable driving need to be connected, to find her, flesh in flesh and bone on bone.

As he spent himself inside her, emotions long outlawed welled up in him, and he wept. He lay heavily, his face buried against her neck, hot wet tears seeping out onto her skin while his body juddered against her. Nan's arms contained him, her hands stroked his hair. Nothing else mattered. At last, the crisis was passed and he was at peace. He lifted his head and met her eyes, knowing his face reflected the tenderness in her own. He sank

160

back again and tightened his hold on her.

'Well....' he said. 'This is a complication.'

Lisa had got through Christmas but she had entered the new year in an angry mood. She had been prepared to make the best of Andy's marriage to Tracey, and the fact that he avoided so much as looking at her during the hours she spent there on Christmas Day left her resentful. She found it difficult to concentrate on her work as the spring term got under way, and eventually located Mrs Thompson after school to ask if she could talk to her.

'I'm sorry, Lisa, I have to get back. My mother-in-law's not well, and we're going to see her in hospital this evening.'

'What about lunchtime tomorrow?'

'I've already got someone coming to see me. Sorry. Have a word with me on Monday, and we'll fix something up.'

'Don't bother,' Lisa said sulkily. 'It don't matter.' She stomped away, convinced that her only ally among the staff had turned against her, and rejected all Mrs Thompson's subsequent attempts to encourage her. She did badly in her work, got placed on report for disrupting a lesson, and a week of detention for something she hadn't done, or hadn't meant to do. In the middle of the week, she decided she couldn't hack school anymore, hung around the streets near the school until she knew her gran would have gone to work, and took herself back home.

The morning passed slowly. Lisa lay on the sofa flicking between the morning chat shows on television, and washing down crisps and Mr Kipling pies with sickly diet lemonade. Martini would have been preferable, but Gran had done her nut when she'd nicked some a few months ago, and she wasn't going to risk it. She was half asleep when she heard the key in the front door, and thought she must have slept till five, except that it was still light outside. She'd have to invent some story about being taken ill at school, and hope Gran didn't check.

But instead of coming into the living room, the footsteps went upstairs, and a male voice could be heard saying 'Watch your back, Stella,' and Gran laughed in answer, the throaty laugh of a woman with her lover.

All the emotions Lisa had been combatting over the last weeks and months focused on that sound. Cold fury flooded her, and she climbed the stairs after them, her fists clenched and her jaw set.

They were standing in Gran's bedroom, arms round each other, and Gran was undoing the man's shirt. Lisa recognised Len, the man who owned the garage on whose forecourt Gran had been working for the last two years.

'You shit! What d'you think you're doing? You're disgusting!' she yelled.

Gran sprang back, her jaw sagging. 'Lisa! You should be in school.'

'Well, I fuckin' well in't!'

Len advanced towards her. 'You don't speak to your gran like that.'

'Wha's it got to do with you, you pervert?'

Len raised his hand and struck her smartly across her face.

'Len, no! Don't go, Lisa,' Gran called.

But Lisa, with one apocalyptic stare at the man who had dared to lay a hand on her, turned, and slammed out of the house with a force that shook the whole terrace. She was so angry she could have done murder. How dare Len treat her like that? How dare Gran take up with Len, behaving like a teenager when she was a dried up old cow? She was never going back there again. She kicked his parked Mercedes as she walked, setting the alarm to shriek satisfactorily after her as she hurried down the street. Bending down, she picked up a stone, and scored it along the side of the other cars she passed: that would serve the smarmy bastards right, whoever they were. Unconsciously, she was following the route she usually took to school, and before long she found herself outside the gates. She made her way inside, and along to the first lesson of the afternoon, her anger ready to spurt indiscriminately, like champagne from a shaken bottle.

Mrs Thompson stopped her as she heaved herself in through the door and tried to slouch to a table at the back of the classroom.

'You're very late,' she said sternly. 'I was told you weren't here today. Have you reported to the front office?'

'No.'

'Well, would you do so please. And if you are late, I expect an apology at the very least, and an explanation would be nice. "Sorry, Mrs Thompson, but I was temporarily kidnapped by aliens". It's your big chance to be creative.'

Lisa's classmates giggled, and she hated the lot of them. 'You can fuckin' well shut up,' she shouted, glaring at them.

'That will be detention, Lisa. You don't use language like that. Now, I think I told you to go and report to the front office.'

'Well I'm bloody well not goin' to.'

'Come on, Lisa, don't spoil everything by picking a fight. You've been doing so well this term.'

The change of tone had no effect on Lisa; she was beyond caring. 'I in't moving.'

A look of resignation crossed the teacher's face. 'Sarah, could you go and fetch Mr Jewson, please?'

Fear crept around Lisa's anger. If the Head was brought in, it would mean Gran getting involved, and she was in enough trouble already. She couldn't cope.

'Piss off, you bloody great cow,' she yelled, pushing past her bemused peers and heading for the door.

Mrs Thompson moved to stop her, but Lisa thrust her away, knocking her off balance, and escaped down the corridor, and out of the school gate before anyone could apprehend her.

Out over the pavement, across the street in front of the school, and on towards the green she hurried, not feeling the wind that blew through the thin bomber jacket she wore over her baggy sweatshirt and leggings. For a long time she sat on the seat where Mrs Thompson had watched her boys play, nearly two years before. Lisa lit one of the three fags she had in her pocket. Mothers pushing infants on the swings in the play area at the edge of the grass, disappeared to collect older brothers and sisters from the local primary school; the first sight of older children told Lisa that her own school's day must have ended.

'You're really for it,' said a year eight girl, coming up to her. 'Old Jewson had your gran in, and she looked like she was going to kill you.'

'Piss off, Justine,' Lisa said mechanically. She hated Gran and school and Nottling and everyone in it, but where could she go? The complications with Andy meant she could hardly go home, but her family were away in any case; Andy had taken them all to Florida.

She didn't want to see any of her mates, so she dragged herself up off the seat, and headed for the main road. A bus was heading towards her with Greathampton picked out in fluorescent yellow on its destination board, and it catapulted the thought of Michael into her mind, with all the kindness he'd shown her over the last few months.

Lisa had no money on her - all she carried was a lighter and her one remaining fag in its crumpled pack - but she determined she would go to Greathampton to find the one adult she could still trust. She set out along the main road, her thumb extended to the rapidly moving traffic.

'And then she called me a bloody great cow, and stormed out,' Alison said as she drove Michael to St Barnabas that evening. 'We'll have to exclude her, and given what she's been up to lately, it could be permanent. It's so depressing. She really seemed to have settled down since you've been involved with her. I wish I'd reacted differently when she came in, but I've been under a strain myself with Steve's mum being ill. I didn't register she was ready to explode until it was too late.'

'It's not your fault. You couldn't let her get away with it. You had a lesson to teach.'

'I know that really, but I suppose I feel responsible for Lisa, with all she's been through, and with you knowing her. Ah well, perhaps she'll turn up at school tomorrow, suitably ready to be chastened. Which reminds me, you haven't heard about Nan, have you? Caroline told me when I saw her yesterday that Ridgefield found out that Nan did that Eucharist last week, and he went ballistic. He dragged her into his study at lunchtime on Thursday, and they were bawling each other out with all the Barney boys listening in, and now she's probably going to get the sack.'

'Oh my God,' Michael said. 'She said she'd get crucified if it got out. How did he find out?'

'I don't know. Someone must have seen us through the blinds. Anyway, it ended with Nan yelling at him to eff off, and he's not going to forgive that. Nan was ever so upset. She told Caroline she just flipped, because she doesn't usually lose her temper in public like that.'

They arrived at St Barnabas that evening unsure whether Nan would be there, but at five-thirty, she emerged from a meeting with Ridgefield looking emotional and pink with the embarrassment. But he had accepted her grovelling apology, she said, accepted that she'd been under stress, and the matter was at an end. Ridgefield made an announcement to that effect in the chapel, while the Programme students and the Barney boys sat suspicious in their separate groupings once again, eyeing each other with dislike.

'He's been nobbled,' Tyrone muttered to Michael as they came out of the chapel. 'I bet the Bishop's told him to lay off her. She's quite Derrick's blue-eyed girl, you know.'

'But it would have been terrible if she'd gone. It might have ruined everything, just when we're all getting on so well.'

'Yes, terrible,' Tyrone agreed as he walked off, rather as if he were disappointed.

Several of the Programme students stayed for a drink in the bar after the evening's lectures, trying to make sense of the eruption that had hit them, and the unsatisfactory anticlimax of its solution.

'Jenny thought it was awful when I told her about the Eucharist,' Michael said to Alison, turning to where she sat on the edge of their circle. 'She likes Christopher, and she thinks it's most unfair he should have to put up with aggressive women breaking all his rules.'

'Yes, but Nan's not at all aggressive when you know her. Has Jenny ever met her?'

'Only briefly at the introductory weekend.'

Jackie and Pam were teasing Gerald, who had come over to take away their empty glasses.

Michael lowered his voice. 'It's personal as well, though. I was going out with Nan's daughter while I was lodging with Jenny, and Becky stayed the night with me rather noisily, when Jenny had said I wasn't to have guests of the opposite sex in my room, and she blames Nan for that, too.'

'Bit of a lad, weren't you?' Alison murmured.

He met her eyes, and the sexual awareness that had flitted between them on the weekend surfaced again. He tried to ignore it, as he leaned forwards with his drink, his elbows on his knees.

'Not really,' he answered. 'There's only been Becky and a couple of others, and I was engaged to one of them. What about you?'

'Worse than that. I haven't counted. But then, I wasn't a Christian when I was sleeping around.' She leaned forwards herself, mirroring his position, and regarding him intently. 'There are odd occasions when I wish I still wasn't. Then I could feel quite happy about going to bed with a man simply because I fancied the pants off him.'

Michael looked down at the glass cupped between his hands. The surface of the lager was quivering, picking up the tremor that had run unbidden through his hands at her words. 'But you are a Christian,' he said slowly, 'and an ordinand, and married, so there's not much scope...' He met her eyes again. 'I'd never be unfaithful to Jenny either. However tempted I was.'

She held his gaze for a few seconds, then she leaned back in her chair, and the spell was broken. 'I should think not. You're practically still on your honeymoon.'

Michael straightened himself to drain his glass, and told himself it was going to be alright. They were responsible adults, who had recognised and rejected the attraction between them; that done, they could continue with their friendship. Nonetheless, he tried to pick on neutral topics of conversation as Alison drove him home.

'How's Steve taking the worry about his mum?' he asked, as they picked up speed along the bypass.

'He says it's one of those things. Women get breast cancer, nothing you can do about it. He's so matter-of-fact, it might be the dog for all he cares. If it was my mum, I'd be in a terrible state.'

'Maybe he finds it difficult to talk because it does matter so much to him.'

'Maybe. So I ought to be able to get him to open up, and help him, but I don't seem to be much good at it. In fact, to be honest, I wouldn't know what to do if he started getting emotional.'

'It's a good thing you're not married to me. I burst into tears at the drop of a hat. You should have seen me when Jenny and I watched Shadowlands. She practically had to wring me out.'

As the road curved downhill, the flash of bright orange hazard lights appeared in the distance. Alison slowed down until they had resolved themselves into a broken-down car and breakdown truck safely pulled into a layby, and accelerated away.

'Oh, you're different,' she said. 'I'd never feel uncomfortable if you got emotional - it's because it's out of character for Steve. I wish I was married to someone who *was* in touch with their feelings.'

Michael looked across at her uneasily, but her face was concealed by the confessional dark. 'I don't think Jenny would say that,' he said lightly. 'She finds it a liability most of the time.'

'Then she doesn't deserve you. She should appreciate what she's got. Some of us would give our eye teeth to have husbands who were as kind and sensitive as you.'

'Don't stop. I like a bit of flattery,' he said, trying to make a joke of it; but his discomfort grew. Perhaps it was time to draw back.

'It's been very good of you to give me so many lifts,' he said, as Alison negotiated the trafffic lights, and turned towards his road, 'but I don't like to inconvenience you all the time. I could easily go back to getting the bus, or cycle, once the weather's better.'

'Oh, don't say that. I wouldn't survive without you to talk to like this. It's no bother, it really isn't. I can't tell you how much I appreciate having you as a friend.' She turned to him as she pulled up at the kerb in front of the house. 'You *can't* take the bus.'

Michael released his seat belt, and put an arm round her shoulders to hug her affectionately before he got out. Immediately she clung to him, and he held her for a few moments, relieved that the absence of Jenny's car meant she was away on call. He kissed Alison's cheek, his lips lingering on the smooth surface of her skin.

'Oh Michael ...' she whispered.

166

'Friendship's all it can be,' he said, letting go of her, and putting a hand on the door.

'I know.'

He forced himself to break away from her gaze. 'I'll see you next week. Goodnight. Thanks.' He got out and made his way to the front door, fumbling for the key in his pocket.

He made himself coffee, switched the television on, and sagged onto the sofa, deeply perturbed. The knowledge that he had behaved perfectly properly when Alison had thrown herself at him did nothing to counteract his shock at the intensity of the errant desire that had flooded him at the contact. He'd wanted her. This was no incidental attraction, to be dismissed with a sad smile, and agreement to forget; this was real, and he was in trouble.

By the time Alison arrived home, Steve was sitting up in bed reading a book. He didn't speak as she came into the bedroom and began to undress; she didn't hazard conversation either. 'Will you please stop interrupting me when I'm in the middle of reading,' he'd say if she asked a question or made a comment about her evening. 'You're always doing it, and you know I hate it. It's not as if you're saying anything important.'

She watched him as she unbuttoned her blouse. The hair around his thinning patch was lank and greasy, his beard concealed the fact that he was getting a double chin, and the buttons of his striped winceyette pyjamas were strained over his stomach. Ageing she could accept, but he never bothered any more. She removed the last of her clothes, and instead of diving straight into her nightdress, went over to the mirror to brush her hair, keeping an eye on his reflection.

He raised his eyes from his book for half a second. 'Bit cold for that, isn't it?'

'That's not what you used to say. I simply don't do anything for you anymore, do I?'

'I'm *trying* to read.'

Alison walked to the bed and pulled her nightdress out from under her pillow. Wrapped in her share of their duvet, she pretended to read until Steve was ready to put the light out.

Michael loved her. It had been obvious in the way he'd looked at her and held her, for all that he'd struggled against it, and the knowledge delighted her. Of course it couldn't go any further, he was right about that. Only when you lived with a man who never wanted to touch you, and thought about nothing other than computers and his latest Elmore Leonard, you needed someone who could make you feel good about yourself. She wondered whether she might ever persuade Steve to divorce her. It was tricky when you were going to be ordained, but the alternative was to have him go under a bus, and that would upset the boys. It would probably upset her too; she didn't wish him harm. No, Jenny would have to be the one who went under a bus. Miserable old gorgon. Trapping Michael into marriage when he was feeling vulnerable, and then treating him like dirt. She deserved all she got ... Oh, I don't mean it, Lord, she prayed, I don't really wish either of them harm, it's just that Michael means so much to me, and I can't believe you'd bring us together like this without a reason. And you know how unhappy we both are in our marriages, you know what a wonderful team we'd make.

Steve muttered something that might have been goodnight, and turned his back on her to go to sleep. His breathing evened out as she lay sleepless in the dark, listening to the distant noise from the main train line into Leathwell. Once he was asleep, she would conjure up one of her lovers, touching herself as she imagined hands and body pressed urgently to hers. She had been resolutely resisting the intrusion of Michael's image for weeks, but tonight, she allowed him to come to her bed to take her with the utmost tenderness while her husband lay sleeping, and her self-induced climax was more intense than any she had known for years.

Six

The journey to Michael's house had taken Lisa hours, and her feet felt as if she'd walked most of the way. It had been a while before anyone stopped, and then the lorry driver who did pick her up had forgotten to stop on the ring road, and she'd had to walk several miles back into the town centre. She arrived just before seven, hungry, thirsty, tired, frozen and miserable, only to find the house unlit and empty.

After a brief rest, she headed back towards the town centre, and took the risk of lifting a Mars bar and a mini can of cola from Kwiksave. The high street was all but deserted, sunk in a torpor until the pubs and cinema threw people out. She hung about while the stinging wind pierced the marrow of her bones, and her stomach ached with emptiness, then walked back up the hill to try Michael again.

There was a light on this time, but no answer to her knock. She took shelter in the back garden, subsiding onto the step in the angle between the outside wall of the kitchen and the wide glass patio door, until she heard the car, and went to throw herself on his mercy. Only instead, she saw the shadowy figures of the two people inside merging into a single outlined form as they embraced, and parting to reveal themselves as Michael and her teacher. She was aghast. Of course all sorts of people had affairs these days, but she would never have expected it of Michael, he'd always gone on about having standards, and here he was, a bloody hypocrite like all the rest. What made this worse was that it meant all his apparent interest in her over the last few months had been a sham. He'd used her as a means of getting off with Mrs Thompson, and it left her without a friend in the world.

Lisa stepped back round the corner of the house, hugging herself as much against the shock as against the bitter wind. There was no way she could approach him after what she'd seen, but she was too exhausted by the events of the day to take any other initiatives. She slumped back on the step again, wanting to die.

The light came on in the room behind her. Through a narrow gap in the curtains, she could see Michael sprawl on the sofa watching television. The large cat who had investigated her when she had first arrived emerged out of the shadows and wound itself around her legs. It allowed her to pick it up, purring and rubbing its face against hers. Lisa held onto it for its warmth and comfort, and began to cry silently into its fur. It suffered the damp indignity of the girl's sobs for several minutes before disappearing to prowl the garden, leaving her alone.

She heard Jenny return, the light behind her went out, and the night got still colder. The garage loomed away on her right, with its metal up-and-over door shining in the faint illumination from the street lights, and another small door set into a windowed area at the back. She had tried the doors, but they were both locked. Sensation had long since departed from her feet, she was too cold to think or move. Time passed. Far-off noises reached her. A train, several miles away. A motorbike's roar from the main road. A dog.

She didn't know whether she had fallen into a doze or not when she was startled into alertness by the banging of a door. A light shone out of the kitchen window, casting its pattern on the grass. The car started up, and drove away. Of course, Jenny was a doctor, she would have to go out at night sometimes. Supposing she hadn't locked up, perhaps there'd be a key to the garage, and some shelter?

Lisa walked unsteadily on cramped limbs round the side of the house to where the kitchen door opened under a corrugated plastic carport. Trying the door silently, she was relieved to find it opening under her pressure. The kitchen was very small, and well organised. A rack of keys hung on the wall by the door, and she took the likely ones out into the garden to try them. With the small garage door unlocked, she could return the key with no one the wiser. She was thinking more clearly, the adrenaline-fuelled fear of discovery sparking ideas in her formerly sluggish mind. Quickly she scanned the cupboards, extracting some slices of bread from a packet, crisps, a packet of chocolate biscuits, a carton of long-life milk, and, as an afterthought, a spare, back door key. She would like to have searched for a rug, or extra coat, but didn't dare. Then she quietly stepped out of the house, shutting the door behind her.

Once inside the garage, Lisa used her cigarette lighter to get her bearings. She was in luck. She spotted Michael's bicycle propped against the wall by the main door, and there was a light on it. With its aid, she inspected her temporary home. The end of the garage had been partly partioned off from the main area, and was filled with garden furniture:

170

two loungers under plastic covers, and a white plastic table with four chairs and a parasol stacked against it. Lisa arranged the plastic covers over one of the loungers, put her provisions under the cover of the other, returned the light to the bike in case Michael missed it in the morning, and made her way back to the lounger with the aid of the lighter. With the plastic covers wrapped round her, and food inside her, she felt better. If she knew deep down that none of her problems were solved by this absconding, at least she had gained a temporary respite. She was asleep when Jenny returned and let herself back into the house, unaware of any intrusion.

'I wonder if I'm relying too much on the friends I've made on the Programme,' Alison said to Caroline the following evening, sinking back into one of the armchairs in Caroline's front room. 'It makes such a change for me to meet people I can really talk to about how I'm feeling, and church, and the academic work, and I worry that I might be being disloyal to Steve.'

'That's one of the good things about the training, that you're part of a group. And I don't think many people these days would say you have to share everything with your spouse. As long as your marriage is sound in other ways...'

'Oh, yes. Well, Steve's too absorbed in his work to have a lot of time for the family at the moment, but it's OK.'

Programme students were expected to link up with someone who would oversee their spiritual development, and Nan had steered Alison towards Caroline. The arrangement would have worked better, had Alison been able to bring herself to be entirely honest, but she could not bring herself to do more than make oblique sallies in the direction of her sins.

'Michael's been a good friend, and he's been coming over to school to do some assemblies for me. Do you think it's alright for me to do such a lot with him?'

'Good heavens, don't worry about exploiting Michael! He loves to help out, and he's always been a friendly soul. He's loved getting back into school work.'

'You don't think his wife minds?'

'She's glad he's got plenty to do. Don't worry about them,' Caroline added, with a reassuring smile, 'they're a very strong couple. Very much in love. You can see how well they understand each other.'

I'm in love with him, that's what she should have said. Help me not to be. But it needed someone far more inquisitorial than Caroline to wrest that acknowledgement from her.

'Are you managing to set aside time for prayer, like you planned?' Caroline continued.

'Reasonably well.' Alison answered the question with half her mind elsewhere. A strong couple ... very much in love. Michael saying he'd never be unfaithful. Surely he felt what she did, though? Surely she could not have misread what had happened the previous evening? What if she'd merely embarrassed him, or worse, he was even now laughing with Jenny about her?

Such thoughts continued to distract her during her final half-hour with Caroline, and stalked her as she drove away from the vicarage. A minute later, she had stopped her car opposite a row of shops, while her longing to drive the short distance to visit Michael struggled with her sense that it wasn't quite appropriate to go straight from a meeting with her spiritual director to see the man with whom she'd been committing adultery in her heart for the last twenty-four hours. But it was no use, she couldn't wait another week to find out how he felt, and she had a good excuse to call tonight, to tell him about Lisa.

At the counter of the chip shop, one or two people leaned on the counter, watching television as they waited for service. A group of lads rolled past her car; one of them tapped on the window and called out as they headed across the road to the off-licence, its interior shrouded by the collage of special offers stuck to the window to tempt its patrons. They had no real interest in her, though they'd probably all know Michael. She let out the handbrake, and drove slowly up to the traffic lights, to cross the junction, and head towards his house.

Michael kissed her cheek without any trace of self-consciousness as he drew her in. 'Allie! How great to see you! I've been trying to get to grips with the Pentateuch all evening, and Jenny's writing reports, so she's not much fun. Come in, and entertain me.'

'I was going to be highly apologetic about disturbing you, but perhaps I needn't bother. I've been at Caroline's,' she added, as he helped her off with her coat

Michael led her into the living room where Jenny was curled up in an armchair with a mound of paperwork on her lap, filling in forms. She looked up as Alison came in, and greeted her without enthusiasm.

'I didn't realise doctors had to bring work home, too,' Alison said.

'They shouldn't have to, not when they're working twelve hour days as it is,' Jenny said, 'but it has to be done.' She sighed and thrust a hand through hair already tousled from frequent disturbances. 'However, I've had enough for tonight. I'm not thinking straight anymore.' She pushed her papers together and dumped them on the floor. 'Can I make you some coffee?'

Alison sat back on the sofa, and began to tell Michael about Lisa. He had flopped back into the corner of the sofa, his legs extended and his body relaxed, but his eyes, deep brown and intense under his dark fringe, watched her attentively as she spoke.

Jenny came back with a tray of drinks and a packet of digestives. 'I'm sure we'd bought some chocolate biscuits, but I can't find them,' she said. 'You haven't eaten them all have you, Michael?'

'No. I wouldn't dare,' he said, helping himself to a mug.

'Perhaps we left them in Sainsbury's. Ah, well. Did I hear you say Lisa had gone missing?'

'She ran out of my class yesterday afternoon,' Alison said. 'Apparently she never went back home, and no one's seen her today either. Her gran's worried out of her mind - they had a row yesterday before she got to school, and me being cross with her was the last straw. She was seen wandering round town, but the last sighting was of her hitching on the road to Greathampton, and someone reported seeing a lorry stop.'

'I do hope she's alright,' Jenny said, curling up in her chair again.

'The police say she's probably gone to a friend's, but her gran's contacted everyone she can think of, and there's no sign.'

'And she's not gone home, or to a friend's here?'

'No. Her mum's away, and there's no sign anyone's in the house. I'm really worried. It's times like this I feel like getting the fags out again.'

'I didn't know you'd given up,' Jenny said, frowning, as if she'd approved of the addiction.

'I could ask around tomorrow,' Michael said, 'see if anyone's seen her.'

They talked over the possibilities, none of them liking to voice out loud their fear that girls who were last seen hitch-hiking often turned up dead.

'I think we should pray for her,' Michael said at last.

'You do sound parsonical,' Jenny said, standing up. 'Even mixing with ordinands is clericalising you. You do what you like. I'm going to have a bath and go to bed.'

'Don't go,' he said.

'I need an early night. I barely got any sleep last night. You can be holy by yourselves.'

Alison raised an eyebrow when she'd gone.

'Jenny doesn't always think a lot of clergy,' he explained.

'Well, she ought to be more supportive. I know I've said it before, but you'd make a wonderful vicar. She should be encouraging you.'

'She says her parents pray together religiously, and look at them, so she doesn't rate the idea. It's just as well you're here.' He took her hand. From upstairs, came the sounds of Jenny moving about, setting the pipes thrumming as she drew her bath. It may be her bed he'll share tonight, Alison thought, but it's me he's really communicating with, me he shares his deepest thoughts with.

She got up to go when they heard Jenny's bathwater begin to gush out through the drain by the back door.

Michael stood up with her. 'Thanks for calling,' he said, showing her to the door.

'Don't I get a hug?' she asked.

Michael glanced upstairs. 'Of course,' he said awkwardly.

His embrace was brief, and his lips merely skimmed her forehead, but she was encouraged as she drove home. Caroline is definitely wrong, she told herself. He couldn't keep his eyes off me, and Jenny's really unpleasant to him. I suppose she managed to bully him into marrying her because he was feeling vulnerable after his fiancee left him, but she's no good for him. A strong couple who understand each other indeed! He's desperate for someone to take care of him, and I'm sure I've been sent to do it.

That night, she allowed him to make love to her again.

By the light from the landing, Michael could see Jenny hunched up under the covers. She seemed to be asleep when he got into bed himself. The sheets on his side were icy, so he snuggled up to her back, and put an arm over her.

'Get yourself a hot-water bottle if you're that cold,' she said, without stirring.

'That's what I have you for. You always used to sleep in my arms.'

'Wrong. I used to lie awake waiting for you to drop off so I could get away from you.'

'Would you rather I wasn't friends with Allie? Is that what the trouble is?'

'I couldn't care less who your friends are. Talk to her all you like, the more the better. At least it saves you from pestering me.'

Michael withdrew his arm and rolled over to lie with his back to her, a chilly chasm between them. He was a patient soul, but Jenny's frequent sniping at him for doing no more than trying to be close to her was wearing him down. What was he supposed to do when his wife rejected him without explanation, and would not even admit there was a problem? A wraith of thought pointed out that it would serve Jenny right if he kissed Allie the way he'd wanted to lately, winding his tongue round hers, feeding off her desire for him, instead of holding back because his vows to his wife still meant something to him. It might do her good to be jealous.

Jealousy, Jenny decided grimly, as she picked at her breakfast, was like living permanently in the hour before a vital exam. Your stomach tumbled continually inside you, your nerves were strung a notch too taut, and you wanted nothing so much as to lock yourself in the toilet and never speak to a human soul again. Since that option had not been available to her in the new year, when she had first started brooding about Michael's interest in Alison, she had coped by immersing herself even more deeply in her work. It wasn't in her nature to challenge him about it; she merely tried to distance herself from him, to pretend she didn't care.

Her alarm had woken her at seven on Saturday morning, two days after Alison's visit, and she groaned as she reached to turn it off. Michael, lying on his back, as always looking about fifteen with his face relaxed in sleep, opened an eye, focused vaguely on her, and shut it again. A few weeks ago, he wouldn't have let her get up without holding her closely; the fact that he was no longer bothered by the strain between them depressed her intolerably as she left to provide the morning's emergency cover at the surgery. She would have welcomed the distraction of a rash of interesting diseases, but relatively few patients awaited her, and she was back home by twelve.

Michael was out. With Lisa still missing, Jenny presumed he was off investigating her old haunts, as he'd done the day before. At least the lorry driver who'd given her a lift had been tracked down and cleared of any ill intent, so Alison had said when she'd rung on Friday. It made it more likely that Lisa was merely with a friend.

Jenny went into the kitchen to get some lunch. She was grumbling at Michael under her breath for taking so much bread and cheese for his lunch, and using a whole carton of milk for his breakfast, when she noticed that the box he always used for his packed lunches was still by the sink.

She stood for a moment, thinking. There had been several odd things happening over the last few days, food that disappeared with more rapidity than usual, the rug that had walked off the spare room bed, the magazine that had vanished from the downstairs toilet before she'd had a chance to read up on how to spot whether your man was cheating on you. She walked round the house thoughtfully, noting that there were no signs of forced entry, but that the spare back door key was missing from the rack.

It seemed a foolish flight of fancy to suppose that Lisa might have holed out in the garage, but once it had occurred to her, Jenny had to go and check it out. The side door of the garage was unlocked, and as soon as she opened it, it was clear that the garden furniture carefully stacked at the end of the summer, had been disturbed.

'Lisa? Are you in here?' she called gently. There was no reply, but she thought she saw movement under the covers of one of the loungers. Jenny walked over and pulled the thin green sheet away.

Lisa blinked grubbily up at her, and burst into tears. 'Don't let them arrest me!' she sobbed.

'No one's going to arrest you,' Jenny said, raising her up. 'We've all been terribly worried about you. Michael's out looking for you at the moment. Have you been here ever since Wednesday?'

Lisa nodded. 'I heard the helicopter, an' I thought the cops'll have been lookin' for me and they'll stick me in prison for wastin' their time.'

'The helicopter wasn't for you. The police thought you'd probably gone to a friend's. Why on earth did you come in here instead of calling on us?'

'I did, only you was out, an' then Michael come back, an' he was snogging with Mrs Thompson in her car, so I couldn't talk to him, could I?'

Jenny led her into the house. 'I'm sure he wasn't snogging her,' she said with more confidence than she felt. 'He's always hugged and kissed his friends, I'm sure that's all you saw. He wouldn't have done it outside our house if there'd been anything wrong about it.'

'Yeah, I suppose so. It didn't go on that long, anyway.'

'You poor thing, you're frozen. Why don't you have a bath and a hot drink, and then you can tell me why you ran away, if it would help.'

While the girl bathed, Jenny phoned the police and Stella, and looked out an old tracksuit to replace the soiled clothes Lisa had been wearing when she'd left home. Sitting in the living room with the gas fire warming them, Lisa explained falteringly about Andy, and why she couldn't go home.

'So it was *Andy* who got you pregnant? Oh, Lisa, you should have told me. He shouldn't have been allowed to get away with that. You were only fourteen.'

'He didn't mean to. You mustn't tell anyone, or he'd get done, and me mum'd kill me.'

'I can't promise that, Lisa. What about your sister?'

'He only did it cos I loved 'im, an' he was drunk. And then he never touched me again, even though I tried to get him to. And he's a good dad to Kelly an' to Darren. If you tell, an' he goes to prison, they'll all say it's my fault. Michael said it was OK, an' he never told no one.'

'You told Michael? But he had no right to decide not to tell. You can't know Andy wouldn't touch Kelly. I shall have to tell someone for her sake.' Jenny bit her lip as she looked at Lisa's round, anxious face. It was just possible that Lisa's interpretation was correct, and though she could understand Michael being persuaded, any professional would immediately have had alarm bells jangling at the story.

'I'll deny it, if you tell,' Lisa said.

'I'm afraid that won't make any difference, once I've reported it. It's for Kelly's sake, Lisa, you must see that. Social services won't be heavy-handed.'

'Yeah, but my mum'll kill me for gettin' off with Andy, won't she?'

'She's more likely to kill Andy. He must have known it was very wrong of him.'

By the time Michael appeared, Lisa seemed to have accepted that something had to be done about Andy, though she remained nervous as they drove her to Nottling to deliver her to her gran.

'Why didn't you tell me that it was Andy who got Lisa pregnant?' Jenny asked when Michael got back into the car after going in to tell Alison the news. 'Didn't you think I had a right to know?'

'I didn't see it needed taking further.'

'*You* didn't! And what do you know about it? Nothing you might talk over with *me*, of course, though I suppose you discussed it at length with Alison.'

'Not all the details, no, only what Lisa said I could tell her. I could hardly break Lisa's confidence to you, Jen,' he said reasonably, 'it's not as if you were her doctor, even then.'

'God, you're such an amateur! You think you're so gifted, but you've got no qualifications, no training, you blunder about going purely on instinct. Don't you realise there's men out there who attach themselves to

177

families like Tracey's, simply so they can get access to children? Didn't you stop to think that he might be raping her sister?'

'That wasn't what happened to Lisa. I'm as concerned about Kelly's welfare as you are, but there's absolutely nothing to suggest Andy's a danger. He's a man who got carried away, and regretted it, that's all.'

'And you'd have to excuse *that*, wouldn't you?'

'Why do you always have to drag my mistakes with Becky into everything?'

'I wasn't thinking of Becky, actually.'

'Then what were you thinking of?'

Jenny was silent, regretting her impulsive accusation.

'I said, what *were* you thinking of?'

'Nothing.'

'I haven't done anything with Alison, if that's what you're banging on about again.'

'Not that you'd regret it, in any case,' she muttered.

Michael sighed loudly. 'No, perhaps I wouldn't. Not with the way you're treating me these days.'

Jenny looked out of her window, shielding her face from him with her hand. She had no reply to make.

'Could you drop me at the surgery?' she asked as they came into Greathampton. 'I've got some telephone calls to make. It's my duty, Michael,' she added, as he raised his eyebrows.

'And what if he's innocent, and you're breaking the whole family up, just because you feel you've got to watch your back?'

'It's not about that, as you'd know if you were more than a naive, well-meaning volunteer.' She got out of the car almost before he'd stopped, and stalked up the path to the health centre to make her call.

Michael came into the hall to greet Jenny when she returned from the health centre at teatime, with his arms hesitantly extended towards her.

'Forgive me for being a bungling amateur and not talking to you about Lisa. I hate it when we argue.'

'So do I. I didn't need to lose my temper with you. I'm sure you were trying to do the right thing.' She put her arms round him, resting her head on his shoulder.

'What I don't understand is why you treat me as if you hate me half the time. It's almost as if you *want* me to take up with someone else, but that's not what I want, Jen. I want to have *you*, enjoying being with me like you used to.'

'I don't understand it either,' she whispered. 'I do love you, only I get jealous, and that makes me want to lash out at you. I know it's silly, I'm glad you've got friends like Alison, really.'

'You were doing it before there was anyone to get jealous about, though.' He paused, but she had no explanation to offer. 'Look, even if I was tempted to get involved with Allie, which I'm not, it would be stupid to do anything about it. She's an ordinand, for God's sake. So might I be, one day. We wouldn't do that sort of thing.'

Seven

'We wouldn't do that sort of thing.' The phrase came back to Jenny with a hollow sound as she sat in the family planning clinic later on that month, listening to Nan Patten talking about her lover. For some months, Jenny had combined her General Practice with three sessions a week at the clinic.

When Nan turned up for a consultation, Jenny automatically assumed that it was some general gynaecological problem that had brought her, and greeted her with an attempt at warmth. As Nan replied somewhat vaguely to her opening remarks, it dawned on her that Nan had no idea who she was. The absence of Jenny's heavy glasses, and the fact that she still practised under her maiden name, stopped Nan making the connection between the doctor she was consulting and the woman she had met once as Michael's wife. Jenny was about to explain, when Nan brought her up short with her question:

'Am I right in thinking that I could get pregnant if I were to be sexually active again?'

'Are you still having periods?'

'Yes.'

'Then you certainly could get pregnant. How old are you?'

'Forty-seven.'

'Obviously you're not as fertile as a younger woman, but it would be a possibility. Do you have a partner?'

'Yes.'

'You should make sure he wears a condom, to protect you against AIDS and other sexually transmitted diseases.'

'He's not very keen on that. He's rather conservative. What I really wanted was a diaphragm...'

As a doctor in a family planning clinic, Jenny had learned not to be judgemental, but Nan's request shocked her nonetheless. She had assumed that to be a priest required some degree of integrity, and that despite her daughter's laxity, Nan kept some moral standards. Yet here she was, Michael's mentor, a woman he greatly respected, and she'd taken a lover.

Jenny mulled the encounter over afterwards, wondering who Nan had got involved with, and the implications for herself. For if a priest like Nan could behave like that, what guarantee was there that Alison and Michael would resist temptation? The fear that it was only a matter of time before Michael abandoned her made Jenny distant with him, led her to repulse the advances that should have told her of her importance to him, while she worked and worked and wished she'd never taken on something as complicated as marriage.

Jenny returned home from a Friday afternoon session at the clinic towards the end of March to find that Michael had left a note explaining he was at a meeting up in the Rows, and wouldn't be back until half five.

Alison was due to pick him up to give him a lift to the Programme's final weekend of the spring term, and when the doorbell went at ten past five, Jenny assumed that she had arrived early for some reason. She pasted a polite smile on her face as she opened the door. She barely had time to focus on the man who stood on the step, before he pushed her back over the threshold, and followed her in, slamming the door with unsuppressed fury.

'What do you think you're doing?' Jenny said. Her mouth had dried, and her stomach knotted under her blouse, but she tried to assert herself. 'Get out of my house!'

'I want a word with you,' the man said, stepping up to Jenny as she backed away. Pale eyes bored into her with contempt from under cropped, gold hair.

'Who are you?'

His next words told her. 'Lise says you're the bleedin' interfering busybody who shopped me to the fuckin' social workers.'

Jenny made a break down the hall, into the living room, hoping to escape through the back door. He was too quick for her. Strong hands seized her by the throat, and he threw her against the wall by the kitchen. Her head hit the plaster with a thud that whirled her senses.

'Right, you bloody interfering cunt,' he hissed. 'What the fuck do you mean by settin' the social on me?'

Jenny was too dazed and terrified to reply.

'Answer me, you fuckin' bitch.' He tightened his grip on her throat and thrust her head against the wall again. Her knees gave way, but he hitched her up, pinioning her to the wall with his left arm braced against her chest, while his right hand maintained the hold on her throat. She could

181

feel his breath on her face, tainted with hate and alcohol.

'I was worried about Kelly', Jenny managed to say, her voice thick and unrecognisable against the pressure he was exerting.

'Kelly's none of your fuckin' business. I don't do kids. I made one fuckin' mistake with Lise, and tha's it! I'm married, right? I'm Kelly's an' Darren's dad now, right? I don't need no stupid, fuckin' bitch to fuck the whole thing up for me.' With each expletive, he shook her head back against the wall, as if her neck were cloth.

'Please, let me go,' Jenny whispered. 'Oh God ... Oh God...' Oh, where was Michael?

'Scared, are we? You thank Christ you're an ugly old cow, or I might really do you.' He seized her breast as if he was trying to unscrew it, and she cried out.

'Shut up!' he spat, increasing the pressure on her throat until the blood pounded in her head. In a last, desperate effort to free herself before she passed out, she tore at his hands, scratching, trying to prise his fingers away. She must have hurt him, for he let go of her throat suddenly and grabbed her left hand instead, bending her little finger back until the cartilage tore with searing agony. She heard herself moan, and to her shame, her bladder emptied down her leg to drench her trousers and spatter onto the carpet in a hot and mortifying stream.

At this final humiliation, he seemed to lose interest.

'You disgust me,' he said, taking her throat again and banging her head against the wall without venom, as if she was barely worth the waste of his effort. 'You're shit.'

He let her go suddenly, and she lurched forward over the arm of the sofa as his tread receded down the hall. Then the front door slammed shut and he was gone; he had been in the house scarcely three minutes. Jenny groaned and rolled off the sofa arm to collapse into a heap on the carpet, panting, shaking, hurting, alive, destroyed.

It was many minutes before her disordered senses began to reclaim her, insistently telling her of the torn agony of her left hand, the raw pounding of her head, the bruises on her crushed windpipe, the ache in her breast, and the cold, stinking wet of her trousers against her legs. The sodden patch of carpet accused her, and her first act on staggering to her feet was to fetch a towel from the kitchen to soak up the shameful evidence. Then she dragged herself up the stairs to the bathroom, threw the damp towel into the washing machine, painfully removed all her clothes with one trembling hand, and set the machine going on its hottest setting. For five minutes she stood under the shower, holding onto the wall for support, as if water alone could remove the hurt.

Downstairs again, she swallowed a generous dosage of strong pain-killers for her head, and made herself a mug of tea, lacing it with sugar because that was supposed to be good for shock. The journey to the kitchen meant passing the spot where the assault had taken place, and she had to force herself to move over it. The last thing she wanted was to stay in the room, but if she let herself give in now, the fear might develop into phobia, so she made herself go to her armchair, and curl up in its familiar depths; but she averted her eyes from the stain on the carpet and the wall against which she had been hurled. The joint of her little finger was red, swollen and throbbing, and she knew she ought to bind it up, but she had spent all her energy. Celestine jumped onto her lap, and settled against her chest. Jenny shut her eyes and sipped her tea, and waited for Michael.

He appeared half an hour later, poking his head round the living room door as he eased his small rucksack off his back and tossed it on the sofa.

'Sorry I'm late. We had a meeting about fundraising, and Baz wanted me there. I'd better go and pack - Allie will be here in a minute.' He had left the room before she could speak.

A few minutes later, the doorbell rang, and Jenny heard Michael thud downstairs to open it. He was making the explanations for his lateness with much laughter, and when he showed Alison through, she was smiling broadly.

'Look after Allie a moment, I won't be long,' Michael said, before disappearing upstairs again.

'I'm probably a little early, but you never know what the traffic'll be like on a Friday,' Alison said, sitting on the sofa.

Jenny couldn't think of anything to say, wasn't even sure a voice would emerge from her throat if she tried. She could only sit, her left hand limp in her lap, her right holding Celly to her, waiting for Michael to reappear, and notice.

'Michael did a brilliant assembly for us the other week. He had the kids in stitches.'

Jenny kept her eyes on the cat. A rustling told her Alison had given up the attempt to engage her in conversation, and had picked up a paper from the rack under the coffee table.

'I'm ready,' Michael announced in the doorway. He crossed the room to Jenny and squatted down beside her. She wanted above everything to throw herself into his arms and weep and be taken care of, but Alison was watching. In any case, Jenny's first instinct when hurt had always been denial; even with such a need as this weighing on her, she did not know how to ask for help. She raised her eyes to his, thinking he must see the distress in her face, but he had given all his attention to bidding Celestine farewell, bringing her to ecstasy as he stroked the long fur under her chin.

He kissed Jenny absently. 'I'll see you on Sunday,' he said as he stood up. 'We're going out in the evening, aren't we? Can you book us a table? The Italian place would be nice.'

'Yep.' The sound of her voice was rough.

'Are you OK?'

'My head...'

'Can I get you something?'

'I've had some pills.' She looked directly at him again, but he merely smiled, and laid a second perfunctory kiss on top of her head.

'Never mind, you've got the weekend without me, it's bound to help.' He turned away. 'Let's go.'

'Michael?' Jenny called. 'Michael ...' but no sound came out. The living room door shut behind them, then the front door, then came the sound of Alison's car engine fading away.

He had left her here alone in the silent house, oblivious to her anguish, and she didn't know how she would survive the next hour, let alone a night, a day and another night. She sat on, thinking that surely Michael would realise something had been wrong, would return somehow, or ring, and ask a question that broke through her defences, but there was nothing.

'What's up with Jenny?' Alison asked Michael as she drove away. 'She completely ignored me.'

'Sorry. She's been in one of her moods lately, and I'm still in her bad books for not telling her about Lisa. I suppose if she's got a headache, it's made her worse.'

'I was beginning to feel like something the cat brought in.'

Michael smiled wryly. 'Jen is a mistress at the art of conveying disapproval without a word. I don't feel too approved of either.'

'You're very patient.'

'She always comes round in the end. I used to try very hard to make up with her immediately, but I've come to the conclusion that it's better to let her find her own way out of her moods. Anyway, it's our first wedding anniversary on Sunday, I can always turn on the charm when I get back, if she's not dug herself out of it by then. In the meantime, I shall let you cheer me up.'

Alison took her eyes off the road for a second, to smile at him. It was nice to have attractive friends to lean on when your wife was treating you like dirt.

Saturday was fine and bright, but a chill had set in when dusk closed over the clear skies. 'It's a bit nippy, isn't it?' Michael said, thrusting his hands in his coat pockets and shivering as he followed the dimly lit path towards the St Barnabas sports hall.

Alison, muffled in her thick jacket, took his arm. 'I needed some fresh air. It's felt like such hard work this weekend. I can never take much at the end of term, and this one's been worse than usual with all the fuss about Nan, and worry about Lisa.'

'But it was only a temporary exclusion?'

'Yes, in the end. Once we'd had a case conference, it was clear permanent exclusion wouldn't solve anything.'

It was late. They had sat in the bar until well after eleven, when Alison had asked him to accompany her on this expedition to clear her head before bed. They had the grounds to themselves.

'How's Steve? Did you ring him?'

'I haven't bothered. The cancer hadn't spread, so his mum's got a good chance of recovery, but he still won't talk about it. I shouldn't complain, he was pretty much like that when we married, steady and silent, and all that.'

They left the college buildings behind them and slowed as the path before them became less clear.

'But back then, you thought it was romantic.'

'Maybe. I was pretty manic at college, I needed someone like him to calm me down. Then he managed to get me pregnant. I'd had a bad stomach, and didn't realise it would stop my pill working. So Steve very nobly offered to marry me, and I thought, why not? We'd been together for two years, I loved him well enough. We told our families, and got everything set for a hasty little ceremony, and then I lost the baby. I was only about eight or nine weeks gone, and all I felt at the time was relief that I'd be able to finish my teaching course after all. We still got married as we'd planned, though.'

'Do you ever think about it now - the baby?'

'Not really. Except that I'd have liked a daughter, and I sometimes wonder if it would have been a girl. I wanted another baby after Josh, but Steve said no. He never did like kids that much, especially now they compete with him for time on the computer.'

They passed the sports hall, a towering block on their right, and went cautiously ahead in the darkness. 'You sound bitter,' Michael said. 'Are things not going too well at the moment? I don't mean to pry, but...'

'Pry all you like. It could be a lot worse, I suppose, but I get fed up being married to someone who isn't in the slightest bit interested in anything I do, and who thinks I'm so downright repulsive that he doesn't come near me for months on end. I'm not sure he's ever made me feel good about myself. You know, when you kissed me in January, it was the best I've felt for years.'

They stopped by the fence at the furthest edge of the college grounds, leaning side by side on the cold, rough wood. It was dark here, only the faint neon glow from Thorleigh allowing them to see each other, pale shapes against the darker shadows. Michael looked across at Alison, and his heart went out to her. She was in his arms before he could think, and he was kissing her passionately, mouth and tongue aching from the intensity with which they came together.

'I didn't mean to do that,' Michael said, breathlessly drawing back from her many minutes later.

'I didn't mind. I'd forgotten kissing could be that erotic. Oh God, I want you, Mikey.' She reached up with her gloved hands and pulled his head to hers again.

Nan tiptoed down the stairs from her attic bedroom, glanced quickly about her, and slipped quietly through into Christopher's house. The door which gave access from his first floor to the first-floor landing was usually locked, with a key in a small, glass-fronted box on the wall beside it for use in an emergency. He had his own key, however, and had oiled the door and left it unlocked, so that she could visit him once everyone else had gone to bed. A little more fraught with risk, this, than their usual meetings. Christopher, stealing to her house under cover of darkness, and disappearing all too soon in the early hours, while she crept back to a bed still warm from their passion, to fall asleep in the memory of his arms. She'd have given anything to be able to wake with him too, but they had to accept the restrictions their situation demanded.

'We'll have to keep our distance in public for a little while,' he'd told her that first night, as they lay together on her spare-room bed.

'How long?' she'd asked. 'Are you ashamed of me?'

'No, of course not. But I shall get an enormous amount of flak once people know.' He'd been silent for a minute. 'This has come at a very bad time for me. Things are at a delicate stage with the St Barnabas Trust Fund. Donors are coming forward because they see it as a way of making a stand against women priests - if they discover I'm involved with you, they'll pull out. Once it's all formally set up, once the money's in, it won't matter if the donors disapprove of me. I'd like to keep quiet about us until then, that's all.'

'That sounds a little deceitful,' she'd told him. 'Maybe you ought to resign as Principal.'

'I'm not being hypocritical. I'm still as much against women priests as ever, and loving you isn't going to make any difference to that. *I* know that, but I can't expect others to see it that way. And I can't resign. It wouldn't be fair to back out at this stage.'

'But we can't have a secret affair ...'

The arguments had occupied too many hours of their precious snatched time alone together, but they had reached a rapprochement of sorts. She felt no stirrings of conscience as she made her way down the passage to his bedroom.

Christopher was sitting up in bed with a dark-green dressing gown round his shoulders, reading. He put the book down, and smiled his welcome.

'Sorry it's so late, but I wanted to be sure everyone had gone to their rooms.' She took off her robe and squeezed into the narrow bed beside him.

'I've got the villa,' he said. 'Two weeks, starting in the middle of August. I persuaded one of my former students to change the dates he was taking his family.'

'I've never been to Crete...' Nan could see herself already, relaxing in the Mediterranean sun in the small villa that had been donated to St Barnabas years ago by a Greek Orthodox monk who'd studied at the college. Two weeks, just herself and Christopher, and a double bed, with any luck.

She began to explore his body, from his shoulders, straight and broad with the muscles firm beneath slackening skin. Along his back, running her fingers down the line of his buttocks. Back to caress his chest, with its coarse, scanty hair; feeling the thickening of his waist, and his soft, flat stomach. She rolled on top of him, laughing.

'What's funny?'

'"In sexual activity, the male takes the initiative and the female receives. The male is active and the female passive". Christopher Ridgefield, Collected Works.' She kissed his nose, and he pushed her over onto her back, nearly sending them both crashing to the floor. Nan squealed.

'Ssshhhh! One sound from you and I'm dead,' he hissed, and stopped her mouth with his.

By the time Michael and Alison got back to the main building, the outside lights had signalled midnight by extinguishing themselves. Though one or two of the bedrooms were still illuminated, there was no one else around downstairs. Above and to the right of the front door, a faint glow came through the curtains of Ridgefield's bedroom.

'I'm frozen,' Alison said, as they went up the steps. 'Do you want a hot drink?'

They emptied their pockets for change and bought coffee from the machine, then went through to sit side by side at a table in the abandoned bar, with its stale air and ghosts of conversation. It was strange to look at each other with the memory of their embrace written across their faces. Michael studied her over his coffee, poleaxed by intolerable desire.

'I don't understand this,' he said, 'I shouldn't be feeling like this about you. I love Jenny. I'm still in love with her. I make love to her. Things aren't great between us at the moment, but that's because we're still adjusting to being married, not because we don't care about each other.' He spoke slowly, holding Jenny in his mind, and frowning slightly. 'I couldn't bear hurting her. And yet I find myself wanting to go to bed with you.' His voice was unsteady. 'I really want you, Allie, and I don't know what to do about it.'

'Don't look so worried. The last thing I want to do is to break your marriage up, or mine. I have got two kids, after all, and they need their dad. And adultery's hardly OK behaviour for ordinands - which is what you're going to be as well, one day. On the other hand,' she said, taking his hand, 'we can't help loving each other, and I can't see it would be so very wrong to show it with a little kiss every now and then.' She leaned forward and touched her lips to his, and when he put his arms round her, the energy of her response robbed him of sense, so entirely different was it from Jenny's diffident passion.

It was past one when they eventually rose from their seats to go to bed. The college was quiet but for the creaks that echoed occasionally as it settled for the night. Under the faint luminescence of the secondary lighting of the first-floor landing, they kissed for a last time before parting to go to their rooms.

Michael got himself into bed, and lay on his back, trying not to think about what he'd done. He mustn't be alone with Allie again, that was for sure. God, he'd wanted nothing more than to bring her to his bed, and he didn't know how he'd managed to say goodnight. He'd got an erection as big as a telegraph pole, and she must have noticed, wound around him as she had been.

A small sound startled him from his ragged prayers. A strip of light ran down beside the door, was filled by a shadow, and disappeared. A rustle of movement whispered across the room, and suddenly Alison was there kneeling by his bed, tugging at him.

'Michael? Michael, wake up!'

He turned onto his side. 'What is it? What are you doing here?'

'Guess what I've just seen? Nan coming out of Ridgefield's house, and kissing him! They're having an affair. They must be.' Her voice was low but excited. 'Oh, why should we resist, while they do what they like? Let me get into bed with you, Mikey. I'm freezing.' She slid in under his covers before he could object, and pushed herself against him. 'Make love to me. If they can do it, why can't we?'

'They're not married to other people for a start,' Michael whispered, rolling over to lie face down on the bed to conceal his state, with his head on his arms. He could feel the wall, cold and hard against his side through his covers, and Allie, soft and warm squashing up against him, her arm creeping across his back. He spoke to her from under the shelter of his elbow. 'Surely you're mistaken. Perhaps there was an emergency of some sort.'

'I tell you, I saw them kissing. I came down to use the bathroom, and I was tiptoeing back to the stairs so as not to wake anyone, when I heard a sound. Then that fire door from Ridgefield's house opened, and he was standing there in his dressing gown, bare legs, bare chest. I thought he might have heard me, and come to check up, but then Nan appeared, in her pyjamas and dressing gown, and put her arms round him. They were kissing really passionately. She's sleeping with him, she must be. And if they can think it's OK, why shouldn't we? I love you. Oh, Mikey, make love to me. It can't be wrong.'

Eight

Michael had no time to be shocked at the thought of Nan having an affair, with Christopher Ridgefield of all people. Alison's hands were taking his head, bringing his lips to hers, and her every touch increased his arousal until his body was screaming at him to take her. He dared not move. The slightest inclination towards her and he would be on her and in her, careless of the consequences. Fighting himself with reserves he had not suspected, he pulled his mouth away from hers.

'I can't. I'm not going to be unfaithful to Jenny. For God's sake, Allie,' he said, as she slipped her hand inside his boxer shorts and caressed his buttocks, 'it's my bloody wedding anniversary this weekend, and I'm not going to spend it making love to another woman. Look, we'll talk about this in the morning. You have to go.'

Alison moved her hand back to clutch his arm. 'Now you hate me. I can't help loving you. Please don't send me away. Mikey, please, I can't bear it.'

'I don't hate you. You know what I feel about you, but you have to go. Don't torture me. Please.'

She left his bed slowly, dragging her feet to the door, and then she was gone, trailing her disappointment and bitterness and the promise she had offered him of ecstatic consummation.

He remained frozen, face down on his bed long after she had gone, except that his body was trembling from the ordeal. He wanted two things in equal measure: for Allie to come back and silence his objections with her passion, and for his wife magically to appear, to forgive him, and exorcise him of this excruciating infatuation.

It did not require Michael's turmoil to leap the miles to disturb Jenny's rest, for she had not slept at all. She had got through the previous evening by keeping the television on, watching anything remotely distracting: gardening programmes, comedies she might have laughed at the week before, news bulletins on four different channels. Tonight, too, the doors had been locked and bolted all evening. She left the lights on all night, and took a sharp kitchen knife with her to bed, knowing it to be a melodramatic gesture, but needing to feel she could do something if Andy came back.

Michael had failed her. She'd tell him one day, and he would be sympathetic and guilt-ridden, but nothing would ever make up for the fact that the one time in her life she had really needed him, he had been too caught up in his own affairs to notice. And without Michael, she had nobody. Well, there was God. But what use was a spirit who shared the pain, without warm, solid arms to hold her, real hands to wipe her face? There were no friends she could call on, only people who would come to her because they were professionals, and paid to care: her colleagues at work, her own GP, Caroline and Peter. She would have to be much more badly hurt before she'd feel able to enlist their services. As she lay in bed, holding a cat who wouldn't stay long, she looked into herself and at the world she had created around her, and realised that she was and always had been, fundamentally alone.

Bright sun through thin curtains woke Michael earlier than he would have liked after a restless night. He got up and dressed quickly, before heading for morning prayers in the chapel, where he was playing the small organ. From where he sat, he could see Alison at the back, pale and drawn, and avoiding looking in his direction. Because he was watching both Nan and Christopher closely, he saw them looking round for each other with studied casualness, and exchanging a single glance and snatched smile. It confirmed for him that, however unlikely it seemed, Allie's story was true. Which all feels like something of a mess, he thought. Nan's the only one I'd have felt able to talk to about Allie, but here she is having an affair with a man ... that surely isn't how she kept her job? I can't believe that ... and Allie's right. When you see someone you respect being underhand like that, it makes it much harder to resist temptation yourself. Oh God. I don't understand why I feel like I do about Allie, it's just as well I got the strength to hold her off last night, because it was a close-run thing. I'd be safer avoiding her in the future, but look at her. She's feeling awful, and she hates herself, I can't let her suffer like that. I've got to do something to show her I still care about her...

Whether by chance, or by her own design, Michael had no chance to speak to Alison alone until they met up to take their cases to her car after lunch. She talked determinedly about the morning session as they walked towards the car park, but once inside the car, he placed his hand over hers as she reached for the gear.

'You mustn't feel too bad about last night, Allie. I really wanted you, it's just... I couldn't, for your sake and for mine.'

Her head was bowed, and he could barely hear her reply above the idling of the engine. 'I'm so embarrassed. What you must think of me.'

'What I think is that you're gorgeous, and you're my friend. I want it to be like you said before - we keep on being close, and maybe you let me kiss you sometimes, only we keep our clothes on.' He hazarded a smile, and she returned it nervously.

'Do you really mean that?' Her face lifted. 'I thought you'd never want to speak to me again.'

'Why on earth not? Maybe if it had happened, I'd have been so shocked with myself I wouldn't have dared to be alone with you again, but we managed to control ourselves, and I'm sure we can find a way of dealing with it. Anyway,' he grinned, 'I'm relying on you to give me lifts.'

He let go of her hand, and she manoeuvred out of the car park and drove towards the main road.

Michael's predominant feeling as he kissed Alison's cheek, and got out of her car outside his house, was of achievement. He had resisted almost overwhelming temptation, and could greet Jenny without guilt. The flowers he'd bought from the garden centre on the way home were not a sop to his conscience but, he felt, a genuine gift of celebration for their first year of marriage. Whatever else went on, she would always come first.

He let himself in quietly through the front door, wanting to surprise Jenny with his offering, and walked softly into the living room. The first thing he noticed was that the furniture had been rearranged, with the sofa drawn forward from the wall, so that they would have to walk behind it to get to the kitchen, instead of in front. Secondly, he noticed Jenny, standing looking out of the patio window at the garden, her arms folded in front of her. When he said hello, a few feet behind her, she jumped violently, turning round with terror on her face. As soon as she saw it was him, she struggled to control herself, but her eyes remained wide and fearful, and she was breathing rapidly through dry, parted lips.

He dropped the flowers on the table and put his hands on her shoulders. 'Sorry. I didn't mean to startle you. What is it? You look as if you thought I was an evil axe-murderer come to ... Jenny, what's happened?' Far from smiling at his joke, she had started to shake, and he noticed how pale she was. Her left hand began the journey towards her throat, then dropped, but not before his attention had been drawn to the strapping around her fingers, and the brutal purple indentations on her throat.

He lifted her chin with his fingers, and examined the bruises underneath. 'What's happened?' he asked again. 'Has someone attacked you?' She shut her eyes. 'Oh God,' he whispered, 'you've not been raped have you?'

She shook her head, and opened her eyes again. 'It was Andy,' she faltered. 'Lisa's step-dad. On Friday afternoon. He burst in and ... and threw me around. I'm alright. It's sudden noises. I keep thinking he's coming back.'

'Friday? Not before I went to Thorleigh? Is that why you were ...? Oh, Jenny.' He took her in his arms, and she buried her face in his shoulder. His hands, gently stroking her hair, found the massive lump on the back of her head, and felt her wince. 'Your head too?'

'He got me by the throat, and kept hitting my head against the wall. I thought he was going to kill me.'

Michael led her to the sofa and sat her down, keeping his arms around her. 'Why on earth didn't you tell me? I can't believe you let me go away for the weekend without saying anything.'

'There wasn't any chance,' she said, her voice thin and uneven. 'Alison was there, and you were in a hurry. And I didn't know what to say. I was so pathetic, and it was all my fault. You told me not to interfere. I thought you'd say I got what I deserved.'

'You can't believe that.' Michael felt a tear roll down his face. 'Oh, Jen, stop behaving as if you don't matter to me. I love you. I die when something like this happens to you.'

He nuzzled her curls as he held her to him in bed that night. Shudders of memory ran through her as she lay in the dark trying to sleep. Even in his presence, she jumped at the familiar noises of the house creaking around them. Sex would be on hold for a while, he understood that, and even so it was nothing, what he felt for Alison, nothing, compared to this gut-rending love he bore his wife.

As Michael waited for Alison to arrive to take him to St Barnabas for the first weekend of the summer term, he was conscious of how nervous he was about seeing her again. He had spoken to her briefly on the telephone towards the end of the Easter holidays to arrange the lift, but it hadn't been possible to tell how she was feeling. For himself, he was determined to re-establish their friendship on a safer footing, to take a step back from the physical expression they'd fallen into. He was still concerned about Jenny, and the determination with which she had tried to put the attack behind her. She had refused to report it to the police, saying she couldn't cope with making her humiliation known to so many strangers, and had dived back into her arduous routines on Monday morning as if nothing had happened. Michael had, however, begun to understand her profound need to feel in control of her life, and had learnt not to take all her statements at face value. He had taken her away for a few days, but though she claimed the rest had completed her recovery, she was frequently woken by nightmares that sent her creeping, trembling, to his arms.

When Alison's Escort drew up, he was talking with Jenny in the front garden, discussing the possibility of turning the threadbare patch of grass outside the dining room window into something more decorative. He waved a hand at Alison, and turned back to Jenny, standing by the front door with her arms folded.

He put his hands on her shoulders. 'Are you sure you'll be alright? I can come back overnight if you want.'

'I'll be fine. Really.'

Michael brushed the hair lightly back from her face, and kissed her lips. She hugged him briefly, then stepped back, a solid figure in a long blouse over wide, patterned trousers, her hair back in her eyes again. Then he got into the car.

'Hi. It's good to see you. How are you?' he asked as Alison drove off towards the main road.

'Fine. Steve came to church on Easter Sunday. He's never done that before.'

'Brilliant! What did he make of it?'

'He said it didn't do anything for him, but he wanted to see the sort of thing I was going to be getting up to. He was actually being quite kind over the holidays - he had a week off, and took us all out a few times, and he even took me out for dinner.'

Alison was definitely looking less tense. Her smile lit her eyes, and her hair shone. He wondered if Steve's kindness had extended to making love to her. The question framed itself in his mind as a jealous accusation, and he bit it back.

'What have you been up to?' she asked.

'We went over to Croydon to see my ex-fiancee get married, and then we had a few days in Scotland.'

'Oh, lovely. A spontaneous thing, was it?'

'Yes. We hadn't done anything for our wedding anniversary, so we had a holiday instead.'

'A romantic second honeymoon?' Alison said lightly.

'Not exactly.' Jenny had let him make love to her again while they were in Callender, cautiously, as if testing whether she still belonged with him, but one night with a tense, anxious woman was hardly a second honeymoon.

Alison parked in the car park at St Barnabas, and looked across at him before she opened her door. 'Do we get to meet this weekend?'

Michael hesitated.

'You've changed your mind, haven't you? I knew you would.'

There were tears in her eyes, and he reached for her hand. 'It's not that. Only things have happened since the last weekend. I don't think we should go to each other's rooms.'

'Have you told Jenny or something? Or - she's not pregnant, is she?'

'No to both those things. Oh, perhaps I'd better tell you.' He let go of her hand. 'Lisa's step-dad beat Jenny up for reporting him to social services. He'd barged in half an hour before I got home on the Friday you picked me up to come here. She was in pain, and in shock, and I never noticed. I went off and left her for the whole weekend.'

'How awful. That's why she seemed to be in a mood. Oh God, how crass of me not to realise something was wrong. Is she alright now?'

'Yes, but she was very shaken.'

'That's why you were being kind to her when you left home just now - you were worried about leaving her on her own.'

'I don't need an excuse to be kind to her, Allie. She's my wife. I love her.'

'Of course. And you're feeling so guilty, you daren't touch me. I understand.'

'I do want to talk to you, I just don't feel comfortable about being alone with you. I don't think I should kiss you again. You're too damn sexy.'

So she wouldn't be resting in his arms this weekend, Alison sighed to herself as she followed him into the college. All her anticipation at seeing him had come to nothing. He had never been far from her thoughts during the holidays, visiting her and making love to her in the elaborate fantasy world she had painstakingly constructed around him. Steve's belated attempt to reestablish their relationship had passed her by. She hadn't even

195

been sure whether she'd wanted him showing an interest in church: this, after years of praying for it. When he did want sex, she closed her eyes, kept her face from his beard, and pretended it was Michael. She settled her scruples by telling herself that her relationship with Michael was divinely inspired, and would have its fruition through some miraculous intervention in the future. If only Andy had been armed - no, that was a terrible thought. Far better if Jenny and Steve could decamp together, so that she and Michael could, after a suitable period of devastation, comfort each other with perfect propriety. Unlikely, perhaps, but God moved in a mysterious way. More often than was comfortable, her conscience pricked her, but it could make no inroads on her passion. Sometimes she thought she'd do anything for one night in his arms.

According to his own lights, Michael knew, he should not have objected to Nan's relationship with Ridgefield. They were free agents, and he had always maintained that sex was perfectly acceptable if you were in a loving relationship. Yet he felt betrayed by Nan's actions. Perhaps it was the clandestine nature of the liaison, perhaps simply the complications it had introduced into his friendship with Alison, perhaps the fact that he no longer felt comfortable about confiding in Nan when he had so much to confide about. While affable enough in her company, he was slightly uncomfortable with her, especially when he observed the interplay between herself and her lover.

'Here's the man who has the answers!' cried Jackie, beckoning Ridgefield towards the dining-table where she sat with Michael, Alison and Nan. 'Canon Ridgefield, do come and settle a dispute for us. What exactly is the point of a celibate priesthood?'

Ridgefield stood beside the table with his Sunday lunch on a plate in his hand, and looked embarrassed. 'What a question. I'm not sure I can say.'

'Of course you can, you've written a book on the subject, haven't you?' She pulled out a chair for him. 'Sit down here, and tell us!'

Ridgefield, hesitated, scanning the faces at the table. Nan, who had been studiously concentrating on removing a strand of gristle from a slice of roast beef ever since Jackie had called him over, glanced quickly up at him. As if that were a signal permitting him to stay, he took the seat Jackie had indicated.

'Yes, *The Celibate Heart*,' Jackie continued. 'With that wonderful chapter about women being better at celibacy because they don't have the same sexual urges as men. Don't you remember, Nan, you read us extracts? It was hilarious.'

'I don't remember...' Nan said.

'Of course you do!' Jackie proceeded to summarise Ridgefield's arguments, oblivious of the discomfort she was engendering among the others at the table.

'No, I wasn't at my best there, was I?' Ridgefield admitted. 'My publisher insisted I needed something about women at the last minute, but given I was living in an all-male theological college at the time, I didn't have much chance for research. I'd stand by the rest of it. There are circumstances in which it's right to be single-minded, free from the responsibilities of family life, and from the distractions of sex.'

'Why should sex be a distraction? It's what life's about, isn't it?' asked Jackie. 'Doesn't it make you a proper human being? Come on Michael, Alison, you're both married, you don't think sex distracts you from the real business of life, do you?'

'Doesn't that depend on how good it is?' Ridgefield asked, before Michael could reply.

They all stared at him.

'So I'm told,' he added, his eyes amused. 'Can I fetch anyone dessert?'

'I think Ridgefield's up to something,' Jackie told Tyrone later that afternoon when he returned to college for the new term. He joined her on the bench by the front doors where she had been sitting reading, awaiting his arrival. 'I saw him a few evenings ago at the petrol station on the bypass, wearing an open-necked check shirt and brown trousers. I hardly recognised him. He didn't notice me - he was being very quick, he only put in five quid's worth, and he was off.'

'That is interesting,' Ty said. 'His sort never leave off their black suits and dog collars. They say in college they had an outing to the seaside a couple of years ago, and he sat in a deckchair with the temperature in the eighties, complete with clerical uniform. Except that he took his shoes and socks off in honour of it being a day off. If he's going round in casual clothes, it must be because he's doing something he's ashamed of.'

'There's definitely something different about him. He was joking at lunch today about having a good sex life, and he's much more cheerful and relaxed than he used to be. I said to Nan, didn't she think he seemed different, but she put it down to him having had a good holiday.'

Ty rubbed his mouth thoughtfully. 'It'd be worth keeping an eye on him. We might not have got anywhere with getting the Programme out of

197

here, but if we dug up some dirt on Ridgefield, and got him chucked out, it'd be worth something. You know, there were a couple of times at the end of last term he was out, and came back in the early hours. I can see the drive and his car-parking space from my room, and I was up late finishing off essays, so I saw him. D'you reckon he's got a woman somewhere? Or a man?'

'I think it's a woman. Nan said something about how he'd got into trouble with a woman in his first curacy, but she wouldn't give any details.'

'I wonder if we could find out?'

The summer came with a heatwave that melted tarmac, dried up reservoirs, and multiplied wasps in plague proportions. Wednesday evening lectures at St Barnabas were conducted with the windows open to the languid air, as the sun lowered itself behind the trees. Michael loved the warmth. He took to cycling to Thorleigh on Wednesday evenings, and to Nottling for his continuing work in Alison's school. What with running the youth club, helping Baz to set up a summer play-scheme for the Rows, playing the organ at St Martin's for a glut of summer weddings, and playing tennis, he sailed through the term getting browner, happier and fitter as the days wore on.

The only drawback was how little he saw of his wife. Jenny had added cases of severe sunburn to the normal surge of infections, allergies and depressions that filled her surgery, and struggled with paperwork late into the night, even when she wasn't on call. She denied that there was anything wrong, other than pressure of work, but he continually felt himself to be pushed away, physically and emotionally. The understanding that had once been between them had departed like a dream exposed to daylight. He guessed that, like a child who cries and learns no one will come, her trust in him had been fractured by his neglect after Andy's attack, and his only hope was that his patient loving might restore her to him.

In the meantime, though he talked to Alison at length in the safety of the St Barnabas bar, or the school common room, he managed to avoid being alone with her until the summer school at the end of July threw them together for a week. The heatwave had continued. Students spent sleepless nights in the airless heat of their sun-warmed rooms, and fanned themselves as they sat in the lecture rooms attempting to concentrate on their theology. In the afternoon breaks, many of them simply lay out on the grass in the sun, or under the trees, or sought refuge in the pool. Only a few, like Michael, were more energetic. He had just come back to his room after showering away the excesses of sweat he'd gained on the tennis courts when Alison tapped on his door.

'Can I talk to you?'

'Sure. Close your eyes while I get my shorts on.' He swapped his towel for some shorts, and draped it over the rail by the sink. 'Do you want to go outside?'

'No, not really.' She shut the door behind her. 'You don't object to me coming here, do you? I wouldn't like you to feel compromised.'

'I don't,' he said, surprised at the note of bitterness in her voice. He combed his wet hair in front of the mirror as she sat down on his bed.

'You seem to have been avoiding me over the last few weeks,' she said. 'I don't like being treated like a leper.'

'I didn't think I was. I've talked to you lots of times.'

'You know what I mean. It's not been the same. I think you owe it to me to tell me if things have changed for you. It's not fair to shut me out suddenly, and leave me feeling awful, really awful, for letting you know what I feel about you, and then you don't care any more.'

Michael pulled a chair away from the table under the window, turned it round, and sat astride it with his arms on its back, watching her. She was wearing shorts and a cotton vest that clung to her small breasts, and her bare limbs were tanned. He tried to keep his attention on her face.

'It's not like that. I still think you're fantastic, and you know how much I like talking to you about things.' He smiled, but she didn't respond.

'Then why are you avoiding me? I miss you, Michael. I miss you never hugging me any more, I miss us not sharing personal things like we used to. You were the one person I felt valued with, and now I don't have anyone.'

'I thought Steve was being nicer to you these days.'

'That was short-lived. He's gone back to his usual state. All picture and no sound, till I want to kick his bloody screen in. Anyway, having you hold me is worth a dozen bouts of sex with Steve. I want affection from you, Mikey, that's all. I know it can't be anything more than that. I want to talk to you, and feel you still care about me. I hate it when you shut me out.'

Michael was moved by her misery. 'I don't mean to do that. Come here.' He got off his chair and held out his arms, hugging her to him with compassion. It was a mistake. Memory flooded his senses as she clung to him, her scent, the taste of her lips, the feel of her breasts against his chest, and her low voice whispering irresistibly *make love to me*. Her mouth was very near to his, and it was a long time since he had been able

199

to kiss anyone properly.

Alison returned his kisses hungrily. 'I could take it off,' she breathed, as Michael's hands strayed over the the thin cotton rib of her top.

'No,' he said, moving his hands back to her waist, 'this is as far as we go.'

'Why? Nan and Christopher didn't stop there.' Her lips nuzzled the smooth skin of his chest, crept down towards the dip of his stomach. Michael ran his fingers through her hair, and gently dragged her back.

'I mean it, Allie, no further.' He disentangled himself from her and propped himself on the edge of the table. 'I really want to carry on being your friend, but I can't do that if you keep trying to seduce me. I'm not strong-minded enough. And however much we might wish it was different, the fact remains that you're Steve's wife, and I'm married to Jenny, and adultery isn't an option - not unless we want to jack in our faith as well as our marriages, and I'm not prepared to do that, even if you are.'

Alison smiled meekly, and he took it for acceptance. They went outside to sit under the trees and talked more deeply than they had for many weeks, but from behind her dark glasses, Alison was thinking: next time, I won't let you stop me, next time.

Nine

On the final Saturday of the summer school, students' families were invited to supper and a barn dance. Though Michael would be busy providing the music for much of the night, he had wanted Jenny there, and, after a week away from him, she had felt obliged to agree. She drove over to Thorleigh late in the afternoon, dressed up in a fitted floral dress, determined to make amends for being out of sorts on her visit nearly a year before.

To her surprise, Tyrone was in the office, directing visitors to the appropriate places.

'I didn't expect to find you here,' she said, leaning over the hatch.

'I've been helping Gloria out in the office for the holidays. Earns me a few brownie points, and besides, I'm keeping an eye on what Ridgefield gets up to.'

'What do you mean?'

Voices behind her indicated another party of visitors. 'I'll tell you later. Mike's practising for tonight - follow the noise if you want to find him.'

Jenny walked round the main building, with the faint notes of an Irish jig growing stronger as she made her way across the grass. A cable had been run out through an open window to power the electric keyboard at which Michael sat, energetically accompanying three other students on violins and flute. Jenny sat down on the dry grass to watch. He'd lived in shorts this summer, and his chest and back were almost as bronzed as the skin beneath the dark hair on his arms and legs. At this remove, her desire for him was as intense as it had ever been; she didn't understand why it should evaporate so quickly when he took her in his arms. The musicians were playing faster and faster, laughing with each other until the flautist collapsed, out of breath.

Michael got up, stretched, and came over to see her.

'Hi,' he said, sliding his hands round her waist as she stood up, and kissing her enthusiastically. She could feel his body through the cotton of her dress, sweaty, sticky and warm against hers. He undid her top button. 'Do you want to come and see my room? I need to shower and change.'

'I don't think I'd better. I'll wait here.'

'Sure? This hot weather makes me horny, can't you tell?'

She could. He was looking at her with eyes narrowed by lust, and she wanted to run away. 'No, Michael. You'll be home tomorrow. Maybe then.'

'It's been a long time, Jen.'

'I know. I'm sorry, I can't seem to relax ...' He was looking hurt, and it made her feel all the more uncomfortable. 'Tomorrow night. I promise.'

'You've promised before. I know,' he held up a hand as she began to protest, 'I'm not pushing you. I'll go and have a cold shower.'

It was growing dark by the time the dancing got under way. The remnant of the day's sun had reddened the western skyline, and bats were darting under the trees. Gradually, the skyline faded as the lights in the college grounds grew brighter.

Jenny sat with Michael and his friends after the buffet supper, drinking, laughing, and slapping mosquitoes with loud claps in the evening air, until he got up to set the entertainment in progress. For much of the evening, she continued to be a spectator, smiling as the staff, students and their families essayed complicated patterns of country dances with more enthusiasm than skill. From where she sat, she saw the moment when Ridgefield appeared, walking through the grounds to be annexed by an exuberant Jackie. He stood, a black-suited figure blending into the night, smiling as he resisted Jackie's attempts to drag him towards the dancing. Roly and Nan approached them, and Ridgefield gave in, taking his place with Jackie in the next set to the accompaniment of mild cheers. At the end, he came to sit on the vacant seat beside Jenny, dabbing sweat from his brow with a folded white handkerchief.

'Never again! I haven't done that for years. I was afraid I'd do myself some damage, and that wouldn't do. I'm supposed to be off on holiday in a couple of days.'

'Anywhere nice?'

'Crete. The college owns a villa near Rethymnon, so I'm going to get away from everything for a couple of weeks. I've been before, but it doesn't pall. How about you?'

'We're not going anywhere until the autumn. Do you let your villa to Programme students? I'd quite like to try Crete.'

Ridgefield stayed for several minutes, discussing the villa and the countryside around it, then excused himself, saying he needed to get a drink. Within a short time, his place beside Jenny had been taken by Tyrone.

'You look like you're having fun - having the pants bored off you by old Ridgefield, were you?'

'No. He was telling me about the college villa in Rethymnon, in Crete. He's about to go there on his holidays. He was saying Michael and I might be able to use it.'

'Very generous!'

'He is,' Jenny said. 'I like him. I don't agree with him on everything, but he's got a lot of integrity.'

'Integrity? Him? Hypocritical bastard, more like. All that stuff he bangs on about with us, how we're not allowed to have relationships while we're in training - yet there he is, screwing some poor woman night after night. That's why I've been watching him, hanging around here, trying to get some evidence. He goes off in the evenings, dressed casually, which is unheard of for priests like him, and comes back at two in the morning. I've tried following him once or twice on my scooter, but he speeds off in his bloody great Audi, and I've no chance.'

'You don't know he's having an affair,' she ventured. 'He might be visiting someone in hospital miles away, he might be seeing someone without sleeping with them. And why shouldn't he have a relationship? He's not a monk.' Across the grass, she could see Alison bending over Michael at his keyboard, laughing with him. Jackie was taking Ridgefield's glass from his hand, and pushing him towards Nan. Excited voices could be heard urging him to dance with her; to Jenny's surprise, given his earlier complaints, he succumbed.

Ty smirked. 'Don't be naive, Jen. I know what he's like. He's had affairs before. There was this married woman when he was a curate. Mum talked to this old priest who was his incumbent, and got the whole story out of him. I bet he's done that kind of thing all the time, only he's got away with it. It's not right, it brings the whole church into disrepute, and I can't stand seeing people like that being respected, getting promotion. I'm going to get proof, and then he'll have to resign, and serve him right.'

Jenny had stopped listening. She was watching Ridgefield and Nan whirling each other down the centre of the set, and instinctively knew that she had discovered the identity of Nan's lover. A man who'd been known to have relationships. A conservative sort of man who didn't like the idea of condoms. An obvious candidate really, someone Nan had worked with daily for months, and an attractive man in his way. To think she'd liked and respected him! She had always had doubts about Nan, but to discover that Ridgefield had sacrificed all his principles to have an affair with a woman priest felt like a personal betrayal of her trust in him. Ty was burbling on. Some spy - he had no idea. The dance ended. Alison had her hands on

203

Michael's shoulders, fondling him as he collapsed over the keyboard. Oh God, and they'd had all week together... all those nights ...

'Could you get me another glass of wine?' she asked Tyrone.

As he walked off towards the makeshift bar, Nan came and took the vacant seat, breathing heavily.

'Whew, I shouldn't do too much of that at my age!'

'You seemed to be enjoying it. You obviously get on very well with Ridgefield.'

Nan scrutinised her more closely under the garden lights, and Jenny waited patiently for recognition.

'I know your face, but I can't put a name to you ...' Nan said, frowning.

'I'm Jenny Turner, Michael's wife. You met me at the introductory weekend, and then again at the family planning clinic in February. As I say, you and Canon Ridgefield seem to have developed a good relationship. Some might say intimate.'

Nan's hand went to her mouth. 'How do you know? You won't tell?'

'Nobody told me. I have eyes in my head, and I can put two and two together. Don't worry, I'm not in the habit of broadcasting my patients' contraceptive arrangements.'

'No, but... Excuse me.' Nan got up and walked off. Jenny watched her seeking Ridgefield in the crowd, and speaking briefly to him. He looked once in Jenny's direction, and a few seconds later disappeared in the direction of the college, back to the safety of his house.

Ty came back with their drinks. 'Having a cosy heart-to-heart with Nan, were you? I thought you didn't like her.'

'I was merely commenting on how enthusiastically she was dancing with Ridgefield,' Jenny said disingenuously. 'I said they seemed to have formed a good relationship. But she walked off.'

Ty turned towards her frowning; the lights reflected in his glasses like oncoming headlights. 'You don't think ... not Nan ... that's not possible. Even he couldn't be that hypocritical. And everyone knows they can't stand each other. Look at that fight they had ... he practically kicked her out ... only he didn't. My God, that explains everything! Ridgefield's having an affair with Nan! God, if I could catch them together, he'd be ruined. What's the betting she's going off to Crete with him? I could follow them, I could take my camera...' His forehead had begun to glisten with sweat.

'No, Ty, don't interfere. Or go and have a quiet word with the bishop if you have to do something. You don't want the papers to get hold of it. They'd have a field day.'

Ty smiled and patted her knee. 'Don't worry, Jen, I won't do anything I shouldn't.'

Lisa had never been abroad before. Tracey hadn't been able to afford it, and now that she'd chucked Andy out, the chances of them all holidaying together somewhere exotic had nosedived. Len's offer to take her and a friend along with Gran for a week in the sun had filled her with excitement.

'Is there anywhere you specially fancy?' Stella had said over tea shortly before the end of the summer term. 'Spain? Greece? I wouldn't mind Greece myself, I fancy myself as Shirley Valentine.' Lisa had got used to the idea of her gran having a boyfriend by now, especially now she'd got to know Len a little better, and decided that he was OK. She was so excited at the prospect of adventure that she talked about it constantly at school the next day. Mrs Thompson put the idea of Crete into her mind during a chance conversation over lunch:

'The Principal of the college I go to was telling me that Rethymnon in Crete was really good. Do you remember me talking about the Minoan civilisation...?'

Lisa didn't remember, but when they went into the travel agent in Leathwell and saw a special offer of a week in Rethymnon, it seemed like it was meant. They'd booked up immediately, Len and Stella, and Lisa and her friend Julie, and three weeks later, they'd been decanted from a crowded plane into the searing heat of a Grecian summer.

'The idea is to shag everything in sight,' Julie told her as they got dressed up for their first evening out on the town. It sounded like a recipe for a good time to Lisa, and she spent four nights in a row groping sun-struck, drunken lads from Tyneside, Essex, and who cared where, until Julie went down with a stomach-bug, and she found herself alone for the evening, while Stella and Len went out to visit an English-style bar.

Lisa went to sit outside under the vine-covered trellis near the hotel pool. The local band that provided live music each night was playing, and several older couples were dancing. Looking round for an empty table, she noticed a man she'd seen once or twice around the hotel. He wasn't much to look at - youngish, but plump, with a sun-reddened skin, greasy, light hair and metal-rimmed glasses with naff black shades that clipped on to them - but he seemed familiar. Tonight he sat on his own with a glass of beer in front of him, typing into a laptop computer. Lisa decided to investigate.

'Not bringin' your work on holiday, are you?' she asked. 'You should be out enjoying yerself.' She sat down, and crossed her legs, noting the way his eyes lingered on the expanse of thigh her movement had exposed below her short, tight, white dress. 'So what are you, a writer or something? Are you gonna put me in it?'

'I'm a journalist,' he'd said icily. 'I'm working on an important story, tracking down some fraudsters.'

'Are you? I got in the papers once. I ran away when I was a kid, an' it was headlines in the Nottling Echo.'

He looked at her with slight interest. 'I know Nottling. I live in Leathwell.'

'I'm sure I know you. D'you ever go to Charlies?'

'I don't go to nightclubs. I've got better things to do.'

'What, like working?'

'Yes.' He bent over his screen again, and recognition suddenly hit Lisa. She'd met this guy on Michael's doorstep, when he'd been having that party for people off the course he and Mrs Thompson were doing, so if this bloke was there, perhaps he was going to be a vicar too. Poor little sod, here all by himself with his computer, but even he hadn't been able to keep his eyes off her.

It crossed her mind that it would be a good laugh to get off with him. 'You oughta take a break some time. Come on, have a dance with me.' Lisa smiled encouragingly, and leaned forward to add emphasis to her already prominent cleavage. He stared at her, flustered and struggling for words. In the end, he let her persuade him, and put his arms awkwardly round her waist to sway slowly to the sickly music issuing from the band. His hands strayed over her, and she pressed herself closer to him, arms around his neck, attempting to kiss him.

He pulled away. 'I can't. Got to keep an eye on my stuff.'

'Why don't you take it to your room? It'd be safe there.'

'Right. I will,' he said in a thick voice.

'I'll give you a hand,' Lisa said.

It was ridiculously easy. They got their things, and she followed him to the lift, where she snogged him for the time it took to climb to the fourth floor. It was hot in his room, despite the shutters that had kept the sun out all day. He switched on the light above the bed, and set the air conditioning to fill the room with its low buzz. Lisa pulled her dress off over her head, removed his glasses, and pressed herself against him. A second later, they hit the bed. In what seemed like another second, he was rolling away from her to throw himself face down on the barely crumpled sheets.

Lisa exhaled loudly. 'Gawd, tha's as well I di'n't blink, I might've missed it.'

He ignored her. She pulled herself up and observed the sprawl of his unresponsive figure. Pale, fleshy buttocks mooned up at her, a shade lighter than the skin which had been under his tee shirt, shorts, and socks. The red of his sun-touched arms and legs formed a deep contrast, and Lisa couldn't help laughing.

'Piss off!' he said.

'Oh, don't be like that,' she said, regretting her unkindness, and poking his back.

He lifted his head and glanced at her, shame, disgust and yearning fighting in his face.

Lisa thought she understood. 'You've never done it before, have yer?'

'I said piss off!'

She shrugged, got back into her clothes, and went back to their room to tell Julie all about it.

It amused her, the next day, to think of the poor bloke, thinking himself so holy, and racked by guilt at having had it off with a girl he'd picked up in the bar. When she saw him at dinner, however, looking sick and upset, she began to feel guilty.

'Maybe I should have a word with him, see if he's OK,' she said to Julie.

'Give over, Lise, don't waste your time. There's men out there simply waiting to shaft you, and it'll be a lot more fun than that fat old git.'

'I know, but he's a friend of this guy I know, and I don't wanna leave it like that.' She arranged to catch up with Julie later, and went to look for him.

'Sorry about last night,' she said, sitting down next to him in the bar again. 'Seemin' like I was laughin' at you. I didn't mean it. Can I get you a drink?'

He looked at her angrily through his glasses, and said nothing.

'How's your story going? Have you caught the villains?'

'Stop wittering on about things that don't concern you.'

Lisa nibbled her thumbnail, and considered him. She could follow Julie, and get off with some bloke down on the beach, or stay here, and see if she could bring a smile to the face of this bad-tempered man who thought he didn't want to know.

'You're a pal of Michael Turner's, aren't you?' she said. 'Tha's where I see you before, last year.'

'No.'

'Tha's alright, I won't let on what you bin up to. You're not a journalist, you're one of them trainee vicars, aren't yer? Tha's why you don't like havin' sex.'

'No, I'm not. I don't know what you're talking about.'

'Let's go back to your room again, then. If you in't holy, we could have another go.'

He was less afraid of her this time; the encounter stretched into minutes. Lisa felt curiously tender as she stroked the pimpled flesh of his back.

'I don't even know your name,' she whispered in his ear. 'I'm Lisa.'

He turned his head away from her. 'Who needs to know names? We aren't going to see each other again.'

'We could do. We live near each other, don't we? I'm going to college in Leathwell in September, I'm gonna do a course on childcare so's I can be a nanny. I do babysitting a lot, I like kids.' She got off him, and lay down next to him, propped on her left elbow, while she idly fondled the pale strands of hair on his chest with her other hand.

'How old are you?' he asked.

'Nearly seventeen.'

'God. You act like you've had sex with hundreds of blokes.'

'A few. It's good for a laugh.'

'You haven't done it with Michael, have you - I mean whoever this bloke is you keep on about.'

Lisa smiled at his transparency. 'Nah, he was never interested in me. More like a big brother. Have you got any brothers or sisters?'

She stayed with him for an hour, telling him about herself, and throwing questions at him which he generally managed to evade. He was rather sweet, though.

'You ought to go,' he said eventually, looking at her with pale-blue eyes that seemed at last to have registered that she was a person. He pulled her to him, and kissed her with fleshy, moist lips, and a new stirring of passion.

'D'you wanna do it again?' she asked, beginning to caress him.

'No, I'm tired. Go on, go.'

'At least tell me your name.'

'Tyrone,' he said huskily. He cleared his throat. 'People call me Ty.'

'Will I see you tomorrow before I go?'

'I don't know.'

'I'll leave you my phone number, in case I don't.' She found a piece of paper and wrote on it in a round, childish hand; then she gathered her things, and left him.

Nan and Christopher had flown to Heraklion on separate flights. He met her at the airport in a hired car, and drove her through the sapping heat of a Mediterranean night over the mountainous road that spined across the island. The stretched-out resorts of Heraklion had faded into the distance, the dark was interrupted only by the tourist buses ferrying people to and from the airport, and the distant lights of the small towns down by the sea. They were alone together, and oh, the bliss of being here, not having to pretend, not having to part at night.

The risk of being recognised seemed so remote that they hardly bothered about it. Dressed in shorts, hats and sunglasses, they looked no different from all the other couples wandering the streets of Rethymnon. They spent their days in visits to the nearby beaches, swimming in the velvet water with the sun searing their faces. Hiring sunbeds to read, or to lie back under a parasol squinting at the jet skis and the parascenders, while their bodies drank in the sun. When it got too hot, they would retire to their villa up its isolated track on the outskirts of Rethymnon, and make love languidly while the net curtains billowed in the open windows. In the small pool at the back of the villa, on loungers in the shade of the vine that clambered above the patio, scarcely bothering with clothes as they learnt one another's bodies and histories, talked of almost everything except the issue that most divided them.

Nan raised it once, coming out onto the terrace by the pool with a loose skirt wound around her waist, waving two long bread rolls to ask Christopher what he wanted putting in them. Suddenly she became conscious of striking the pose of Minoan goddesses, her breasts exposed, her arms extended sideways, though waving bread instead of snakes.

'Is this how you'd prefer your priestesses?' she laughed. He didn't smile. They looked at each other.

Nan lowered her arms. 'I'm sorry. I know it's not funny. I only wish we could talk about it.'

'What is there to say? We're not going to change our positions.'

'But what are you going to do and say about it when we make this public?'

Christopher shrugged. 'I don't know. I'll see when we get there. The Trust Fund's not going to be completely tied up for another few months.'

209

'It's suited you, keeping me a secret, hasn't it?'

He held out a hand to her. 'Bear with me, Nan.'

She came up to him and kissed his forehead.

'I thought we might go to Knossos tomorrow,' he said.

Though few tour buses came on a Sunday, the site was packed. Bright-red Britons dragging whining children across the stones. Tour guides repeating the official myths in a myriad different languages. Nan stumbled around in Christopher's wake trying to work out whether any of the walls and paintings were genuine, her head beginning to ache in the oppressive heat. Weary, she made her way to the foot of the hill where fewer people strayed, and sat under the trees while Christopher went to re-examine the frescoes. For a moment, she felt the song of the past, insistently calling into existence the shadows who once walked the hill under the searing sun.

Her reverie was interrupted by Christopher rushing up to her, his face drawn. 'We have to go!'

'What's the matter?'

'I've just seen bloody Tyrone Nixon, that's what.'

'Here? At Knossos? Did he see you?'

'He came up and spoke to me. He's followed us here. I'm sure he knew. Perhaps he's been spying on us at the villa...'

'Don't be silly, it's a coincidence,' Nan said with more assurance than she felt. 'How could he possibly know we were here? He's probably more upset than you are - fancy meeting up with your Principal while you're on holiday.' She squeezed his hand. 'Don't look so worried. No one's even been suspicious about us. The only outside person who knows is Jenny Turner, and she'd never say anything. She doesn't think much of me, for some reason, but she likes you.'

'If it got out now, it would be a disaster.'

They took separate, circuitous routes back to the car, and drove over mountains spectacular in the evening sun, back to Rethymnon and away, as they thought, from any danger.

Ten

'Bugger!'

Nan was lying drowsy in their bed when Christopher's exclamation of horror alerted her to the catastrophe that had struck them. She sprang out of bed, grabbed a robe to cover her nakedness, and went through to the living room. Christopher was standing with his hands holding the patio doors tightly together. Outside, the closed shutters prevented her from seeing anything, but she could hear voices:

'Where is she? ... Come out. We only want to talk to you.'

'What is it?' she asked Christopher.

'There's a dozen reporters out there. I was right, Tyrone's been spying on us, and he's told them we're here.'

'What are we going to do?'

Hands rattled on the shutters. 'Come out! Canon Ridgefield!'

'We'll have to talk to them. Keep out of the way, they've got cameras.'

Nan put a hand on his arm, and stepped out of the line of sight as he reopened the doors, and the shutters, and stepped outside to a chorus of clicks.

'What exactly is it you want?' she heard him say.

'We want your story,' they called back. 'Where's Nan?' 'How long's this been going on?'

'I'm not quite sure what you're talking about.'

'This,' said one of the hacks.

'Can you give me a few minutes to read it,' Christopher said politely. 'Then I'll come and answer your questions.'

He stepped back inside, drew the door shut, and pulled the curtains across. In his hand, he held a thick tabloid newspaper which he tossed onto the low table in front of the sofa. Nan sat down beside him, and together, they stared in horror at the front page:

TV Star's mum in church sex scandal ran the headline. Below it, a colour photograph showed Christopher rubbing suncream into Nan's back as she lay face down on a lounger.

The Church of England is in chaos again today as two senior clergy are discovered having sex-romps in a Cretan love nest. Blonde Reverend Nan Patten (48) a leading campaigner for women priests, and mum of BBC Children's Television presenter, Becky Patten, flew to the island last week to join lover Canon Chris Ridgefield, 52, Principal of St Barnabas Theological College and well known for his opposition to women priests. The bubbly vicar had been working alongside Father Ridgefield, but colleagues and friends say they had no idea she was converting him to her cause...

And so on. A senior churchman discovered bonking on a Greek island made a good story. A bonking cleric who wrote advice books on how to be celibate was an added bonus. But to have a cleric well known for opposing women priests, bonking one of their number in a secret hideaway, complete with unambiguous photographs, had made a story that must have moved the paper's editor to ecstasy. Christopher turned the pages in silent fury.

Inside, further pictures showed them both relaxing by the pool, embracing uninhibitedly. Worse still, Tyrone's camera had captured Nan's priestess pose, and there it was, reproduced next to a picture of a Minoan figurine under the headline:

Church boobs again.

A cartoon underneath portrayed a topless female priest at the altar, with the caption *'Ever since we got that new priest, our members are on the up ...'*

'I'm so sorry,' Nan told him, fighting tears, unable to see how they could survive this crucifixion. Christopher had lived a careful life for years; celibate, ordered, not necessarily liked, but respected by many. Tipped to be a bishop, as the paper said; now overnight he had become a laughing stock. The personal opprobrium was bad enough; the cartoon, showing her denigrating the Mass, was surely unforgivable. She put a hand on his knee.

He stood up, shaking her off. 'I shall have to tell them, now they know this much. St Barnabas is finished either way.'

'I'll come with you.'

He opened the doors and they went outside hand in hand, blinking in the glare of the sun as the cameras raked them once more. 'It's not what it looks like,' Christopher said. 'Nan is my wife. We haven't done anything wrong.'

The sun that had so burned Tyrone's skin during his reconnaissances in Crete was sinking into the Atlantic, turning the sky to fire. Steve and Alison, sitting out on their Eurosites plastic chairs in front of their tent, paid little attention to the spectacle. After a strained fortnight's camping in the Vendee, the truce they had endured for the sake of James and Josh had finally broken down.

Alison was not sure how they had arrived at the point at which Steve put the question, but she was suddenly tired of pretending.

'*Is* there someone else?' he asked again.

She took another gulp of the cheap red wine Steve had bought from the nearby Hypermarche.

'Yes there is, if you really want to know.'

'It's Michael Turner, isn't it?'

'Yes.' She kept her voice low, for there were several other family groups gathered in earshot under their awnings.

Steve stared at her, his lips tightening, though whether to prevent an outburst of anger or grief, she couldn't tell. He refilled his glass before he replied. 'I might have guessed, you've never stopped talking about him all year - except that I thought you Christians weren't supposed to believe in adultery. I presume you've slept with him?'

'It's not about that. He talks to me, he makes me feel like I'm worth something.'

'You should have said if you weren't happy.'

'That's the whole point. I shouldn't have to tell you. You should know.'

'So what are you planning to do?'

'I don't know. He hasn't told Jenny yet, and I won't be moving in with him - I still want to be ordained. Only he's made me realise how different my ministry could be if I had someone supporting me, rather than sniping at me all the time like you do. I'm tired of you never being interested in me. I deserve to have someone care for me. I want a divorce.'

'You're a selfish bitch,' he said, looking at her with distaste. 'As long as you're happy, it doesn't matter about me, or the kids. Or Michael's wife.'

'His marriage has never worked - he only married her on the rebound, and she's really horrible to him.'

'So you've been consoling each other in bed. Very nice behaviour for a vicar, I must say. What happens if I make a fuss?'

'I don't know, Steve. I wasn't going to say anything yet. I'll talk to Michael when we get back, and see what he says.'

The sound of tears heralded Josh's arrival, clutching his arm. James ran up to her. 'This big kid pushed him off the trampoline, an' he went right over on it. Kerpow! Can I go back now?'

Alison took Josh onto her knee. 'As long as you're back in half an hour,' she called after James.

'I'll go and keep an eye on him,' Steve said, getting up from the table.

Alison hugged Josh, soothing his hot, tired head, and wiping away the tears that trickled from his eyes. He had not yet acquired his father's skill at denying pain.

Michael was left on his own as August neared its end, for Jenny had gone to a conference in Edinburgh. As he called in at the newsagent's for his *Observer* on the way back from church, he glanced at the tabloids, vaguely noticing the photographic exposure of some poor woman caught *en flagrante* with an inappropriate lover. His eye travelled across the accompanying headline, and his attention was caught:

TV Star's mum in church sex scandal.

As he scanned the page more closely he realised with a stomach-churning shock, that the woman in the pictures was Nan, her affair with Ridgefield uncovered at last.

Over the next few days, Michael's living room was taken over by newsprint as he bought newspapers by the armful to discover what was being said. By Monday, the story of Ridgefield's liaison with a married woman in his first curacy had been introduced. Mercifully for some poor family, she remained unnamed. Tuesday proclaimed the news that Ridgefield and Nan had in fact been married for some five months. Married by Peter at St Martin's, with none of them suspecting a thing. Wednesday revealed that, the marriage notwithstanding, Ridgefield's hopes of establishing a trust fund to ensure the independent and female-free future of St Barnabas had been dealt a fatal blow by the public withdrawal of all his various backers. It wasn't, so they said, merely that the Principal of the college would have a wife who called herself a priest, though that was bad enough. It was not even the stories of his past, embarrassing though they were, for past sins could be forgiven. Rather, it was the underhand way in which he had concealed his marriage, duped people into promising donations which he knew would never have been forthcoming if the truth had been known. Thursday quoted the Bishop of Leathwell saying that while he was delighted about the marriage, he regretted the lack of honesty and the damage done to the reputation of St Barnabas.

The stories troubled Michael greatly. He could barely recognise the individuals being pilloried and ridiculed for their relationship, their work, their commitment to their causes. With a lack of other news, the papers exulted over the scandal, and with so many of Nan and Christopher's friends and allies away on holiday, there seemed to be no one to speak for them. Michael consoled himself with extended conversations with a horrified Jackie and with Becky, who'd been at the wedding, and was now having to lie low to avoid reporters desperate for her personal angle. When Alison rang on her return from holiday later that week, he was grateful for someone else with whom to talk the whole thing through.

'Why don't you come round?' she suggested. 'Steve's taken the children to his parents for a couple of days, so we wouldn't be disturbing him. Or are you and Jenny planning something?'

'No. She's away as well.'

'Come and have lunch, then.'

Michael hesitated before he agreed. Visiting Alison alone at her home might not have been wise in the past, but surely now they had come to terms with the inconvenient attraction that spiced their friendship? As soon as Alison opened the door to him, he knew at once that she was entirely the wrong confidante for a man whose wife turned her back on him night after night.

'Excuse the get-up, I've been sunbathing,' she said, waving a hand at her bikini bottoms, and the short vest she wore above it, through which the outline of her breasts left little to imagination. He was acutely physically aware of her as he kissed her cheek, and allowed his hands to linger round her bare waist for longer than was strictly necessary.

'You're looking well,' he said, striving for a casual tone.

'So are you. Come through.' She tied a sarong around her waist as she led him through to her living room. 'I'm afraid it's only sandwiches, but I've opened a bottle of wine.' They sat side by side on the sofa, mulling over the story and its implications.

'Imagine,' Alison said, 'all that time we thought they were having an affair, and they'd married after all. I suppose they realised how strongly they felt about each other, and decided it would be wrong to sleep together unless they were married. It's just as well you held me off when I thought it would be alright for us to sleep together because they were.' She put her plate on the table. 'And we haven't got an excuse now, so you'll never kiss me again.' She gazed at him, lips parted, and whispered, 'Unless you'd kiss me one last time, for old time's sake.' She was too close for him to refuse.

'I only hope there's no photographers lurking in your back garden with long lenses,' he said, pulling back from the embrace.

Alison got up and pulled the curtains across the window, then came back and sat down next to him again.

'The doors are locked as well,' she whispered. 'You're quite safe.'

Michael put his arms around her as her mouth closed on his again, and suddenly he was back where he'd been when she had come to his bed the first time, wanting her with every fibre of his body. Only this time, Jenny was too distant from him to alter his course. He pulled Alison's vest up over her head, cupped her golden breasts in his hands, and lowered his mouth to tease at them with fevered lips. A few seconds later, his polo shirt had joined her top on the floor, and the only sound was of their hurried breathing, and whispered invitations. Make love to me, Mikey ... I want you so much ... Oh, God, Allie ...

Jenny's flight was late leaving Edinburgh. She hadn't understood exactly what the problem was, she only knew that after a long delay in the terminal, they stood on the tarmac for another forty-five minutes waiting for permission to take off, and since their scheduled departure was at ten, she wouldn't now be home till well after midnight.

She fell asleep shortly after take-off, exhausted by the intense input of the last week, the heated, draining discussions over meals, and the sickening sight of the newspapers spied in the shops all week, gloating self-righteously over Nan and Ridgefield's sins. Though she had known, and been critical, of the relationship, it had still shocked her to see it splashed across the front pages like that. However wrong you were, no one deserved to have the most intimate details of their lives held up for ridicule. What had Ty been thinking of to sell his story to the papers? There'd been no need. A quiet word with the Bishop would have secured Ridgefield's removal; publicising it like this did immense damage to the church Ty had said he was protecting. It was almost as if he'd wanted to ruin Ridgefield; and why should he want to do that, except at Deidre's instigation? Assisting one of Deidre's schemes was the last thing Jenny had intended. And now that she knew that Ridgefield had tried to preserve some integrity by marrying Nan, she bitterly castigated herself for her part in it all.

Jenny dozed until the pain in her ears woke her to warn her that the plane had begun to descend. Landing safely accomplished, she made her way towards the exit, her ears tight and her eyes gritty from sleeping in her contact lenses, feeling as if it were four in the morning.

Michael was waiting for her, his tan washed from his face by the dull neon lights that illuminated the concourse. The news about Nan would have hit him hard, she realised, coming out of the blue as it must have done.

'I'm sorry I'm so late,' she said, handing him one of her bags to carry to the car.

'It's hardly your fault.' Michael kissed her, and turned towards the exit.

'Are you OK? You look worried.' She took his arm, and he gave a half smile.

'It's been a long day. We've got company - I hope you don't mind. Christopher Ridgefield rang me this evening, and asked whether I could possibly pick Nan up, because she wasn't flying back until tonight. He's been plagued by reporters, and he didn't like the thought of them covering his reunion with her. I had one or two, wondering who I was and trying to get her story.'

They found Nan waiting in the car, lying back against the seat, washed out with fatigue.

'I'm sorry,' Jenny managed to say, taking her place in the front.

'It wasn't your fault. Or was it? You said you wouldn't talk.'

'Did you know?' Michael asked Jenny.

'Nan came to the clinic. I didn't realise who it was she was seeing until I saw them together at summer school.'

Nan sighed. 'I suppose Tyrone saw us then as well. And we thought we were being so careful. We'd no idea anyone would be watching that closely.'

'Ty had been suspicious for months. He'd noticed Christopher staying out late,' Jenny said.

'How do you know that?' asked Nan.

'He was talking about it at the summer school.'

'I didn't realise you knew him.'

Jenny said nothing, realising she had drawn too close to revealing her part in the story.

Michael said casually, 'He's Jen's cousin.'

'Are you sure you didn't tell him about us?' Nan asked Jenny.

'Jen wouldn't do something like that,' Michael said. 'She's very hot on confidentiality.'

'Like you said, he saw for himself.' Jenny said. And then, in case it came out at some stage, she added, 'I mentioned what Christopher had said about going to Rethymnon. I didn't know Ty would go to the papers. I thought he'd write to the Bishop.'

'It's as if he wanted to humiliate us. I don't understand why he should have been so vindictive - what had we ever done to him?' Nan was silent for a minute. 'Your cousin? You don't mean that he's related to Deidre Rutt as well ...'

'He's her son,' Michael said. 'Only he uses his dad's surname.'

'My God! That explains everything. Chris would never have let him into St Barnabas if he'd known.' Again, she was silent for a minute. 'I suppose Deidre was behind him going there. No wonder he was being so uncooperative - she'd told him to be. She probably thought that if there was enough antagonism against the Programme, we'd have to move out, and she'd get us after all.' She began to laugh sourly. 'Whereas in fact, all Tyrone's done is to make sure that Christopher's trust fund collapses, so he's still reliant on the Programme staying. If Tyrone hadn't gone to the press, the Trust would have been set up, and Chris would have kicked the Programme out. Deidre can't be too pleased with her darling boy now.'

'She might not mind too much if Christopher ends up having to leave St Barnabas,' Michael said. 'Do you think he will?'

'We don't know. He's got a meeting with his governors in a few days.' She sighed. 'Oh, God, why did I have to put him through all this?'

But Jenny could not allow herself to care.

They delivered Nan to her house, and ten minutes later, were back home and making their way to bed. As soon as Jenny got under the covers, Michael reached across to put out the light, and gathered her into his arms.

'Not tonight. I'm tired.'

'But I've missed you. I need you. It's been months, Jen.' He kissed her again, then rolled on top of her, pinning her head against the pillow, and forcing his tongue in her mouth.

'Michael! No!' She tried to push him away, but he was insistent. His left hand dived between her thighs, and massaged her.

'Please, Jenny, please. I can tell you want to.'

She gave up resisting. It was true, her body was already responding to his caress, and it had been a long time. She held him to her as he grunted and gasped, again and again. It seemed an age before he reached his climax, and she registered how odd that was, for he was usually quick when they had not made love for some time. Her lips were on his ears, her nose in his hair, and for a moment she thought she caught an indefinable trace of unfamiliar perfume there. He couldn't have been cheating on her while she was away, surely? Visiting Alison, or worse, having her here with him in their bed? He surely wouldn't have turned to her tonight so urgently out of guilt alone?

'Did you do anything today?' she asked as he lay with his head on her shoulder.

It was a while before he replied. 'I popped in to see Allie to talk about Nan, but I didn't stay long. We knew as well, you know. Allie saw Nan coming out of Christopher's house in the middle of the night. We'd no idea they were married.'

His breathing became regular, and he slept. Jenny lay under him, wide awake, wondering whether she would ever be able to trust him whole-heartedly. She had tried so hard to believe his assurances that Alison meant nothing to him, but what if they'd decided to follow Nan's example? The nightmarish picture niggled back into her mind: Michael lying naked with Alison, caressing her, exploring her body, penetrating her with those little groans he gave when he was aroused. He *wouldn't*, she told herself. He's *said* there's nothing going on, he's not like that. He loves me, he's got a conscience. She's married, she's got a family, she's going to be ordained, for God's sake. Only none of the reassurances worked any more; she knew, simply knew, that he had made love to Alison, and she would never be able to trust him again.

It was nearly twenty-four hours before Jenny realised that, in the hassle over her plane journey, she had forgotten to take her pill that evening, and by then it was already too late.

'I understand you'll want my resignation. I've brought a letter with me,' Ridgefield said, passing an envelope across to Derrick, who chaired the St Barnabas Board of Governors.

'Now, Christopher, don't be hasty,' Derrick replied, pushing the envelope back towards him. 'We're here to look into what's happened, and to make some decisions. I don't see everyone baying for your blood.'

Though not baying, the other seven men sitting in Ridgefield's study did not look him in the eye, preferring to fiddle with their papers, or to take unnecessary sips from their coffee cups. He could well understand their embarrassment, given the mortifying details spread across the papers all week. He had forced himself to read what was being said so that he could rebut the malicious imputations, and had given a press conference with the Leathwell Diocesan Press Secretary guiding his responses, but the mud stuck. Clung mercilessly to him, plaguing his waking thoughts and haunting his nights, colouring the expressions of everyone he met, destroying the delight he'd once had in loving his wife.

'I've brought the college into disrepute. I've married a woman priest. I can't possibly stay on.'

Gerald, on the Board of Governors as senior student, raised a hand, and said, 'I've been ringing round the students, and they're three to one in favour of you staying. I know we weren't happy about Nan being around the place at first, and there was a lot of ill feeling about that Eucharist, but they're up in arms about the way the press treated you and the college. They don't see why you should be driven out by a creep like Tyrone.'

'I've nothing against Nan personally,' another of the governors chipped in. 'My problem is with the way you kept it a secret from everyone. I can see you thought it would be awkward because it might put people off making donations to the Trust Fund, but in that case, why couldn't you have waited until it was properly set up before you married her? It would only have been a few months, and that way we'd have had none of this nonsense with the papers.'

Ridgefield scanned them all, considering how much he could tell them. He saw Nan in his mind, her clothes awry, her arms around his neck, breathing, 'I can't help it, I want you too much, I can't last for who knows how many months, being near you and not being able to ... and what if someone sees you leaving here? They'll think the worst whatever we say.' He'd made love to her - how could he resist? - and afterwards, intoxicated with desire, he'd said, 'Let's get married. Privately. Then it doesn't matter.'

'We did intend to wait, but we didn't think we could,' he told the governors. 'We thought if we married, we'd avoid any scandal if someone found out. And then, we knew the fact that Nan thought of herself as a priest and I couldn't accept it, would put a lot of strain on our relationship. I thought if we were married, I'd have to find some way of living with it. We'd be tied together, and I wouldn't simply be able to walk away when things got difficult. I knew I still opposed women priests just as strongly, so I didn't feel I was being hypocritical in continuing to gather donations from people who wanted St Barnabas to keep its integrity. I knew there'd be some objections once they knew about Nan, but from the college's point of view, that didn't matter so long as their donations were secure and the Trust Fund was set up. I can see now why they feel angry that I deceived them, but at the time, I convinced myself I was doing the right thing.'

'You have made errors of judgement,' Derrick said, 'but I'm not sure that debars you from continuing as Principal. You did have the interests of the college at heart. We also ought to bear in mind that it looks as if you were deliberately set up. We shouldn't speculate about it outside this room, since there's no direct evidence, but it does look as if Deidre Rutt encouraged Tyrone to cause trouble between the Programme and St Barnabas, so she'd get another chance of taking over. And that he went to the papers at her instigation because she wanted to damage Christopher's reputation. She denies it absolutely. I spoke with her after Christopher told me about his suspicions, and she claimed to be shocked by Tyrone's actions. Indeed, she's thrown him out of the house. I've also discussed matters with Tyrone himself, and he insists he was acting on his own initiative throughout. So while we may have our suspicions, there's nothing we can do. But I would be loth to lose Christopher because of it. What do the rest of you think?'

The Archdeacon coughed. 'I agree, I'd be sorry to see Christopher go. But I'd understood last year that he said he'd leave if he couldn't guarantee St Barnabas' independence. And since the Trust Fund has fallen through, it looks as if we'll be stuck with the Programme for the forseeable future for financial reasons. How does Christopher feel about that?'

'You'll probably all shoot me down in flames for saying so,' Ridgefield said, 'but I think on the whole, it might be a good thing for us to have them here permanently. I'd got it in my head that the only way of protecting the interests of ordinands who oppose the ordination of women was to train them on their own. Yet having female ordinands, and Nan, around the place over the last year hasn't been as bad as I thought. As Gerald says, there have been problems, but we've all been forced to be more rigorous about why we object to women priests, because we've met them, and seen that they're not all bug-eyed monsters. If we know we're right theologically, we don't need to be exclusive. We don't need to be frightened of hearing other points of view. I also think it's important for those of us on the more traditional catholic wing of the church to integrate as far as we can, otherwise our insights and traditions will be marginalised. It strikes me that if I personally can be committed both to Nan and to opposing women priests, maybe St Barnabas and the Programme can learn to respect each other.'

'I'm sure you're right,' Derrick said. 'And who better than yourself to oversee that process?'

General murmurs of agreement issued from the other governors.

'So I can tear up this letter?' Derrick asked, picking the envelope up.

Meeting no objection, he ripped it in two, and handed it to Ridgefield for disposal.

Eleven

A week, two weeks, four weeks, eight weeks. As each interval passed, it lessened the likelihood that the nightmare would end of its own spontaneous accord. Jenny had known almost at once. Her body had always been ordered in its rhythms, and when her period failed to appear at the appropriate time, she'd known that her missed pill had had catastrophic consequences. Pregnant. Oh God. She didn't believe in abortion, couldn't contemplate deliberately killing the embryo taking root in her, but she didn't want it, and willed it to die. She didn't want to be a mother. Not now, not ever.

Michael always talked as if they'd have several, once she felt able to take a break from her career to have them. He was exactly the sort who'd enjoy the whole process: sharing antenatal classes, coaching her to give birth, going to church with an infant in a sling, showing it off to his friends and family, pushing the supermarket trolley with a toddler in the seat, playing in the park.

'I'd be quite happy staying at home to look after them,' he'd say. 'I'm good at nappies, and getting up in the night. I used to have holidays with Sarah when hers were little, so I'm pretty experienced.'

Jenny's own feelings had always been more ambivalent. When she watched her mothers giving birth in the GP Unit at the hospital, and it went well, she could feel the yearning to bear her own creased and bloodied infant, to catch it to root at her breast. When mothers sat exhausted in her surgery with tantruming toddlers, beyond caring, she saw herself submerged beneath a weight of responsibility that would destroy her spirit and turn her into a nit-picking, carping, ungenerous-spirited mother who would destroy her children even more thoroughly than she herself had been harmed by her own childhood. Somehow the thought of Michael taking over and doing the job to perfection made it all even more difficult, and she had been happy to put the whole thing off.

The sheer panic which the knowledge of her pregnancy induced utterly confounded her. She did her best to maintain a calm demeanour, but inside, a knot of terror grew with each cell that was forming her baby's heart and lungs and limbs and brain. At first, she said nothing to Michael, because she hoped that a late period would save her. Then she told herself she ought to wait until the pregnancy had properly established itself. When I get to eight weeks, I'll tell him then, she promised herself, only before she could reach that point, he came home from the Programme brimming with delight because Alison was having a baby, and Jenny needed no guesses about its parentage.

'This'll interest you,' he'd said, sitting down on the sofa and calling to Celestine. 'Allie's pregnant.' The cat roused herself for a transfer from Jenny's lap to Michael's, hopping lazily down to the carpet, and up again to drape herself across his chest.

Jenny picked up the television remote control from the arm of her chair, and switched it on. 'Is she? When's it due?'

'End of May. She's going to bring it along to lectures, and lend it out for students to practice baptisms on.' He smiled. 'Perhaps I can get some practice with it. You don't fancy having a go yet, do you?'

'I don't feel ready...' she said hesitantly.

'That's OK, I'm not pushing you. Are you feeling alright, Jen? You look like a ghost. That holiday was supposed to perk you up, not leave you iller than before.'

'I couldn't help getting a stomach bug.' She'd been sick for the first time during the week's holiday they'd taken in Germany, and had spent most of the time throwing up or thinking about where the next toilet was. Michael had no suspicions, he'd said his own stomach felt odd, and it must have been something they'd eaten, and she'd not been ready then to disabuse him.

Is Alison's baby yours? she wanted to ask. Is that why you made love to me with such difficulty, because you'd already exhausted yourself impregnating her? Only she couldn't face hearing his answer. Holding back the news of her own pregnancy was a way of hurting him, of showing she didn't need him, didn't care what he got up to.

Patterns ran through her brain.

The track of deception: get up early to throw up in the kitchen sink where he won't hear. Pretend to keep taking the pill. Add tampons to the list when he did the shopping, mutter about it being 'that time of the month'.

The track of logic: he is going to have to know at some point. This is psychotic behaviour - crass enough in an ordinary person, crazy for a doctor, for God's sake. Sit down and tell him.

The track of fear: oh, help me, help me, help me. Oh, please, Michael, notice!

Working helped to block the voices out, and as the winter months worked their way into December, she was grateful for the flu season, and the increase in patients housebound by the weather; anything that filled her life, and allowed her to divorce herself from everything that was going on inside her.

On the day before Christmas Eve, Michael drove Jenny to Croydon. He glanced at her profile as he negotiated the ill-tempered holiday traffic, remembering the Christmas two years before - was it really only two years? - when they had got engaged. She had still had an air of reserve about her, but her eyes and skin and hair had glowed, she was in love, and happy. What had he done to turn her into the strained, silent, pale woman she had become? It wasn't as if she had real grounds for suspicion about Alison, or could have any idea of the pictures that still flashed through his mind from to time: the curve of her golden breast, the taste of her skin, the throaty whisper of her voice. *Make love to me, Mikey...* And hadn't he fought free of Allie for his wife's sake? Hadn't he always been constant in his attentions to her? He couldn't understand why his attempts to love, understand and support her never seemed to be enough. The barriers she erected between them withstood all his attempts at infiltration. He'd not even been certain she'd come with him on this trip.

'You are *not* going to be on duty again over Christmas,' he'd told her firmly, when she spoke of it. 'You're overtired as it is. You've been on call far too often recently, and you did it last year. I want to have Christmas with you, and we're going to my parents. Sarah and Ruth will be there, and I want to see them.'

'I've already volunteered,' Jenny had replied, with a set chin.

'Then you'll have to tell them you were wrong, you hadn't realised your husband had already made arrangements. I'm serious, Jen. You need a break. I need a break, with you.' He wasn't sure what he'd actually do if she refused, but as if she had no energy left to fight him, she acquiesced. He knew that Jenny's miserable appearance would expose the state of his marriage to his family, but he hoped that in some way their concern might help.

Meg clearly saw at once that something was wrong.

'My poor dear,' she said, putting an arm around her daughter-in-law's shoulders, and leading her into the sitting room. 'You look all-in. What has he been doing to you! You're not to do a thing while you're here. You definitely look as if you need spoiling!'

She questioned Michael obliquely in the kitchen, as he helped her produce cups of tea for everyone.

'Jenny seems a little down - is everything OK?'

'That's a mother's leading question. Are you about to get divorced? No. Is she pregnant? No. Does she want to be pregnant? No. She's tired, that's all. She's been overworking as usual. Nothing a few days' holiday won't cure.'

He was pleased to see that Jenny seemed to be making an effort in response to Meg's care. She became friendly to him in front of his family, talked to them, and played games with the children if not enthusiastically, at least without looking as if she was under sentence of death.

'I can't believe that,' Ruth said to Sarah, waving the remote control at the local news she had uncovered on teletext. '"A London woman who thought she had indigestion from too much turkey, gave birth to a healthy, seven pound three ounce baby girl on her bathroom floor. Mother of three Sandra Gill had no idea she was pregnant, but called the latest arrival the best Christmas present she'd ever had". How can anyone not know they're pregnant?'

It was the evening of Boxing Day. The younger children were in bed, and the older ones helping their fathers come to terms with a new computer game, while Michael, Jenny and his sisters relaxed in the living room.

Michael looked up, read the story for himself, and went back to his magazine.

'Have you ever had a case like that, Jenny?' Sarah asked her sister-in-law.

Jenny wrote something on her crossword. 'I haven't, but there was a woman who gave birth at the surgery before my time, when she'd thought she'd only got a bad back.'

'But how?' Ruth persisted. 'They must know their periods have stopped, and that they're getting fatter, let alone anything else.'

Jenny put the crossword down. 'Some women have very irregular periods anyway, and their weight goes up and down. And even if you got sick, you might put it down to a stomach upset.'

'There are other signs, though, aren't there?' Ruth said. 'Your boobs change for a start. You fill out and go dark.'

'That's more with a first pregnancy.'

225

'I remember falling asleep all the time, and having to go for a pee a lot,' Sarah said. 'It got quite embarrassing at work.'

'Mike's sitting there looking innocent,' Ruth said, observing his attention straying from his page. 'What do you know about pregnancy, little brother? Do you think you'd spot the signs?'

'I should think so. One of my friends on my course is pregnant, so she's been telling me all about it.'

'Would you mind if I went for a bath?' Jenny asked, 'I'd like to try out some of that bubble stuff Rachel gave me. I'll be down in half an hour, if you're wanting to do something.'

'I wasn't being insensitive, was I, talking about pregnancy?' Ruth said after she'd gone.

'No, that's OK.' Michael said.

'Are you planning to have children one day?'

'One day.'

'It won't be easy for Jenny, with her career,' Sarah said, and she and Ruth began to talk about the difficulties of combining work and family, while Michael stared at his page, and wondered if it was possible that he had been being rather dense? Jenny was very tired. She was off her food. She had needed to stop for a toilet on their journey, though they never usually bothered. That morning, noticing him watching her dress, she'd commented that either her trousers had shrunk, or she'd had too much Christmas dinner. He hadn't seen her without clothes on for a long time - she changed in the bathroom, or on the rare occasions she allowed him to make love to her, insisted on having the light out. She'd implied she was having periods, but he couldn't remember seeing any physical evidence, now he thought about it. Only surely she was still taking the pill? And surely even Jenny wouldn't be that underhand, keeping it a secret from him - as if she possibly could in the end. It didn't make sense, but then Jenny could be a pretty strange woman.

'I think I'll go and see if mum needs a hand,' he said, leaving the room. Instead of going to find Meg in the kitchen, however, he went upstairs.

Jenny was standing in a long candlewick dressing gown in front of the mirror, putting cream on her face. Michael came up behind her, putting his hands on her hips as he held her gaze in the glass. Grey, frightened eyes stared back at him from a face pale despite the warmth of the bath she had rushed through. He turned her round to face him, untied her robe, and slid it off her shoulders. She stood in front of him mutely, her hands

226

clenched by her sides as he studied her body. With a light finger, he brushed her breast, with its darkened nipple and tiny swellings around the aureola that hadn't been there before. His fingers tracked down to stroke her belly, unsure whether it was only his imagination finding the faint swelling above her pubic hair. Unsure, until he met her eyes again. He pulled the dressing gown back round her.

'When?' he asked.

'The end of May.'

'Like Alison's.'

Jenny sniffed, and bit her lip.

He pulled her to him. 'Why didn't you tell me?'

She turned her face away. 'I don't want it. I hate it! It's a parasite! I feel ill all the time. I hoped I'd lose it.'

'Jenny! This is our baby. It's wonderful. Oh, *why* didn't you tell me? I could have been looking after you.'

'I thought you'd leave me.'

'Why should I want to do that? You know how much I want a baby.'

'But you've already got one, haven't you?' Jenny said, raising her head and speaking very rapidly. 'You've got Alison having your baby, and you're only biding your time till you leave me and go to her. I didn't want to use this as a bargaining counter.' She looked away.

'What are you talking about?' Michael asked. 'Jenny?' He pulled her face round to look at him.

'What I said. You've been having an affair with her. She's having your baby. Why should you want me when you've got someone beautiful and pleasant like her? '

'I have not been having an affair with Alison. Come and sit down, Jen, let's have this out.' He led her over to the bed, sat her down against the pillows, arranged himself next to her and pulled the quilt around them both.

'I have not had an affair with Alison,' he said, slowly spacing each word. 'What on earth makes you think I have?'

She shrugged her shoulders, wanting to retreat from the consequences of her outburst.

'Hmm? What, Jenny?' He put an arm round her.

'I've seen you together. I've smelt her on you. You talk about her all the time.'

'That's not true. I like her a lot - she's a good friend. Maybe I fancy her a bit, but I haven't ever slept with her.' He leaned his head against hers.

'You haven't seemed to want me around a lot of the time, so perhaps I turned to her more than I should have done. If you want the truth, I have kissed her a few times, but that's all. I've not had sex with her. I wouldn't do that to you, Jenny.'

'Wouldn't you?'

'Of course I wouldn't. Anyway, what would I want to be getting her pregnant for? She's married. She's not going to leave Steve. It's you I want a baby with. You know that.'

'Accidents happen. *Would* you be honest with me, if you had slept with her?'

He was grateful that she wasn't looking at him. 'I think so. But it doesn't arise. Before God, Jen, I've not slept with her. And even what there was, me kissing her, that's over. When I saw her over the holiday, when all that stuff about Nan and Christopher came out, we agreed that we were beginning to be tempted more than we should, so we wouldn't let ourselves be alone again. I think she must have decided to patch things up with Steve by having another baby. And ... if you're due at the same time, it must have been around then that you conceived - only I thought you were on the pill.'

'I forgot to take it that night. Oh, Michael, I smelt her on you, and you couldn't finish, and I was sure you'd been having sex with her, and it was your baby.' Jenny put her head on his chest. 'I hated you so much, and I wanted to hurt you by not telling you, and I suppose I thought it might all go away if I didn't tell anyone. I can't cope with it, I'm terrified of being a mother. I've probably damaged the poor little mite for life with hating it non-stop for four months.' She clung to him, while he circled her with his arms, trying to calm her turbulence.

'I'm sorry, Jenny. I've let you down. I should have noticed long before this. Is this why you've not wanted to make love? Surely it can't hurt?' He bent to kiss her, and she smiled at him with love in her eyes for the first time for months.

'No, it can't. You .. you could pop in to say hello if you want to,' she whispered.

Michael slid his hand under her dressing gown and caressed her stomach as he pulled her down to lie next to him.

'Michael?' Meg called through the door with a knock a few minutes later. 'Are you coming down again? Sarah's wanting to play a game.'

'We'll be down in five minutes,' he shouted. 'Can I tell them?' he asked as they dressed.

'They'll guess you didn't know. I am sorry, making you look silly.'

'Don't mind me. I've never had much pride. I'll leave it to you, when you're ready.'

Downstairs, they occcupied themselves playing Scrabble until it was past midnight.

Sarah yawned. 'Oh, well, back home tomorrow. And no more fun till August. Are you going anywhere exciting in the summer, Mike?'

'We're not sure,' Michael said, hesitantly.

'We're expecting to be otherwise occupied,' Jenny said. 'From the end of May onwards.' Michael flashed a smile at her.

'Do you mean ...?' Meg started, and stopped, in case she was thinking the wrong thing.

'I haven't wanted to say anything, because there's been one or two problems,' Jenny said. 'Only Michael's been persuading me I can't go on being cautious for ever - that's the trouble with doctors. I'm pregnant.'

Michael felt them all looking at him with surprised delight, and decided they probably guessed that he had been in ignorance until half an hour ago, but in the end it didn't matter. He was going to be a dad, and he was too thrilled to care about anything else. It was, he thought naively, high time he had a more straightforward vocation.

PART THREE

TO BE A PILGRIM

No goblin nor foul fiend
Can daunt his spirit;
He knows he at the end
Shall life inherit.
Then, fancies, fly away;
He'll not fear what men say;
He'll labour night and day
To be a pilgrim.

John Bunyan 1628-1688

One

The phone rang on. Michael stood staring out of the window onto the flower beds in front of St Barnabas, imagining the shrill summons filling the hall back home. Of course, when you had a new baby to deal with, it wasn't always easy to get to the phone.

Behind him, he was aware of Pam watching impatiently from the end of the hall. Programme students who came to the summer school without mobiles always competed for the public phones at this time of the evening, and Michael was about to give up when a click broke into the ringing.

'Hello?' Her voice was colourless, and his heart sank.

'Jenny? Why have you gone back home? Your mum said you left this morning.'

'I couldn't stand it. They were awful. Everything I did was wrong, and Lyddy wouldn't settle, and they ignored her except when she cried, and then they blamed me. I hardly slept for two nights, and then yesterday, I was expected to help out in the kitchen all day because they'd got a parish supper. Oh, God, there she goes again.'

A thin wail insinuated itself down the phone line, haunting his nerves with its insistence. He could visualize the tiny face crumpling into red passion, the lips white-blistered from over-zealous sucking quivering into rage as she remained untended.

'Hold on,' he said. 'You can't be on your own all week. What the hell were your parents thinking of, damn them? I told them you needed looking after.' He heard her sniff.

'I'll have to go.'

'Don't cry, Jen.' He was acutely aware of fellow students, unable to avoid eavesdropping as they began to gather outside the dining room for supper. 'Look, I'll try and get back after the session tonight, and we'll see what to do. Will you be OK till then?'

'Yes.' The phone went dead.

She wouldn't be all right, he could tell. She had been feeling fragile enough before the visit to her parents. Now, exhausted, alone, with an unsettled seven week-old baby, she would be in a desperate state in three hours' time. It had been a mistake thinking that her parents would suddenly have turned sensitive, but Jenny had wanted to go, convincing herself they sounded keen to see Lyddy, even if they couldn't possibly get away to Greathampton themselves to see their latest grandchild because Diana was coming to stay in a fortnight.

Jenny had dropped Michael off at St Barnabas on Saturday, and she'd seemed happy as they showed Lyddy off to all his friends. He'd never been prouder of her, dough-skinned though she was under a grey tee shirt and in a skirt that didn't yet do up around her thickened waist. Even newly-washed, her curls were limp, and there were shadows under her eyes that matched his own, for he too woke every time Lyddy wailed for food and comfort. He'd kissed them both goodbye with the utmost tenderness before waving Jenny goodbye, yet here she was, back home again on Tuesday, with her nerves shot to pieces.

A long time ago, before Lydia Margaret made her way into the world, Michael had expected that, with a competent medical professional for a partner, fatherhood would be a doddle. After the tension of the first few months, the second half of Jenny's pregnancy had been fairly unproblematic. She retained some ambivalence about the baby, but Michael's delight had rubbed off on her, and as she stopped feeling ill, she had seemed to be looking forward to the birth. That Jenny had her own demons to fight, he knew, but he had not expected that the birth of their baby would loose them in such quantity.

'It's only my hormones,' she'd say, fighting back tears after shouting at him, or screaming at Lyddy. 'It'll pass. I don't want to start taking drugs, which is what my doctor will suggest if I say I'm finding it difficult. My mother got put on tranquilisers after having me, and she's still on them. I'm not going to risk ending up like her.'

'I thought you could have drugs that weren't addictive now,' Michael had said, vaguely alarmed by her refusal to acknowledge that she might need help.

'You can, but I'm not taking anything. I'll be alright.'

She insisted she'd be fine if he went away to St Barnabas for the summer school - there was Caroline down the road, or the health visitor on the end of the phone - but both he and Jenny had seized on the idea of her taking Lyddy to her parents as an ideal solution. Now that had failed, and he wasn't even sure that having him back overnight for the rest of the week was going to be enough.

Michael went into the dining room, collected a plate of food and sat down at an empty table, preoccupied and anxious. He had hoped to find Alison there, knowing she would be sympathetic. She'd brought Luke with her, a dark-haired, dark-eyed baby a week older than Lyddy, who lay placidly in his buggy at the back of the lecture room, sleeping, or watching the patterns of the shadows on the walls, or nursing quietly at her breast, entirely unperturbed. Michael had taken his share of holding him, though he found him a poor substitute for Lyddy, for all his wide, heart-wrenching smile.

His intention of never being alone with Alison hadn't quite worked out, for he'd sprained an ankle playing tennis, and had to ask her for lifts soon after the autumn term started, unable to cycle or hobble to the bus stop. By mutual consent, they had kept their conversations impersonal, and though they remained physically aware of each other, there seemed no danger in him continuing to travel with her once his ankle had healed. Alison's pregnancy made him feel safer with her; these days, they talked about babies and their studies rather than themselves, and their changed priorities took the edge off any lingering attraction, or so he liked to think. She had been taken aback when he had told her about Jenny's pregnancy in the new year, especially once she had worked out the likely date of Lyddy's conception.

'She's only just told you, hasn't she?'

'She thought I was having an affair with you. She thought I'd fathered your baby, and was going to leave her,' Michael had said, looking steadily at her. 'Now I've cleared that up, I think we understand each other.' He had never asked questions about Luke's hasty begetting; and by unspoken agreement they had never referred to that August afternoon as they constructed a safe relationship out of the dangerous ruins of their first year of friendship.

He didn't notice Jackie take the chair next to him until she spoke. 'How come my favourite man looks so gloomy, when he's managed to leave all the shitty nappies and disturbed nights to his wife for a week?'

Michael pushed his plate away and put his head in his hands.

'Oh, Mike, I'm sorry.' Jackie put an arm round his shoulders. 'What's up?'

He ran his hands through his hair and turned to face her with smarting eyes. 'Jenny was supposed to be at her parents', but she's gone back home, and I don't think she's coping very well. I don't want to be here.'

'Go home, then.'

'I thought I'd get the bus back after the session, and drive back over before breakfast, but I keep wondering what's going on. Lyddy was howling

235

while I was on the phone, and I feel I should be there.'

'What's to stop you going now and staying there? It's not going to matter that much if you miss the rest of the summer school, is it? You can catch up.'

'I suppose not, but I'm beginning to think it might be right for me to try for ordination again next year, and it was partly because they doubted my commitment that they turned me down last time. If I've walked out simply because I don't like hearing my baby crying, it won't look very good.'

'Bugger that,' Jackie said, with the assurance of someone who knows they have only two months to go before clearing the final hurdle. 'Nan, could you come here a minute?' she called across to a neighbouring table. 'Michael's getting in a state about his family,' she said, when Nan sat down with them. 'Tell him to go home.'

Nan listened while he explained. 'As long as you get the work done eventually, there shouldn't be a problem, and your commitment to the Programme is hardly in doubt. Besides, you're not going to get much out of the week if you're constantly worrying about what's going on back home. I'll run you back now if you like - I've got some stuff I want to collect from home. Sort things out, and if you can't get back again, don't worry.'

Half an hour later, Michael was approaching a front door through which he could already hear Lyddy's howls. She was lying in her carrycot in the hall, a howling, sweating bundle in a yellow Babygro, arms held out rigidly from her trembling body, and her face screwed up in a creased, red mass. What the hell was Jenny playing at? He picked Lyddy up and held her damply to his shoulder, patting her back and stroking her hot head on its unsteady neck.

'It's alright, Lyddy. Calm down. There, there.' It didn't seem to have any effect. He put his little finger in her mouth, and she gummed at it desperately, then pulled away, yelling furiously. 'Are you hungry, little one? Is that what the problem is? We'd better go and find Mummy, hadn't we?' He went through to the living room, fighting off apprehension about why Jenny had abandoned the baby. She was standing looking out over the garden, her hands clenched into balls by her sides.

'She wouldn't latch on properly, and I was tense and the milk wouldn't come, and she howled and I got so cross I wanted to kill her. So I put her in the hall for two minutes while I tried to calm myself down.' She turned to him, her face contorted by anxiety. 'I'd only just put her there.'

'It's alright, I'm not accusing you. Sit down, let's try again.' Jenny sat down on the sofa, lifted her tee shirt, and unhooked the front of her bra. Her breast was heavy, the nipple dark and protruding now from frequent use, though her shape had not made feeding easy in the beginning. Michael passed Lyddy to her, and the baby made a brief attempt to suck, but finding nothing immediately available, arched backwards yelling with inconsolable anger.

Jenny let Lyddy fall onto her lap. 'Oh, God, I'm such a failure. And the shop'll be shut, we can't even buy a tin of milk.'

Michael knelt beside her. 'You're tense, that's all. Relax.' He stroked her head, though Lyddy's bawling was screwing him up in knots, too. 'I thought you were supposed to flow with milk automatically when she cried.'

'Well I don't,' Jenny flared angrily, trying to stroke the milk down with a rough hand.

'I could do that,' Michael said suddenly, moving her hand aside. He lowered his lips to her breast, as he had not allowed himself to since the birth. The rhythmic stimulation worked, milk began to spurt into his mouth. He took his head away quickly, and Jenny put Lyddy in his place. The baby sucked, shuddered with relief, and settled to her work; gradually the panic faded from her eyes and they began to close. There was peace.

'Sorry if that felt wrong,' he said.

'It worked, anyway. I'm wonderful, aren't I? I can't even breastfeed on my own.' Jenny sighed. 'Thanks for coming back. I'd got into a state. I'm not normally this pathetic.'

'I know you're not.' He put his left arm round her and caressed Lyddy's back with his right hand. 'I'm not going back to Thorleigh. Nan says I can catch up later. I missed you, and it's not fair leaving you on your own.' Jenny kissed his cheek. 'Shall I make a cup of tea?'

Michael went into the kitchen. Unwashed, half-full mugs and plates with food dried onto them by the day's sun, cluttered the surfaces. How disruptive a baby was to every aspect of life. He'd found it easier to adjust than Jenny, since he had never been one for routines and order, while she hated the fact that she could make no plans that were not liable to un-scheduled interruption.

'You ought to be used to being on call,' he'd joked.

'It's not the same. I got time off then. I can't escape Lyddy. She's there, draining me dry all the time. I knew I should never have been a mother.'

Michael waited for the kettle to boil, remembering Lyddy's arrival in the world. Jenny had faced the birth with nervous courage, controlling herself in front of her colleagues in the maternity unit until near the end when she'd screamed and taken huge draughts of gas and air to manage the final contractions that expelled her baby's head into the world. He wasn't the sort to stand with a video camera in hand, but the image was imprinted in his mind as clearly as with any film. The squashed head with its crown of wet, black hair, bloodied and disembodied between Jenny's legs. The body slithering out, to be placed on Jenny's stomach. He'd held Lyddy while they'd cleaned Jenny up, amazed at how heavy and solid she felt, at the way she gazed without tears on a bright new world, with one eye closed. He hadn't known he was crying until he saw the tear fall onto his baby's face, and thought: I have christened her already, with love.

Which was all very well, he smiled to himself, as he remembered the euphoria, but it's bloody hard work. His three nights uninterrupted sleep would have to see him through the next three years, and God knew when Jenny would want sex again. Lyddy began to wail again as Jenny changed sides, and he went back through to hold her hand, anticipating a long night.

Tyrone caught Lisa's nipple between his teeth, and closed them.

'Ow! That bloody hurt!'

'Then stop rabbiting on when I tell you. You never stop.' He sat up, and retrieved his tee shirt. Lisa was lying back on his bed looking hurt, but he wasn't particularly bothered. She might think of herself as his girl-friend, but as far as he was concerned, sex was the sole purpose of the relationship. The last thing he wanted in his current state of ennui was to have to be sensitive to some girl's every whimper. Thrown out of St Barnabas and disowned by his mother, Ty had needed someone on whom to vent his bitterness. He had contacted Lisa soon after Michael and Jenny had tracked him down to the malodorous bedsit he'd found for himself in downtown Leathwell, and been surprised at how eagerly she'd responded. She'd turned her nose up at the neglected state of his room, but it hadn't stopped her having a good time flat on her back on his bed. She'd taken to calling several times a week after the nursery nurse course she was doing at the college. They had sex, maybe shared a takeaway, she'd do some tidying up and cleaning, or take his washing to the laundry, and then she'd be off. He despised her for her devotion, while knowing he would have been lost without her. She was the only friend he had left, apart from Michael and Jenny, and with their baby arriving, he saw very little of them.

His social life consisted entirely of Lisa talking to him about her inconsequential, boring life. Her chatter grumbled past him like the noise of his neighbour's television; after the first week, he scarcely noticed it. He never let information slip about himself if he could help it; only in unguarded moments when he held onto her after sex did he ever come close.

'Why don't you never talk about your family?' she'd asked that evening, stroking his cheek with its neatly trimmed beard. 'Does your mum know about me?'

'There's nothing to know. Anyway, I haven't spoken to her for months.'

'I know what you mean. I wouldn't speak to my mum for a year after she chucked me out. Now she's blamin' me fer bustin' up her marriage, stupid old cow. I went with her boyfriend when I was a kid, and when social services found out, they said he had to get out in case he done my sister too. My mum did her nut.'

'Oh, do shut it, Lisa.'

'You get so you want to get in touch, but you want them to make the first move, cos it hurts, don't it, thinkin' yer mum hates you? Even if you know she's a bastard, blaming you when it's all her own fault really.'

That was when he'd bitten her. Hatred of Deidre still burned his soul. He had forbidden Jenny and Michael to tell her where he was living, though his mother sent periodic messages through them, inviting him home.

'Tell her to fuck off,' he'd tell Michael as they sat over a pint in the nearby pub. Lisa was too damn right. Nothing hurt like rejection.

Lisa sat herself up, rubbing her nipple. 'I wish you'd take me out sometimes, Ty. You're ashamed to be seen with me, that's the trouble. I didn't know I was that ugly.'

He looked at her, the round face with those beautiful greeny eyes, and the soft hair that swung into his face when she lay over him. Full breasts, plenty of curves, maybe overweight, but then, he was no wraith himself. 'You're not ugly.'

'Then is it because you'd be in trouble if you was seen with me? Are you worried someone you know might see us? You've never let me meet any of your friends, 'cept Michael, have you? P'raps you in't got any others.'

'Just shut it, would you? I'll bloody take you out. Here,' he said, throwing her bra at her. 'Get some clothes on, and we'll go down town if that's what you want.'

He'd got himself a job in the run-up to Christmas, a sales assistant on hi-fi and computers, helped by the convincing reference that Michael had somehow prised from Ridgefield.

'He still feels strongly about what you did, but that's not surprising,' Michael had said. 'It's tough enough being married to Nan, without having his sex life splashed all over the tabloids. Fortunately, Nan came in while we were talking, and she was more sympathetic. Said that anyone with a mother like yours deserved pity, not more punishment. "Come on, Christopher", she said, "at least write the lad a good reference, give him a chance. There must be *something* good you can say about him. Like mentioning his interest in photography." Christopher looked daggers at her, but he's agreed, and from what he said when he gave it to me, he's been far kinder than you deserve.'

Since Ty actually knew something about the goods he sold, he had done well, and was kept on after the new year. It helped to pay the rent while he rebooted his journalistic career at Radio Leathwell, and it allowed him to offer excursions to Lisa if he felt like it.

'Can we? Brilliant.' She began to get dressed, inexplicably delighted by the meanest of his gestures towards her.

Ty walked ungraciously beside Lisa as they left the building, allowing her to put her hand through his arm, while trying to give the impression he was nothing to do with her. It was late August, and the early evening streets were still dotted with late shoppers, and tourists thinking Leathwell had more to offer them than a bus tour and the muted delights of the cathedral's architecture. They passed the cathedral during their meanderings. Lisa spotted the open doors, and led him towards them. The noticeboard outside announced that Evensong was at 4.30. Proximity to the church, the all too familiar sound of the organ inside playing an introit made Tyrone shake, and he pulled her away.

'I want to go in,' she said.

'Don't be stupid. They don't let slags like you in there, anyway.'

'Yes they do. Tha's not what you've done in the past, tha's what you do in the future - we had this weirdo bloke telling us when I was in Michael's youth club. Please, Ty, what's wrong? You used to go to church, you're not scared, are you?'

The truth was, he was shit scared, but he couldn't admit that, and she was already inside the door. As he followed her, his stomach knotted, and he felt dizzy and sick. He couldn't even stop her going up to sit with the meagre congregation towards the front as a thin choir sang the opening responses.

A woman across the aisle turned to see the late-comers, and stared hard at them. Ty did not return her gaze, he was concentrating on getting his legs to stay firm beneath him. The last time he had been in a church had been the day before he had gone to Crete. He had been so sure of himself then, of the mission laid on him to expose Ridgefield and Nan; sure he would end up basking in his mother's approbation. He'd been going to be a bloody vicar too, had led his life with rigid discipline. God, what a mess.

Lisa was gazing around the building wide-eyed.

'It's bloomin' big, in't it? I hope it don't fall down.' She took his hand, but he shook her off.

He forced himself to relax, to look around. He'd come here often enough with his mother over the years, lending support to her campaign to be appointed as a canon in recognition of her devotion. Old Ridgefield had effectively torpedoed that plan. Deidre had loathed him ever since.

Across the aisle, the grey-haired woman two rows in front had turned to look at him again, and this time he met her eyes. Of course, she would be here. One of her leisure activities was showing tourists round the building, and she'd stay on for the service. He had not known you could hate someone and long for them so acutely at the same time. He tore his gaze away and looked at the altar; a child again, longing for his mother's approval, and not a man justifiably angry at the way she had manipulated him; a man who was making his own way in life, and with a docile mistress to prove his maturity. He looked at Lisa, and she smiled lovingly at him. It made him sick.

'I'm going for some air. You stay here. Really,' he added as she started to follow him. 'I'll be back.'

He strode down the aisle without looking at Deidre again, but there was a lighter echo behind his steps, and she caught him up as he tried to close the heavy door behind him. They stood on the forecourt under the shadow of grey stone looking at each other. She was wearing a horrible pink suit with a grey clerical shirt and collar, and her hair was sprayed into its usual neat, grey perm, but she was far more lined than he remembered.

'Well?' he said.

'Why haven't you been in touch? I wrote so many times.'

'I never opened them. You disowned me. Why should I want to be in touch?'

'I've missed you so much, darling.' The thin, queenly tone that had irritated him beyond measure for much of his life cracked as she stretched out an arm towards him. Her hand dropped as he failed to respond. 'I'm sorry. Darling, I am sorry. It would have caused such complications if people had thought I had anything to do with what you did, and it was generous of you not to say anything. I never wanted to lose you altogether, you must believe that.'

For the first time in his life he saw her unsure of herself, and took a step towards her. They embraced awkwardly, for Deidre had never been a demonstrative parent.

'I like your beard,' she said, stepping back, and trying to get the conversation back to normal. 'Can you come back and have supper, or something? What about your friend?'

He had forgotten Lisa, obediently waiting for the end of the service. 'Oh, she'll be alright. She'll be having to catch a bus home herself soon. She's not important, just someone I bumped into.' He followed Deidre to her car, resolutely crossing Lisa off the cast list of his life.

Two

Michael was lying on the sofa when Jenny came into the room after an afternoon at the clinic, with their new cordless telephone cradled against his right ear, talking in a relaxed, intimate voice to whoever was on the other end. Lyddy was curled up on his chest, her face a pale pink against the white muslin cloth on his shoulder, and her mouth sucking the air in her sleep. Celestine lay further down his body, stretched out with her paws extended down his jeans, twitching as she dozed.

'I need to go, Jenny's just walked in. Let me know how it goes. I'll see you at the weekend. No ... Yes.' He chuckled down the phone. 'Cheers, Allie.' He rang off and smiled contentedly at Jenny. 'Hello, you're back in good time.'

He's allowed to talk to her, she told herself, stamping on the spark of jealousy that still glowed when she heard Alison's name. 'You look very comfortable,' she said. 'You haven't needed me, obviously.'

Lyddy was nearly four months old, and lasting long enough between feeds now for Jenny to do some sessions at the family planning clinic. It made sense to leave Michael to care for Lyddy. Jenny needed her work, he revelled in fatherhood, taking the physical care and the emotional strains in his stride, and so proud of his daughter he was getting boring. He was, however, still an organist, continued to run the Thursday night youth club, had got involved in running the St Martin's parent and toddler group, and was talking about doing a parenting course for some of the young men up on the Rows who had been inadvertently saddled with fatherhood. All this, and he was about to start his third year on the Programme. For all his current appearance, he could hardly be thought lazy.

'I always need you. I've definitely found my role in life at last, don't you think? A human mattress. Celly's dreaming of catching birds, so do you think Lyddy's dreaming of mammoth breasts, like in that Woody Allen film?'

'That's probably her nightmare.' She sat down in her chair, feeling slightly redundant.

'There's room for you too,' Michael said, patting the sofa beside

243

him as if he had read her need for reassurance.

Jenny shook her head. 'I'm not risking waking her up.'

'What was it like being back?'

'Wonderful. I felt intelligent for a change. What did Alison want?' she couldn't help asking.

'Her school's being inspected this week, and she needed moral support, especially with only just having gone back after Luke. It's the first time I've spoken to her since summer school. Oh, and Lisa rang earlier, as well. She says Ty's walked out on her, and she's desperate to get in touch with him.' Lyddy stirred, and Michael patted her nappied bottom through her dungarees to lull her back to sleep, while he reported the story Lisa had told him.

'It must have been Deidre he went off with,' Jenny said. 'She's made it up with him. I wouldn't have expected her to be that maternal, but I suppose Ty was her little baby once, and that means something, even for a Rutt.' There was an edge to her voice, she realised, and Michael was looking at her oddly. She rushed on. 'What did you tell Lisa?'

'I gave her Deidre's number at Diocesan Church House - I didn't think I ought to give Ty away if he's wanting to split up, though he's behaved like a complete bastard. He sent the few things she had in his room back in a parcel, together with presents she'd given him, without even a note. She'll be much better off without him, but she doesn't see it that way, of course.' Michael nuzzled Lyddy's hair, and stroked the back of her neck with his finger. 'I love their smell, don't you? Anyway,' he continued, 'I've asked Allie to keep an eye out for her.'

Lyddy woke up properly and began to cry. Michael shifted her so that she was lying in his arms, and stroked her cheek and talked and smiled at her until she grinned back at him. Celly jumped down, and stalked to the cat flap, superceded. Jenny, watching Michael distract the baby, with the heel of her hands pressed hard against her nipples to stem the flow that Lyddy's cry had instigated, knew exactly how the cat felt.

'I'd like to go back full-time fairly soon,' she said. 'I'm sure I could work my hours round feeds, and she'll be going onto solids soon.'

'Don't take it too fast. You don't want to make yourself ill.'

'I'm more likely to make myself ill staying at home. There's nothing for me to do, and let's face it, I do love Lyddy, but I'm not very fond of the baby stage. Whereas I am a reasonable doctor, and you like babies. We ought to play to our strengths.'

'That's fine by me.' Lyddy began to fret more volubly, and Michael swung his legs round off the sofa, and handed her over to Jenny. He waited until the baby had settled to the breast before he spoke again.

'I've been thinking that I'd like to try for ordination again this coming year,' he said. 'It feels like it's the right time, and it would mean I could do more with the kids and families at church.'

'Have you talked to Peter and Caroline?'

'Yes. It was Peter who suggested it might be time to try again. He's been using me to help with services, as well as with the music, and he thinks I've matured a lot, and he'd welcome having me on the staff. What do you think, though?'

Jenny thought many things. She thought that the only time she felt like any sort of competent mother was when she was feeding Lyddy, but that that stage would soon have passed. She thought that Michael, ordained, would lose a vital part of himself, but if it was what he wanted, who was she to stand in his way? She thought that he would have less time for her once he was under Peter's direction, but that it might be no bad thing, for they should never have married, and she had nothing left to give him.

She gave him her most confident smile. 'Push a few doors, and see what happens.'

The wind gave up tormenting Lisa as she slipped inside the cathedral. She went through the doors into the interior of the gloomy building, and put her bags down to smooth her hair back down. She had had it cut to swing just above her shoulders, in a vain attempt to cheer herself up with a new look, but it hadn't helped. It was the second time she'd been to evensong since the day Ty had left her with the woman she now knew to have been his mother. She had spoken to Deidre Rutt on the telephone a couple of times, and suffered a curt dismissal.

'My son does not wish to have anything to do with you. Goodbye,' she had said the first time.

The second time, her message had been even more bleak. 'Tyrone has a job in London, and he won't be coming back. He's forgotten you; you really must forget him.'

Subsequent attempts to speak to Deidre had been thwarted by the receptionist at Church House, and Lisa had decided to tackle Ty's mother in person. She'd visited the cathedral and managed to discover when Deidre would be helping with one of the services, and here she was, fighting the late autumn winds, to achieve her goal. Whatever the evidence of his actions, it was still impossible for Lisa to believe that Ty really had excised her from his life. For nearly a year she had endured his treatment without complaint, believing that the rare signs of tenderness and interest in her were truer to his nature than the surly boorishness he usually adopted. She loved him, and he needed her, whether he knew it or not.

The cathedral still seemed an alien place to her, but she entered it bravely, and took her place in a pew towards the back. A pale-faced, grey-haired man intoned the largely incomprehensible service in a gentle northern accent that might have been restful had Lisa been less preoccupied. She wasn't sure how you were supposed to pray, but she knelt and thought about Ty, and how unhappy she was. Deidre Rutt was reading a lesson, and it didn't take much imagination to cast her as the villain who had severed lovers for her private ends. Lisa tackled her after the service with a searing anger in her heart.

'I wanna know where Ty is,' she said, grabbing the woman's arm.

Deidre shook herself free. 'Remove your hands from me! I presume you are the young ...' - she looked Lisa up and down disdainfully - '... lady who has been telephoning me so importunately. I have told you already that my son does not wish to have any further contact with you.'

'He does! He must! Oh, please tell me where he is. He loves me.'

'If he loved you, he would have got in touch with you. In any case, he hardly knows you.'

'That might be what he said to you,' Lisa said, her voice growing high as she panicked. 'He's been screwing me for a whole bloody year. I call that knowin' someone.' Several people looked at them, and hurried away down the aisle, anxious to avoid being contaminated by an ugly scene.

'This is the house of God. You really must watch your language!'

'I'm not bloody well watchin' anything till you tell me where 'e is!' Lisa shouted, seizing Deidre's arm again roughly, and holding a fist to her face. 'Tell me where 'e is, or I'll do you, you fucking cow!' Two hands gripped her arms suddenly from behind, and pulled her away.

'I suggest you leave, Deidre. I'll deal with this young lady - unless you have anything you wish to say to her?'

'Indeed not!' Deidre stalked out indignantly.

'Get your hands off me,' Lisa yelled to her captor, struggling against his grip.

The man who had taken the service was holding her firmly, though there was a half-smile on his mouth. 'Many of us wish to speak like that to Deidre Rutt, but few of us dare. Can I let go of you, or are you dangerous?'

Lisa made another attempt to pull away, but the fight had gone out of her. She crumpled into tears. She'd failed to do anything except antagonise Ty's mother, and he was never going to come back to her.

The man let go of her arms and rested a hand on her shoulder. 'Come through to the vestry.'

'Can I help, Chris?' A woman came up to them, looking at Lisa with concern.

'She's a girlfriend of Tyrone's, or ex-girlfriend, from what I can gather. She thinks Deidre's been keeping them apart. Am I right?'

Sobs prevented Lisa from speaking, so she nodded.

'I'll look after her,' said the woman. 'I'm Nan. Come with me, and I'll get you a cup of tea.' She led Lisa gently through into a small room, and sat her on a chair.

'That was Canon Christopher Ridgefield you were talking to. He's the Principal of St Barnabas Theological College in Thorleigh, and I'm his wife.' She tore off a paper towel from the case that hung over a small sink, and passed it to Lisa to blow her nose. 'We live in Greathampton. Where are you from?'

'Nottling.'

'Are you? I had a student from Nottling. Alison Thompson.'

'Oh, yeah, she used to teach me. I babysit for her.'

Nan filled a kettle and plugged it into a socket behind the robes that hung against the wall. 'Am I right in thinking you're Lisa?'

'Yeah. How'd you know?'

'I know Michael Turner, and he's talked about you and Tyrone.'

'He's walked out on me, an' I'm trying to find him. D'you know where he is?'

Nan poured boiling water onto tea bags in smoked glass mugs, prodded them gently with a spoon, and added milk. 'Here's your tea. I haven't seen Tyrone for over a year.' She drew up a chair and sat down. 'He was responsible for doing a lot of damage to me and Christopher while he was a student at St Barnabas, and he had to leave under a cloud. That makes me a little prejudiced against him, but I suppose he had his reasons. You helped to stop him going too far downhill, from what little I've heard from Michael.'

'I still love him, even though he was a bastard most of the time. I thought if he took it out on me, he might get to feel better, but he never did.'

'No,' Nan said. 'He was lucky to have some good friends, like you, and Michael.'

Lisa began to feel more at ease. 'He's OK, Michael is. I used to see him a bit, when he come over to see Ty, and he took me out for a burger a couple of times. So why's Ty gone off without saying nothing?' Lisa bit back a second eruption of tears.

'I would guess he needed time to sort himself out after what he did last year, and now he has, he'll be wanting to take up the threads of his old life again: get a decent job, get back with his mother - after all, he's all she's got. Unfortunately for you, he'll want to forget everything that reminds him of the last year, including you. I'm sorry. It's bound to hurt.'

Lisa sniffed. 'That was the first time I've ever had anyone need me, you know. I s'pose tha's why I kidded meself he loved me, but I don't s'pose he did.'

'Do you want to talk to me about it?'

'I wouldn't mind - if you've got a day or three.' Lisa said, attempting a smile.

'Come in,' Michael said, answering the door to Nan on an early November afternoon. Lyddy clung to him, crying at the cold rain gusting across her face. 'I thought I'd put her to bed as soon as you arrived, and then hopefully she'll give us an hour or two before she wakes up.'

'Hello, Lyddy,' Nan said, removing her damp coat, and hanging it on the rack in the corner of the hall. 'You are a beautiful baby. Have you got a smile for me?'

Lyddy buried her face in Michael's neck. 'She's tired. You wouldn't like to put the kettle on, would you, and make some coffee while I put her down?'

Nan went off to ferret around in the kitchen, while Michael tucked Lyddy in her cot. He produced a dummy from a box on the window sill - Jenny didn't approve, but she wasn't the one having to deal with Lyddy's howling these days, so he did as he pleased. He patted her bottom under the quilt, while her eyes drooped and closed, feeling again the surge of love that her round, pink cheeks and dark, baby curls aroused in him. He'd always liked babies and children, but he had not known he would feel so passionately about his own. Rain spattered against the window of the little room, and a car raced past on its way to the main road. When he looked back into the cot, Lyddy was fast asleep, and he left the room quietly to join Nan.

She was sitting in Jenny's armchair, looking at a file through the glasses perched on her nose, while Celestine sat unblinking at her feet, evaluating her lap.

'I'm still self-conscious in specs,' Nan said, taking them off. 'Makes me feel old.'

'You don't look it,' he said. Whatever strains there were in her marriage to Christopher - and he knew their differences still caused tension between them - it continued to do her good. She had left the Programme in the summer, after her appointment as Diocesan Director of Ordinands. It was a high-profile job; the exposure in the tabloids the year before didn't seem to have damaged her career prospects, as it had done Christopher's. He had immediately ceased to be regarded as a candidate for episcopacy, and though, with Roly retiring, he had been asked to take on being Principal of the Programme as well as St Barnabas, he remained bitter.

'Flattery will get you everywhere,' said Nan. 'I made some coffee.'

Michael sat down on the sofa and picked up the mug she had left on the table in front of him.

'Is it working out alright, Jenny being back at work full-time, and you looking after Lyddy? Does she find it a wrench, leaving her all day?'

'Seems to be OK so far. Jenny says she's a lot happier, though I reckon she's still feeling a bit fragile. It's as if her emotional skin has got thinner, and she doesn't seem to be able to distance herself from everything as much as she used to. She gets upset about patients, or blows her top about them, and she never used to do that. She says it's her hormones, and it's only when she gets home that it shows. I do worry about her sometimes, but we manage.'

'Good.' Nan drained her mug and put it back on the table, looking at him thoughtfully. 'As long as it doesn't put too much strain on you. I guess you're the one who gets kicked when things go wrong.'

'Everything leaves a strain,' Michael muttered, leaning back, and running his hands through his hair. 'But you expect that with a new baby. I survive. And I get some time off for good behaviour.' Celly leapt onto his lap, and he caressed her as he spoke.

'What does Jenny think about you seeking ordination?'

'Oh, she says go for it. She's known it's what I've wanted ever since I met her, and she's got no problems with it. Having grown up in a vicarage, she knows what's involved. She doesn't want to be a full-time vicar's wife, but as long as she can carry on with her practice, she's fine.'

'I shall need to talk to both of you together at some stage.'

'I know, that's OK. She's happy to do it.'

'Right, tell me why you want to be ordained.'

'I've told you often enough.'

'I know, but this time you want me to do something about it, and I'd like to hear it as if I didn't know anything about you.'

Michael settled himself back on the cushions and revisited his life history. 'I was pretty knocked back by being turned down, as you know,' he said at the end, 'though I can see now it was probably a good thing. I've grown up in the last few years. Got married, got a family, settled down, shown I can do the academic work. And I've done a lot more at St Martin's. Peter and Caroline both say they think I have a lot of gifts.'

'I'm sure you do have a lot of gifts, but there again, the Harts have a vested interest in pushing you forward. They'd like to have their protege become a minister, and they could do with an extra pair of hands at St Martin's. Besides, just because your parents and godparents tell you to do something, it doesn't mean it's right for you.'

'It isn't only that, of course it isn't. Can I tell you about what I've been doing in the church recently?' He launched enthusiastically into a description of his work and his motivations for it, striving to get the interview back on course. 'I *know* it's right for me,' he concluded. 'What else am I supposed to do? I can hardly bum around looking after my kids, and doing odd spots of voluntary work all my life.'

'No?'

'A vocation has got to be more than that, hasn't it?'

'Has it? There are hundreds of ways of having a vocation, and if they don't include bumming around doing different dead-end jobs, or making cars or cleaning toilets, or changing nappies, come to that, then most of the population is excluded. Ordination isn't the answer to everything, or for everyone.' Nan looked at him with a furrowed brow. 'I'm sure there'll be something you should do, but I'm still not clear exactly what you want to be ordained *for*.'

'I'm not explaining myself very well today,' Michael said.

'Which is odd, because normally you're very articulate.'

'I wasn't expecting you to interrogate me so aggressively.'

'Can't friends be challenging? I didn't expect you to be quite so uncomfortable.'

'No, I didn't either. I think it's because it matters to me.'

A thin wail came from upstairs, and Michael immediately jumped up. He grinned wryly at Nan. 'She's got me well trained hasn't she?'

'We can leave it there if you like. I'll need to talk to you again, and you'll have to see Bishop Derrick, of course. I'll be in touch about seeing you with Jenny.'

Michael showed her to the door, and went to see what Lyddy wanted, not altogether displeased by the interruption.

Both Nan and the Bishop turned him inside out in the meetings that followed, and Michael was thoroughly pessimistic about his chances after Nan had spoken to him with his wife. There was something unctuously false about the enthusiasm Jenny had shown, as if she were a mother promoting her particularly untalented child. They had a bewildering and bruising altercation afterwards.

'What were you playing at?' he demanded, after Nan had gone.

'What do you mean?' Jenny replied defiantly, looking across at him as he sat back down on the sofa. 'I said I'd support you, and I did.'

'You didn't have to sound so bloody patronising about it. You know what I mean. You keep saying you want me to do it, but you won't talk about it, you're not really interested.'

'Of course I am. It's what you've always wanted. Anyway, you always used to say you loved me because I didn't tell you what to do. I know the love bit's more questionable now, but I'm only trying to be how you want.' She sat rigidly, hugging herself inside her thick arran sweater, keeping him at bay.

'I'm going to bed,' he said, standing up.

'Oh for God's sake don't creep out looking hurt and pathetic. Who's the one who won't talk now? Next I suppose you'll come crawling to me in bed saying "I love you, hold me closer" as if I'm your mother and you'll die without me. Stop being so wet.'

Michael turned to look at her with his hand on the door. 'That's hardly fair. Why shouldn't I feel hurt when the person I love doesn't seem to want me, or even to like me very much? I'll tell you what, I'll save you the embarrassment. I won't crawl to you, I won't even touch you unless you request it in writing, how's that?'

He pulled the door to firmly behind him, and went upstairs. When she joined him in bed, he pretended to be asleep, lying with his back to her, wondering why she pushed him away so brutally, as if her survival depended on it.

'I know you're not asleep,' Jenny said, when she'd turned the light out, and was lying beside him. 'I'm sorry for what I said. I can't help it if I don't feel like sex. It's natural, lots of women don't after having babies.'

Michael didn't bother to point out that her aversion had set in long before that, before pregnancy, before Andy's assault, before he'd got to

251

know Alison. She had never loved him, and there was little point in reminding her of it.

'If you're that desperate, I can lie here while you get on with it.'

'Sex isn't the point,' he said roughly, his eyes smarting. 'Sexual frustration I can deal with. I want someone to hold me. God, I wish I was a baby, so I could howl till someone cuddled me.'

They lay miserably in a dark disturbed only by the orange glow of Greathampton creeping past the curtains, and the muted traffic noise from the ring road ebbing and flowing through the opened window, until Jenny tentatively put her arms around him. He couldn't help himself growing hard as he embraced her.

'I thought you said this wasn't about sex,' she whispered.

'I said I could deal with it. But I'd rather make love to you than to myself. Hmm?' He kissed her, and for once she didn't turn away. So, for only the second time since Lyddy's birth, he was able to lose himself inside her. They said no words, but for a few minutes, he could pretend that he was loved, and it had to be enough.

Soon afterwards, Nan rang to say she was recommending that Michael go to a selection conference.

'Wow! I didn't expect that,' Michael said, sitting down abruptly on the bottom stair.

'Why not? I know I've seemed hard on you, but I needed to be sure it was something coming from inside you as well as from everybody around you. Now it's up to them. I expect your selection conference will be at the end of April.'

The months passed quickly, as their lives fell into a routine. Jenny picked up her practice again, her only concession to Lyddy's existence that she tried to come home for half an hour at lunchtimes, and usually managed to be back from the surgery in time to give her daughter a breast-feed before bed. Her practice's enrolment with a deputising service had freed her from the necessity of being on call at nights, although Michael suspected she might have welcomed the extra distraction. He carried on with his work, Lyddy in tow, his delight in her a small consolation for the loss of his wife's affection. It was as if an explosion had left a crater in the centre of their marriage, a deep hole which they circled circumspectly, lest it swallow them up. Though they talked in a friendly enough manner about Lyddy's antics, or their work, Jenny rebuffed any further approaches

Michael made towards emotional or physical intimacy, and he left for his selection conference still baffled by her attitude towards him.

'Stop behaving like a mother hen, Michael,' she laughed, as he explained for the second time how Lyddy likcd to be settled for her afternoon nap. 'You act as if I'd never had anything to do with babies before. I'm on holiday, and we'll enjoy it. You go off and do your best. I might even pray for you.'

'You better had,' he said, kissing them both goodbye. Jenny held Lyddy, encouraging her to wave, while Celestine sat at their feet washing herself. The glimpse he had of the three of them together in his rear-view mirror was the last he would ever have.

Though Lyddy was scarcely a difficult baby, being solely responsible for her left Jenny's nerves jangling, and she was not at her best when she answered the door the following evening and found Alison standing there.

'Oh,' Jenny said, swinging a grousing Lyddy round onto her other hip.

'I had to come to Greathampton, and I thought I'd drop these books off for Michael,' Alison said, with a quick smile.

'Thank you.' Jenny took the bag with her free hand, and tossed it onto the hall floor behind her. 'Did Michael ask you to check up on me? Oh, do be quiet, Lyddy!'

'Well, he did say you'd be on your own.'

'Do you want to come in?'

'No, I won't, I've got Luke asleep in the car.'

Apart from a visit with Michael just after Luke's birth, and a brief introduction at the summer school, Jenny had not seen Alison's son. Go on, take an interest, she told herself. 'Can I see?'

She followed Alison down the path. In the back of the car, slouched in his baby seat, a dark-haired child slept contentedly, his face pink in the evening light.

'He's coming on,' Jenny said politely. 'I suppose he's into everything?'

'When he can be bothered. He prefers to sit and watch the world go by. As long as he's got someone to cuddle him and talk to him, he's perfectly happy. He's obviously going to be extremely laid back. Still, that's not really so surprising, considering...' She paused to disentangle her car keys from her jacket pocket, and Jenny, observing Luke's long, thick lashes, and remembering Meg's stories of Michael as a baby, finished her hanging sentence for her.

'Considering who his father is, you mean?'

Alison turned slowly and stared at her for several seconds. 'Well, there is always that,' she said, neutrally.

'He *is* Michael's ...' Jenny whispered, backing away.

'He loved me. If it hadn't been for her,' Alison nodded at Lyddy, 'he'd have left you for me.'

Jenny gasped, whirled round, and headed back towards the house.

'Jenny...' Alison called after her, but she could not stand hearing more.

The slam of the door set Lyddy off howling again, and Jenny thrust her down on the floor, and leant against the hall wall, with her forehead pressed to the cold plaster. The doorbell rang; Alison, wanting to gloat. Jenny ignored her, and eventually Alison gave up and left. Jenny remained where she was, muttering to herself. 'He was lying to me. I knew it. I knew it. Oh, God, they were lovers. I hate her. I hate him. Oh God. Shut up, Lyddy, you horrible child! I wish you were dead!'

Another wailing sound merged with Lyddy's, and Jenny looked down to see Celestine triumphantly stalking down the hall with a bird in her mouth, mewing her delight.

'Oh, you disgusting animal. Get out. Get out!' Jenny opened the front door, and pushed the cat out with her foot. Celly tried to double back inside, but Jenny stooped, scooped her up and threw her down the steps onto the driveway. The cat shot off towards the road. Cars passed only infrequently, but Celly was unlucky. A youth, putting his foot down to create a satisfactory roar before braking sharply for the junction with the main road, neither saw nor felt the blow of his front wing catching the cat. The shriek Jenny gave as she saw the two hurtling towards collision was lost in the noise of his radio booming through quadrophonic speakers.

Jenny rushed to the kerb and knelt down beside the cat as the car sped unconsciously on its way. Celly lay on her side, entirely still, a trickle of blood apparent at the corner of her mouth.

'No! Oh, Celly.' White-faced, she gathered the cat up, a warm, limp toy, drained of all its magnificent life. She'd murdered her.

By the time Michael rang two hours later to see how things were, Jenny had everything under control. She had put Celestine in a box awaiting burial, while she bathed Lyddy, watching as the baby splashed unconcerned, soothed by her familiar routine. Jenny nursed her before putting her in her cot. Though Lyddy had been using a cup and eating solid food for some months now, they were both reluctant to give up this bedtime feed. Jenny would sit on her bed with her feet up, and her daughter cradled hair to head in the crook of her arm, looking at her baby's soft, pink cheeks, her dark lashes fluttering and closing with perfect contentment, and think: I can do this. Even tonight, when her mother was drained of all feeling, Lyddy still fell asleep content.

When she had tucked Lyddy under her quilt, Jenny went outside and opened the box to gaze on her cat. The body was cool and heavy by now, dust had settled on the retina of the half-open eyes. As Jenny caressed the long fur, a ball of misery lodged in her throat, so she could scarcely breathe, but she would not allow the tears to reach her eyes. Her own guilt and grief were harsh enough, but how could she tell Michael? So many of her early memories of him had Celestine in them, sprawled across his lap as he'd opened his heart to Jenny in those early days, stalking him sedately through the grass when he dug the garden, nuzzling inconveniently against his head as they made love in their new bed on their return from their honeymoon, mewing for attention. Pull yourself together, she told herself. It's only an animal. You can get another one. She pushed her sorrow to the back of her mind and took refuge in practicality. With a set face, she selected a place to bury the cat, and dug a hole under the huge pink peony where Celly was wont to lie in the summer. She found one of Michael's old gardening jumpers in the shed, and kissed the cat before she wrapped her up in it and laid her in the earth. She had only just sat down when the telephone rang.

'Everything OK?' Michael asked.

'Lyddy's fine, but I'm afraid there's been an accident to Celly,' she replied calmly. 'She got hit by a car. She's dead.'

'Oh, no! Oh, Jenny, how awful.'

'These things happen. She was trying to eat a bird by the front door, so I chased her off. I threw her down the steps and she ran straight into the road. Just her bad luck there was a car.'

She heard Michael draw breath on the other end of the line. 'That's terrible. I can't believe it.'

'Never mind, you can always get another one.'

'You sound as if you don't care at all...'

'Of course I care, but there's no point in being over-sentimental about animals. Anyway, how are you getting on? Impressing them with your high Christian standards?'

'Doing my best.'

His response was half-hearted, and he returned to talk about Celly before he rang off.

'I can't imagine coming back, and her not being there to welcome me. Have you buried her?'

'Under the peony. You'd better go, there must be other people wanting to use the phone. I'll see you on Thursday.'

'I'll ring tomorrow. Love to Lyddy. And to you. Jenny...'

But she had put the phone down. He always sounded concerned and loving, a fine Christian man, passing himself off as a perfect candidate for ministry and yet he'd betrayed her, and lied to her, over and over again.

That night, she barely slept, seeing the accident again and again whenever she woke, and tormented by nightmares while she slept. Michael and Luke, Lyddy and Celestine, ran through her dreams, until she gathered them up like an armful of Lyddy's toys and hurled them onto the road to be crushed by the oncoming traffic. She woke at six-thirty, flooded by tears, to the sound of Lyddy's wailing, and it took her some minutes before she could nail her emotions down enough to tackle the day ahead. She survived only a few hours, until like water bursting through a hastily patched dam, the chaos she had been holding at bay for so long erupted and swept her away.

One minute she was a normal mother, taking Lyddy upstairs to help empty the washing machine in the bathroom. The next, she was standing on the half-landing, with the world whirring round her, and the only fixed point a limp, lifeless body lying at the foot of the stairs. Somewhere between those two moments, she'd done something to Lyddy. There'd been that high, terrifying shriek of pain and fear, and the harrowing thud of Lyddy's head hitting the sharp corner of the post at the bottom of the bannisters, jerking back, still. And all Jenny could do was stand and stare.

And stare. And stare.

Three

Michael had been shaken by his conversation with Jenny the previous evening. He woke with an urgent, irrational desire to get back that refused to disperse as he joined the other candidates for prayers before breakfast. He phoned Jenny to reassure himself, but she had the answerphone on, and all he could do was to leave a message for her to ring him if she had the slightest cause.

'I need to go home,' he explained to the chief selector after breakfast, as his anxiety grew more intense.

'Your cat's died, and you need to go home? I hardly think that's as important as testing your vocation for ministry.'

'I know it sounds trivial, and I can't explain it, I just know I have to.' He knew he'd made a mistake as soon as he'd said it, marking himself out as arrogant or misguided, or both.

'Surely there's someone you can ask to call in? You'll be back tomorrow. I have to say, Michael, that one of the question marks against you in the past was your degree of commitment, and if you walk out like this, it will be noted.'

Michael turned away, and went to prepare himself for his next interview. Half an hour in, however, and he could stand the struggle to concentrate no more. He stood up.

'I can't stay. I've got to go home. I know it's the end of my chance of selection, and I'm sorry for wasting your time, but I have to go.'

He left his interviewer gaping after him as he left the room, grabbed his bags, and headed homewards.

The drive took Michael a little over two hours, and he arrived home to find two or three of his neighbours standing outside the house looking serious.

'Where've you been?' asked Stan from across the road. 'The coppers have been asking for you. Your kid's got took off to hospital in an ambulance, ooh, about half an hour ago. And Jenny went off after them in a police car.'

Michael put a hand on the gatepost to steady himself. 'Why? What's happened?'

'I don't know, they didn't say, did they, Stan?' Norma from next door chipped in, shocked but excited to be present for the most dramatic incident the road had seen in years. 'She must've got taken ill, or perhaps there was an accident. You'd better get to the hospital...'

But Michael was already opening the car door, starting the engine, swinging the car in a kerb-crunching circle to speed back towards the main road. He was barely conscious of the traffic around him. Something had happened to Lyddy. Jenny had not gone with her in the ambulance. He could think of only one explanation, and it engulfed him with terror as he drove to the hospital, praying in a mantra: oh God, let her live, God let her live!

A hundred miles away, the chief selector for Michael's conference screwed up the piece of paper on which he had been drafting critical notes about him, and deposited it in the waste bin. He had known candidates who claimed direct divine guidance before, and they rarely got through. He wasn't sure what to make of someone whose forebodings preceded by several hours a call from his local police force, summoning him home because his baby had been whisked to hospital in an ambulance.

The journey through the town centre to the hospital took forever. Michael got caught by every traffic light and reversing delivery lorry possible, and then it took him several more minutes to find a parking space before he could at last get to the Accident and Emergency Reception.

There were several people waiting, and nobody at the desk. Everybody looked more on edge than usual, and he realised that this was because a baby was screaming, a shrill, terrified screeching that pierced heart and skin to stretch the nerves beneath to breaking point. His whole body shook with recognition: Lyddy! Alive! He knew it instinctively, though the cries she gave were unlike anything he had ever heard from her before. He followed the sound to a small cubicle.

Lyddy was in the arms of a pale nurse in a short-sleeved uniform, emitting her high shrieking from a body rigid with rage and pain. A splint was attached to her right leg, and a grey lump with a deep red line across it, bulged from her left temple.

The nurse was trying unsuccessfully to persuade Lyddy to take a dummy. 'Calm down. Come on, you'll wear yourself out,' she was saying, a trifle crossly. She looked up as Michael came in.

'Let me take her,' he said, reaching out.

The nurse drew back with undisguised suspicion. 'Who are you? What do you want?'

'I'm her dad.'

He tried to take Lyddy, but the nurse retreated once more. 'I'll need to check,' she said, pulling open the door at the other end of the cubicle.

'Let me take her,' Michael said again, more urgently. It was a nightmare to arrive to find Lyddy in such distress, and not to be allowed to hold her. 'Where's my wife?'

A doctor appeared, positioning himself between Michael and the nurse as he consulted with her in a voice inaudible above Lyddy's screaming. He glanced at a file in his hand and turned to Michael. 'We'll need to take a few details. Can you tell me your name and address?'

Michael complied with the questioning, his eyes constantly on Lyddy, an arm's reach away from him. Only when he had spread his wallet before them, confirming his identity with his credit card and driving licence, was he finally permitted to take her. At last he could enfold her in his arms, could seek to still her flailing limbs, and comfort her anguish with his familiar presence. He stroked her humid cheek and touched the dummy to her lips, pressing his cheek to hers as he murmured reassurances:

'Lyddy, Lyddy, it's alright! I'm here, precious. Shhh.'

But she was beyond response to any of his techniques, and her screams continued unabated.

'Can't you give her anything?' he begged the nurse, who had remained to observe his failure to soothe the child he had claimed.

'Not till we've assessed her head injury.'

'When will that be?'

'I don't know.'

'Do you know where my wife is?'

'I'll see if there's a doctor free to talk to you, shall I?'

There were doctors in plenty as the hours lengthened, though none of them could tell him what had happened to Jenny. Doctors, nurses, staff in white coats or casual clothes, their badges of identity swinging meaninglessly before his eyes as they looked at Lyddy, and asked him questions, and gave him forms to sign, before leaving without having made the slightest difference to her plight.

Lacerated by the baby's constant screaming, Michael was too distracted to take in more than fragments of what they told him. Talk of a fall downstairs, of broken limbs and pins and hairline fractures of the skull, of scans and X-rays, all passed him by. Delays for the scan, delays for the theatre. Michael could only sit or stand or walk with his distraught daughter, utterly impotent in the face of her misery, enduring with her the interminable stretches of an unimaginable hell.

The theatre was finally free. Lyddy was given an injection, and gradually all sound faded as her body stilled into unconsciousness in his arms. He could hardly bear to relinquish her to the trolley that would wheel her through the double doors and away from him, for what if she never woke to cry again? And, oh God, where was Jenny?

As he stood staring at the last shudder of the closing doors, a voice broke into his thoughts. 'Hello, Michael. Could we have that word now? Would you like to come to my office?'

He turned to see a sensible-looking woman with dark skin and curly black hair, smiling sympathetically at him. 'I'm Faye Hooper,' she said. 'I spoke to you earlier. I'm the social worker here.'

He frowned, having no recollection of her.

She set off towards her office. 'Have you had anything to eat or drink since you arrived?'

Michael tried to think, and failed.

Faye looked at him closely. 'You don't know whether you're coming or going, do you?'

He shook his head. 'I don't think she ever stopped crying. It didn't feel like it. I'm worried sick about the operation, and I've no idea what's happened to my wife.'

Faye put a hand on his arm. 'You have had a horrendous time. I'll get you a cup of tea, and let you catch up with yourself, then we can talk.'

Faye's office housed a small desk and two low chairs set at an angle to each other under the window. A dispirited spider plant trailed from the bookshelf above the desk, brushing the piles of paperwork with the dusty green of its leaves. She sat Michael down, and left him while she fetched two plastic cups of steaming tea.

'It's pretty horrible, but it's hot,' she said, placing his cup on the corner of the desk. 'I sugared it, I thought you might need it.'

He took a sip of the scalding liquid, needing the jolt it gave him. Nothing had passed his lips since his nervous breakfast with a group of would-be ordinands back in a world he no longer recognised.

He met Faye's eyes. 'I'm ready.'

'It looks as if Jenny's had some kind of a breakdown. She's in the Linthorpe Psychiatric Hospital, the other side of Leathwell. Seeing as she's a GP, they didn't want to take her somewhere local where she might bump into one of her patients.' Faye waited while he took another gulp of his tea. 'I'm afraid this is going to be difficult for you, Michael, but you'll need to know. When Jenny rang for an ambulance, she said she'd killed your baby, so they sent the police along as well. The paramedics found poor little Lydia unconscious in the hall. From her injuries, it looked as if she'd fallen downstairs and knocked herself out.'

Michael kept his eyes on Faye's face, wishing he could avoid hearing what must come, knowing he had to hear, and somehow to bear it.

'They found Jenny upstairs, staring out of the back bedroom window, taking no interest. All she'd say was that she'd thrown Lydia downstairs and killed her.'

'No... She wouldn't,' he whispered.

'She wouldn't listen when they told her the baby was alive,' Faye continued, 'and she wouldn't come to the hospital. The police arrested her on suspicion of causing actual bodily harm, and took her down to the station...'

'Arrested! They can't. Jenny wouldn't hurt anyone, especially Lyddy. She loves her. She's a doctor, she ...' Shakily, he placed his cup back on the desk, and put his head in his hands. A normal Jenny might not hurt anyone, but she had been on edge for so long, how could he know what she might be driven to do?

'She was obviously in no state to be interviewed,' said Faye, 'so the police doctor called in a psychiatrist, who suggested she go to Linthorpe. They'll assess her, and then the police will want to interview her as soon as she's well enough. The police notified the local authority straight away, of course, which is why I'm involved.'

Michael jerked upright. 'You can't take Lyddy away!'

'No one's planning to do that. Don't panic. Certainly no one's suggesting you shouldn't have care of her.' She smiled reassuringly. 'I've spoken to your health visitor, and she says you're doing a great job, you even do some work with dads at the clinic over in the East End Rows, don't you? It's Jenny we need to assess, but Lyddy's going to be in here for a few days, so that gives us plenty of time to get reports from Linthorpe.'

'What's going to happen to her? Will she be charged? Could she go to prison?'

'I can't tell you that. No one can until we've been able to talk to Jenny, and get some psychiatric assessment.'

'I have to see her. She must feel awful.' He tried to make sense of the picture Faye had given, to imagine Jenny hurling Lyddy down the stairs to certain injury and possible death. Impossible. She wasn't like that. He put his hand to his head again. 'If somehow, she did do something,' he said slowly, 'it would be because she was ill. She wouldn't mean to.'

'If that's the case, she'll be given help.' Faye leaned forward. 'I know this has all been a tremendous shock for you, Michael. I am going to need to ask you a few questions at some stage, but I suggest we leave that until you're feeling stronger. Do you have family around? Does Jenny?'

'Not nearby. I could ring my mum, she might be able to come for a while.'

'I think you should ask her. I'll help all I can, but it's a lot to cope with.'

'I have to see Jenny,' he said. 'But how can I? I have to be there when Lyddy comes round, and it's at least forty minutes' drive. What shall I do?'

'My impression when I talked to them at Linthorpe was that Jenny wasn't necessarily ready to receive visitors, but why don't you ring them yourself? You can use my phone.'

Several minutes later, Michael was sitting at Faye's desk with the phone to his ear, listening to Rose Johnston, the consultant in charge of Jenny's case, explaining that one of the few things Jenny had said was that she didn't want her husband, and wouldn't see him.

'But come over tomorrow, she may change her mind. You might bring a few things in for her - she only has what she stands up in. I'd certainly like to talk to you tomorrow, though if you've a minute now, perhaps you could give me a few details.'

'What do you want to know?' He leaned on the desk, mechanically answering the questions being put to him, packaging his wife's life into a series of boxes: full name, age, address, occupation, children, parents, marriage. When he put the phone down, he was feeling even more inadequate. Once before, he had failed his wife when she was most in need. Let her turn him away, when he should have known she wanted him to stay. Yet here he was, abandoning her again. Leaving her to her lonely battle with fear, grief and guilt, and a humiliating public collapse that must feel like her worst nightmare. And yet how could he leave Lyddy to wake from her operation confused and in pain, deserted by her parents yet again?

It was a crucifixion, one hand nailed to Lyddy, the other hammered to Jenny in Linthorpe, too far to sustain. He was tearing apart.

Her operation successfully completed, Lyddy was transferred to a cot in a four-bedded children's ward. Michael found her with her eyes shut, but whimpering fitfully as she fidgeted in her sleep, disturbed by the plaster encasing her leg from hip to ankle. He talked to the nurse at the desk next to Lyddy's cot, then fetched himself a sandwich and coffee from the Hospital Friends canteen, and began his long vigil by her bed.

Lyddy stirred and cried frequently as the evening wore on, and he patted her bottom, or retrieved her dummy, or simply stroked her face and spoke soothingly until she had settled again. He passed the night on a thin foam mattress on the floor beside the cot, with the curtain drawn around them to shut out some of the light and the muted night-time activity of the ward. Lyddy continued to be restless, afraid in the unfamiliar environment, and, despite medication, upset by the ache in her head and leg. After the fourth time of heaving himself up to deal with her frightened cry, he carefully lifted her from the cot and lay down on his pillow with her on his chest. The nurses would undoubtedly object, but Lyddy seemed reassured by his presence, and the feel of his shirt under her face as she nestled under his chin. They had spent countless hours like that in her early weeks. Finally, both of them slept.

Four

Subdued light reached Jenny's bed from the corridor outside. It gave her something to stare at as she lay wide-eyed on her bed, trying not to listen to the relentless litany reeling through her head ... godgodgodgod what have I done what am I doing here? Lyddy's dead and I did it, threw her down the stairs to tumble tumble, screaming, screaming, striking her head with that thwack wrenching her neck and jerking her body until she lies lifeless, lying still, still lying on the floor, and she'll never smile at me again. I can't stand it. I want to lie here till I die, wherever I am, with these people who sit me up and make me drink and ask me things I can't answer and watch me all the time I don't know why, I never want to move or think or do anything again for ever or ever ... I've killed my baby. I never had a baby. I didn't want her, she never existed, my breasts aren't tender with needing her, she wasn't mine she was Michael's and he's got his son to go to now, he doesn't need me any more, he never did, he never even came and no one wants me, I'm disintegrating, I should never have been born...

The night was lightening into dawn when the nurses discovered Michael and Lyddy. He resisted their desire to get her back into her cot, however, tightening his hold on her as he pointed out that they were both actually getting some sleep this way. In the end they left him for a couple more hours. As he came to consciousness at the start of the ward's day, there was a moment when the child he held in his arms was not Lyddy, but his wife, tiny, fragile, dependent on him for life itself. It took him a while to collect his senses, and focus on Lyddy once more. He changed her, fed her breakfast, and managed to coax a tentative smile from her before he left her in the care of the nurses, and took the main road out towards Leathwell.

He was almost at Linthorpe before he remembered he was supposed to have brought things for Jenny. He had to turn and head back to the superstore he'd passed a few miles earlier, where he could buy clothes and toiletries, before finishing his journey.

The hospital itself was situated at the approach to Linthorpe village, and easy to find. Michael followed the signs down a driveway and found a pleasant set of single-storeyed buildings set in the large garden of the dilapidated country house that had been demolished to make way for it. One or two people sat on seats in the April sunshine, whether patients or staff he couldn't tell.

A nurse with wavy grey hair and a freckled face came to meet him in reception. 'Hello, I'm Angela. I'm the nurse assigned to your wife while she's here.'

How is she?' he asked, shaking her hand.

'Not much change. Still very withdrawn, not saying anything much.' She studied his face.

Michael was becoming used to the appraising looks given him by the professionals with whom he'd come into contact over the last twenty-four hours, the attempts to judge his own level of complicity in Lyddy's accident and his wife's breakdown.

'Could you come and have a word with Rose Johnston first, then you can try and see if your wife wants to talk to you,' Angela said. 'Her office is through here, and when she's finished, she'll call me, and I'll take you along to Jenny.'

She led him down a short passage, tapped on a door, and ushered him in. Rose Johnston turned out to be a short woman with dyed-blond hair in a bun, a tendency to stoutness, and bright lipstick out of place on a weather-beaten face. She shook his hand firmly, sat him down, and invited him to tell her about his wife's state of mind. He answered as best he could, though the questions became more difficult.

'Was Lydia planned? How did Jenny feel about the pregnancy?'

Michael hesitated. He could hardly say she had hated it so much she'd not even told him for months. Surely it was not for him to betray the frailties Jenny worked so hard to disguise? But he had been opening himself up to questioners of one sort or another all week, and he had in any case no energy for dissembling.

'She was upset at first,' he said. 'It disturbed her, and she wasn't completely sure why. And it came at a time when things weren't very good between us. I was thrilled, of course, and once she got used to the idea, so was she. A little anxious, but that was natural.' He described Lyddy's birth, and Jenny's ambivalent response to motherhood. 'She was very competent at the practical things, and she breastfed Lyddy - she still does at night-time. She's really loving, and does lots of things with her when she's not at work. Anyone can see she's a great mother. If I didn't think that, I'd never have gone away and left them. Only I get the feeling it still disturbs her at some level. She never takes it out on Lyddy, but she's always sniping at me.'

'Is she jealous that you spend so much time with the baby?'

'She arranged it that way. She couldn't wait to get back to work. To be honest, she's been a bit strange with me practically since we got married. Maybe it's my fault, but she won't discuss it, so what can I do? It's like now, saying she doesn't want to see me, but I honestly can't figure out why. I'm the only one she's got, and I really love her. I can't bear it when she pushes me away.'

'Does that apply to your sexual relationship as well? I don't mean to be intrusive, but I'm trying to build up a picture.'

'What sexual relationship?' he said gloomily. 'She's not been specially interested since Lyddy was born, though I suppose you expect that. But Jen's never really been that enthusiastic, apart from the first two or three months. You must be thinking there's something wrong with me, but I've had long-term relationships before without problems.'

'And has Jenny had previous relationships, or a bad experience, perhaps?'

'No. We used to talk about that kind of thing a lot before we were married, and I think she would have told me. And I'd have said she enjoyed that side of things at first.' A sense of loss hit him for the wife he'd once had and needed to recover. He looked at Rose appealingly. 'Could I try and see her?'

Airy corridors, open doors and intermittent people passed by Michael like views from a slowing train as he followed Angela to the unit where Jenny had been taken. Doors opened off a short corridor, and Angela pushed one of them to reveal a modest room, reminiscent of St Barnabas or student accommodation anywhere: the small combination wardrobe, table and chair, and a sink in the corner by the window. Michael's attention went immediately to the bed up against the wall on the left, and the hunched figure curled on its side with its back to the room.

'Jenny!' he whispered, kneeling down beside the bed and putting his arm over her. Her body was tense as steel, her hands clutched her head, and her eyes looked blankly at the wall. As he held her, he could feel her rocking herself with infinitesimal movements.

'Lyddy's alright. She's going to be OK. She misses you, so do I.'

Jenny made no response. He rubbed her shoulder. 'You wouldn't hurt her, I know you wouldn't. Jenny. Please talk to me. It's Michael. I love you.' He stroked her hair, and laid his face against her shoulder, trying to communicate with his physical presence where his words could not pass. She seemed to tighten in on herself even more, so that he was startled when words issued from her in a low, lifeless voice.

'Go away.'

'Don't say that. I want to help you.'

'I hate you. Go away.'

Her voice held a note of distress. Angela touched his shoulder. 'Perhaps you should for the moment.'

Michael stood up, limbs cramped, and knees aching. It tore his heart to leave Jenny there, like leaving his own flesh impaled on a stake, but what could he do?

'Couldn't I bring Lyddy in?' he asked Angela as she led him back down the corridor. 'I'm sure it would help if Jen could see her.'

'Well, not really,' Angela replied awkwardly. 'We can't be perfectly sure how she'll respond, can we? We don't want to distress Lyddy any further.'

'Oh.' Michael went cold. He had been so concerned about Jenny that he had temporarily forgotten the seriousness of the accusations that hung over her.

'You could take a photograph and bring that,' Angela said. 'That would show Jenny the baby's making progress. As long as Lyddy doesn't look too awful.'

He smiled briefly. 'That depends which side you look from.'

Before going back to the hospital, Michael drove home. He had been wearing the same, rather formal, trousers and shirt for the last thirty hours, and he felt the need for change, as well as having items to collect for Lyddy.

The emptiness of the house chilled him as soon as he closed the front door behind him. No Celestine to wind herself around his legs. No Lyddy, grinning as she crawled determinedly towards him down the hall. No Jenny to wrap her arms around him and restore his wholeness - not that she had done either of those things for many months now. He went upstairs slowly, wincing as he imagined Lyddy's fall, and the harsh contact of her tender body with the angles of the stairs, wall and bannisters. The upstairs stair-gate was leaning against the wall on the half-landing. Michael carried it up with him, wondering why it was not in its normal place. As he set it down at the head of the stairs, he was transported back to Sunday afternoon, packing for his conference, with Lyddy crawling back and forth on the landing. She'd pulled herself up on the gate, and stood tugging and pushing at it with a mischievous grin on her face.

'You're a monkey!' he'd said, sweeping her up in his arms.

There was no danger from her antics. He always checked that the gate was immovable, its extended rods screwed as tightly as they would go in the gap between wall and newel. Jenny would do the same, abnormally safety-conscious. Yet he could have understood an accident happening; Lyddy attacking the gate with more gusto than usual after Jenny, distracted, perhaps, by grief over Celestine, had left it insufficiently secure. She'd sounded unconcerned, but surely she'd wept as she curled Celly up in the friable earth, and shovelled the soil over her?

Michael stepped into the back bedroom, and gazed down the garden at the raised mound of earth beneath the peony, and tears rose to his eyes for the loss. The police had found Jenny here, indifferent to Lyddy lying unconscious in the hall below. She'd stood at the window, Faye had said, and confessed to throwing Lyddy downstairs and killing her. Rather as she'd confessed to responsibility for Celly's death the evening before: I threw her down the steps.

He was thoughtful as he showered and shaved. Was it possible that Jenny had been confused when she made her confession? Could the shock of a genuine accident to Lyddy have unhinged her in some way? He had not thought to ask Faye for Jenny's exact words, or to get a precise report on what had been found at the house. He had been too shocked by Lyddy's distress and the news of Jenny's breakdown, to think intelligently about what he was being told.

Michael pulled on jeans and a clean tee shirt, collected nappies and a couple of bright dungarees and tops from Lyddy's drawer, and drove back to the hospital with hope stirring faintly in his heart.

Lyddy was crying when he arrived back on the ward, refusing to be comforted by the nurse who rocked her, and tried to persuade her to take her dummy. He took over, and Lyddy clung to him tightly, as if he was her only defence against being abandoned again to the pain, the alien smells and prying strangers he had rescued her from the day before. She was reluctant to let him put her down, so he sat with her on the chair by the cot, cradling her to him. Oh Lyddy, Lyddy, he called silently as he stroked her cheek, and gazed at her shocked eyes, smile at me again. Struggle against me, wanting to be put down and away in the corners, grinning while you cause mayhem. Recover your zest for life, because I'm not sure I'm strong enough to protect you much longer, not while I think of Jenny curled up against the world, and with no one to bring her back.

He sat back staring out of the second-floor window at the tops of trees waving against a blue sky, waiting until Faye was free to see him. Somewhere below, the town rattled along with its routine business. In the corner opposite him, a child watched videos of the Sooty show, and ever afterwards, the sight and sound of the puppets could make Michael shiver with memory. As Lyddy fell asleep, he too closed his eyes. Interviews with selectors, with social workers, doctors, nurses and psychiatrists confused themselves in his mind, all intent on uncovering his deepest motivations, and all finding him wanting. He woke to find his mother sitting in the chair on the other side of Lyddy's cot, knitting.

'I didn't like to wake you,' she said, coming round to kiss him. 'The nurse said you'd been up with Lyddy half the night. A social worker came, and said you should go to her office as soon as you woke up, but she'd be gone at five.'

Michael embraced Meg, laid Lyddy gently in her cot, and promised to back in ten minutes. Then he made his way to see Faye.

She was extremely interested in his idea, especially once she had consulted the reports in her file.

'Lyddy's injuries are consistent with having got tangled up with the stair-gate, certainly. The police report noted it was found halfway down the stairs. The question has been whether Jenny pushed, or threw her, deliberately. You can understand we have to take action when we find someone saying they've hurt a child. But you're saying when she said,' Faye read from her file, '"I threw her down the steps, and she's dead", she was looking down the garden at the place she'd buried your cat the evening before, and you think that's what she might have been referring to?'

'That's right. When she told me about the cat on the phone, she talked about throwing her down the steps. If Lyddy fell downstairs, it could all have been too much for Jen. She confused things, or she blanked it out. I don't know, but it makes a lot more sense to me than that she should have hurt Lyddy deliberately.'

'We'll have to see what she says, won't we?'

Michael returned to the ward to find Lyddy still asleep, and Meg explaining to the nurse at the desk that he'd always been caring, even as a child, and 'he was away being interviewed about being a priest when all this happened. I expect he'll get another chance.'

Michael doubted it, but he wouldn't tell her that yet. Her comment had reminded him of something. 'Oh, God,' he said. 'It's Wednesday, isn't it? Allie will be calling for me to give me a lift to the Programme. I'd better ring and explain.'

He rushed to the telephones, fumbling for change, and caught Alison as she was preparing to leave. Comforted by her sympathy over Lyddy, he went further and explained that Jenny had had a breakdown as a result of the accident. 'Only please, don't tell anyone - she'd be mortified.'

'I am sorry. She's been a bit depressed all year, hasn't she?'

'Nothing like this. It's awful, Allie. She wouldn't speak to me at all when I saw her. Just told me she hated me, and I should go away. I know she's upset, but I hate it when she treats me like shit. I might have deserved it once, but not now.' There was silence at the other end of the phone. 'Allie? Are you there?'

A further few seconds went by. 'I think that may be my fault,' she said. 'I called on Monday evening to leave you those books, and I think I may have said something that gave her the impression you were Luke's father.'

'But you put her right straight away. Allie -' he said with horror as she hesitated, 'you told her not to be silly, didn't you?'

'I ... no. I said you loved me, and you'd only stayed with her because of Lyddy. I'm sorry...'

'My God! Allie, how could you? No wonder she flipped. I've always sworn nothing happened. She must have thought she could never trust me again. Didn't you think? Didn't you care what it might do to her?' He had raised his voice unconsciously, and several faces turned towards him. The public phones in the corridor by the main lifts at the General were hardly the most appropriate place for such conversation.

'I really am sorry,' Alison said. 'I didn't intend to mislead her, only when she jumped to the wrong conclusion, I saw a chance to hurt her. I'd had an awful weekend at home, and I was jealous. I tried to take it back, but she rushed into the house and slammed the door. I rang the bell, but she wouldn't answer. I'd no idea it would push her over the edge.'

Michael hardly heard. He could think only of Jenny lying in despair in the hospital, imagining he'd betrayed her. No wonder she wouldn't speak to him.

'My money's running out,' he said. 'We'll have to talk about this later.'

He rang off, reflecting that every fragment of his family's suffering could be traced back to his own foolhardiness one way or another, and it was just as well that he'd finally blown his chances of ordination.

'I know how difficult this is for you.' The sympathetic words slithered over Jenny's mind. They meant nothing. She used such empty phrases herself with patients when she wanted to con them into talking to her.

'Can you tell me what happened?'

It was too humiliating even to look up, let alone to speak. She was stripped naked and slit open, pinned out like a rat to a dissection board while they picked over all her inadequacies. 'It's got a womb, it's female, it's given birth' - a baby girl who squeezed into the world and thudded out of it ten months later because of her mother's carelessness or anger or deliberate malice - Jenny wasn't quite sure now, but the picture was always the same: the scream, the crash, the silence, and the white face ... She'd reach that point and long to howl and wail but she dared not begin lest she dissolve in the sadness, so she fought it down to a tolerable despair.

'The heart is very small,' they'd say, pulling it away from its accompanying vessels. No wonder she was never any good at loving. No wonder she drove her husband into the arms of his mistress. Because even if what the whisperers said was true and Lyddy hadn't died, by some miracle was somewhere in this world, laughing and nestling with her pliant lips on someone else's cheek or breast, then her mother had still failed her, caused her agonies, let them take her away in a shrieking ambulance when she should have known, she was a doctor, she should have *known* that her baby wasn't dead, and not left her desolate. So Michael had a baby one way or another, and she'd lost him to a woman who didn't run a mile whenever he tried to love her because she couldn't stand it.

'Not much of a brain, either.' She'd thought she had once, passing examinations, and qualifiying, and pretending to heal people. Not now. You couldn't have mad doctors, doctors who got carted off by police and admitted to mental hospitals - you weren't supposed to use those sort of words, but everyone saw it like that. Talk to me, they said, tell me about it: your childhood, your friendships, your marriage, your sex life, your feelings about your baby, your husband your job your mother your father your sister your broth... NO! No, I've got nothing to say.

The thoughts ran to and fro like currents below the waves. With all her energies she tried not to let them surface to consciousness, blanked them out, strove for containment, so that she could reconstruct her life the way it had been, oblivious, and safe. But still they kept nagging away at her in their gentle, insistent voices.

'Your husband's had the main care of the baby, hasn't he? How do you feel about that?'

'Alright.' Damn, she'd spoken.

'You might have felt jealous or left out.'

Tears trying to get through, don't let them rise. Oh the shame of breaking down like this, what if they tell everyone? You know that nice Dr Furlong? Went completely crazy. Shameful. Pathetic. Wet. Despicable. An entire thesaurus of contempt.

'We'll leave it for now. Do you think you could try some lunch? Angela ...'

Lyddy was allowed home on Thursday morning. Michael drove her back to find Meg in control in the house, cot freshly made up, the washing Jenny had abandoned two days before hanging on the line.

Stan, and two or three other neighbours, wandered over when they saw Michael's car draw up, and exclaimed sympathetically at the plaster on Lyddy's leg.

'Jenny's having a rest for a couple of days,' he told them. 'She needed it after all that worry with Lyddy.' He contrived to make it sound as if the police had taken her to hospital to be with Lyddy on the morning of the accident, and hoped he would be forgiven the lie.

After lunch, Michael left Lyddy with Meg and drove to Linthorpe.

Jenny was sitting on the bed, dressed in the peach-coloured tracksuit he'd bought for her the morning before, hugging her knees, and staring impassively at her feet.

'Jenny?' She didn't even look at him as he sat down next to her, and covered her hand with his own. 'Lyddy's back home. You should see her trying to crawl with her leg in a plaster. Look, I've brought some photographs of her.' He got out the prints he'd taken that morning with a disposable camera, and held them in front of her, one after the other. Lyddy smiled weakly out of them, her bruise prominent, her plaster mostly covered by her dungarees. 'You can see for yourself she's alright. Have a look.'

Jenny turned her face away. Her arms came up to grasp her shoulders, hunched and tight.

Michael put the photos down and took a deep breath. 'Why won't you speak to me, Jen? Is this about Allie? What she said on Monday?' He put an arm round her. 'Alison lied to you. I'm not Luke's father. I know I've got my faults, but I try not to lie, and I haven't lied about this. I've told you before. I've never slept with her.'

Jenny remained inert; limp, lustreless hair shielded her face from him.

'You jumped to conclusions,' he said. 'She let you, because she was jealous. She tried to put it right, but you'd slammed the door, and you wouldn't answer when she rang the bell. Jenny, there's no way Luke could be mine.'

Very slowly, Jenny turned her face towards him, and he stared into her eyes, dull and grey as the North Sea under winter fog. She looked as if she were about to speak, but no sound came out.

Michael stroked her pale cheek with his free hand. 'I can understand you hating me because you thought I'd lied to you, but I didn't. I love you. Please talk to me. Tell me what happened. You needn't be afraid to think about it - Lyddy's alright now. Look, didn't you see the photos I brought?' He picked one of them up, and held it between them.

Her eyes focused slowly on Lyddy's battered smile, and he heard her sharp intake of breath. 'I want to see her,' Jenny whispered.

Michael tightened his arm around her shoulders. 'I know you do, but you'll need to explain what happened, before you can do that. You told everyone it was your fault, you see.'

'It was,' she said. 'I threw her down.'

'You threw Celly. Did you throw Lyddy as well?'

He had to wait for an answer. Her face contorted, and she made a new effort, speaking slowly as if she were piecing the facts together from splintered fragments of knowledge. 'I took Lyddy upstairs to get the washing. I started doing the gate, then the phone went. I thought it might be you, so I was going to leave it for the answerphone. Then I thought it might be Caroline, because she'd said she might invite me round, so I rushed to the bedroom to answer it.' She paused, closing her eyes. 'I suppose I didn't fasten the gate tightly enough. I didn't know she'd climb on it. There was this crash, and she screamed, and there were thuds ... I ran out, and I saw her hit her head. She went so quiet and still, I thought she was dead. I couldn't stand it. There's nothing worse than losing a baby. You never care about anyone after that.' She turned to him, anguished, her hands gripping his tee shirt. 'I wanted to die.'

Michael drew her to him, holding her head to his shoulder. 'Oh, Jen...'

'I didn't think you'd care, you'd got Alison, and Luke. I didn't know what to do. I don't know what I did. I couldn't think about it. I couldn't.'

One of the points from her narrative assumed importance in his mind.

273

'So you were on the phone when Lyddy fell downstairs?'

'Yes.'

'Do you remember who it was?'

'I don't know. One of these junk telephone calls. It doesn't matter, does it?'

'Well, yes, it does. You see, you dialled 999 and told them you'd killed your baby. And then when the police came, they found you in the back bedroom saying the same thing.'

Jenny lifted her face and stared at him, aghast. He did not need to spell it out to her; she knew only too well what processes were set in motion when a child appeared to have been injured deliberately.

She put her hands to her face. 'Oh God, what have I done? I must have brought everybody down on us, the police, social services ... they'll say Lyddy's at risk, they'll make me stay here ... Oh, God, I'll never live it down. What will they think at the surgery? I'll be struck off!'

He held her more tightly, trying to soothe her rising panic. 'Hardly anyone knows. I told the surgery you're ill. And no one's done anything as yet. They're all waiting for you to tell them what happened. Once they're sure it was an accident, you'll be able to come home.'

'I want to go home now. I want to see Lyddy.'

'I know you do, but you can't do that immediately. You'll have to talk to Rose Johnston, so she can make a report. There'll have to be a case conference about Lyddy.'

'That could take days to set up. I'm not waiting that long to see her.'

'I'm sure we could arrange something. Only, Jen, if you did stay here a little longer, they might be able to help you understand why you've found it so difficult being married, and having Lyddy. It might be connected...'

She flung his arm from her. 'No! Stop bringing your own problems into this!'

'I'm sorry.' They sat in silence for a minute. Michael took her hand.

'I'm here voluntarily, aren't I?' Jenny said. 'Tell them I'm intending to go home tomorrow, that might persuade them to have the case conference early.'

Jenny was right. Her determination to go home prompted Faye to convene a hasty case conference the following morning. Michael called to collect Jenny from Linthorpe so that they could both attend. He was not entirely happy with her state of mind as the two of them went hand in hand to Rose Johnston's office to take their leave. His wife was speaking too brightly, too eager to show that she was in control after her shameful collapse.

'I am sorry to have been a nuisance,' she said. 'You'd think a doctor would be better at coping with emergencies.'

'It's entirely different if it's your own child,' Rose said. 'And it sounds as if there have been some difficult emotions bubbling around for you since you married. Michael also said some things that suggest you've been suffering from post-natal depression - not sleeping, irritable, forgetful, over-sensitive, not interested in sex ...'

'Men!' Jenny interrupted cheerfully, gripping his hand more tightly as she included him in her smile. 'They practically expect you to make love in the delivery room, don't they! No, I'm no different from anyone else who's just had a baby on that score. Anyway, I could hardly have done my job for the last few months if I was in that sort of state.' She smiled, as if trampling that other despicable Jenny underfoot, and wiping her from her shoes.

'I think you may find it more difficult than you think to put all this to one side,' said Rose. 'You've had a very unpleasant experience. You may get flashbacks. You may find yourself being over-protective with Lyddy. You won't help yourself by pretending it never happened. And I repeat, I think there's more going on here than the shock of Lyddy's accident and your breakdown, and it'll keep resurfacing until you pay attention to it. I'd be very happy to help you get to the bottom of it. Otherwise, I'm afraid the same strains will build up again, and you're risking more problems.'

'I don't think so,' Jenny stated firmly. 'I'll take things carefully for a while, of course, but I can't see the point of digging around in my past to try to come up with some spurious reason why I lost it in an emergency because I'd had a bad night. So thank you for everything, and now we'll be on our way, so you can get on.'

Michael exchanged glances with Rose as he followed Jenny out. It was an unsatisfactory ending, but there was nothing more either of them could do.

The case conference considered the welter of reports on Lyddy and her parents, and listened sympathetically to Michael and Jenny's plea to be able to resume their normal family life. The telephone call should be traceable, but even without that evidence, there was no reason to think that Jenny's story was untrue. Their health visitor would call regularly over the next few weeks, and Jenny would have to return to the police station for the case to be formally closed, but there were no grounds for preventing her from going home to her daughter.

275

'I can't wait to see Lyddy,' Jenny said, breathless as an expectant lover, as they turned into their road. She clasped her breasts. 'I've been getting quite sore.'

Michael put an arm round her, and guided her into the house. It took a further effort of will for her to shut out the remembrance of her last hour in it, but finding Meg ensconced in the living room knitting and guiltily watching an afternoon soap, made it easier to survive.

'Hello, dear. I am glad to see you home. Lyddy's due to wake up shortly - would you like me to fetch her down?'

'It's OK, Mum, I'll do it,' Michael said. A few minutes later, he appeared holding Lyddy, red-faced and blinking after her sleep.

'Who's this, Lyddy?' he said, lowering her towards where Jenny sat, apprehensive.

Immediately Lyddy started to struggle, calling out frantically, 'Mum Mum Mum,' and reaching out with wildly waving arms. Jenny stretched out and took her, wrapping her arms around the baby, and kissing her hair, her cheek, beaming with joy.

'Lyddy...' She breathed the single word ecstatically. She held Lyddy a little away from her in gentle, unbelieving hands, tracing her fingers across Lyddy's cheek and brow, pausing over the bruised temple, and white plaster, the signs that this was truly her own, living child. Her eyes were bright as Lyddy, grinning toothily and dribbling, clutched her mother's face, and clothing. Meg smiled, and tactfully left the room. Jenny lifted her tee shirt, pushed her bra aside, and at last held her child to her breast again.

Lyddy gave little grunts of contentment, like the small baby she had regressed to being through her long days in purgatory, and nestled to her mother as easily as her plastered leg would allow.

Michael dropped to his knees, encircling them both with his arms as he buried his face between them. Jenny stroked her fingers through his hair, as if he were Celly come back to complete their return to normality.

'We'll be alright now, won't we?' she whispered to the back of his neck. His arms tightened around her, and in the stillness, they both believed it might be true.

Five

Alison forced herself to meet Jenny's eyes. 'I misled you, because I was jealous,' she said. 'I swear Michael isn't Luke's father. He couldn't be. We've never had sex. They do look a little alike, but that's only because Michael and I are fairly alike. Lukey has got a similar temperament, but I think third children often are more placid. That's what I was going to say to you, but when you misunderstood, it seemed a good chance to hurt you. I'm sorry.'

She looked at Michael, sitting on the arm of his wife's chair, a hand on her shoulder. In the days since Michael had rung Alison from the hospital, she had, for the first time, been fully facing up to the irresponsibility of her behaviour and its far-reaching impact on his family. After a serious talk with Michael, she had offered to come to his house after the Programme's evening session to tell Jenny the whole story of her relationship with him.

'How do I know this is going to be the truth?' Jenny had asked. 'There've been so many lies, how do I know you haven't fixed up some story between you?'

'Oh, I think you'll know,' Alison had said. 'Why should I make up something that shows me in such a bad light? Anyway I want to get this sorted out before I'm ordained. I've been very wrong, and I want to say sorry.'

'I didn't sleep with him,' Alison repeated, 'but I was in love with him. My marriage was going down the tube, and it really knocked my self-esteem. I was scared enough about joining the Programme, and I should have realised how vulnerable I am to temptation when things get difficult. I guess I was ready to fall for the first attractive man who had time for me - and there was Michael. He used to talk about you a lot, and say he loved you, but I never saw any evidence you cared about him. So I kidded myself I wasn't doing any harm by wanting him to care about me, and make me feel good about myself for a change. Then he kissed me in the bar at college in the new year - it started out as a joke, but I could tell he fancied me. After that, I began to want him so much I didn't care about anything else.'

277

'But you were going to be ordained,' Jenny said. 'How could you think like that?'

'I told myself we were both miserable in our marriages, so it must have been God bringing us together.' Alison grimaced. 'You can convince yourself of anything if you're self-interested enough. I used to find myself hoping something would happen to you or Steve. I know that's terrible, but I'm trying to tell you how desperate I was feeling. Then Michael kissed me again at the weekend in March, and I thought he couldn't possibly care about you if he could be that passionate with me. We agreed we mustn't go any further, but ...' She took a deep breath. 'I went to his bed that night. I saw Nan coming out of Christopher's house, and I couldn't see why Michael and I should resist our feelings if they could be doing that. So I went to his room and tried to persuade him to sleep with me, but he wouldn't.'

Jenny turned to Michael, and whispered, 'Wasn't that the weekend Andy ... oh, Michael...'

He sought her hand. 'I know, I know. I felt terrible about it. But I told myself at least I *had* resisted, so all I'd done was kiss her. And what's a kiss between friends?' He met Alison's eyes. 'I hadn't reckoned on how strongly it would make me feel about her.'

'That's been the story of it, Jenny,' she said. 'Me throwing myself at him, and him saying no. If he'd had any sense, he'd have dropped me completely, but he didn't want to be unkind. He could see how unhappy I was without him around. I managed to get him to kiss me a couple of times, but that was all. Only I persuaded myself that he was in love with me really. So when Steve asked me if there was someone else, I said yes. I said Michael and I loved each other, and eventually we'd both get divorced so we could be together.'

'You told Steve that?' Michael said, horrified, sitting forward on the arm. 'Oh, Allie, you fool. I *never* gave you reason to think I'd ever leave Jenny.'

'No, but I thought if I could once get you to sleep with me, you'd realise how much you loved me, and then you would leave her. So I invited you over, and tried my damnedest. We got as far as taking our clothes off. And then he got up and walked out on me.' A high colour spread across Alison's cheeks, and she came to a halt as memory accused her.

She'd set the scene for her seduction of Michael with such care, locking her conscience in a box, because once they'd made love nothing would matter, he'd never be able to go on denying the depth of the love between them. At last, she'd thought, as he removed her vest, and pressed

278

his bare skin to hers ... only it had all gone wrong. Michael had suddenly torn himself away from her, and, ignoring her pleas, had escaped with his clothes to the bathroom. Nearly two years on, she could still recall the pain of that day in all its anguish.

'But you love me,' she'd said when he came back. 'I thought you could tell Jenny, and...'

'Why should I tell Jenny that I've stupidly let myself get carried away with you? I've been a lousy enough husband to her without piling this on her, too.'

'You're going to leave her, though. You must. We love each other.'

'There's never been any question of me leaving Jenny, I've always told you that.'

'But God's brought us together, Mikey, I'm sure he has.'

He'd looked as if he was about to cry. 'God doesn't lead us into this kind of mess, Allie.'

'I didn't sleep with you before we were married,' Michael told Jenny softly. 'I didn't sleep with Alison.'

'I see.' Jenny eyed her across the room. 'So when you swore you'd never done more than kissed her, you were lying?'

'Well, there's how you kiss, and where you kiss, isn't there?'

'And yet you swore you weren't unfaithful... Isn't that being unfaithful?'

'Yes. I'm sorry, Jenny. At the time, I felt I'd achieved something by walking out, but it was just as bad as if I'd actually gone through with it.'

'I can't tell you how hurt and humiliated and cheap I felt after he'd gone, Jenny,' Alison said. 'I made out to Steve I'd had a change of heart, and that I'd stay with him as long as he'd agree to another baby. Hence Luke.' She shrugged her shoulders. If anything, Luke's arrival had worsened things between herself and Steve, but she wasn't going to say that to Jenny. 'That's the story. I'm so ashamed of myself, I can hardly believe how badly I behaved. I thought I'd done my repentance, and got over it, and then I go and mislead you about Luke ... I know sorry isn't enough, but it's all I can say. Michael always wanted to be true to you, and you're very lucky to have him so devoted to you. But I guess you know that.' She smiled philosophically and stood up. 'I'd better go now. Steve isn't too happy being left in charge of Luke, even if the poor kid does sleep all evening. No, don't get up,' she added as Michael began to move. 'I can find my own way out.'

'Does that help?' Michael asked Jenny, as the front door shut behind Alison.

Jenny sat forward in her chair, and rubbed her face. 'It's about what I expected. Not as bad as I once thought, but... I suppose you'll say it was my fault for being horrible to you all the time.'

'No, I wouldn't say that. It was my responsibility, mine quite as much as Allie's. But it has been over for nearly two years. Can you forgive me?'

'I have to, don't I? I've caused you enough trouble this last week to cancel anything out. Let's forget about both things, and start again.'

Michael put a hand on her shoulder and, finding it tense, began to massage it. 'I'm not sure it's that easy to forget about Lyddy's accident, and what it did to you.'

He spoke gently. Jenny had shied away from any discussion of it since her return, preferring to lose herself in extended hours at the surgery or family planning clinic. As she'd shown after Andy's assault, throwing herself into her work seemed to be the only way she could manage to deal with emotional turmoil. Discreet enquiry proved Dr Furlong to be perfectly in command despite the worries she had over her daughter, but Michael remained anxious about her real state of mind. She had declared it impossible now to get home at lunchtimes, and as a consequence saw little of her daughter. Michael sensed an ambivalence in her, guessed at the nightmarish flashbacks to the point at which she thought her baby dead, but she shared nothing of it with him.

'Oh, don't you start,' she replied, shrugging him off. 'It was a temporary disorientation, brought on by tiredness, that's all.' She stood up. 'And speaking of tiredness, I'm ready for bed.' She faced him, and attempted a smile. 'I appreciate you getting Alison round. You're forgiven, and we won't talk about it again.'

Michael took her in his arms as they lay in bed. He wanted so much to prove his commitment to her, for the clearing away of the questions about his relationship with Alison to have abolished the tensions between them. Yet, though she made a dutiful attempt to return his passion, he sensed she gained no pleasure from his embraces, and longed only for him to be done, so she could get some sleep.

'I blew my selection conference,' Michael told Nan, when he finally had the leisure to contact her about it. 'I knew I had to get back, and I walked out.'

'Don't worry about it. I'm sure we'll be able to sort something out. They can hardly object if you have a family crisis.'

'But I came away before the crisis had happened. I don't really understand it, but I had such a strong feeling that I had to get back that I couldn't resist it. It seems arrogant to put it down to divine intervention, and I suppose it was just picking up the strain Jenny was under when we spoke on the phone, but it's a little difficult to explain to people who have some doubts about you anyway.'

'Yes. We can't have ordinands who obey the voice of God, can we? Where would the Church of England be then?'

Nan got him squeezed into another conference in July, however, through a combination of her persistence, Bishop Derrick's influence, and some bullying by Deidre Rutt. Jenny had enlisted her aunt in his cause at the last minute, pronouncing herself more thoroughly in favour of his ordination than she had ever been in the past.

With Lyddy cared for by a friend during the days he was away, and Jenny, so she assured him, in complete control, Michael was able to concentrate on his interviews. He was conscious of confessing to more doubts and vulnerabilities than he had shown either five years before, or at his more recent abortive conference, and he was stunned when he got through.

'Good news, Michael,' Nan said. 'Congratulations. Recommended, and in glowing terms.'

Euphoria set in. He phoned round everyone he could think of, rather as he had done to announce Lyddy's birth. Everyone except Jenny, for he didn't like to interrupt her surgery, and he would see her that evening. His ordination was set, appropriately enough, for Michaelmas, and he had a few weeks in which to fill in the tiny gaps in his training, and to finalise arrangements for his work as an unpaid minister at St Martin's.

It should have been the culmination of all his ambitions, he should have been able to be happy at last, but as the days went by, he found himself sinking deeper and deeper into depression.

At the end of July, he stood in front of a mirror in the Harts' house, trying on Caroline's strip of white plastic under the collar of his denim shirt, and wanting to weep. In two months' time, he'd have the right to wear one of his own, and he wished he didn't feel so petrified at the thought. His face stared back at him from Caroline's dressing table mirror; his hair shorter these days, so that the angles of his face were more apparent. If he looked closely, he could see the lines around his eyes, two for sorrow, one for joy. He laid Caroline's collar down, and picked up the bottle of tablets he'd originally come into the room to collect for her. Sunday lunch at the Harts' for the potential new curate and his family. It was strange to be in this new, formal, relationship with them.

Back in the Harts' living room, Lyddy was sitting in the middle of the floor with Jenny, concentrating hard on putting round pegs into the square holes of the red plastic pillar box Caroline had produced from her cupboard.

He handed the bottle to Caroline, and sank down onto the sofa next to her. 'How do you think my sermon went?'

'Not bad. The content's reasonable, but you sound constrained. There's not much of you coming through.'

Hardly surprising. He'd lost the habit of being himself. 'Peter's always saying there shouldn't be a lot of yourself in a sermon.'

'You need a balance. You can bring your own distinctive approach, without sounding as if you're on a chat show. You'll develop. I expect you still feel nervous.' Caroline left the room to check up on her roast chicken.

'What did you think?' he asked Jenny.

'I thought it was fine,' she said, without looking up. 'Though I do find it odd seeing you robed up like that. I hardly know you,' she added, lifting her head to smile brightly.

Michael scratched his knee through the navy cloth of his trousers. 'Sometimes I wonder if I'm doing the right thing. I get this absurd impulse to fling off my cassock and all the paraphernalia, and leave it in a heap on the floor, while I run out of the building. I feel stifled sometimes, even though Peter's good about everything.' His need for her help left his voice shaky, and he thought from the expression in her eyes that she had recognised it.

Her reply, when it came, merely nailed the door more firmly shut against him. 'Come off it, Michael. This is what you've always wanted. You look wonderful dressed up, very authoritative, and you'll have a very worthwhile ministry. You dare get cold feet after all we've been through to get you here! Now, perhaps I'd better go and see if Caroline needs any help.'

She headed for the kitchen, a perfect potential curate's wife: poised, friendly, supportive; Jenny was playing the role exactly right. What did it matter that she wouldn't listen to him, never talked to him about anything other than Lyddy and the practicalities of his new role, that she had found one excuse after another for not making love since the night of Alison's visit? He would turn to gather her into his arms, longing to love her back to life, his poor, bruised wife, to tangle with the spring of her hair under his fingers, to be warmed by her lips, comforted by the broad softness of her belly, to taste the sweet drops that would still come to her breasts when he kissed them. Only she didn't want to know. She never wanted to know.

The same friend took care of Lyddy while Michael attended his final summer school on the Programme. The other students, whom he had not seen since his selection conference, were all over him, thrilled that at last he had achieved their own status. He worked hard, concentrated on providing music for the services, played more tennis than the dullness of the weather deserved, and forced himself not to phone Jenny too often, in case she thought he was treating her like an incompetent child.

Michael was alone at a table, belatedly finishing his after-lunch coffee, when Alison came over and sat beside him. 'Could I talk to you, Michael? About something personal? Would you mind? I need some advice from you.'

'Sure.' Michael drained his cup. 'Shall we go for a walk?'

The path they took wound under the trees past the sports hall, the same track they had trodden in the dark to end in each other's arms over two years before.

'Has Steve got a job in Wellesley yet?'

'No,' she replied. 'I don't think he's trying very hard. He's not likely to move when I and the boys do, because even when he gets a job, he'll have to give three months' notice, and we haven't put the house on the market. I'm not convinced he wants to come, to be honest. He's realised how much he dislikes having a baby in the house, and he feels I bamboozled him into having Luke, which is fair enough, I did. I can't say I shall hate being on my own. You've no idea what it's like tiptoeing round someone else's fragile ego all the time, and knowing they'll explode if you do the slightest thing wrong.'

Michael wasn't going to respond to her final remark. 'What are you going to do about Luke?'

'I thought I might ask Lisa to come and be my nanny. She should be finishing her course this summer, and she knows the children because she's been doing quite a bit of babysitting for me.'

'That sounds like a wonderful idea, if you can afford it. Or can you get her on the cheap, as a friend of the family?'

'I probably could, now she's got religious. Did you know she's going out with Colin Blatherwycke? She met Nan, and Nan sent her along to St John's in Leathwell, because there's lots of young people there, and she got converted.' A guilty smile came over Alison's face. 'I shouldn't tell you, but it sounded funny. Bernie Blatherwycke suggested people come forward to tell their stories, so Lisa went to the microphone and started explaining in graphic detail exactly what kind of life she'd been saved from. Bernie had to wrestle the microphone from her hand before someone called the vice squad. Colin came to the rescue, and it's been true love ever since.'

'Is she likely to want to move to Wellesley, in that case?'

'I don't know. I'll have to ask.'

'What was the advice you wanted from me?' Michael asked.

'I didn't really need any. I wanted to tell you how things were. Do you mind?'

'No.' They had reached the fence, and were leaning on it, looking at the cows grazing on the other side. 'This is where we were before, isn't it?' Michael said. He took her hand. 'I'm not sure I've ever said sorry to you for messing you about, but I am sorry. I should have been stronger.'

Alison shrugged. 'It was my fault. I felt awful telling Jenny, realising how stupid I'd been.'

'And yet, you know, Allie, you're still important to me. All my happiest memories of the Programme have you in them. I'll miss not seeing you. I'd like to keep in touch.'

'It might be safest not to,' she said, placing his hand on the fence and letting go. 'Supposing Steve and I do finally split up, and I was to start hankering after you again? I'm not safe to know. And it wouldn't be fair on Jenny, either, would it? We'll say goodbye at the end of this week, and who knows, maybe we'll meet somewhere in years to come, when we're both respectable clergy, and none of this will matter any more.'

'I hope so.' He put a hand on her shoulder briefly. 'We'd better walk back,' he said. 'I'm seeing Nan.'

'All my life, ever since I can remember, I've thought I should be ordained,' he said to Nan, sitting outside under grey skies. 'And everyone else has believed it, you, the selectors, my church, and here I am, with it all about to come true, and I feel as if I'm making the biggest mistake of my life.'

'It's not unusual to have doubts about being ordained - big day nerves is par for the course.'

'It's worse than that,' he said, gazing back along the path that he and Alison had lately walked.

Nan sat at the other end of the wooden seat, studying him. 'Is it something in particular, or a general foreboding?'

'It's everything. I keep going, because I think it might be alright once I get there, and I tell myself people always have some doubts, like you say, but Nan, I feel dreadful. I've always thought I was born to wear the shoe of ministry, and here I am all ready and putting it on, but it doesn't fit. It pinches me in all the wrong places. I tell myself that eventually my foot will stretch the leather, and the fit will be comfortable, and that it's much better to be shod than to go barefoot. Only then I think - if you wear a poorly fitting shoe, you can end up with such agony in your feet that you can't walk at all, and I'm afraid that's going to happen to me.' He leant forward, with his head in his hands. 'I shouldn't be saying this, not after all the time and effort you and everyone else has put into getting me this far...'

'Good heavens, of course you should. Like pulling out of a wedding - it's a bloody nuisance laying off the caterers and returning the gifts, but what's a week of trouble compared to a lifetime of misery? What does Jenny say about it all?'

'I haven't said anything about this to her.' A minute passed. He looked up to find Nan's eyes on him. 'We don't seem to talk any more. She's been really enthusiastic this time round. She keeps saying how much she's looking forward to me being a curate, but she behaves as if she's playing a role. She's not real. I suppose it's to do with her being ill, but I don't know how I'm going to cope with ministry when my marriage is such hell.' He broke down as he spoke, finding relief in the bitter tears that seeped from behind his hand.

'My dear boy,' Nan said, moving across and putting an arm round him.

'We'd had some misunderstandings, and I thought it had all been sorted out, only now it's worse than ever. Jenny barely speaks to me except about Lyddy, and she won't let me touch her, I feel absolutely trapped, and I don't know what to do.'

'We need to sort this out, don't we? You and Jenny need to talk to someone about what's going on between you, and then we might be able to sort out more clearly whether your doubts about ordination are genuine, or because you're unhappy in your marriage.'

Michael sniffed and nodded.

'Do you think Jenny would agree to see a counsellor with you? I could recommend someone very good.'

'I don't know. She'd probably insist there wasn't a problem.'

'But there *is* a problem for *you*. I think you need to be insistent yourself.'

'I'll have a go,' Michael said, without enthusiasm.

'I'd like to talk to you,' he said seriously, on his first evening back, after Lyddy had been put to bed. Jenny sat in her chair with her arms folded, and stared impassively at him. 'I'd like you to see a counsellor with me.'

'What on earth for? I'm perfectly alright now.'

'But I'm not. I'm miserable. I spoke to Nan last week, and...'

'Spilling your soul out to Nan, were you?' she interrupted. '"I'm a poor, sensitive, misunderstood man, boo hoo". You'd better not have been talking about me.'

'And just what am I supposed to do? I'm lonely, and I'm unhappy, and you don't want to know. This ought to be a wonderful time for me, leading up to my ordination, and I try and put a brave face on it, but I can't stand the way you're shutting me out. We've not been happy for years, have we, Jen? I thought once you understood about Allie, everything would be right again, but you seem more distant than before. You won't let me touch you, you don't need me, and you won't let me need you.'

'I'm the same as I've always been.'

'No you're not. Oh, Jen, I didn't marry you for this.'

'No, you married me because I was there, and you didn't want to lose your access to my home and income. Anyone in the same position would have done.'

'That's simply not true, and you know it.'

She picked at her fingernails, saying nothing.

'Would you rather I moved out, then? Stopped sponging off you?' The chill that gripped his stomach spread slowly over his whole body as he waited for her response.

Jenny shook her head.

'Then for God's sake make it worth me staying! I always seem to have wanted you much, much more than you've ever wanted me.'

'That's not exactly true. Sometimes there've been other women you've wanted. No,' she held her hand up to prevent him speaking, 'that's all in the past. I'm trying damn hard to forget it, and to be supportive about your ordination, I don't see why you're complaining all the time. I don't know what more you want.' She got up to go through to the kitchen.

'I want to be able to love you, but you won't let me near you.'

'I don't *want* to be loved!' she shouted, turning back to him with her hand on the door. 'I want you to leave me alone!'

For a few seconds their eyes met, and he saw her horror at her outburst. She pulled the door open. 'And I *don't* need to see any well-meaning counsellor,' she said. 'You go if you're that desperate. *You're* the one with the problem.'

She slammed the door behind her, and Michael thumped the sofa next to him once, very hard, in a sudden surge of anger.

Six

'Hello, Lisa. How lovely to see you. You're looking very well,' Jenny said. The young woman on her doorstep that early September evening had shining silvery hair pinned back from her face to sweep onto her shoulders, and a wide smile lighting up her eyes. Ty, throwing himself into his new radio job in London, didn't know what he'd missed.

'You know Mrs Thompson? I'm off to Wellesley tomorrow, to be her nanny. Is Michael in? I was up at me mum's, and I thought I'd drop in on the off chance to say goodbye.'

'I'm afraid not, he's at church, but come through.'

'Yeah, I've really fell on me feet. Hello.' Her comment was addressed to Lyddy, who had toddled out into the hallway, trailing her muslin. 'You're a lovely girl, aren't yer?'

She picked Lyddy up and followed Jenny into the living room. 'Ooh, you're gorgeous, you are,' she exclaimed, kissing the baby. 'I love the smell of baby powder. Mine would've jus' been coming up to four now,' she added, matter of factly.

'You still think about that, do you?'

'Yeah, a bit. Like when its birthday would've been. I s'pose I'd have had it adopted, but you don't forget, do yer? It must be terrible to lose a real baby. You'd wanna kill yerself, I should think. You're a little treasure, aren't yer, Lyddy?' Lisa lifted a giggling Lyddy into the air and kissed her stomach.

'Cor, I in't been in here for years,' Lisa continued, looking round the room with interest. 'Do you remember when I run off? Wha's happened to that lovely cat of yours? I cried all over it, I did, but it didn't seem to mind.'

'She died. It wouldn't be fair to get another one until Lyddy's older,' Jenny started to say, in the emotionless tone in which she always referred to Celly. But she couldn't finish the sentence. As a father, buried up to his neck under levelled seashore sand by his children, first makes the surface quiver, then crack, then break apart as he rises to freedom, so loss erupted to shatter Jenny's smooth facade. The world around her blurred, and it

287

took her a full minute to realise that the cause was her own tears welling up and falling heedlessly down her cheeks.

'Here, are you alright?' Lisa came over to her, full of concern.

Jenny could neither move nor speak, only continue to weep, in loud, choking sobs that shook her whole body. Slowly, she crumpled to the floor and lay in a heap, overwhelmed by an unbearable grief, with all the sorrows of her life coursing out through her eyes. She didn't register Lisa's attempts to help her, or the girl's efficient comforting of a puzzled Lyddy. If she had known Lisa was going to the telephone to dial Nan's number, as the only local person she could think of who might know what to do in such a crisis, she would have objected, but the tears kept falling, falling, and she was paralysed.

Nan arrived five minutes later, and, after a whispered conversation with Lisa in the hall, came through into the living room and knelt beside Jenny. The first Jenny knew of her presence was the warm arm that circled her and held her without speaking for a long, long time. The muted sounds of Lisa putting Lyddy to bed and leaving the house to fetch Michael, failed to penetrate Jenny's consciousness. Little by little, she had inched her head along until she was sobbing into Nan's skirt like an abandoned child. She didn't know how long she wept in the security of Nan's arms, only that she could no longer fight the emotions forcing their way out.

She hardly knew to whom she spoke when at last words croaked from her. 'They shouldn't have hated me. I was only a baby, I couldn't help it. I should have been special.'

'Can you tell me about it?'

'He died before I was born. They only had me because he'd gone, and then they hated me because I wasn't him.'

'Your brother?'

Jenny pulled herself up, and looked directly at her rescuer for the first time. She should have shied away from this woman whom she'd always disliked, but all she could think, when she registered who it was who had come to her, was that everything was alright because Nan knew her. Knew and cared about her, because she knew and cared about Michael.

'Yes.' Her throat was dry, and she choked on the word.

'Let me get you a glass of water,' Nan said, getting up and heading for the kitchen. By the time she came back, Jenny had dragged herself across to lean against the sofa. Nan produced a warm, wet towel, and wiped her face with gentle strokes. It was the first time in her life that Jenny remembered being embraced with warmth by a woman. As a child with blotched face and streaming nose, she'd have been told crossly to pull

288

herself together, and not to come back until she'd found a handkerchief. Accepting Nan's ministrations and encircling arm, meant an unfamiliar surrender to female care that liberated her to acknowledge, for the first time, the pain of her forlorn childhood. Nan listened intently, until Jenny faltered to a stop.

'And how do you think all that might have affected your relationship with Michael?'

Jenny looked at Nan consideringly. 'I suppose I've felt torn between being desperately afraid he hates me and is about to leave me, and hating him for seeming to care for me too much. Sometimes I want to lash out at him, and really hurt him, and I feel awful, because everyone says how nice he is.'

'I know the feeling. I'm an expert in being married to someone you love and hate in equal measure.' Nan smiled, and Jenny managed a half-smile in response.

'One day I look at him, and there he is, a sensitive wimp, besotted with Lyddy, bursting into tears at the drop of a hat, and gazing at me with that hurt, pathetic look because I haven't wanted him slobbering all over me, and I hate him. I despise him. Then other times I feel I couldn't survive without him. I want to run to him and curl up on his lap and have him take care of me because I'm the pathetic one, and he's strong and kind.'

'Have you always felt like that?'

'I don't know. I fell in love with him because he wasn't like anyone I'd met before. He was good-looking, and fun, and friendly, and open, and caring - I'd never had anyone that nice take an interest in me, and be so patient about getting to know me. I couldn't believe it when he said he loved me, and started being all over me, passionate, romantic, treating me like the love of his life. We married three months later, and it was too quick. I hadn't had time to get used to the idea. Then Michael seemed to fall more and more in love once we were married, and sleeping together, and it made me uncomfortable. It really hit me when he came back home from a summer camp because he said he missed me so much. I mean, he was supposed to be the strong one, not weak and dependent.'

'If you don't feel lovable, you end up having to doubt the judgement of anyone who gets that attached to you.'

'That's right,' Jenny said. 'I guess I put him on a pedestal, but the more I got to know him, the more I saw his faults. He'd do stupid things, or turn out not to be as dependable as I'd thought, and that's when I started despising him. I mean, I like helping people, but I couldn't face being married to someone weak.'

'It's frightening, isn't it? You open yourself up to someone, then they turn out to be fallible, but you can't get back your old self-sufficiency. You must have felt very lonely.'

'And confused.' Jenny sniffed.

Nan passed her a sheet from the roll of paper towel she'd brought from the kitchen, and she blew her nose.

'Did you talk to Michael about how you were feeling?'

'I couldn't do that. He was so happy, I couldn't hurt him. I suppose I coped by pushing him away, getting him to take up other interests, like starting the Programme. He made lots of new friends, and I threw myself into my work, and it felt more manageable. Except that he got so friendly with Alison, that I thought they were having an affair.'

'And were they?'

'As good as, though they never went all the way. It made me utterly miserable. Jealous as hell. Yet for all I want to blame him for being such a heel, I know I pushed him into it. I felt comfortable, in a strange sort of way. I was the one on the outside, watching someone I loved loving someone else, excluding me.'

'That's interesting, isn't it? If I wanted to be naughty, I could suggest that you've set things up so that Michael's caring for Lyddy full-time, and you're on the outside there, too.'

'Maybe. I don't know. I'd have said that was practical necessity.' Jenny took another sip of water while she gathered her thoughts. 'How can I escape it, if that's what I'm doing? I can't change the way I've thought about myself all my life.'

'Yes, you can, only it will take a long time. Nobody can make up for what you lost as a child, but you can learn to accept Michael loving you. You try it - next time he looks at you with those gorgeous brown eyes and tells you he can't live without you, take a few deep breaths, let go of the waspish reply, put your arms round him, and enjoy it. It's like sex. It hurts the first time, and feels downright odd the next few times, but once you get the hang of it, it's really quite fun. And you'll find if you let him need you, he'll flourish, and that way he'll be able to support you.'

The front door opened as Nan spoke. 'I sent Lisa for Michael. Do you want me to leave?'

'No, stay.' Jenny held Nan's arm, 'I don't know what to say to him.'

Michael came into the living room with an anxious expression on his face, uncertain what he might find, but expecting it to hurt.

He had been surprised to recognise Lisa at the back of the church for their midweek service, despite what Alison had told him about her recent involvement at St John's. She'd waited until the end, and then grabbed him.

'Jenny started crying her eyes out, an' I didn't know what to do, so I rung Nan Patten, and she come over. I put Lyddy to bed, then I come an' got you. Is that right?'

'Thanks, Lisa,' he said. His robe had been off by the time she finished speaking, and he had cycled back up the hill, wondering which development surprised him the most, that Jenny should allow herself to cry, or that she should allow Nan to comfort her.

The first thing he noticed when he walked into the living room was the air of calm, so different from the atmosphere Jenny usually created around herself. The two women were sitting on the floor, legs crossed, with Nan's hand enclosing Jenny's as if they had been friends for a lifetime.

'Lisa said you were upset,' he said to Jenny.

She looked up at him, the traces of her crying still evident, but with the tension gone from her face.

'I am,' she said, getting up. 'I needed to be.' She came over to him and put her arms round his waist. The gesture had become so unfamiliar that it took him aback, and it was a few seconds before he tentatively hugged her to him.

'What's happened?' he asked over her hair.

'Could you tell him, Nan,' Jenny said. 'I'll make some coffee, or something. I don't think I can go through it again.' She kissed him as she drew back from his embrace and went into the kitchen.

'You're going to need to take a lot of care of her,' Nan said, when she'd explained what Jenny had told her. 'This business about her brother is all tied up with how she's been treating you, but she's got a lot more work to do on it. I wonder if you ought to take her to talk to her parents - it might help to put things into perspective for her. Meanwhile, listen when she needs it, and bring her to see me any time, if that's what she wants. And I mean any time.'

'Thank you.'

Nan patted his shoulder. 'And then I think we'll be able to sort out what should happen about your ordination. It's all coming right. You don't know what a miracle it was that I was actually in when Lisa phoned.'

Michael drove Jenny to her parents on Saturday afternoon. She had rung in sick the day following Nan's visit, without guilt, knowing herself to be in a strange state of mind in which she could never have coped with patients

291

or paperwork. Instead she slept for hours, and sat quietly in the garden with Lyddy and Michael playing around her. She wasn't ready to make love to him, but she sought his hugs as she gathered her strength for the encounter with her mother.

'I need to speak to you,' she'd said on the phone to Joan. 'I'm coming over - would the morning or afternoon be better for you?'

Joan made many excuses, but in the end agreed to be there if Jenny came at three. 'But I have only got an hour, dear.'

It was too warm a day for comfortable travelling. Lyddy was restless in her seat in the back of the car, whining as the sun burned through the glass onto her face, but unwilling to stop pulling off the shade Michael had carefully fixed to the glass beside her.

Joan took her time in coming to the door when she rang the bell, and greeted them with a set face. 'I can't think what could be so important as to bring you out onto the roads in this heat. Lydia looks quite burnt. She has your colouring, of course, not like Diana's family. I'm afraid your father's busy with his sermon, so don't expect to see him. It is a working day for us, as I'm sure you appreciate.'

Jenny sat down opposite her mother in the living room, while Michael took Lyddy over to sit by the window, where he tried to distract her from the range of breakable objects littering the room. His job was to provide moral support, Jenny had told him. To say nothing, but to keep Lyddy out of mischief.

'We could leave her with someone,' he'd said.

'I need her there,' Jenny had replied.

'I was in a psychiatric hospital at the end of April,' Jenny began. 'I had a breakdown. I thought I'd hurt Lyddy deliberately. I even thought I'd killed her at one point, and we had the police and social services investigating us.'

'Keep your baby away from the shelves, please, Michael, some of that china is valuable.'

Michael met Jenny's eyes, and said nothing. He merely removed Lyddy from the vicinity of the shelves she had been eyeing, and sat down with her again.

'I couldn't understand why I cracked like that. But now I look back, I can see how I'd been building up to it, ever since Lyddy was born, and before that too. I'd been driving poor Michael mad because I find it so hard to accept anyone loving me. I'm sure it's because of Jeremy.'

'Don't be ridiculous. You have no business bringing that up.'

'But I do. Didn't you ever think what it would be like for me, never

292

being wanted? It's not surprising I've never been able to cope with being a mother. I've hated Lyddy half the time, I've left her to Michael. And then I thought I'd killed her, when she was about the same age Jeremy was when he died, and I'm sure it wasn't just coincidence. I've been talking to someone, and it's all begun to make sense.'

'Don't be ridiculous,' Joan said again. 'You should know better than to listen to people who want to fill your head with that kind of rubbish.' She drew her knees closer together, and pursed her lips, a red scar against her powdered skin.

'I've always suffered for not being him. Did you ever get to mourn him, Mum? You had me so quickly afterwards, and I was a girl, and you've always said I was a difficult baby. When I thought Lyddy was dead, I couldn't cope. My world ended. And you went through that, but for real. It must have done something to you.'

Joan looked at her angrily. 'Keep that child under control,' she snapped at Michael. Since Lyddy was merely standing holding onto his knees, he looked baffled. 'I had my faith,' Joan said eventually, 'and Austin, and a healthy daughter. If God willed that we lost one, then who was I to go to pieces? When these things happen, we have to put a brave face on it, and get on with life. You can't give in to these things. We didn't have all this psycho babble and counselling industry then. And of course your father and I loved you. You were rebellious, that was the trouble. Quiet, but stubborn. You can't blame us for any problems you've had later. You've made your own choices.' Joan stared at Michael with hostility.

'I understand,' Jenny said calmly. 'There's no reason behind it. You simply don't like me. Well, if that's the case, perhaps we should stop being hypocritical, and not pretend we're all part of the family. Let's go, Michael. We won't invite ourselves again, and you don't need to bother getting in touch with us. After all, you've got Diana.' Jenny stood up. 'Is that what you'd prefer, Mum? To have me go away, and not see me again?'

'I would prefer,' Joan said, standing up and whipping a small table mat out of Lyddy's grasp, 'not to have you coming here raking up things that are firmly in the past. It's none of your business. And if you can't control that child, I should prefer not to have it here, wrecking my house. Diana's children were never that destructive.'

'Very well.' Jenny helped Michael gather up Lyddy's things, and, gesturing him to silence, led him out of the house.

'How do you feel?' Michael asked as they strapped themselves into the car.

'Dreadful. I can hardly go back now, and I can't see her coming round.

293

I kind of thought she'd fall on my neck and beg me not to go.'

'You got to her. I was watching. She was looking at Lyddy almost hungrily. Does Lyddy look like Jeremy at all?'

'I don't know. I've never seen any pictures of him. I don't even know if they kept any. Oh, Michael, it's so sad. Fancy locking all that away for so long.'

They sat in silence for a minute, then Michael said, 'You've got to go back.'

She regarded him steadily. 'Why should it be any different?'

'Trust me, Jenny. You've got to go back.'

Obedient to his promptings, Jenny got out of the car and made her way round the house, one hand caressing the rough, warm brickwork as she rounded the corner. Through the french windows, she could see Joan, still in the same seat as if she hadn't moved, but she held a small piece of card in her hand. Even at a distance, Jenny could see the track of tears running down her face from closed eyes.

She entered quietly, knelt at her mother's feet, and put an arm around her shoulder. Joan opened her eyes, and raised her head slowly. Anger, pain and memory fought each other across her face. 'How dare you?' she whispered. 'How *dare* you make me remember?'

'Tell me about him, Mum. I need to know.'

'It's nothing to do with anything.'

'It is. It affects me, and it stops me being a decent mother to Lyddy.' Jenny took the small studio photograph from her mother's hands. 'He's lovely isn't he? Do you think Lyddy looks like him?'

Joan sat back in her chair and closed her eyes again. Jenny thought she was going to stay like that for ever, then her mother's lips moved. 'Not so dark,' Joan said, 'but the same expression, when she smiles. He was such a lovely baby, so happy. He'd taken his first steps. And then in the morning, he was dead.' She turned a wrecked face on her daughter. 'I blamed myself. And Austin wouldn't talk about it. He said we had to have another baby to replace him, but I couldn't replace him. He made me get pregnant, and then you arrived, and you weren't even a boy. I didn't want you. All the time I was carrying you, I didn't want you, God forgive me. There's not a day passes when I don't think about what he might have been doing. I'm sorry, Jennifer. It's not your fault.'

Seven

All these years,' Jenny said as they drove back an hour later. 'I never really thought about it from her point of view - how could I? I was a child. I only felt excluded.'

'Does it help you?' Michael asked.

'I understand, and I guess that's half the battle. It wasn't me being fundamentally horrible after all. Actually to hear her admit she didn't want me ought to have been awful, but somehow it makes it better. I mean, if you start from that, the times I did manage to please, or get some affection, were big advances. And I can understand that she didn't dare to let herself love me, because it felt like betraying Jeremy. If there'd been someone to talk to about it, she might have worked it through, but my dad wouldn't acknowledge there was a problem, and she thought vicars' wives had to be pillars of society, so she wouldn't seek help from anyone. It would have been letting the side down, and she was of the generation that thought clergy wives shouldn't have friends in the congregation. I suppose she was left with Deidre, and she always felt herself to be in competition with Deidre - she wouldn't have wanted to show weakness in front of her. And then Deidre had a son a few years later, which must really have been rubbing salt into the wound.'

They broke their journey to have tea at a Little Chef. Lyddy refused to sit in the high chair, and instead wriggled on Michael's knee, sucking chips and showering the drink in her trainer cup across the floor and her father, with joyful prodigality. Jenny watched them, not an outsider, but content, because they were hers.

'Put her in the chair, you can't get at your food,' she said, seeing Michael snatching a bite from his burger with expert timing.

'She's been stuck in chairs all day, haven't you, little one? Sometimes a girl needs her freedom.'

Jenny smiled at them, and thought about Michael, about to strap himself into the Church of England, safe and separated out to fulfil his mission. It was exactly where she'd wanted him, but for whose sake? She was thoughtful for the remainder of the journey, and said little until they reached the outskirts of Greathampton, and she could ask to be dropped at Nan's house, to solve the final puzzle of her strained relationship to Michael.

'I've had an awful thought,' Jenny said, sitting on Nan's sofa with a mug of coffee in her hand. 'What you said I do - pushing Michael to be involved with other people because I feel comfortable being on the outside - I'm doing the same with the church, and him being ordained. I know you're probably the last person I should say this to, especially when I haven't said anything to him yet, only I've got to get it sorted in my own mind before I talk to him.'

'I don't think you can do any harm if you tell the truth. Michael's been tying himself up in knots over it, and I haven't known how to help him. I wasn't sure if he was worried about ordination because your marriage was in trouble, or whether his doubts really were pointing to something. I've always thought you were the key to it. Forget who I am, and tell me what you really think.'

'He mustn't go through with it. I know it's what he's always wanted, and you've all backed him, so I haven't felt I could say anything - I thought my anxiety about him being ordained was because of not wanting to repeat what I grew up with, so I'd have been selfish to object. Only I can see now that pushing him into doing something I'm not happy about is another way of distancing myself from him. I can feel jealous of his work, feel sorry for myself when he doesn't have time for me, or when he's the one who has a breakdown because he should never be tied to an institution.'

'He does have a great many gifts,' Nan said. 'He gets on well with everyone, he's good at communicating, kind, caring, always willing to go the extra mile for people, and to turn his hand to anything. He's had a real impact on the Programme and St Barnabas over the last three years.'

'I know all that, but he's been free to be different. He wasn't an ordinand, he was doing lots of different things. That's when he's at his best, when he's simply being himself, free to respond wholeheartedly to whatever happens to come his way. I see him now, dressed up in robes at the front of the church, putting on his best clerical voice, and leading worship and preaching sermons as if that was what it was all about, and I could weep for him. He says he'll have a lot of freedom while he's non-stipendiary, but he's still putting himself under other people's authority, and when it comes down to it, what clergy are really there for is to keep the structures of the church going. It's such a waste. He's a maverick at heart, it isn't right to tame him and organise him. It's like the butterflies that emerge from their chrysalises in church. You see them up in the skylight, flapping against the glass and trying to escape into the daylight, but they can't, so they die. That's what the church does to creative people.'

'Ministry doesn't have to be that constrictive.'

'But it would be for *him*,' Jenny said. 'I'm probably being silly, but that's how I feel about it.'

'And you've never said that to him?' Jenny shook her head. 'My dear girl, didn't you think he needed to hear it?'

'He used to say he loved me because I didn't tell him what to do, like everyone else.'

'Surely that's a matter of degree? If you truly love someone, you don't stand by while they blindly head off towards the edge of a cliff. If you know they're going wrong, you have to do something. I sometimes wonder what would have happened if I'd tried to persuade Chris to drop his plans to kick the Programme out. I might have saved us both a lot of agony, but I didn't like to interfere. I thought I was biased. I thought he'd be angry, or leave me. But I should have tried. You have to warn people if they're heading in the wrong direction, you can't let them destroy themselves, not if you love them.'

'But I haven't been confident about loving Michael, so I haven't dared.' She paused. 'He never asked much of me beyond understanding and a cuddle, and I couldn't give either. I've failed him. I should never have married him.'

'Not at all,' Nan said. 'You're exactly what he needs. You've always felt like an outsider, so you can let him be different and unconventional. Traditional old buggers like me insist on fitting people into some neat, pre-existing category. I can remember telling him when I interviewed him that there were hundreds of ways to have a vocation other than being ordained, but once I saw how admirably he fulfilled all the criteria, that was where I thought he must belong. It's you who sees the other possibilities for him. No wonder he picked you out. It's funny how there've always been questions about him, always some obstacle cropping up when he takes steps down the road to ordination. We've all got it wrong. It's not that he'd make a bad priest, but that he'll do even better being something else. You need to tell him, Jenny. I suspect he'll feel liberated.'

As Jenny got up to go, Christopher came through to the living room.

'I'll run you home,' he said.

'I can walk.'

'I'll walk you home, then.' Jenny was about to object that she had been out alone at night in far worse places than this Greathampton suburb, but she thought she might as well practice accepting kindness.

'Thank you. I'd like that.'

Nan hugged her as she left. 'Come and see me, you and Michael together, when you've talked.'

The street lights guided them down the hill towards home.

'I don't know what you've been talking to Nan about,' Ridgefield said, 'though obviously I've had some conversations with Michael, and I know there have been some problems between you. I'm not asking you to say anything, but I would like you to know I've thought of you often over the last four years, prayed for you.'

'Have you?' Jenny looked at her companion's profile. 'Why?'

'When you talked to me about my sermon, it encouraged me to think I was going vaguely in the right direction. Encouraged me to be a little more bold in some of the decisions I took. I'm grateful. And I was touched by you, and your story. I felt for you. I was intrigued when you turned up at St Barnabas having married this wonderful man you'd said you'd fallen in love with, and looking thoroughly miserable about it. Once I got to know Michael I found him very impressive. Yet there were you, looking as if you were in purgatory on the odd times you turned up at college.'

'I sometimes feel I've made a complete mess of everything ever since I met you. If I'd not told Michael how I felt about him, we might both have been a lot happier.'

Ridgefield shook his head. 'No.'

'But I've done nothing but make things difficult for him.'

'I seem to recall we agreed at the time that the difficult option might sometimes be the most creative. It's not that suffering is sent to try us, but surely any worthwhile learning involves conflict and discomfort? That's one thing living with Nan's taught me, anyway.' They exchanged a smile. 'Remember, even messiahs don't fly, Jenny. They trudge. Uphill, with swollen feet, bare-soled over flint-sharp stones, or ice or fire, hardly knowing what route they should be taking. And we have to follow, damn them, scarcely seeing them in front of us for the fog, with not the faintest idea where we're going. Stumbling, and swearing at the merest suggestion that such foolish adventuring might be divine. As for me, I'd rather give up half the time. Go back home to sit by the fire with a good book, because I'm much too old and lazy to be a pilgrim.'

'That's not true. You've kept going, however tough it's been. You've taken risks, like you said you would. Letting yourself get involved with Nan to start with. Staying on at St Barnabas when a lesser man would have run away. Staying on in the Church of England, even.' She laughed. 'You've been a glutton for punishment.'

'Ah, but you see, Jenny, I've discovered there are compensations along the way. Occasional times when we're permitted to enjoy ourselves, to let go. Like struggling to the top of a rise, and getting to coast downhill for a while before we tackle the next ridge.' He looked at her. 'Is that what you're going to do for Michael? Give him some freedom?'

'Yes,' said Jenny. 'If he'll take it.'

It was nearly eleven when Jenny let herself into the house. The living room was dark, suggesting that Michael had already gone to bed. She went upstairs quietly, and tiptoed into Lyddy's bedroom. The curtains were drawn, but in the light from the landing, she could see her daughter curled under her quilt, one hand clutching her muslin. Jenny bent over and kissed her warm cheek. Lyddy stirred, and carried on slumbering as Jenny went out, pulling the door to behind her. To her left, she could make out Michael's shape under the quilt on their bed. In the bathroom, Jenny removed her contact lenses from tired eyes, and brushed her teeth. Slowly she removed her clothes, folding them neatly to lay them on the chair by the bath. The mirror by the door reflected her naked figure, a particularly fleshy pear-shape, with wide hips and drooping breasts. Hardly lovable, hardly desirable, and yet he always had, he said, wanted her so much more than she'd wanted him. No, it wasn't quite true, there had been wanting enough on her part. But in the past she had always been afraid of what intimacy might lead her into.

She stepped across the landing, switched off the light, and felt her way towards their bed.

'Are you asleep?' she whispered as she knelt down on the floor beside him.

'No.'

Jenny switched on the bedside light, and Michael threw a bare arm across his eyes to shield them. Self-conscious at her nakedness, she lifted the edge of the quilt and slid into bed with him. He shifted onto his side to hold her, still blinking in the unaccustomed illumination. For a full minute, Jenny forced herself to look into his eyes, to trust that what she found there would not destroy her. Then she lifted her hands to cup his face and kissed him.

'I love you,' she whispered, realising with shame that she had not said the words for years. 'Forgive me for being so slow to sort myself out.'

Michael clutched her to him, arms locked round her, and buried his face in her neck.

'I could have survived anything, if only you'd held me like this sometimes,' he answered softly. 'I know you think I'm wet, but ...'

'No, why shouldn't you want affection as well as sex. I presume you do still like sex,' she added in a low, and, she hoped, husky voice. 'I'm afraid I haven't given you much chance to know recently.' She rolled over on top of him as she spoke, and looked down at his face. 'You're laughing at me. I'm trying to be seductive, and you laugh at me, even though you know how shy I am.'

'It's the way you bite your lip and look so anxious about it. Do you remember when you threw a condom at me, and lay there like a sacrificial lamb?'

Jenny blushed violently, and would have escaped him, but he was holding her too tightly. 'You're beautiful and I adore you, and I certainly do still like sex, if you can remind me how it's done.'

There he was, gorgeous brown eyes sharing his amusement with her, dark hair falling away from his brow to show the lines she'd left there, parted lips waiting for her. Forget the awkwardness and embarrassment, Nan had said. Jenny bent her lips to his, and let herself go.

'Shouldn't we be using something?' he murmured, his voice muffled by her breast.

'No,' she said. 'I want another baby with you. I want to enjoy it this time.'

'I need to tell you something,' Jenny said as she lay in his arms at peace again. 'I don't think you should be ordained.'

His face took on an anxious frown, and she smoothed the lines away with a finger. 'It's never been right for you, Michael. We both know that. I'm sorry, I've been pushing you towards it because it was another way of keeping my distance from you, but I don't need to any more.'

'I thought I had a vocation.'

'Well of course you have.' Jenny propped herself up on her elbow, and looked down in his face. 'But vocation is simply what you do next, it's no big deal, it isn't a long-term commitment to one role for life, with no escape clauses. For you, it's carrying on being yourself, without making long-term plans, or saddling yourself with lots of possessions and distractions. Do what's necessary for today, and take no thought for the morrow. I'll keep you clothed and fed. And hugged.'

Michael smiled. 'It sounds too easy.'

'No, it won't be. You'll get things wrong sometimes, you don't always weigh situations up accurately. Your gift is to live life through your senses and your feelings, you're not necessarily wise. People will doubt your commitment because you're laid back and refuse to take life seriously, or they'll think you're big-headed, because you prefer to trust your intuition, rather than being logical.'

'In short, I'm thick, arrogant, self-centred, undisciplined, naive, immature and a drifter, and the selectors were right the first time after all.'

'No. They sensed some of the right things about you, but they could only see the negative side.' She frowned. 'Am I being too dogmatic?'

'I like it. It's how you used to be, when you were my friend.' He drew her down into his arms again. 'It's time we went to sleep. I'm supposed to be leading the first half of the service tomorrow.'

'Make it for the last time?'

He gazed at her for a few seconds, and whispered, 'Alright, for the last time.'

On Sunday afternoon, Jenny walked with Michael up the hill to Nan's house, swinging Lyddy between them. Michael had played his part in the service that morning with such vigour that she had begun to wonder whether she'd been wrong to suggest he withdraw from ordination.

'I was demob happy,' he explained. 'I told Peter afterwards, and he was pretty cross at first, but then he said since he and Caroline and my parents have never yet succeeded in getting me to do the orthodox thing, he shouldn't have been surprised.'

Jenny's eyes met his across Lyddy's head and they laughed. No, he wasn't one of them, he was hers, in a conspiracy with her against everyone who painted by numbers.

Christopher greeted them at the door.

'Nan's in our bedroom,' he said. 'She's decided that a year of having a fallen hem on the curtain is long enough, so go and talk to her there, or she'll have an excuse for leaving it another twelve months. Would your daughter like to come and see our squirrels?'

Lyddy eyed him suspiciously, but on being assured that daddy would wave at her from the upstairs window, went out to the garden holding his hand.

'Is Christopher practising his grandfather act?' Nan asked. 'Damn!'

She shook her hand as she misjudged the force the needle needed. 'There's going to be so much blood on this curtain, I'll have to take it down anyway to wash it.'

'I'm not sure how long Lyddy will go along with it, she's getting shy with people. Must take after me,' Michael said, waving out of the window. He turned round. 'I'm not going to be ordained. I can see I've been trying to do what everyone expected of me, rather than finding a path that was right for me.'

Nan let go of the material, and studied him. 'I think you're right,' she said. 'Have you any idea what you will do?'

'Look after Lyddy. And perhaps another one, in nine months' time.' He grinned at Jenny, a look which Nan intercepted, and, Jenny thought, understood. 'Meanwhile keep going with what I've been doing, the youth club, the stuff with dads up on the Rows, take up the organ again. Perhaps I should try and get licenced so I can still preach and...'

'No,' Jenny interrupted firmly. 'Other people can do the formal things. You wait and see. No plans. No licences. Nothing for the journey, no stick, no food, no money, no spare shirt, sandals on your feet, go where you're welcomed - there's a definite precedent.'

'It all sounds far too chaotic for me,' Nan said, 'but I guess that's how you've lived when you've had the choice, isn't it, Michael?'

Outside, Lyddy's enthusiam for the squirrels was turning to annoyance that her father was not there to feed them with her. 'I guess it is. Christopher's making faces at me, I'd better go and help.' He kissed Jenny's forehead, and headed out of the room, humming.

'Is everything OK now?' Nan asked. 'Is he really happy about it? Or should I say, accepting it, philosophical?'

Jenny held up a hand. They could hear Michael's feet on the stairs, springing lightly down. He bounded the last two or three steps to land with a thump, and they could track him from the sound of his singing as he made his way out to the garden.

'I think he's happy,' she said.

The End